PLUM DUFF

VICTORIA GODDARD

UNDERHILL BOOKS

CHAPTER ONE

On the northern approach to Ragnor barony along the old imperial highway, you cross a fine stone bridge over the Temby, a tributary of the River Rag, and almost immediately enter the dark and dim fastness of the Arguty Forest.

An ancient woodland of that sort seems wilder, at least to a country boy such as myself, than the true unpeopled wilderness of the mountains. The Arguty Forest is not merely thickly wooded: it is *dark*.

In Ragnor barony and those lands around, you once could reach Astandalas the Golden and still can reach Fairyland through the Woods Noirell in the south. There, if you stray off the path, you might find yourself caught in a faery circle or lost in the woods between the worlds.

In the Arguty Forest, you are much more likely to find yourself in a pit trap, caught by any of a variety of gangs of highwaymen, tumbling into the Magarran Strid, or visited by a hermit saint.

Or perhaps that's just me.

On our way back from collecting books, sundries, and my best friend Mr. Dart's niece Jullanar Maebh from Orio City, we had given a lift to a highwayman dressed as the Hunter in Green—to ignore, at least for the moment, all the other events that happened between collecting said books, sundries, and niece, and actually arriving at the edge of Ragnor barony.

(There had been two deaths, a resurrection, and a unicorn. Amongst other things.)

I had discovered during the past week that the ostensible Hunter in Green was actually the Honourable Roald Ragnor, Baron Ragnor's son and general aristocratic layabout. I had yet to determine the point of his masquerade.

Whatever his purpose, he bade us halt the coach just inside the woods so he could go on his solitary way.

"As you wish," Mr. Dart said; he was sitting with his back to the driver, and he rapped smartly on the dividing shutter to inform the coachman of our plans.

Mr. Fancy, my grandmother's coachman, had taken a fancy to Mr. Dart when he'd picked us up after our precipitous escape from Orio City's infamous prison. If *I'd* tried to persuade him to stop at the edge of the forest he would have been most sarcastic in manner. He merely tipped his hat to Mr. Dart and muttered something that could be taken as polite.

The enormous falarode groaned under the weight of all the books, Winterturn supplies, and passengers as it slowed to a ponderous halt. Thankfully, the old highway was well-laid stone underneath a scattering of dead leaves and dirty slush. I regarded the slush thoughtfully. On the other side of the Crosslains there had been a blizzard, which had trapped us in the country house of the eccentric and somewhat murderous Master Boring and forced us to go quite around rather than over the pass between Lind and south Fiellan. On that side of the mountains they held that snow before the Lady's Day—the winter solstice—was bad luck.

On our side we said it was sign of a good winter. *Good*, for us meaning a season of a fair snowfall that stayed and protected all the overwintering crops and nourished the ground. The solstice was not even a week away now, and it appeared the snow had begun to settle. There were ample signs that the coming winter would be a hard one politically, so I was cautiously hopeful that the weather would prove less catastrophic.

4

A little before we reached the unremarkable path where the Hunter in Green had requested we deposit him, the coach slid to a halt in a sudden wild whinnying on the part of the six horses drawing it.

We jerked and swayed with the abrupt cessation of movement. Jullanar Maebh, who was sitting next to Mr. Dart opposite the Hunter in Green, shivered and drew her shawl closer about her shoulders. Hope, my friend from Morrowlea and the most recent addition to our party, was sitting next to me, and she put her hand on my knee for balance.

"Why are we stopping, Jemis?" she asked softly.

"I don't know," I admitted cheerfully. "Shall we go see?"

The Hunter in Green scoffed. "I'll go see. You stay here."

Jullanar Maebh, who had not been entirely pleased with any of us, and certainly not the addition of a man pretending to be the Lady's Hunter, scoffed in turn, more loudly and sincerely. The Hunter swung his masked face around, his entire bearing suggesting amusement; Jullanar Maebh merely said, "We await your report, sir."

He actually laughed before swinging himself out of the carriage in a blast of chill air. I took my hands out of my pockets and wished I'd thought to buy a pair of good gloves when in Orio City. Theoretically I had three pairs on order in Ragnor Bella, but there was no telling whether I would return to find one, two, or all of them ready for the winter.

From outside came a jumble of words, the Hunter's strange accent —a mimicry, I now knew, of the Solaaran accent of Zunidh—and robust timbre rumbling through the horses's continuing noises. Mr. Fancy's voice raised up sharply, followed by another man, whose voice was so fruity and rich we all turned with one accord to tilt our heads in curiosity.

Even Ballory the unicorn foal left off her drowsy communion with Mr. Dart's side and the remaining three kittens to prick her ears forward and listen. The Hunter had left the carriage door ajar, letting in both a draught and their voices.

"Ballory, no," Mr. Dart said, half a moment too late—the unicorn had scrambled to its feet, unceremoniously dumping the kittens, and clattered out through the gap. I reached down to collect the kittens, knocking my head against Mr. Dart as he made to stand.

We both tumbled backwards into our seats. Jullanar Maebh made another savage scoffing noise and Hope said, "Oh dear, are you all right?"

"Yes, thank you," I said, even as Mr. Dart nodded hastily, said something that might have been, "Just fine," and clambered out.

The carriage was intended for ten, but Mr. Dart's valet Cartwright and the coachman had rearranged the seating to permit the inclusion of large quantity of books and other items I'd acquired in Orio City.

We had been expecting Jullanar Maebh and her mother, so they had left enough space for four passengers; the addition of the Hunter in Green, who was a large man, had been something of a squeeze. With him gone, however, and the ladies' feet and skirts drawn back, Mr. Dart was able to exit without having to do more than duck his head.

I glanced at the two women and then, when they both shrugged, followed suit. Hope had mentioned she'd not slept well the night before, and Jullanar Maebh had contracted a cold at some point along our journey, and was quietly sniffling into a handkerchief.

Outside the carriage it had started again to snow, a fine sifting powder that could likely keep up all day. It washed out the forest around us and eliminated shadows, so we and the carriage seemed to stand in a ghostly wood: all tall oaks, their bark darkened by humidity, their rusty leaves rattling above us.

Roald Ragnor stood foursquare, his costume a viridian mass bright against the black carriage. Mr. Dart was in deep grey, as if he'd strayed out of the woods himself. Mr. Fancy and Mr. Cartwright were in heavy black greatcoats, Mr. Cartwright's almost as rusty as the oak leaves with age and wear.

Ballory stood out against the snow as if she were formed of pure moonlight. She was rubbing her nub of a horn against the knee of the man who had stopped the coach.

A soft wisp thumped over my foot; I looked down to see the orange kitten had made its way out and was now trotting unconcernedly across to join Ballory in fawning over the man's feet and twining around his legs.

The grey kitten sat at the top of the carriage steps and mewed imperiously until I picked it up and pet it. The tabby had claimed Hope's lap and was purring audibly.

The man before us, caressing the unicorn's ears with an expression almost as wondering as the rest of us sported, was undoubtedly the Wild Saint of the Arguty Forest.

~

I had grown up—Mr. Dart and the Honourable Roald Ragnor and I had all grown up—hearing stories of the Wild Saint. He asked for nothing, people said: he received all gladly, and gave what he received even more gladly still.

He had been an ordinary enough monk in his youth, my father had said, belonging to the order whose chapter house was in Temby in middle Fiellan. Like so many, the order had become corrupt and worldly, seeking their own aggrandizement over their spiritual duties.

The monk who became the Wild Saint had been travelling, my mother had told me, between Fiellan and Lind, through the passes in the Farry March, when he had a vision of the Lady.

She had told him to mend his ways for the good of his own soul, and when he asked the goddess how he might, she laid upon him the instruction that he needed to learn what a gift the world was; that he should seek for nothing, but receive with joy what was given, and give with abundance in his turn.

He had, so everyone said, wandered in the mountains for many days until he found himself in a glade deep in the heart of the Arguty Forest, not far from the Magarran Strid or the caves where they found the tippermongeramy.

There he came to a wild crossroads.

The wild crossroads, in fact.

Crossroads are a matter of great superstition and deep lore in my part of the world. Long before the Astandalan Empire came with its roads and its binding magics, we held that crossroads were places of fear and wonder: places where the dead might walk, or the Dark Kings come calling.

Places where you might meet the Lady; or find a path opening to another world, or the Lands Beyond.

At a crossroads you might find grace or disaster, adventure or any form of a change of direction.

Most of the crossroads in southern Fiellan had long since been anchored into the Schooled magic of Astandalas, the old tracks covered over with the great slabs of stone and linking chains of the wizard-engineers of the empire. The crossroads were still marked by standing stones, and the superstitions lingered, but it had been said—it had been *believed*—that much of the old, deep magic of Alinor before the coming of the Empire was gone.

The Fall of the Empire had made it clear that that magic was only quiescent, bound by the Schooled wizards. When their bindings broke, that terrible day *when the lights went out*, our crossroads ... woke.

But never mind that.

Of the three baronies that comprised Southern Fiellan—Temby, Yllem, and Ragnor—Ragnor was the most isolated and the most ... shall we say, traditional.

It was the one where the cult to the Dark Kings had progressed to the point of sacrificing people. Or at least attempting to do so; I owed my life to Mr. Dart twice over on that account.

Only the fact that the imperial highway to Astandalas cut through the middle of the barony, on its way to the passage between worlds on the other side of the Woods Noirell, meant that we were not entirely *backwards*. We had had travellers passing us by, everyone from half the armies of Astandalas to the Red Company themselves.

Few of them made the two-mile detour to visit Ragnor Bella itself, unless they'd mistaken their stages and instead of stopping at the Horned Man Inn just north of the Arguty Forest and then the Bee at the Border in St-Noire, they found themselves needing a rest-halt in between. Even then the Green Dragon was closer to the road, if in those days nearly as obviously dangerous and wild as at present.

Nowadays, the highway leads nowhere. It stops unceremoniously in a field, the circular arch that once marked the passage a haunted relic. The Woods Noirell (my mother's legacy to me) are as full as twisting and convoluted magic as they ever were, and the Good

Neighbours press ever closer. But the Bee at the Border has shut up more than half of its great wings, as no travellers come there now.

And the Arguty Forest, that deep and dark forest full of mortal dangers, is wilder and darker and deeper than ever it was during the days of the Empire. Even in Imperial days the forest was not *safe*. The highway was patrolled by companies of soldiers, because no one could ever plumb every cave and every gorge and every millennium-oak's canopy.

The places where trails cross in the Arguty Forest were never caught and bound by Imperial wizards. I had read, in a class on History of Magic at university, that most Schooled wizards intensely disliked the forest precisely because it was so alien to them and their magic.

There is, deep in the forest, a crossroads where two ancient roads meet. It is called, by traditional immemorial, the Savage Crux.

The roads are so ancient no one now knew who had made them. They are not paved, not bound in chains of iron and magic and stone, but their tracks scar and shape the landscape.

The east-west path is said to have been made by giants, long and long ago when the world was young. The eastern terminus is in the Farry March, up in the long narrow valley between Fiellan and Lind, where a huge monolith, fifty feet high, stands on the brow of a hill, marking no one knows what. To the west, on the other side of the valley of the River Rag, is the Gap of the Gorbelow Hills, which was said to have been broken by giants.

The Giants' Road is still visible, if one stands on certain heights in the barony, as a raised dyke running across the valley. There is a ford across the Rag where that line crosses it, requiring a portage for any boats that might want to go downriver from Ragnor Bella, and a huge tumbled pile of stones that people call the Giant's Castle occupies the entire pinch of the valley floor between the river and the trees: that is why the highway had to go straight through the Arguty Forest.

If the Giants' Road seems to run across the general line of the valley, the north-south track that crosses it at the Savage Crux defies common human or animal practice entirely. It runs along a clear line that does not quite follow any magnetic compass direction, ignoring cliffs and mountains, gorges and waterfalls, bogs and sinkholes and all the other mass of miscellaneous terrain that is tumbled across the foothills of the Crosslains.

This route—it is hardly a path; no one has ever actually been able to *follow* it, certainly not on horseback or even on foot—is called the Lady's Way. It is said that it was made by Sir Peregrine, the Lady's first Champion, when he chased the Good Neighbours out of Fiellan. He rode his unicorn companion along the route, harrying those whose steeds were made of wind and shadow when the Wild Hunt came hunting in the mortal countries.

I looked at the six Ghiandor horses drawing my grandmother's falarode, which had a certain viridian sheen to their flanks and which could travel far faster and longer than any truly mortal horse of my knowledge; and then I looked at Ballory, barely larger than a cat, more *real* than anything else in that shadowless light of a snowy day, and I wondered.

There had been a fair amount of time, driving up the length of the Crosslains to the northern pass and then back down through Fiellan again, to think about what it meant for my friend, Mr. *Peregrine* Dart, to find and befriend a unicorn.

He stood there, auburn-bearded and dressed as befit a young gentleman not so lately up from university, in grey and sober plum, and nothing but the unicorn now gamboling at his feet suggesting anything was odd. No magic was apparent around him; even his stone arm was hidden in its sling.

Facing Mr. Dart, the Wild Saint wore brown leggings and a long green woollen habit over it, and over that a great cloak made apparently of mink pelts. He held a long wooden staff in his hand, which he was leaning on as if it were a walking aid but which I thought was actually a hefty quarterstaff—if the nicks and flattened spots where it had clearly hit things heavily were any indication—and his hood was down, showing him both fully bearded and with the sort of baldness that looks like a tonsure. His hair and beard were both rich brown; his skin was ruddy and tanned rather than naturally dark.

He lived, so barony rumour had it, in a small hut right at the Savage Crux.

It was not done to build at crossroads, not in southern Fiellan. Inns and pubs and churches and villages alike were all built at least a furlong away from any crossroads, safe from the walking dead or the Dark Kings or the Gentry's interest.

The Wild Saint had been sent by the Lady to learn what a gift and a grace the world was, and at the Savage Crux of the Arguty Forest, it was said, he had found a man so injured he could not be moved at all.

This being the first Finding, the man who would become the Wild Saint listened to the Lady's words and worked to heal the injured man where he was. The man recovered, in a way quickly hailed as miraculous, and in return gave the Wild Saint a pot.

He was a tinker, so he'd seemed; but the pot was enchanted, and no matter what was made in it, there was always enough for all who were there to eat from it.

After the so-called tinker left, the Wild Saint was preparing to leave from the Savage Crux when a tree fell across one of the roads. He was perforce obliged to clear it, but he had no tools—no axe or saw—and so he built a fire to burn through the trunk.

Long before he had been able to cut the tree in half, another traveller had come by, this one with a handaxe they left in return for the meal and directions and some unspecified advice.

And so it went. Each time he might have continued, something happened: a gift was given, or needed to be given on.

It was said that he was still working through the great oak, though the road was now cleared, and still living at the Savage Crux, the only person in the whole of southern Fiellan who dwelled at a crossroads.

"So this," the Wild Saint said out loud, "is Ballory."

I was startled out of my thoughts and looked again at the man in front of me. Ballory was regarding him with not quite as adoring an attitude as she showed to Mr. Dart, but with clear affection.

It occurred to me, not for the first time, to wonder just how intelligent the unicorn foal was.

Mr. Dart was regarding him with little less intrigue, if less outright pleasure. The Hunter in Green had his arms folded in a gesture of definite smugness. I decided to ignore him for the moment and, since no one else was saying anything in response, asked, "Were you expecting her?"

The Wild Saint lifted his head from gazing down at Ballory to pierce me with striking blue eyes.

"This is Jemis Greenwing, the Viscount St-Noire," Roald said.

The Wild Saint nodded, his eyes not leaving my face. "The son of Mad Jack Greenwing, recently come home out of durance vile. The son of the Lady Olive, a fine lady and a finer woman, friend to all. Yes, I know who you are, Mr. Greenwing."

I bowed to the saint, deeply as if for Hal.

He laughed, richly and royally. "Yes, you have your parents' blood in your veins," he declared. "In answer to your question, young sir, all of us on the Lady's side have been waiting this long age for the coming of a unicorn to the world. All the signs were pointing towards an imminent change: for that is what a unicorn portends, you know, here in Northwest Oriole. Change."

I nodded, but I refused to let the question go unanswered. The Hunter in Green (*the Honourable Rag*) had also known the name Ballory.

"By name?" I persisted.

The Wild Saint settled back on his heels, his hands sliding on the quarterstaff until he was completely and fully balanced for movement in any direction.

I watched him but did not shift my own position. I was well enough balanced to respond to an attack if one proved forthcoming, but I could hardly see myself attacking a saint of the Lady. Now that I was looking at him I could see quite clearly that he *had* seen the Lady in truth. There was an air about him—something in the look in his eyes, perhaps—that was … not exactly *fey* … but …

Perhaps the word I was looking for was *holy*.

He said, "Who are you to ask?"

The Lady's voice was in my ear, that laughter that had caused all the trees in the Wood of Spiritual Refreshment to bloom, all the faces of the souls of the waiting dead to blossom. I smiled at the Wild Saint, certainty falling into my voice, my mind, my bones.

"I died in sacrifice and came back to life by the Lady's grace and the work of her Champion." I put my hand on Mr. Dart's shoulder, just above the knot of his sling. "I stand behind and beside him."

The Wild Saint started to laugh, a booming noise that echoed in the silent, still, grey trees. Somewhere not far away a jay cried out, answered by another. Grey jays, I noted, remembering another passage through the Arguty Forest, and the Whiskeyjack gang. They were not close, not yet, if the jay-calls were theirs.

"Then I will tell you, young sir," the Wild Saint said, "that if you truly want to know the answer to that question, you must follow your champion where he leads. We are nearly come to the Lady's Day, the shortest day of the year, the longest night, when the world turns on its axis. Are you patient enough to await what comes?"

Mr. Dart gave a short hitch of his shoulder, which I interpreted— possibly incorrectly, but I did know him quite well—as a request to say nothing further, so I merely stepped aside and bowed again to the Wild Saint.

"Thank you for the lift, Lord St-Noire," the Hunter in Green said, and I could hear the grin in his voice.

CHAPTER TWO

The rest of the journey to Dart Hall was uneventful.

We climbed back inside, minus the orange kitten—which the Wild Saint had scooped up with apparent delight, kissed on the nose, and declared a gift of the Lady—which asseveration I did not in the least deny—and settled ourselves into our seats.

"Any trouble?" Hope asked tentatively.

"No, just the Wild Saint," I replied. Jullanar Maebh sighed in extravagant disbelief and turned her head firmly to look out the window as we scrunched back onto the main highway and started off again.

Despite a week in Mr. Dart's and my company she had yet to reconcile herself to the mad adventures befalling us. Mind you, six months of them had not fully led *me* to reconciling myself with them, so I could not entirely blame her.

We arrived at Dart Hall just as the grey was gradually becoming the deep, luminous blue of a snowy evening. The windows in the Hall were well-lit, and it looked greatly welcoming as we trundled up the long drive at a smart trot. I brushed my hand down my coat, wishing I had not lost my hat, and smiled encouragingly at Hope, who had expressed her concern at imposing on the Squire.

Jullanar Maebh was very pale and still. She had braided her copper hair back tightly, so only a few tendrils framed her face. Mr. Dart patted her hand gently. "All will be well, cousin," he said softly. "My brother is eager to meet you."

She jerked her head in barest acknowledgement. She had not been willing to share the impetus behind her mother's pleas for sanctuary, nor explained why her mother had not accompanied her to meet us, except that it was not due to her death. I had been sufficiently preoccupied with my own affairs—not to mention the small fact that she disliked me—to have not pressed. It was mere inquisitiveness on my part; if it were more important than that, Mr. Dart would tell me.

Someone in the house had clearly been looking out for us, for by the time Mr. Fancy drew the falarode up before the entry the great oaken doors had opened, and the Squire, Sir Hamish, and my own father had gathered at the top of the steps to meet us.

Mr. Dart and I looked at each other, and then down at Ballory.

"Why don't you and Hope go first, Jemis?" Mr. Dart suggested.

It was his family, so I nodded agreement and exited the carriage first. Mr. Cartwright had already moved around to the side to start handing the luggage down to some of the Hall servants, while Mr. Fancy remained perched on his seat like a large crow.

I ensured the steps were locked into position and turned to hand Hope out of the carriage. She was dressed in a heavy wool cloak lined with fox fur, and looked with a mixture of apprehension and curiosity at the Hall and the men assembled to greet us.

I glanced back in, but Mr. Dart was whispering to Jullanar Maebh, so I took Hope's arm and led her up the stairs.

"You're back safely, then," Sir Hamish said when no one said anything at first.

"Yes," I replied, smiling thankfully at him. "Master Dart, this is a friend of mine from Morrowlea, Hope Stornaway—the Ironwood heiress. She agreed to act as chaperone for Miss Dart, as it happened that … Mrs. Dart was unable to join us."

All three gave me a sharp look. I smiled back as guilelessly as I knew how, which wasn't particularly. Hope gave a small, nervous curtsey. "I hope you don't mind the imposition, M-master Dart."

The Squire started and then gave her a kind smile. "You are welcome, Miss Stornaway. I look forward to knowing you. Jemis's friends from university have all been ... most interesting."

Hope gave me a puzzled look. I grinned at her. "Hal, Violet, and Red Myrta."

Hope stifled a giggle, no doubt for that combination: Hal, the Imperial Duke of Fillering Pool; Violet, an Indrilline spy (albeit truthfully the Lady of Alinor's daughter and loyal agent); and the daughter of Myrta the Hand, chief of a gang of brigands.

The Squire grunted an acknowledgement, and managed not to stare longingly at the carriage for a moment longer.

"This is Sir Hamish Lorkin," I added to Hope, and then indicated my father. "And this is my father, Major Jack Greenwing."

"Sir Hamish. Major Greenwing." Hope curtsied again as the two made short, polite bows in return. My father's eyebrows had gone up, though I couldn't imagine what there was in my polite phrasing to astonish him so.

Hope and I shuffled over to stand next to my father. He set his hand on my shoulder and gave me a quick, comforting squeeze. I felt for a moment as if my heart would overflow entirely.

"There they are," Master Dart said, eager as a boy, as the carriage door swung open again.

Mr. Dart came out first, followed by Jullanar Maebh. She was still pale but it was less pronounced than earlier. Her cheeks flushed as she came up the steps, and her eyes skimmed anxiously over Sir Hamish, the Squire, and my father before settling on the Squire.

There was no doubt they were related. Her hair was a brighter copper and far curlier, but her nose and the shape of her jaw and her eyes were all clearly derived from his side. She walked up beside Mr. Dart to stand uncertainly before her father.

She curtsied, as politely and impersonally as Hope had not five minutes before. The Squire responded with a curt bow, then his face changed and he stepped forward, arms wide, expression suddenly beseeching.

"May I?" he said, and at her tremulous nod embraced her.

Beside me, Hope was sniffling back tears. I pulled out one of my store of clean handkerchiefs and offered it to her silently. She took it with a small smile, no doubt remembering my absurd collection of handkerchiefs from Morrowlea.

Mr. Dart stood next to Sir Hamish, who put his hand on my friend's shoulder in just the way my father had done for me. For the first time I did not feel a pang of envy for Mr. Dart. I smiled over my shoulder at my father on that thought, startling him again. My father smiled slowly, and his hand gripped me, just as if he understood exactly what I was feeling.

The Squire released his daughter, and they stood back, teary-eyed and smiling brilliantly. All of Jullanar Maebh's fears seemed to have fled, and Master Dart himself's uncharacteristic bout of anxiety had passed.

"Come inside, daughter," he said, his voice warm and welcoming. "Come in and be welcome to your new home."

～

Inside, we doffed our various outer garments, stamped the small bits of snow acquired on the stretch of drive between carriage and stairs on the doormat, and were guided into the friendly morning room.

I'd always felt Dart Hall to be a second home, far more welcoming than my uncle's house. I had a bedroom here, where I kept a few books and a change of clothes. The morning room was my favourite of the daytime rooms: it was a snug space, the walls covered in wallpaper striped in pale blue and cream.

Sir Hamish's portraits of his parents and those of Mr. Dart and the Squire were the most prominent artwork, along with landscapes from their collection. I went to examine the portraits, seeking the Petronelle and Master Ricard I had met in the Wood of Spiritual Refreshment.

These had been painted when they were older than in that life after death, but I could see the Petronelle I had met in the portrait's eyes and mouth. I had seen that Master Ricard's face had relaxed from stern lines; his frown was much more obvious in the painting.

"You've never been so interested in those portraits before," Sir Hamish said from beside me.

"I met them," I said without thinking.

Sir Hamish gave me a penetrating, considering stare, as if he were looking not just with a painterly regard—something I had always found unexpectedly difficult to bear, for how *naked* it made me feel— but deep into my soul.

For all that he was my father's cousin and my dear friend's honorary father, I had never truly *talked* with Sir Hamish. I had always felt uncomfortable with him, able to feel how my social status was slipping, unable to tune out my uncle's and his wife's dripping poison enough to believe that Sir Hamish would himself ignore the slander against my father's name.

I shivered. There had been a holy light in the Wild Saint's eyes. Was there something ... fey ... about *me*, now that I had visited the Lady's country and come back myself?

"Something happened," Sir Hamish said quietly. Behind us, I could hear a murmur of voices as Master Dart introduced my father to Jullanar Maebh and they made all the proper greetings to each other.

"Yes."

He held my eyes a few moments longer. I looked back steadily. Was it three days since I had come back from the Lady's Country? Four? Already the subtle inward changes were settling into normality. It was hard to remember why I had been so anxious and doubting of Sir Hamish's opinion. Looking at him now I was absolutely certain that he cared deeply for me.

How many people had I pushed away in my fear of being rejected by them?

Was it magic or simply my own too-cautious nature that had done so?

How insidious had been that curse?

"I met a woman once who had witnessed a miracle," Sir Hamish said, even more quietly. "What lay lightly on her is shining in your eyes."

"I died," I said quietly, but not quietly enough, for everyone else had stopped talking and my words fell straight into that silence.

~

The explanations were complicated, to say the least.

Before we'd even finished describing crossing the Arguty Forest on the way *to* Orio City, my father was trying valiantly not to laugh. The account of how Moo the highwayman from Nibbler's gang had dumped half a dozen kittens on us made him screw up his face in the effort to keep his composure.

"I see you still have one of the kittens," he observed. The second grey—now the only grey one—appeared to have adopted me, and was currently investigating the corners of the room, whereas the tabby was—

I frowned at Mr. Dart. "Where's Ballory?"

Mr. Dart was sitting on a chair between the settee where Jullanar Maebh and Hope sat and the fireplace. There was a distinct lack of unicorn foal, however.

"You named one of the kittens *Ballory*?" my father said, giving up on the struggle and letting himself laugh freely instead.

I glanced at Mr. Dart, who gave me a blandly challenging expression.

"Why does everyone except me know that name?" I asked in exasperation.

"How do you *not* know it?" Sir Hamish said. "It's the name of Sir Peregrine's unicorn!"

"He was an ancestor of ours, you know," Master Dart said to Jullanar Maebh, his voice rounding with pride. "Perry here is named after him."

Jullanar Maebh, Hope, and I all swivelled to stare at Mr. Dart. I'd already heard some of this from the Lady in the Wood of Spiritual Refreshment, but it had gone out of my head like the details of a dream in all the hurly-burly of the subsequent events.

"I thought we could leave Ballory until a bit later in the story," Mr. Dart said. "As there are some important matters to discuss first."

"Yes," Sir Hamish said, "like why exactly Jemis said he died."

"He's not allowed to explain," Mr. Dart said firmly. "He's disturbingly glib about the whole thing."

"I came back."

"That doesn't make it any better, Mr. Greenwing."

Jullanar Maebh suddenly sat forward, folded her hands tightly together on her lap, and stared intently at her father. "May I? I am not certain I can take their—their *whiffle!*"

"My son does have the gift of talk," my father murmured. He was standing next to me, his hand on my shoulder when he wasn't overcome with laughter. He squeezed my shoulder again; I was once again struck by how comforting it was. "Please, Miss Dart."

"I was waiting for you to meet me in Orio City," Jullanar Maebh said, her eyes on the Squire. "I met these two the night before, in a student pub."

"Oh, Perry," the Squire sighed. "*Must* you?"

Mr. Dart shrugged, unrepentant. "We met Jack Lindsary, and Jemis very valiantly refrained from punching him."

"He's got a new play coming out this Winterturn," I said, remembering anew. It felt so very removed. "About the dragon, apparently."

"Excellent," Sir Hamish said. "I've been making notes to what you might do about it, Jack."

"Even more splendid," my father said. "Do continue, Miss Dart."

"I had not heard their names correctly, so I was most surprised to discover them there to meet me. Nevertheless, we made our arrangements to meet the next morning after they had completed their other commissions and I finished my preparations. I was ... discomposed to discover that Lord St-Noire here was wanted by the Governor-Prince of Orio City and that we were all four of us arrested and thrown into the prison as a result."

My father dug his fingers into my shoulder despite the incontrovertible evidence that we were not stuck in the infamous prison.

"I wasn't there," Hope said tremulously, raising her hand. "I ... encountered them later."

"Hal was instead," I explained.

"Hal—the Imperial Duke?" Sir Hamish frowned and looked meaningfully at my father. "They arrested you *and* an Imperial Duke?"

"They had hostages from half of Northwest Oriole. Or rather Lark did." I discovered I had not progressed quite so far in forgiveness and divine charity as all that: I was still rather angry at my erstwhile lover.

"Lark being ..."

"Jemis's sweetheart from Morrowlea," Hope said.

"The bride of the governor-prince," Jullanar Maebh said.

"A dark witch," said Mr. Dart.

I shrugged when everyone looked at me. "The successor to The Indrilline."

My father swore with such pungency I didn't know any of the words. We all regarded his prowess with amazement. It was clear he was much quicker to figure out the political ramifications of the situation than I'd been.

"Sorry," he concluded weakly, nodding apologetically at the ladies.

Hope's eyes were shining with admiration, and she merely shook her head and said, "Please, don't worry about it."

Jullanar Maebh shrugged. "My mother is an Outer Reaches *spákona*. She can scale fish with her tongue when she gets going."

Sir Hamish laughed abruptly. "I'd forgotten that—do you remember, Torquin, when Ingrid brought that moonshine from home for us to try, and then insisted she could drink everyone under the table ...?"

"Which she did," the Squire said.

"It's true," Sir Hamish nodded.

The Squire scoffed. "Like you remember any of that evening."

"*I* remember that evening," my father put in. "I was on leave and we all ended up swimming naked in the fountain in Kinglode—"

The Squire harrumphed and hastily said, "So, you were thrown into the infamous prison of Orio City. Did they let you out when they realized who you all were?"

"No, we escaped," I said proudly. "Everyone made fun of my final paper at Morrowlea, but I was *right*, you know. Ariadne nev Lingarel's poem *is* a cipher describing the architecture and how to get out."

My father started to laugh again. "You successfully *escaped* the Orio City prison by means of a poem interpretation? Oh Jemis, Jemis!"

"Unfortunately there was some messy business with wireweed again," I explained. "Lark forced me to take some ... which was probably good because that was how I'd understood the poem in the first place ... but it meant that when we came to the last part of the riddle— it was a complicated magical riddle, you see—I had to sacrifice some-

21

thing ... and I sacrificed my magic ... but with the wireweed overdose, I ... died."

"And yet," my father said slowly, "you are here now."

"That was Mr. Dart," I said, turning to smile brilliantly at him as my gratitude suddenly surged forth again. Mr. Dart himself stared fixedly at the floor, his cheeks and the tips of his ears scarlet.

"He's the champion of the Lady," I said, "and in a house in Lind he found a unicorn."

∾

Ballory was brought forth from the kitchen, where she had undoubtedly converted the cook and scullery maids and footmen to the meet and right adoration of her being, and promptly won over the hearts of Master Dart, Sir Hamish, and my father alike.

Once that marvel had settled into—not *normalcy*, but a kind of more homely wonder—I felt an increasing urgency to pass on the messages with which I had been entrusted, and begged their leave to tell them.

Sir Hamish bravely agreed to go first, and so we went to the small study on the main floor which they usually used for the business of the estate. I told him whatever I had been charged to say, the words coming clear and clean out of my mind, received by him with astonished, astonishing gratitude. At the end he looked at me with a shattering kind of grace.

I had felt the same on speaking with Ariadne nev Lingarel, my mother, my stepfather, in that Wood.

"Thank you," Sir Hamish said hoarsely when I had finished.

I had explained I would not remember the words, and did not; only the taste of them, of snow and sweet honey, still on my lips.

"Thank the Lady," I replied seriously. "And thank Mr. Dart—Perry —Peregrine—for guarding my way home. I know the Lady would not have left me forever in the wastes between this life and the next, but I had no desire to linger there."

Sir Hamish regarded me once again with his painterly eye.

"May I paint you, Jemis?"

This fell so hard on my own thought that I flushed and looked down. "If you'd like."

"I know it's not your light, Jemis," he said, and surprised me by taking me by both shoulders and then giving me a swift, close embrace. "Thank you."

∾

Master Dart was next; the Squire said very little when I had finished, but his eyes were bright.

"This daughter of mine," he said tentatively.

"A woman of great character," I replied instantly, having already decided what I would say to this obvious line of questioning. "Game despite all the mad adventures we fell into. And brilliant."

The Squire harrumphed, but he was visibly pleased.

"Perry has been cunningly finding out her Winterturn traditions," I added, "so you can surprise her with them."

The Squire harrumphed again. "He's not too upset at being done out of the entail?"

I could only shake my head, for Mr. Dart had never wanted it in the first place.

"I suppose not, eh," the Squire muttered, and patted me awkwardly on the shoulder. "You're a good friend to him. Glad you didn't die, what?"

"Indeed," I said, grinning and knowing that a month ago I would not have been able to see that for the gentle, loving tease it was. How had I ever feared that Sir Hamish and the Squire would reject me even if Mr. Dart didn't?

How had I ever thought Mr. Dart would disdain my friendship because I thought I had lost all the promise of my family and my education? I had sworn fealty to him, for that action at the dark cross-roads between life and death; but he had long since been a loyal friend to me.

∾

I knew my father's messages were from my mother and my stepfather, but nothing more.

When I had finished, he gestured for me to sit down in one of the chairs in the room, and took the other. He clasped his hands, elbows on his knees, and rested his chin on them.

"I haven't been able to tell you how I came to survive Loe."

I shook my head, my heart suddenly leaping into my throat.

"Sometimes," he said, "I think my whole life led up to that point, and I am still waiting there, at the Gates of the Morning, waiting for the enemy to climb the hill."

I could only look at him. I had not known to imagine that scene, not until Hal had come to Ragnor Bella earlier this autumn. I had been told that my father had died ignominiously, running away from a court-martial for treason; and that he had died honourably, lost over the Border on a scouting mission. I had held those two contradictory notifications in my mind and my heart, unable to believe the one and unable to prove the other.

"You will never be quite the same," he said, regarding me intently. "No one I know who has died and returned ever was."

"You've known it to happen before?"

He smiled crookedly. "Not quite so dramatically or miraculously. Perhaps it is always a miracle. A lot of things happen in a battle, Jemis, and there are many forms of dying."

He had died himself and come back to life, in all the ways that mattered: socially, spiritually, emotionally; perhaps even physically, if my dream of the pirate ship being captured was true.

"Jemis," my father said softly, "thank you for coming home."

CHAPTER THREE

I spent the night at Dart Hall, and the next morning prepared to head in to Ragnor Bella and my own little flat over the bookstore.

Hope and my father were the only two to join me for breakfast, which was at the unsociable hour of dawn—all of eight o'clock, this time of the year.

"Good morning," I said brightly.

"Good morning, Jemis," Hope replied, then sighed. "Lord St-Noire—"

"Mr. Greenwing if you must," I interrupted. "Please."

My father laughed. "Good morning, Jemis, Miss Stornaway. Are you off to town this morning, Jemis?'

I nodded and poured them each coffee. Hope, I knew from Morrowlea, took hers the way Mr. Dart did, with lashings of honey and cream. Perhaps it was the Charese manner. My father tended to black. I liked something in between the two.

"If you can stand not running, I'll walk in with you."

It was so much easier than it had been to simply smile at him, acknowledge the small tendril of joy unfurling in my heart, that after all the doubts and loss—we still could have *this*. The simple, homely interactions of a man and his son.

"Do you run around the barony here?" Hope asked. When I cocked my eyebrow at her she smiled, dimples appearing suddenly, and I knew what she was about to ask.

"There are some interesting rock formations, yes."

"I've heard there were standing stones," she asked tentatively.

I glanced at my father, who said, "The False Witnesses. They're a stone circle—nine stones—up above the Darts' land. The edge of the mountains."

I nodded. "There are the ones sacred to the Lady—the Dragon Stone, and … the Ellery Stone …"

My father looked sharply at me, then picked up the conversation smoothly and told Hope about the Giants' Castle. She replied with questions, and I sat back with my coffee, trying not to shiver at the thought of how the cultists had marred the Ellery Stone.

I had not realized the stones were such a specifically local feature, but apparently only Fiellan and northern Ronderell, particularly up by Fillering pool, had any, and it was rare for them to still be in *use* as were those in Ragnor barony.

"We have sacred wells and caves mostly, my part of Chare," Hope said. "People still leave offerings at some of them."

Hal had shown me a grotto up on the coast by his castle, which was nearly carpeted in sea-polished amber.

("It's low in value," he'd said; but gorgeous when the sun hit the wet stones.)

I said, "I will see if I can find a map for you. Miss Dart might be interested in the waterways."

"Don't go to the Magarran Strid on your own," my father interjected seriously.

I shuddered at the visceral memory of being on the rocky islet as the water fell away from the surface and revealed a hideous deep gorge laying beneath what had seemed a shallow surface. "Yes, let's avoid that."

"I've heard of the Strid," Hope said. "It's supposed to be the most dangerous stretch of water in Northwest Oriole, apart from the Maelstrom between the Ghath and the Iarlaich in the Northern Sea."

"I've sailed that," my father said grimly. "It's not as dangerous as the Magarran Strid, for all that there's a hole in the world at the bottom of it."

I blinked at this unexpected tidbit. "I beg your pardon?"

My father laughed, the shadow lifting from his face as I undoubtedly looked deeply puzzled.

"You know how there are passages between the worlds," he said.

"Of course, but I thought they'd … broken … in the Fall?"

"The ones that were bound into the structure of the Empire, yes. But they were never all of the passages, nor even the majority of them. Many only open on specific occasions or for specific people … wild magic can have a will of its own, they say. And at the bottom of the Maelstrom is a window to another world. The Sea-Lord's Eye, they call it up there. No one knows where it leads. Even if the passage goes both ways there's no way to come up through the Maelstrom … you'd have to be an extremely powerful and skilled mage to even think about trying."

"I wonder if Jullanar Maebh has ever seen it," Hope said thoughtfully, and then one of the servants came in with a tray full of toast and porridge and the conversation shifted to other interesting rocks of the barony, of which it turned out my father and I both had some distinct opinions.

～

I had been informed the night before that Mr. Fancy had continued on to Ragnor Bella to deliver my purchases before returning to St-Noire himself. This meant that I had nothing but what I was carrying to take back myself.

I changed into the outfit I'd left at Dart Hall, which was rather too lightweight for the weather. I'd been intending to run and thought it would be fine for that purpose, but since I was walking I added the coat I'd been given by the eccentric Master Boring.

My father regarded the long quilted garment with amusement. It was cut closely around the torso and waist before swinging out to just above my knees. It was made of quilted wool in a fine deep teal—apparently a favourite colour, as there had been numerous outfits in variations of that shade—with embroidery in black and silver. The long line of small silver buttons were, I admit, both deeply fussy and greatly appealing.

"Is that the new fashion in Orio City?" My father asked, his lips twitching.

"Not yet," I replied, not quite embarrassed, but grinning to cover the hint of it. The coat had last been fashionable in the early years of the Emperor Artorin's reign. My father was in a new coat in a sober blue with brass buttons. *Its* cut was solidly fashionable in Ragnor Bella, which was always a step behind everyone else.

"Is this part of the story that went off-course last night?"

"It might be," I allowed.

We left Dart Hall by the front door. It was a splendid morning, bright and crisp. The snow had ended in the night, and the lawns before the Hall presented a smooth white sward marred only by the tracks of rabbits and other small creatures. The rougher grass of the sheep meadows on the other side of the ha-ha showed above the snow; the sheep themselves seemed almost yellow in comparison.

"A fine morning," my father announced, and set off with his hands jammed into his pockets.

I wondered if the rival brother haberdashers of Ragnor Bella had neglected to make *any* of our ordered gloves, or whether he'd just forgotten them somewhere.

We walked silently at a steady, brisk pace. I fell into it fairly easily, remembering the long day spent traversing the Arguty Forest with him and General Ben, all of a month ago and before I'd realized he was my father, come back from the reputed dead a second time.

"Your mother and I used to go for these lovely long walks," he said as we turned off the drive onto the road leading to Dartington and eventually to Ragnor Bella. "We often walked half the night through, when the moon was out. She loved the twilight, Olive did."

I let that new piece of knowledge settle into my heart. My mother, so happy, so healthy, so *herself* in the Wood of Spiritual Refreshment. So much of my sojourn there was hazy in my mind, impression and emotion; but her face was clear. Now *there* was a gift from the Lady.

The road was soft underfoot, as the ground had not frozen before the snow fell. I enjoyed kicking up little lumps of snow as we walked, little conical hats on the toes of my boots building up and then falling off in a tumble of pellets.

"My chatterbox son, so quiet," my father teased.

It was so much *easier* to say these things now, to myself, to him, with a few of the knots in my heart unloosed. "I am so glad you came home, Papa. It must have been hard, when you didn't know what you would find."

"That is why Ben and I came incognito," he replied, smiling crookedly. (I knew that smile; that was my own smile in the mirror, when I could not help but laugh at myself.) "But you know, Jemis, I don't think I would have wanted to come any other way. It was so wonderful to meet you without knowing quite who you were at first."

We fell silent as we passed a cottage along the road. The housewife was in her front yard, gathering kale from a little patch of vegetables. We nodded politely at her; she bobbed a curtsey back, then said, "Well, look at the two of you! Master Jack, you're looking better. Very proud of your boy, I expect?"

"Very," my father said. "How are you, Mrs. Finch?"

"Can't complain, Master Jack, can't complain. Mr. Finch has the arthritis sore bad, but the Squire sees us right."

"He's a good man."

"Aye, couldn't ask for a better landlord." Then she laughed, her eyes crinkling until she looked like an old apple, all cheerful and rosy-cheeked and wrinkled. "At least not for us as are Dartington folks. Your people will be glad to see you home, Master Jack, what's left of them, and your son to come after you."

"Aye," my father said, and tipped his hat to her. "Good day, Mrs. Finch."

I didn't have a hat, so I gave her one of my most extravagant bows, all heel-clicks and curlicue hand gestures. Mrs. Finch laughed again and made a shooing gesture with her handful of curly green leaves.

We kept on, following the tracks of a pony-cart down the road until it turned off for the Old Arrow. We went over the bridge, a hard left to get onto the river-road.

"Not the Greenway this morning?" I enquired.

"Did you want to go that way? I thought it might be a trifle wet."

I would probably have run that way, as I still tended to avoid the White Cross even though I now knew my father had not been buried there as a traitor and suicide. It was hard to lose the fear and disgust the place had so long engendered.

"I wanted to see how high the river was running," he added. "If you don't mind."

"Of course not."

We passed a handful of other people on their way into Dartington from outlying farms, but it was both too early and too late in the morning for there to be much traffic. Neither of us said anything as we approached the White Cross, but my father did bump my shoulder, gently, with his own, as we went past.

"When did you realize it was me?" I asked curiously. "I obviously didn't know it was you until you told me ..."

"You were under a curse and also you thought I was dead," my father replied quickly. "I wasn't surprised or offended you didn't recognize me."

"I'm sure you weren't expecting me to be in Yellton Gaol. *I* wasn't expecting to be in Yellton Gaol."

"While I am somewhat disturbed at the number of prisons you have found yourself in of late, at least you have a high success rate in escaping them. I should like to hear more details about the Orio prison break."

"I'm going to write it up as a proper monograph."

"Of course you are! Jemis, how you are your mother's son!"

I let that settle into my heart as well. My mother had died when I was fifteen, and I had never gotten to know her as a woman with her own interests and skills apart from survival and motherhood.

"I started to wonder when we were in the tunnel waiting for the Knockers to pass us by. You had such a strange tone to your voice when you talked about Vorel ... but I just couldn't fathom *how* it was you, why you were dressed the way you were, why you were in Yellton Gaol ... Then at one point you smiled at something, and Ben told me—when your attention was distracted—that it was just like *my* smile, and after that ... everything you said or did seemed to be further proof. It wasn't one moment," he concluded, with a slightly shame-faced smile. "Just a slow realization that *this* fine young gentleman was *my* son—*mine*!"

I had to do something, but we were walking side-by-side and it seemed odd to stop and embrace him; but that sort of embarrass-ment seemed to be greatly reduced after my sojourn in the Lady's Wood, and after a moment I slung my right arm around his shoulders.

He was a little taller than I, and far broader in his shoulders despite his still too-lean frame, but he leaned into me and let his left arm slide around my shoulders in turn.

"Then you defended me so fiercely … Ah, Jemis, I am so sorry you had to."

"It was not your fault."

"Hamish has been poring through Tor's law-books to see where the line crosses from gossip to slander."

"Libel is a possibility as well," I suggested, "given that there's been more than a few comments in the *New Salon*. And there's Jack Lind-sary's play."

"I am very proud of you for not punching him. I'm not sure I would have been able to refrain, in your place."

That bizarre evening in the hot, colourful, noisy student pub was hard to remember. After a moment I was able to offer this truth: "He had a very silly hat."

"A punishment in itself, indeed," my father replied gravely.

~

We talked of small things for the next couple of miles. The river-road showed little traffic; there were far more animal trails than human or horse tracks. At one point we stopped to observe a slide made in the snow down to the swift, muddy water.

"Otter," my father said, considering the bank.

I was reminded of the Honourable Rag talking about otter-hunting. I couldn't imagine taking any joy in the act. I didn't mind hunting in general, but the idea of tromping up freezing rivers or their snowy banks, following the curly-coated otter hounds as they sought out their quarry, was deeply unappealing.

Besides, I rather liked otters. They didn't do much harm and were a joy to watch.

"I was saved by an otter once, on a scouting mission," my father said. "I was hiding on the bank, and made a noise, and the people I was spying on heard me. They started to search, but then a family of otters came tearing out of a side stream, play-fighting the way they do, and made such a ruckus that I was able to sneak away. Always liked them, even before that."

We regarded the otter slide for a few more moments, but the otters themselves were not to be seen.

This part of the road left the bank, where there was a large stand of willows and a notoriously boggy patch, and climbed to a low rise with an excellent view over the valley.

The Arguty Forest was a dark mass to the north. The opposite bank of the Rag was mostly meadows and leas along this stretch, as they tended to flood in the winter and were slow to dry out in the spring. That was all the Baron's land on that side, anyway.

My father was looking upriver, to where we could see the smoke rising over the brow of a hill hiding Ragnor Bella from direct sight. The river was high, muddy grey from the rain. The mountains encircling Southern Fiellan were snow-crowned, the sun gleaming whitely. A few of the higher peaks had long streamers of snow whipped off by the wind.

"What a splendid place this is. I don't know that I ever want to leave again."

That could have been said by either my father or I, I realized in astonishment a moment after I determined that it had been him, not me, who had spoken.

Either of us would have been considered equally unlikely to voice the sentiment.

"You've travelled farther than I have," I said.

"You've been to the Lady's Country and back," he replied. "It's not a competition, Jemis."

I laughed at that. "I didn't think I was ever going to come back,

32

after university. I went to Morrowlea thinking I would set out to seek my fortune ... I thought there was nothing here for me. I thought it was so *boring*." I shook my head in amazement. "I was so wrong."

My father smiled that crooked smile we shared, and ducked his chin into his collar. I straightened the hang of my long coat, which was, if anything, too warm for the sunny day, and slipped a little as we started down the hill back towards to the bank.

My father caught my elbow. I caught my balance before quite falling over, and so we were posed there, halfway down the hill, his hand on my elbow, me laughing again, when a vixen with two tails appeared out the hedgerow on the inland side of the road, looked at us with her black ears pricked intently, and said, "Beware the false hunter."

Gnomic warning uttered, the two-tailed vixen bounded lightly back through the hedge and out of sight.

My father's hand gripped tight on my elbow. In our silence the river rushing past us sounded very loud.

"Well," I said, recovering my aplomb. "At least it's not another dragon."

CHAPTER FOUR

The two-tailed vixen had certainly been there, and equally certainly had not left any tracks once she was through the hedge.

We examined the few prints in the snow between hedgerow and road. They looked like ordinary enough fox-tracks, except for a certain silvery glitter where there ought to have been shadows in the snow.

I was glad my father was there as a witness.

"As I said: I have learned that I was entirely wrong to think Ragnor Bella boring."

"Indeed," my father replied, and then seemed to shake himself free of his thoughts. "We shall have to look into that. And where better than your bookstore?"

"Really?"

"You do know Mrs. Etaris has ah, an unconventional past?"

"I had gathered that. She went to Galderon, I understand." There were plenty of other odd skills Mrs. Etaris possessed. She had a tendency to lay them all at the feet of her time at Madame Clancette's Finishing School for Girls in Fiella-by-the-Sea, but—the thought came to me—of course, that was simply a *joke*.

So many of her comments suddenly made considerably more sense.

"Yes," my father murmured, as we started walking again.

"Did you know her well ... before? I mean, I know she was friendly with my mother ... the Embroidery Circle ... They were kind to me when I first came back, after Mr. Buchance died."

"They are good women. But no, not so much Mrs. Etaris on my part. She was a good friend to Olive."

We walked a while in silence. The sun was warm, and snow was dropping in quiet thumps off the branches of the trees that lined the riverbank along here. We walked more slowly than earlier, both of us occupied with our own thoughts.

Not that mine were particularly interesting. I could not hold onto serious concern, whether about Mrs. Etaris's mysterious past or the ominous warnings of a magic fox. The sky was bright and robins were singing in the hedgerow, and there were white geese in the river, and my father and I were walking side-by-side.

This was a moment that would not be lost, I swore. This world or the next, this love, this beauty, this crisp air and this bright sunlight, this mud on my boots and the swinging hem of my coat, this—

My father yanked me by the elbow as the Honourable Rag thundered by on his black stallion, once more in his fine scarlet riding habit.

He lifted his whip to his tall beaver in acknowledgment, which he hadn't done the last time he'd thrown clots of mud up against me. Well, my father was here this time.

I'd thought we'd made some progress in our friendship, after the revelations in Master Boring's house in the foothills on the Linder side of the Crosslains, but perhaps not.

My father slowly let go of my elbow. I mumbled thanks, wondering what had happened to my reflexes and spatial awareness. Surely that had not all been my unknown and now extinguished magic? I had practiced long and hard hours at Morrowlea and since to engrain them into my muscles. My father had always told me—

I glanced up at him, the reflexive thought stuttering in his real, living presence. "You're here," I said. "Alive."

"I am." He looked at my face, smiling a little. The eye that had been injured was brighter than the other, the skin around it paler from the patch covering it all summer. He was so wiry, his muscles like hawsers

35

over iron pulleys, no flesh to spare even after a third of year healing from the pirate galley.

I wanted to know—everything. Nothing he was ready to share with me. Nothing I dared ask, if he did not offer.

"Come," he said, "I want to know what you bought in Orio City before you were arrested."

~

I had made the classic mistake of asking people if they wanted me to get them anything from the capital. By the end of the afternoon of my departure, I had a list three pages long which included a winter's worth of food for the villagers of St-Noire in the Woods. I also had five hundred bees with which to buy books for Mrs. Etaris.

All my successful acquisitions were piled in the middle of my flat.

My small, cozy flat.

My father leaned on the doorframe, regarding me with what I considered slightly excessive amusement.

I stood two steps in, as far as I could manage. It looked—well, it looked like nothing so much as the wall of *stuff* that had filled the entryway to Master Boring's strange house.

"I hope there's not another unicorn buried in this lot," I murmured, and then had to explain exactly how Mr. Dart had come across Ballory, last night's explanations having centred more on the connection between Hillend Towers and the ancient legend of Sir Peregrine and the Unicorn.

There was no unicorn, foal, sculpture, or otherwise.

There was, instead: five hundred bees' worth of books, all of which had to be ferried back downstairs for Mrs. Etaris to go through; three crates of exceedingly expensive tea from Ysthar; *five* crates of beautiful clothing originally belonging to Master Boring's (now dead) favoured son, which I'd accepted because I'd been in something of a daze and unable not to reply honestly that I liked the clothes very much and that they fit surprisingly well; a seemingly endless collection of parcels done up in brown paper and jute twine, only half of which were labelled; and numerous sacks and barrels and small wooden crates containing a variety of foodstuffs and other delights.

"Well," said my father, after we finally excavated one of my chairs, upon which he promptly sat down. "I don't suppose you'd be willing to open one of those crates you say is tea and make us a pot? I haven't had tea since ..." His face went suddenly wistful.

Since before Astandalas Fell, I supplied, and nodded.

I went downstairs, because I still couldn't reach the door to my kitchen. Mrs. Etaris was in the store, examining the first box of books.

"You did find some treasures!" she exclaimed happily, pulling out a small stack of books in tooled green leather. "The complete three-volume set of Durgand's *Valiance and Shock: an Account of the Infamous Red Company's Nefarious Deeds.*"

"I wonder why they didn't bind them in red," I said, for want of any better response.

How did I not remember buying *those*?

Well, the rest of the day following the book fair had been rather ... full, to say the least.

"Oh, this was always one of my favourites—the Customs House of Colhélhé, you know," Mrs. Etaris said, her eyes dancing with merriment.

I hummed the opening bars of the relevant song, and she started to laugh. "Oh yes, that's it exactly! But you didn't come down for that, surely?"

I gave her a courteous bow. "I was wondering if I might borrow a kettle-full of hot water, and whether you might be interested in a cup of tea."

She paused with her hand still holding the book open to the spot presumably recounting the nefarious deeds concerning the Customs House of Colhélhé. It a story I knew only from the Fitzroy Angursell song on the subject, which was hilarious but scant on some key details, I'd always thought.

"Bring the tea down, Mr. Greenwing, and I will show you how to make a *proper* brew."

~

Tea was fantastically expensive.

It had been somewhat expensive, but an affordable luxury, in Astandalan days. It was frequently mentioned in the literature: people were forever stopping for a cup of tea, or having an elaborate ceremony involving it, or a full meal.

They had it in the morning—there were special blends for breakfast —at midmorning, in the early afternoon, at tea time, after supper. Sometimes people seemed to drink it just before bed, as a soothing alternative to an alcoholic nightcap.

There were versions that were supposed to be green, and others that were white, or black, with liquor that bore hints of smoke or caramel or pepper or roses.

There had been, it was said, an entire valley that grew tea *only* for the Emperor's table.

There were stories of the valleys shaped by magic, hidden by magic, protected by some of the most powerful spells and enchantments ever devised, all to grow the tea drunk throughout the Empire. Tea plants—I wasn't very clear on what they were like— were the personal property of the Emperor, and were protected accordingly.

It was said there were ice-white dragons, sinuous as snakes, wingless and yet able to fly, who guarded the approaches to the valleys.

I wondered if there was a coherent account of the Red Company's visit to that valley devoted to the Emperor's personal tea in Durgand's *Valiance and Shock*.

They had, so Fitzroy Angursell's song had it, served it to the Crown Prince Imperial, Shallyr Silvertongue, that time they'd kidnapped him.

I had always wanted to know a lot more of the context of that particular adventure.

Mrs. Etaris left me to stoke up the fire in the iron stove that heated the bookshop, and disappeared into the back room where we kept such important supplies as mugs and biscuits. She reappeared in due course with a sturdy stoneware teapot that I had not seen before and the familiar copper kettle.

"I was taught to keep a separate pot for true black tea," she informed me. She set the kettle on the stove and nodded approvingly when some water droplets hissed as they landed on the iron surface. "Very good, that won't take long. Now … the tea?"

I had forced open the crate upstairs, using the boot knife my father had given me before I left for Orio City and which I had somehow managed not to lose despite all the adventures, and presented her with one of the smaller containers we had found inside.

This was a round tin covered in coloured paper showing a pattern of what seemed to be cherry blossoms on a sky-blue background. There was a cartouche in the centre bearing a sigil and what looked like arcane runes; neither my father nor I knew what they said, though my father had recognized them as marks pertaining to the grade and origin of the tea.

Mrs. Etaris clearly knew more than we did, for she examined the cartouche carefully and with satisfaction. "First leaf from the Kzarlin, how *splendid*. Wherever did you find this, Mr. Greenwing? I hope you did not spend your *entire* inheritance from Mr. Buchance on tea?"

"No, I was … given it."

"A princely gift." She paused, considering. "Or a ducal one?"

I set myself to another recounting of the past week. I'd already agreed with Mr. Dart that I should tell her, as Mr. Dart was nearly as admiring of Mrs. Etaris as I was myself—and even Hal had wanted her insight into the overall political situation in Northwest Oriole—but the events did not seem any less odd and magnificent for the third time telling.

Mrs. Etaris listened carefully, betrayed little more than a blink at the account of my death and resurrection, and in the end said: "Well, Mr. Greenwing, do beware of falling into blackmail or bribery as a propensity; they can be habit-forming."

I spluttered a denial, as I had intended nothing of the sort when accepting the gifts from Master Boring. (Surely he'd not intended them for a *bribe*? He'd known, as we had, that there was no *proof* he'd murdered the unfortunate and obnoxious Henry Coates.)

Mrs. Etaris simply laughed and turned to the now-whistling kettle. "Now: to make tea; first you must bring fresh water to the full boil. Then you warm the teapot, like so—" She poured a goodly measure of water into the vessel in question before returning the kettle to the hob.

My mother had taught me to make all forms of herbal teas and tisanes in just this fashion, but I kept my mouth closed and regarded Mrs. Etaris with as attentive an expression as I could muster. She merely laughed again.

"I can see the Scholar in you," she murmured, and opened the tin.

The paper crinkled as it tore, and then a deep, woodsy, fruity, just slightly peppery aroma unfurled.

"This," she said, breathing in deeply, "is very good tea." She took a pinch and dropped it in one of the mugs, then splashed a small quantity of water not from the boiling kettle, but the teapot. She filled the other two mugs all the way with the water from the teapot before adding several heaping teaspoons of the tea to the pot and filling it with the freshly boiling water.

"Now we let it steep," she said, and placed the pot close to the stove, where it could bask in the heat. "I am missing a tea cozy … the cat shredded the old one while you were gone. I think he missed you."

"I may have acquired a friend for him," I said, and explained about the kitten I had left at Dart Hall.

"Gingersnap is getting on in years," she acknowledged, with a fond glance at the cat that lay curled up in a patch of sunlight in the bay window. "He could do with a little shaking up." She wrapped her hand around the teapot and stood there, her expression far away.

I wondered which lost friends of her youth she was remembering. She had the same look she'd had when we'd found the bag belonging to her old friend, the one who *sang going into battle*, in the back of a wardrobe upstairs.

"Try that tea," she directed, nodding at the one she'd made with the hot but not boiling water. I tasted it and made an involuntary face at the ashy, bitter overtones.

"Not what you were expecting? Indeed." She took my cup and tossed the dregs into a slop bucket she'd brought from the back room. "Fetch some milk, will you? There's a jug on the back step."

The back step opened up past the door that led to the stairs up to my flat. I could hear a low rumbling sort of singing, and a few thuds, and guessed my father was continuing to move the new purchases around.

I shut that door and moved a pair of over-shoes out of the way before opening the outside door.

There was a wooden crate containing the glass bottle of milk as delivered of a morning by Mr. Sifton—I would have to ask him to start bringing me one again, and a pat of butter—oh and eggs—and would he bring bacon? The previous milkman had been known to—

I took a breath, stilling my racing thoughts. My fingers snugged into place around the neck of the bottle, resting on the grooves and protuberances of the familiar double B sigil.

The bottle's design had been patented by my stepfather. Some fraction of a penny from this bottle had no doubt found its way into that vast fortune he'd unexpectedly left to me.

I glanced once around the back alley. There was another door, the back entrance to the notary public, who lived above his office. He'd already taken in his milk, with yesterday's empty bottle left in its place.

There was a stack of old wooden barrels beside the notary's door. I wondered what they had contained; they looked like the whiskey barrels Myrta the Hand's gang had requested we convey to Yrchester, on our way to Orio City.

The snow had mostly melted except in the corners and the inverted prints where the milkman and his pony-cart had pressed their marks and compressed the snow. I glanced up as a cloud passed across the face of the sun, casting the alley into shade.

When I looked down again, sitting there in front of me was the two-tailed fox.

"Beware the false lover," she said, before tumbling over and over herself behind the barrels outside the notary public's back door, where she disappeared.

I crouched there with my hand on the milk bottle. The sun had come out from behind the cloud just in time to show that whatever else the fox was, she did not cast a shadow.

CHAPTER FIVE

W e drank our tea in a strange mix of extravagant luxury and considerable upheaval: my father and I sitting on crates, Mrs. Etaris on the singular uncovered chair. The cups were the same pretty glazed stoneware we used in the shop for our elevenses, and Mrs. Etaris had provided some of her biscuits. These were Winterturn sugar cookies rather than her gingersnaps, but still very good.

The tea itself was splendid: rich, full-flavoured, not a hint of ashes at all. I sipped it with great relish.

"I've been making mincemeat," Mrs. Etaris said at one point, her gaze wandering around the room. I had barely started to decorate it; only my father's Heart of Glory hung on the wall in all its splendour.

Had I found an etching in Orio City? I was sure I remembered looking at one, at some point in that afternoon when Hal and Mr. Dart and I had wandered around looking for spices and fabrics and a strangely specific type of leatherworking tool for Mrs. Kulfield.

"I'll bring you a jar," Mrs. Etaris went on. I thanked her even though it took several moments before I could even begin to be sure she still meant the mincemeat. Well, anything that came in jars from Mrs. Etaris was probably worth having.

"What are your Winterturn traditions, Mrs. Etaris?" my father asked politely. "You're from Fiella-by-the-Sea, and went to university at Galderon, if I understand correctly?"

"Indeed," she said, sipping her tea. "I picked up a few unusual ideas during that period."

"So I've heard," he replied, smiling.

I was getting better at realizing there was subtext, but had no idea what on earth they were talking about.

When we had finished the tea—which I was starting to get an unfortunate taste for, all things considered—she returned downstairs to unpacking the boxes I'd so far carried down. My father and I stood in the middle of the room while her footsteps tripped heavily down the stairs.

"What did you mean, just now?" I blurted.

My father regarded me, his mouth tugging up into that crooked smile. "What happens if I lay down the Salmon of Wisdom as my discard in a game of Poacher?"

All the things he had taught me, asking something about Poacher to spark my mind into action, in that long glorious summer when I was nine. All the games I had played at university, testing my skill by teaching others how to play. Those games I had played since, in tavern after tavern across the whole of northern Fiellan and half of Ghilousette, learning from players good and bad, mediocre or with the gift of luck. All the books I had studied, all the puzzles I had laboriously deciphered.

Here was another gift, a small riddle for a fine winter's day.

"At what point in the game?" I asked finally.

He smiled more fully, his eyes and face lighting up: the father I remembered from my childhood, full of life and vigour, full of merriment and cunning, showing me card after card alone, in combination, in endless permutation of sign and sense and significance.

"That's the question, isn't it?"

He left it at that, leaving me to ponder what that particular card would mean as the discard. The general idea of the game of Poacher was to finagle the other player into believing your hand—cards of Chance and Happenstance, of Fish and Other Prey—held a story that overmatched theirs.

The discards were the shape and outline of the story. To discard the *Salmon of Wisdom*, one of the highest cards in the deck—

Well. What *could* it mean?

We spent the rest of the morning sorting boxes and parcels. My thoughts whirled, trying to piece together too few clues.

I needed more information, I decided on the tenth or twentieth run downstairs with a box of books.

On the fifteenth or twenty-fifth I had begun to wonder if the Embroidery Circle might have it.

~

My father took me to lunch at a tiny little public house tucked away on a back street. I had not known either taproom or street existed before he turned down the narrow lane between the old blacksmith's and someone's blocky brick house.

The place consisted of a taproom with a long counter, at which leaned three or four men, and three tables. One was free, and we sat down, my father with his back to the wall and mine to the room. I disliked being so exposed, but my father clearly had the seniority in that respect.

Well, all respects, being my father, obviously.

I subsided as my thoughts tangled over themselves and merely nodded a beat too late when the publican came out and offered us ale and 'the special'.

"I've never been here before," I ventured quietly once the man had returned with two tankards full of a foaming, brown ale.

"I'd be surprised if you had. This is Harry's place for his old comrades."

I sipped my ale. It was cool and nutty, with a pleasant bitterness and a hint of sweetness. "Thank you for bringing me here."

"Jack's son will always be welcome," the publican—Harry, I supposed—said, with a faint emphasis on *Jack*. I startled but managed not to slop my ale all over myself, though the table did not fare so well. My father snorted, the publican laughed, and I flushed and hastily found one of my handkerchiefs to mop up the mess.

"None of that, now," Harry muttered, pushing my hand out of the way and tossing a stained rag down instead. "There. Save your good cotton."

It was not so long ago that my dozen cotton handkerchiefs, all woven by myself on the Morrowlea student looms, had been a major part of my entire wardrobe. I nodded in gratitude. I didn't think I would ever be able to take them fully for granted, not when I knew how long it took to weave even a foot square of cloth.

When I'd first seen the huge sails of the tall trading ships in the Fillering Pool harbour, I had found myself nearly dizzy with amazement at how very much work went into simply the sails. Hal had laughed at me; but I knew he had been even more overcome at the discovery of how much labour and skill went into the things he (an Imperial Duke since he was seven) had always taken for granted.

He had understood gardens, or thought he did, from his own love of botany. He had not, until the first autumn season spent putting up produce for the winter, known just what went into all those jams and jellies, those barrels of apples and turnips, potatoes and onions, garlic and rutabagas and celery root and parsnips and carrots and all the other foods to get us through the winter.

Even learning how much land needed to be given over to seed production, and how to harvest and clean and store the seed ready or the next year ... oh, there had been so much to learn about what underlay a community.

"The food's good, Jemis," my father said suggestively.

I looked down to discover a plate of lamb stew before me, a crusty loaf of bread broken in the middle of the table. Yellow butter—Mr. Sifton's best, I was fairly sure—and a little pot of salt completed the offerings.

It was good.

The conversation at the bar was on the topic of the coming winter. "I hear Jack's son yonder ordered food for the Woods," one said. His voice was not loud, but clearly audible. My back was to the bar, but I could see my father smiling as he sopped at the gravy with his bread.

These were not the manners my mother had so diligently instilled in me. Well, Morrowlea had taught me to always modulate my behaviour according to the local custom.

"Aye," said a second man behind us—surely they hadn't deliberately waited until I was eating again? My father's expression was of no assistance to me whatsoever. "It'll be a hard winter, mark my words. More snow than we'll know to deal with, I reckon."

"It's hard for them folk in the Woods," the first one said.

The third one chuckled with a dark, wet sound. "Better for them to not know aught of the past three years, no? There's been strange stuff afoot."

"More since he came back."

"Aye."

I focused resolutely on the lamb stew, though I could feel that my face was hot and red. My father had already finished his plate, and was now sipping his ale while watching me.

Why *would* someone discard the Salmon of Wisdom?

Some cards could be too good for the rest of your hand. Some stories were too tall to be believed. Sometimes wild magic broke through and transformed everything else.

Some cards in Poacher made all the rest … reverse.

The world lifted around me as if it were about to settle into a new pattern. I halted, the heel of the bread in my hand. Behind me the men were talking about someone they had known once, long ago, when they were soldiers facing the enemies of Astandalas far from Ragnor Bella.

You could not hold the Salmon of Wisdom and the Holy Grail and the Unicorn in your hand at once: only two of the three were permitted, or else all three collapsed into their reversed meanings.

Which you kept and which you discarded depended entirely on what you thought was in your opponent's hand.

This was the deep lore of Poacher, which I had barely begun to be able to study. I knew enough to know the permutations were possible, enough to know that decisions would have to be made, but not enough to know what to do about them.

My instinct would be to keep the Salmon of Wisdom and the

Unicorn. One card from the Fish, the other from the Happenstance deck. To keep two from the Happenstance deck—

Why?

My father wiped his mouth on a handkerchief he pulled out of his pocket, then stuffed it back carelessly. Seven years on a pirate galley had not inculcated a great nicety of dress in my father, if ever he'd been prone to it. I couldn't remember anyone ever saying so.

"Well, Jemis, I must be off—the lawyers are expecting me again. Vorel left a right mess."

My uncle Sir Vorel and his wife the so-called Lady Flora had both been taken by the Kingsford lawyers back to the capital with them, as their crimes were considerable and ranged from attempted murder to false allegations of treason to stealing my inheritance to consorting with the Dark Kings and attempted human sacrifice.

I was glad they were well out of the picture, to be entirely honest. Even if I had no desire to move into Arguty House, my father had fond memories of the place from his own childhood, and he deserved something good after all he had gone through.

Not that one needed to go through hell on earth to deserve something good.

I looked up to see that he was smiling fondly at me. I shrugged, trying not to flush again, and drank down a good portion of my remaining ale.

"I'm going to deliver some of my commissions from Orio City," I said, glancing around for Harry the publican.

"It's on my account," my father said, clapping me on the shoulder with one hand and waving at the men on the bar with the other.

One of them muttered, "It's a long account, three life debts and—"

"Ssh," the second said, elbowing his friend, as he caught me half-turning my head to hear them better.

We went outside. "Three …" I said quietly, not quite a question.

"They were men under my command," my father replied briskly. "I told them to come here, if we all survived the last battles of Loe, and I would see them right. Olive did well to support them as best she could."

I remembered men coming to the dower cottage, to my stepfather's house in town, hats in hand and faces haggard and hopeless. Injured men, most of them, in body and in soul: thin, raggedy, unshaven, scarred.

My mother had never turned them away. She had always welcomed them in, whether our parlour held nothing but mint tea and parsnip cakes from our garden or all the delicacies Mr. Buchance had brought from Chare. They had spoken, these rough and uncouth men, in rough and uncouth accents, of service and secret woes I did not understand until I was much older.

She had always found something for them, no matter how hard our own straights were.

"They served your father in good faith," she would tell me after they had gone. "We have our responsibilities to remember that."

"We don't have anything to give them," I'd objected.

"There is always something, be it only a listening ear and a cup of herbal tea with our own honey," my mother had said. She'd not been sharp, but resolute, firm, steady as the earth under our feet.

She always did find something: a few days of work digging over the garden or chopping wood or rebuilding a wall. Sometimes a few days of food and a safe place to rest was all they needed, these men who had nothing. Sometimes all she could give them was a tiny pot of honey, the pot one of the rough unglazed things we tried to make with clay from the stream at the bottom of the dower cottage garden.

The honey was our own; my mother, lady of the Woods Noirell, was very fond of bees, and hers were kin to those ones who drank the nectar of the Tillarny limes and turned them to the special honey known across the continent.

I had heard stories from those men, snippets and tales of my father's bravery, heroism, humour. They had moderated the stories for my young ears, my mother's tender birth. I had never been able to reconcile their Mad Jack Greenwing with the supposed coward shot in the back fleeing a court martial for high treason.

No wonder he knew half the highwaymen in the Arguty Forest. All those lost soldiers had had to go somewhere.

~

I went back to the bookstore, confirmed with Mrs. Etaris that she didn't need me to work that afternoon, and sallied forth with a basket of the identifiable packages and the goal of finding out the current gossip in town.

It was for once not about me. A few people made gentle mock of how well I was looking for someone supposedly dead these past several days, but most of them were far more interested in hearing all about Mr. Dart's unicorn.

By the time I made it to the second Mrs. Buchance's house, I had heard and done my best to correct a dozen mad rumours that ranged from Mr. Dart being the one who'd died to a rather hysterical suggestion that he was the avatar of the Hunter in Green who'd been seen all around the barony the past few months.

Logical argument did not seem to sway any of them, which I already knew from my own times as the subject of their theories. I corrected them anyway, hoping some of the audience at the baker, the fishmonger, the post office, and the apothecary would at least hear the truth for what it was.

I concluded my journey with Mrs. Buchance's house, knocking on the door before opening it to find it as full of life as it usually was.

The front hall, in fact, was full of miscellaneous children—my half- and step-sisters, their various cousins—not one but two excited dogs, and what appeared to be a professional man, who was trying to browbeat Mrs. Buchance into paying for something she almost certainly didn't need to pay for.

"Oh—Jemis—" Mrs. Buchance said as I entered the chaos. She smiled wanly at me as she bounced the baby. "It's good to see you."

One of my sisters let out an ear-piercing squeal. Lauren, I was fairly sure. Sela was the one to fling herself at me. "*Jemis!*"

"Careful now," I said, swinging the basket out of the way as she tackled my knees. She was followed by one of the dogs and two of the small boys.

"Lord St-Noire," the businessman said, his smile ingratiating.

I decided not to correct him, since I disliked his oily demeanour. "Yes?"

"Mr. Highdar was just telling me about—what was it, again, Mr. Highdar?"

"It's High*door*," he said, his smile slipping briefly until he was able to fix it again with an excessive display of teeth. I hid my own smile. Mrs. Buchance did not need much assistance to see off an importunate lawyer. Still, there was no point in wasting time in kicking him out.

"Mr. Highdoor," I said firmly, "I'm sure Mrs. Buchance will consider your offer carefully and discuss it with her advisors before she makes any decisions." I shooed the dog and the small boy holding onto its collar to one side so I could open the door and gesture at the man to leave.

"The offer is only valid if Mrs. Buchance signs right now," Mr. Highdoor protested. "I couldn't live with myself if she missed such a splendid opportunity because I didn't take the time to explain it fully. There are other people interested in the investment, you know."

I glanced at Mrs. Buchance, who shook her head in a sharp negation.

I smiled at Mr. Highdoor. "I'm sure that we all much appreciate your diligence, even if it does seem rather last-minute to come argue the opportunity the day it must be taken. I seem to recall learning that investments should be made with caution, research, and diligent background work. If you leave your folder of documents, I should be glad to go over them with Mrs. Buchance—you never know, perhaps I might be interested in the investment myself."

I held out my hand, but I could see that Mr. Highdoor was not going to relinquish the leather briefcase he was clutching.

"No? In that case, good afternoon, Mr. Highdoor."

He scuttled out. I shut the door, and Mrs. Buchance heaved a great sigh. Lamissa, the baby in her arms, imitated her and then grinned toothlessly around when the rest of us, children included, all laughed in response.

"Oh, Jemis, I am glad you're back." She handed me the baby in exchange for my basket, which contained a few treats for her and my sisters—most of my acquisitions for them would come as Winterturn gifts—and smiled more genuinely at me.

"He just wouldn't *leave*," she admitted. "I was about to start getting snippy."

I grinned. "I thought you were doing just fine."

Lauren tugged at my coat, but when I looked down she was just examining the buttons with intrigued curiosity. I left her to it after checking that her fingers were not excessively mucky.

Sela said, "Are you here to go gathering greens with us? Please say yes, Jemis! I don't want to go without you!"

Mrs. Buchance said, "It's not Winterturn yet, Sela. If you ask nicely, perhaps Jemis will be willing on the Lady's Day."

"Please, Jemis, *please*?" Sela asked, staring at me with exaggeratedly wide eyes.

I had always loved the whole process of gathering the greenery on the Lady's Day. It was a tradition my mother had been very keen on.

"Certainly," I said, winning a grateful smile from Mrs. Buchance; though I then realized I would probably end up with all the miscellaneous small boys as well.

Perhaps my father would be willing to come with us. Or Mr. Dart. Ballory would be a great distraction.

The children were all chatting excitably about what they liked best about gathering Winterturn greenery—I would apparently supply sweet buns and hot spiced cider at some point, or so Sela confidently declared—when I finally managed to ask Mrs. Buchance when the next Embroidery Circle meeting would be held.

"We'll likely have one in a few days' time." Mrs. Buchance regarded me with a sudden curiosity. "Did you want to come, Jemis?— Not that that's a problem," she added hastily. "I was not aware you were an aficionado of the fibre arts, that's all."

I hesitated, realizing for the first time that going to the actual meeting meant I would need to find some handicraft to do at it, and in the little moment of silence, heard a scratch on the door.

I hesitated again, then opened the door. We all looked out, to find the two-tailed fox standing there, her ears forward and her eyes focused on mine, too-alert and too-aware to be either animal or human.

The children all fell silent in astonishment. The two dogs cowered back behind the boys, tails tucked between their legs and bellies flat on the ground.

The fox looked at Mrs. Buchance, and then at the baby in my hands, and then at me.

"Beware the false friend," she stated, and this time simply vanished.

CHAPTER SIX

M iraculously, the rest of the day was quiet. I wasn't quite sure what to do with myself.

I puttered around, hanging up the new clothes from Master Boring and stacking the tins of tea neatly in the small cupboard that passed for my pantry.

Mrs. Etaris had kindly lit my stove while I was out. It was much smaller than the one in the store down below, and served as my primary heat and cooking surface. I liked it because it not only heated the room much better than an open fireplace, but it was also safe to leave unattended when, for instance, I was interrupted in my late-evening nap over a book about the curious habits of foxes by a commotion downstairs.

I had learned nothing of the folklore but the mundane was nevertheless fascinating.

I slung on my new coat and hastened downstairs in my slippers. My boots were by the door, drying out after an afternoon delivering parcels and gossiping.

There was a unicorn foal in the middle of the bookstore, nudging curiously at the stove door with her horn.

"Ballory," I said, more than a little puzzled. Then, louder: "Mr.

Dart? Perry? *Peregrine?"*

No answer. Ballory continued to nudge at the stove door.

"It's hot," I informed her. She scraped her horn across the glass front, which made a deeply unfortunate screeching noise. I shuddered atavistically. "Please don't."

She paused momentarily, then shifted her head so the horn was scraping down the channel between glass and iron frame. This made a marginally better noise.

"Thank you," I muttered. "And where is your Mr. Dart?"

No answer.

This was a sacred and beautiful magical being, eulogized in song and story across all of Northwest Oriole.

This was a creature, I reminded myself, that had been closed in a box in the middle of a maze of stuff in Master Boring's house.

Ballory continued to scrape at the channel with a singular focus.

"Is there a reason you're doing that?" I asked, not expecting an answer, which was just as well as I didn't receive one.

"Look," I tried, "I really did want to go to sleep at some point tonight."

Ballory paused to roll one limpid eye at me. It shone a warm red-gold in the reflected glimmer of coals from the stove, and was rather mesmerizing.

I cast around for something that might answer the question. "Do you want me to add another log to the fire?" I reached down for a stick, only to find that the unicorn had disappeared when I glanced aside.

I stopped there, looking around at the dim room. There was no sign of the door having opened or shut; no snow on the carpet. The fading hint of flowers might have been from the potpourri Mrs. Etaris kept behind the stove.

I blinked, but there continued to be nothing. I went to the door, but it was securely latched and bolted; so was the back door. There was nothing in the other rooms on the main floor, not even the cupboard under the stairs.

Eventually I gave up and returned to bed, deeply bewildered but increasingly sleepy.

~

In the morning, when I went down to light the stove in the bookstore, I saw a strange rune or sigil carved in silver over the glass door. It glimmered and then faded even as I watched.

My life hadn't been this prone to oddities *before* I went to Morrowlea, surely.

~

Perhaps it is best to back up to the rest of the afternoon.

The uncanny fox uttered her warning and disappeared. All the miscellaneous children started talking at once, and were eventually persuaded by Mrs. Buchance to go play in the back garden with the dogs. This left her, the baby, and me; we went for a cup of tea.

I explained the three encounters with the fox.

Mrs. Buchance, who was not much given to fey imaginings, nodded but seemed to have little to add.

"It's very odd," she said at length.

We could agree on that, at any rate.

"You could tell everyone at the next Embroidery Circle meeting, if you like," she suggested.

I did indeed like, and said so with what I hoped was gratifying rather than embarrassing enthusiasm. Mrs. Buchance was smiling brightly by the end of my effusions, which was a good thing, at any rate.

"How are you, Jemis?" she asked suddenly, after pouring me the lemon balm tea to which she was partial. She passed me a plate of plain shortbread to go with it, which I took gratefully. I'd eaten a goodly lunch but nevertheless found myself unaccountably hungry.

"Very well, thank you," I replied. I did not have a message for the second Mrs. Buchance from the afterlife. I felt no uneasiness over this: it was clear, at some deep level, that there had been necessary limits to the messages I could be given. What the necessity was was unfathomable, but it was so.

"You are looking ..." She trailed off. I remembered the odd light in

55

the Wild Saint's eyes, and smiled at her with what I hoped was a more normal expression. "Very well," she concluded, with a faint air of confusion. "Your trip to Orio City was successful, I take it?"

"In the end, yes." This seemed to be a good moment to offer her the item she'd asked me to acquire for her, a kind of metal mould for making small cakes in the Taran style. "I don't think I'll be going to Tara for another degree. The city didn't agree with me."

"Did you still want to leave?"

I glanced up at her question. She was smiling at me with a slightly anxious expression.

The second Mrs. Buchance, Miss Eleanor Inglesides that was, was only five years older than I. She'd been hired as a nursemaid for my sisters when my mother had died, and by the spring of the year following was my stepfather's second wife, with a baby of her own coming soon after.

It was only that morning that my father had expressed his love of Ragnor Bella, and I had not been sure, for a moment, whether it was not my own thought spoken aloud.

"Not as much, no," I admitted. "I don't seem to need to leave for either adventure or fortune, after all!"

"There's always the question of romance."

I shook my head. "Do you remember my friend from Morrowlea, Violet Redshanks?"

Mrs. Buchance was perhaps the only person I knew who hadn't immediately clocked *Redshanks* as a false name from its use in Fitzroy Angursell's *Aurora*. The poem and all the songs derived from it were equally banned, but that hadn't stopped very many people from contriving to know them. Mrs. Buchance's brother, the town baker, was certainly most familiar with them.

"How could I forget?" She laughed. "I thought she seemed a trifle dangerous ... Do be careful, Jemis."

"She's said I might write to her," I confided, ignoring this. Violet was nowhere near the danger my previous amour had been. Violet had told me she was dangerous; Lark had beguiled, bespelled, drugged, and imprisoned me.

"She is very beautiful and seemed a woman of great character,"

Mrs. Buchance said with due consideration.

"She is so smart," I said. "We both read Classics. Violet studied the ancient epics. She even learned Old Oriolan so she could read *The Knight and the Unicorn* and *The Lady and the Dark*."

Mrs. Buchance made an amused, agreeing sort of noise, and I continued to rhapsodize on Violet for a few moments before she finally laughed and told me to continue on with my errands, as it was time to feed the baby.

I went out smiling, retrieved hat and basket from the front hall, and continued on my way. Even as I delivered nutmegs and awls to Mrs. Kulifeld and grains of paradise to Fogerty the Fish, I found my mind circling back to my first comment about what Violet had read at Morrowlea.

I'd forgotten about Violet studying Old Oriolan, the language of Northwest Oriole from before the coming of the Empire.

I'd forgotten I'd even known the *name* of that language, let alone a handful of words in it, courtesy of Violet explaining place- and surnames that derived from the ancient tongue.

The Knight and the Unicorn had been translated early into Shaian, and was well known as a minor local masterpiece of early Fifth Calligraphic, as that period was called after the dominant court style of the time. The poem, a long narrative epic with definite allegorical overtones as beloved by pre-Astandalan Northwest Oriolese poets, told the story of the first Sir Peregrine and his finding of the Unicorn.

The Lady and the Dark, on the other hand, had suffered in one of the occasional bouts of censorship of regional culture, when the imperial governors felt that some sort of folk religion or movement was proving politically destabilizing. In one such period of foment, all the Shaian translations of *The Lady and the Dark* had been destroyed.

I knew a handful of lines from the poem because it was frequently quoted in Alinorel literature written in Shaian between the coming of the Empire and the destruction of the manuscripts.

I was so caught up in my thoughts that I nearly passed a few regular customers at the bookstore without greeting them, and remedied it with a bow and a smile before heading into the milliner to see if she might have any hats that were not entirely feminine in style.

"Well, Mr. Greenwing," Mrs. Ayden said, pursing her lips as she regarded my unusual coat. "What happened to your tricorner?"

It seemed excessive to explain that in the course of escaping from Orio Prison I'd lost it in a faery islet between Orio City and the hunting lodge of the King of Lind at some moment between dying and being miraculously resurrected.

"I lost it, alas," I said. "Can you assist me, or will I have to go to Temby?"

Yelton was closer, but since I'd been escaping from *their* gaol on my last visit to that town, I rather thought I'd avoid it for a few more weeks at least.

Mrs. Ayden looked down my long swinging coat. She nibbled at her lip. I waited patiently.

"I do have a hat I made years ago," she said slowly, and then, without further comment, turned around and disappeared into the back room.

There had been no one else in the shop when I entered (a crucial part of my entering, if I may be entirely frank), so I sat down on one of the tufted pink velveteen chairs apparently there for the purpose and considered the state of the world, or at least that portion of it involving me.

Apart from how much I was missing a hat—hopefully to be remedied with something not entirely terrible by the good efforts of Mrs. Ayden, as clearly I was going to have to buy it now that she'd gone to, what was it?—nearly a quarter-hour of effort to find it, and there was as of yet no sign of her return—

I forced my thoughts back to the question of my circumstances. I was most confused by the magical talking fox, deeply pleased to be home, and entirely disinclined to leaving Ragnor Bella to go up to Fillering Pool for Hal's coming-of-age ball on Winterturn Twelfthnight.

I couldn't see any way out of attending, more was the pity.

I would have to tell my father about the invitation. Hal had asked me to bring him and Mr. Dart along, though none of us had been able to come up with a practicable way to draw Mrs. Etaris as well. She would have had to make preparations weeks ago to attend the fair Hal was hosting.

My eye travelled around the room thoughtfully. It was a decidedly feminine sort of place, full of pale colours—pastels were all the rage in Ragnor Bella, no doubt derived in some arcane way from Lark's love of icy blue—Violet had been wearing a deep green when I saw her at Lark's court, green and purple to show she was on the Lady's side.

Violet was the Lady of Alinor's daughter.

I considered a bonnet of pale golden straw tied with a pale pink ribbon. Not the sort of thing to appeal to Violet at all.

Did she get tired of the colour puns? I seemed to recall she had, at Morrowlea. "Purple is more of a lordly colour," she'd told me, as we dyed cloth one messy summer afternoon. "I much prefer the Lady's green."

—And where *was* Mrs. Ayden? This was taking far longer than I'd anticipated. I didn't have anywhere particular to be, now that I'd finished all my deliveries bar the ones to the Woods Noirell, but I was ready to go home and investigate my own acquisitions a little.

There were spindles full of ribbons, silk, grosgrain, cotton, satin, sateen, velvet. There were baskets of yarn, as the milliner's shop served also as a sort of place to buy cloth and yarn and other needments for both sewing and other fibre handicrafts.

There were bolts of cloth, mostly the pale sorts one used for lining bonnets. Straw hats by the score in different stages of completion. Mrs. Ayden had several forms on a table in the room, round balls on stands to stand in for human heads. They displayed three entirely different sorts of hats: two were variations on the straw bonnets familiar from the past several years, one was a marginally more daring exercise inclining in the direction Violet's had been, when she came to Ragnor Bella earlier in the autumn.

My thoughts were wandering. My tutor, Dominus Nidry, would not be impressed.

Lay out the facts, he would say. What do you *know*?

(And then, once I had laid them out, he would cackle and say: *What do you* think *you know?*)

The Lady fought the Dark: that was in all our legends.

This time of the year, right before the solstice, was the time when the Dark Kings were supposed to be at their strongest.

I leaned back in the chair, folding my hands on my lap. Surely I had had more than enough to do with the Dark Kings already?

Surely we had enough to do in dealing with Lark's abominable behaviour and terrible government?

I sighed. There were baskets of yarn beside my chair, balls of a thick wool just the colour green Violet liked best. I picked them up, pinching the soft, chunky threads between my fingers. It would make a cozy scarf.

Not that my skill at knitting was anywhere near sufficient for a courting-gift to the Lady Jessamine's daughter. But perhaps I could knit well enough for Violet Redshanks, lately of Morrowlea.

Mrs. Ayden came out then, all plump and pink from her round gown to her mob cap, bearing in her hands a visibly old wooden hatbox.

"Here it is," she said reverentially, setting it on the table.

I had stood to meet her, and now took the few steps necessary to reach the table, all thoughts of the Lady and the Dark Kings flying out of my head. (So easily are we mortals distracted!) "What sort of hat is it?" I asked, though I knew full well I was going to be buying it.

Mrs. Ayden coloured prettily. "When I was a wee young thing, not even as old as you," she said, "I had a beau who was going to Astandalas."

I leaned forward attentively. "Indeed? Do go on."

She rested her hand on the hatbox, eyes starry with bright memory. "Oh, he was a handsome man," she murmured. "Dusky as an autumn evening, and his legs so fine …" Her voice drifted off, and I watched in vague alarm and amusement as she permitted herself a small, very private sort of smile.

If, twenty or thirty years from now, I remembered seeing Violet standing before the bronze mirror at the only available gateway between the public palace and the hidden prison, asking for us to trust her … I could not stop myself, and felt my own lips curve in a similar smile.

"Just so," Mrs. Ayden said briskly, shaking her head. "He went, but he never came home again, for he was a soldier and he was sent where the soldiers went. He was not in your father's regiment," she added, her eyes sharper. "He belonged to the Seventh Army, and they were posted to the far side of the Empire. Voonra or Colhélhé, so they said. One letter, two, and then a note from his parents to say he'd been killed."

"I'm sorry," I said.

"It was a long time ago," Mrs. Ayden said. "And I won't hear a word against my Athol, do you hear?"

Athol Ayden, I presumed. *Athol* was an uncommon name in Fiellan; it belonged to the pre-Astandalan days, like my own Jemis.

"By the Lady's grace I will see him again, my bonny George," she added in a lower voice.

I thought of the quiet, gracious Wood on the other side of the black gate of death, those who waited and those whom we would await, in mysteries of soul touching soul. All those faces shining in the light of the Lady's smile, all the trees laughing with flowers, all the wind remembering the name of my friend on the other side.

"Yes," I said, with what probably came across with uncanny certainty.

Mrs. Ayden raised her brows at me, but forbore comment and instead thrust the hatbox across the table at me. I caught it, and wondered, as my hands raised dust and the faint aroma of cedar, just what this box might say to Mr. Dart, who heard the voices of the inanimate.

"He was a fine dresser, my bonny George," Mrs. Ayden said. "He'd like to see the old styles come back in, he would. He'd heard of your Jack. He'd like you to wear this hat, since he never had the chance."

I was *absolutely* buying this hat. I opened the box with careful hands. The wood was stiff, but after some cautious working at it I was able to pull the lid off. I set it on the table gently.

Inside the round box was a prodigious quantity of tissue paper. It was all figured over with tiny silvery stars.

Mrs. Ayden touched the paper with one trembling hand before lifting it to her mouth. Her eyes were very bright.

I swallowed against my own sympathetic emotion, and slowly, gently, carefully unwrapped the paper.

CHAPTER SEVEN

I t was a round felt hat: black wool, as befit a military man, with one
flat cocked side. It had a silver ribbon around the base of the
crown, and a cluster of silvery-white feathers as fine as they had ever
been, held in place with a silver button. The rim was bound with black
silk ribbon, gleaming dully in the light coming in the window.

I lifted the hat out of the box with all due care. The flat side bore a
cockade, a rosette of gold and green ribbon, echoing the colours of the
Seventh Army without being quite one of their insignia. Under my
hands it felt resting, quiet.

It was … beautifully made.

"Silver aigrettes from the far south of Voonra," Mrs. Ayden said.
"Lined with linen. It was my masterpiece."

She said it simply. I hadn't realized she'd formally apprenticed, but
it was clear her skills were those of a master in her field.

"Go on, put it on. I think it'll fit. Your head is not so far from my
bonny George's."

The thought that she could recall her bonny George's hat size after
—what? thirty years?—was heart-wrenching.

This style of hat went back before the beginning of Artorin Damara's reign, to the last years of Eritanyr's, when there'd been a brief

resurgence of styles most commonly known from the Empress Anyoë's reign. I didn't know the history of fashion, even of men's hats, well enough to pinpoint it more closely than that.

It didn't *go*, in any historically appropriate way, with any part of my outfit. I glanced at Mrs. Ayden as I lifted the hat out of the box. The silver-starred tissue paper rustled, and the scent of vervain and cedar wafted up.

Oh, how she must have loved her bonny George. He would surely be waiting for her, the other side of the Grim Crossroads.

I set the hat on my head. It fit almost perfectly. I wondered what it said about me that I kept meeting people who gave me clothes from their dead beloved's coffers, and they fit properly.

Mrs. Ayden turned around hastily and fumbled with a covered item at the back of the shop. She drew back the cloth to reveal a wide full-length mirror. That was an extraordinary item all in itself, and for a moment I was distracted from my reflection by the carved wooden frame. It was no modern piece, that was certain: it was an heirloom that might have been found in the ducal castle at Fillering Pool.

I stepped towards it, only to be distracted by the motion and catch sight of myself. I straightened my shoulders hastily.

Black boots, well-polished, with a buckle at the widest part of my calves. The stockings were hidden; the plain dark blue breeches were just visible below the hem of the coat.

And such a coat it was! Fine wool in a deep teal, with a long line of silver buttons down the lapels:, a minor lord's court garment. Silver and black embroidery; wide cuffs turned back to reveal the paler silvery-blue lining. I had chosen a black waistcoat figured with silver for the day, and one of my own white linen shirts below it. No gorget but a cravat tied in my favourite Mathematical style.

My hair was braided back into a short queue, tied with a black ribbon. When this hat was in style Astandalan lords would have had shaven heads, and Alinorel lordlings would have worn powdered wigs.

The green in the cockade was the wrong shade entirely. But the hat … well. It was not my beloved Fillering Pool tricorner, but then again …

I looked at my eyes, sharp brown and brighter than I remembered them being.

(The last time I had seen myself had been the double of myself on that faery islet between here and there, when I had faced my greatest fear: that I did not know who I was without the wireweed, the drugs and the spells and the magic that were now all of them gone from me.)

I settled the hat at a jauntier angle. I would never have chosen it out of a collection, but then again, what did we ever get to choose bar our responses to the hands we were dealt?

There was no particular reason this hat could not come back into style. There was no way I was going to follow Jack Lindsary's example! I grinned at my reflection, and for a moment saw a flash of the fey light.

"Here," Mrs. Ayden said briskly, all no-nonsense and practicality once more. I turned to her, still smiling, and saw her falter briefly before she continued on. She was holding a new cockade in her hand, this one teal and silver ribbon. "This will match your coat better."

"Thank you," I replied solemnly, and removed the hat so she could show me how to remove and replace the cockade. I handed her the green-and-gold rosette, and pretended not to see how her hands were once more trembling.

"Might I have some of those ribbons, please?" I asked, pointing almost at random at a selection. Mrs. Ayden laughed, a short abrupt sort of coughing laugh, and pulled over the rack, which I now saw was folded in the style of an indoor drying rack and extended out from the wall when she tugged on it.

There must have been a hundred and fifty different ribbons wound on spools set on the dowels.

"My Athol made it for me," Mrs. Ayden said. "He's a carpenter. Very good with his hands."

I wondered if she meant that with quite the overtones her warm voice had given it. Well, I might blush for her innuendo but I wasn't going to say anything otherwise.

"What kind of ribbon would you like?" At my blank look, she added, "What are you going to use it for?"

Her kind voice did make me blush. I had no idea what to do with

the ribbons, but I needed a project to take to the Embroidery Circle—
my mother had told me that they did not appreciate it when people
came for gossip and not to work as well—

"Winterturn presents," I blurted at last, and ended up half a dozen
yards of silk ribbon in crimson, gold, hunter-green, and icy white.

"If you have any other coats you'd like me to match, I can easily
make you another cockade," Mrs. Ayden said, and then proceeded to
charge me only for the ribbons and the yarn I had set on the counter
when she'd brought out the hat.

I protested, but to no avail.

"I'll tell you what," she finally said, jollied out of her sentiment and
laughing roundly at me now, "I'd appreciate trying the cake you and
your friend made for the Fair. It looked delicious."

There was nothing I could do but bow, as extravagantly as I could,
to that. And buy a set of knitting needles and some purple yarn the
colour of Violet's name.

～

I felt much better wearing a hat. Now when passersby glanced twice
and then whispered behind their hands, I could pretend it was in
appreciation of my odd outfit.

A hat from a totally different period surely made it appear
deliberate.

I acquired a meat pie from Mr. Inglesides, who gave me a thorough
once-over but said nothing as he took my coins, and returned to my
little flat.

I hung the hat and my lovely coat on the hooks by the door, and
wondered at what point one felt like one belonged.

～

By the next morning, the gossip had sped round the town that I'd died
and Mr. Dart had a unicorn. No one believed either report.

Mrs. Etaris had asked me to open the store, as it was the end-of-
term prize-giving at the kingschool and her daughter was being

awarded the prize for Composition, which Mrs. Etaris was clearly deeply pleased about. It was a slow morning, even with the lure of gossip. I was glad when the Honourable Rag flung open the door and brought me elevenses.

"What," he cried, "is all this palaver about—your hat!"

"It's the new style," I said easily, nodding at the hat sitting on the counter, and continued on serving the other customer in the store, an elderly woman who was slowly buying the last copy of last week's *New Salon*.

That reminded me of the stack of notes that I'd left upstairs, containing the transcriptions I'd made of the last year's Etiquette Questions Answered column. There was a code hidden in the column; I didn't think it would take too much more work to break.

"*Is* it now," the Honourable Rag said, with a meaningful inflection.

"It's a very nice hat," the customer said, poking at it. "A bit old-fashioned, I'd have thought."

"Oh, the old styles come circling round all the time," I proclaimed even more airily.

"I thought it was all the triangle hat you were wearing before? Oh," the elderly customer said, her rheumy eyes lighting. "You've just been to the city, isn't that so?" She peered intently at my hat and then the rest of my outfit. "I'll have to tell my boys to come see you," she mumbled. "They always want to be, what's the word? To the point. They were all for saying codpieces were coming back in, which, really, that's a little *daring*, isn't it? Your style is much more becoming."

I smiled at the Honourable Rag, who had been gallivanting round as the Hunter in Green in a green codpiece, amongst other items, and handed the elderly woman her change. "Good morning, ma'am."

She patted me vaguely on the arm and shuffled slowly out with the paper under her arm. I leaned back against the counter and continued to smile at the Honourable Rag. He stared back, less vapidly than had been his wont before I discovered his secret.

"You're going to give away your game," I said eventually, gesturing at his face. "You're looking far sharper than you ought, if you want to be taken for a fool."

"Damn you, Greenwing," he said lightly.

"Best not to suggest it," I retorted, my voice equally light but my intent earnest.

He scoffed, all the Honourable Rag. "Oh, and now must I guard my tongue?"

I raised my eyebrows at him. "I have seen the near edge of Paradise. Pray believe I have no desire to require the Hunter to harry me out of the shadowlands."

He looked away in what seemed an odd sort of confusion for someone who was wandering the region pretending (fairly convincingly) to be the Hunter in Green. After a moment he said, "Fair enough. Here, Greenwing, I brought you a repast."

He set something wrapped in linen cloth on the counter in front of me, along with a dusty bottle of wine. I raised my eyebrows again. "It's a bit early for the wine, don't you think?"

"Never too early," he proclaimed, nudging it towards me. "Go on, Greenwing."

I really did not want wine, not at eleven in the morning, and certainly not while I was actually *at* work. Mrs. Etaris was an easy employer, but I could not imagine she would be altogether pleased with me getting muzzy-headed.

The Honourable Rag continued to watch me with an eager expression. I felt a strange, odd, twinge of unease. There was something … odd about the way he was standing.

He was lounging with his back against the bookcase, his foot propped up on a chair. I'd seen him positioned so any number of times.

He'd changed clothing from when he'd thundered past me and my father that morning, I realized. He wasn't wearing the scarlet breeches and dark riding boots now, but all black: boots, breeches, coat, gloves, hat.

He hadn't taken off his gloves when he came into the store.

"Go on, I brought them specially for you," he said, pushing off the wall so he could extend one long arm and use the black-gloved hand to push the cloth-wrapped bundle so it bumped against the money-box and set the coins inside rattling. He jerked back, as if the noise had shocked him.

It was an iron box, made by Roddy Kulfield, the smith's apprentice.

"You could add another log to the fire," I suggested casually. "Take off your gloves, if you want. They're very fine—kid, are they?"

"Could be," he said. He looked at the iron stove and nearly winced. "I'm quite warm enough. Have your lunch."

That came out with something that was *not* the Honourable Rag's accent.

What had the magic talking fox said?

Beware the false hunter.

Beware the false lover.

Beware the false friend.

It was not so long ago that the Honourable Rag's sister had fallen in love with a man wearing a knife-sharpener's face but who was actually the Earl of the Farry March in fairy-granted disguise.

I slowly unwrapped the cloth. Inside were half a dozen mouth-wateringly beautiful biscuits in the shape of stars.

My mother had warned me about drawing the notice of the Gentry. She had never given me any particularly useful hints for what to do if one *had*.

"Go on, eat." I glanced up, to see the Honourable Rag—to see *whoever was posing as* the Honourable Rag—regarding me with a sharply hungry expression.

"These look beautiful," I said, hoping to stall long enough for someone else to come in. "Where did they come from?"

Another moment of confusion that shouldn't have been there for that question. "The baker," he said dismissively. "Take one."

It was an odd compulsion, not far different from mere social pressure. Perhaps this was all it was. He wanted me to eat one of the biscuits; I did not.

They smelled amazing. Vanilla and sugar and something like nutmeg and something else that was undoubtedly causing that silvery shine. They were a pale gold under the silver glitter, the points of the stars crisp and clear.

He met my eyes, his sharp as cut sapphires. *"Take one."*

My hand reached out without my will consenting. I could see it in the corner of my eye even as my own glance was held by his. *No, I* cried inwardly, but all that happened was that my fingers trembled minutely.

My father had held a Border against an invading army. I had never been able to say *no* when it mattered, except when it came to defending him. I could stand against anyone for love of him, holding up his memory as something good and fine, tarnished though it was by lies and calumny.

Oh, where was my father? I cried in my heart, even as my hand inched towards the biscuits and the false Roald leaned forward, no longer hiding his predatory expression.

I could feel sweat beading at my temples, the strain in the tendons of my neck, the quiver of my muscles as they tried to lock in place. None of it sufficed. He whispered, his voice heavy and soft as an eiderdown, *"Take one,"* for the third time, and my resistance broke.

Just as my hand closed around the biscuit the door opened and Mr. Dart came in.

Cold air washed in with him, crisp and clear and fresh and sprinkled with moisture. It must be snowing again, I thought vaguely, unable to look away from the imposter.

"Halloo, halloo!" Mr. Dart cried cheerfully, stamping his feet on the mat. "What are you doing, Roald, Jemis? Having a staring contest?"

He bustled over to examine the biscuits, nudging me with his good shoulder when I didn't—couldn't—move to provide him room. I stood in the grips of my own lack of willpower, palm and fingers prickled by the sharp points of the silvery stars.

"Go away," the imposter said, not looking away.

Mr. Dart laughed. "Before passing on my message? I just saw your father, Roald—he's expecting you forthwith. He'll not be pleased to find you've been gossiping with Mr. Greenwing here instead of attending your aunt."

I swallowed hard, pushing back against the weight of the imposter's will. He had doubled down, his purpose beating against me. It felt like nothing so much as when Lark had stolen my will with her drugs and her magic.

Was this what lockjaw felt like? All my muscles were locked stiff. I could not blink, could not swallow, could not move; could only breathe and direct all my efforts to refusing to lift the hand holding the biscuit.

Mr. Dart was burbling something. The imposter answered in terse, increasingly snappish bites.

My eyes were watering from the strain of keeping them open. My mouth was watering from the scent of the biscuits. The aroma curled into my nose, my mouth, seemed to send tendrils into my mind. My reason continued to say *no* but my will was weakening as my appetite grew.

Why wasn't Mr. Dart *doing* anything? Surely he could see my behaviour was unnatural even if he couldn't tell the Honourable Rag was an imposter!

But he did nothing. He talked and joked, his shoulder bumping mine, even as my fingers gripped the biscuit and my arm started to bend and lift. I watched it out of the corner of my eyes, unable to look away from the imposter, unable to resist physically as his will over-powered mine.

The imposter's eyes were changing colour. No longer bright blue: the pupils looked as if they were melting all over the iris, black ink pooling outwards. I trembled, but whatever power was in him was stronger than me.

I pushed the biscuits away with all my strength. My hand rose to my lips.

I remembered this aching *need*, this hunger beyond hunger, this mad desire. I had felt it for Lark, for the wireweed, for running. All the parts of my mind and will inclined towards that certain form of temp-tation were falling like skittles in a game of bowls.

After dying, the Lady had healed my system of wireweed, but I had known I would still need to be cautious, for I was still vulnerable. The scars were a part of me, she had said, even if they no longer pained.

I breathed in deeply. Vanilla, sugar, nutmeg, something that tasted of magic.

Of course it was magic. That fox had been a fairy fox, and this man was no man, no true friend to me or any mortal man.

His eyes were fully black now. I could see myself reflected in them, my face white against the darkness of my hair and coat, the multi-coloured blur of the books behind me.

There were so many stories about what happened if one ate of fairy food.

I clenched my mouth shut. The biscuit touched my lips, and I held there, the scent nearly maddening, my mouth salivating, my whole body locked into resistance.

What did the imposter *want*?

What was Mr. Dart *doing*? Every other time he'd rescued me when I needed it—

I opened my mouth to call on his help, and saw the imposter smile.

CHAPTER EIGHT

The next few minutes were deeply befuddling.

There was a crash, and suddenly my leg was damp and I was tumbled in a pile of books at the back of the store.

I brushed my hands together. My hand was full of silvery dust, like the tissue paper Mrs. Ayden had used to store her hat. Her bonny dead George's hat.

Had the paper crumbled in my hand. I brushed my hands together again. They glittered all silvery and felt full of tingling little prickles.

My legs were all silvery as well as damp.

I took a breath, and coughed as sal volatile went all up my nose.

I spluttered until I was standing upright. Mrs. Etaris was holding a phial under my nose; Mr. Dart was crowding behind her with an unrepentant expression.

"How much of the biscuit did you eat?" he demanded.

I blinked at him, and again at the store. Mrs. Etaris stood there. Mr. Dart was there. My father was there. All of them were frowning at me. I leaned against the bookshelf as my head swam. My mouth tasted musty and strange.

There had been the Honourable Rag—no. I frowned. "Eyes. Wrong."

"I do beg your pardon?"

That was Mrs. Etaris. Always so courteous. I tried to smile at her, but my face felt odd, all my muscles quivering as if I had exhausted myself by running all the day and the night in some mad mood.

"All black. Spilled ink," I explained, waving my hand vaguely. My hands barely moved. I slumped down to land awkwardly on a pile of books. "Not good seat," I muttered, but could not find the strength to move the one jabbing me in the posterior. "Books."

I got the sense they were exchanging glances, but the starry dust on my hands was really bothering me. I tried to wipe the dust off again, but my breeches were already covered with the stuff.

"Glittery."

They seemed to look down on me. Mr. Dart squatted next to me, careful not to touch the liquid puddled on the floor. I frowned at it. "Wine?"

"Whatever was in that bottle," he agreed, and peered into my eyes.

I looked away, wincing from the light in them, inexplicably afraid.

"What," my father said, "just happened?"

∾

It was a good question. I tried to come up with some sort of answer, and tumbled into darkness.

I woke up in my own bed, Ballory slumbering next to me. She felt warm and rumbly under my hand, her hide just as smooth and soft as it had looked. I stroked her rhythmically, sleepy and content. She made a soft whuffling noise, stretching all four legs straight out before relaxing again.

She was purring.

I stroked her side, feeling her heartbeat drum steadily. Her mane was very silky.

I fell asleep again.

∾

When next I awoke it was morning: the sun slanted through the windows in my bedroom, pooling directly on the gleaming white unicorn foal. We had both shifted position in sleep, so her muzzle was resting in the palm of my hand. Her warm breath puffed over my fingers.

I stirred in the way one does when perfectly comfortable, then subsided when Ballory snorted and seemed disturbed. Our indolence did not last much longer, however, for there was a soft, delicate pressure on my abdomen as a grey kitten paced up the eiderdown. I watched her come.

She had pale green eyes that looked somewhat myopic as she stopped right on my chest and stared intently at my nose.

The kitten was purring. Ballory was snuffling. That left a mystery as the origin of the soft whispering noise that seemed to be coming from down the side of the bed.

I really didn't want to roll over to find out there were goblins under my bed.

Surely Ballory would wake, if there were goblins under the bed?

They'd be antithetical to her purity and divine grace, wouldn't they?

The whispering continued, this time accompanied but what was much more clearly a girlish giggle.

Ah.

"Well, *powderpuff*," I said, "is it time to get up?"

"Oh, *yes*," came a bright squeal that made me wince almost as much as getting the sunlight full in my face, which I did when two little girls popped up from where they'd been laying on the floor beside the bed and startled the kitten, the unicorn, and me.

We all tumbled off in a tangle of sheets and eiderdowns. Ballory emitted an irritated squeal, almost the first noise I'd heard from her. The kitten *meeped* as it was scooped up by Lauren.

"Powderpuff is a perfect name!" Lauren declared, kissing the kitten on the nose. It meeped again.

I sat up and leaned against the side of the bed as I tried to make sense of the situation. I was in my own bedroom in my flat over the bookshop. Lauren and Sela were sitting on the floor, dressed fit to go outside save for their coats and mittens. Lauren was still wearing her bonnet, but Sela had tossed hers to the side of the room, along with a basket.

There were a quantity of apples on the floor. Red and green stripy ones; my favourite. Sela had picked one up and was trying to persuade Ballory to eat it. Ballory was much more interested in the hair ribbon tying Sela's plait together.

"Powderpuff, Powderpuff, Powderpuff," Lauren chanted, kissing the kitten each time.

Apparently that was the cat's name now. Well, hopefully I could pretend she'd named it.

"What time is it?" I said vaguely. My throat felt sore and raw, and I coughed reflexively.

Sela scrambled up. "Oh, Mama said to give you the honey tea when you got up."

The honey tea had been a near casualty of my tumble off the bed, and was a casualty of Sela's attempt to ferry it over to me.

"Thank you," I said, regarding the new splotch on the carpet. At least it was winter and so unlikely to attract ants.

"It's the Lady's Day!" Lauren cried happily. "Time to cut the branches!"

"Your house is very bare," Sela added critically. "Mama said we should decorate it."

I nodded in something approaching agreement, then staggered up to my feet. I felt a wash of dizziness, which thankfully soon passed.

"Are you growing a beard again?" Sela asked.

I rubbed my chin. "I wasn't planning to."

"Good. It's not as nice a colour as Mr. Dart's."

"Thank you, Sela. Now, you had all best leave so I can get dressed. Is your Mama here?"

"No, but Uncle Jack is, and Mr. Dart, and Ballory, and—and *Powderpuff!*" Lauren said, counting them off on her fingers and then kissing the kitten again.

I presumed Uncle Jack was my father. "Well," I said, gathering my eiderdown up. I was dressed in a nightgown, which was seemly enough even if I'd rather several more layers to ward off the chill.

"Take Ballory and the kitten out and see if someone will put the kettle on, please."

"Do you have any cocoa?"

I had no idea. "Why don't you go see?" I suggested, and that got them all out of my bedroom at last.

There was water in the ewer. It was cool rather than cold, which was ... bracing. I washed my face and shaved, wincing at the scrape and chill. Ablutions done, I turned to my wardrobe. Without a hat—

Or no. I had a new hat.

I turned the memory over carefully. Yes. I had met with Mrs. Ayden, the milliner, and she had given me the hat she had once made for her beau before he had been killed.

I had come back to the bookstore and spent the evening reading about foxes.

In the night I had had a dream, or a vision, or just possibly a real encounter, of Ballory coming in and scratching her horn along the door of the wood stove.

The next morning I had been manning the store when the Honourable Rag had come in and tried to make me eat some sort of magic biscuit, and I had resisted.

It hadn't been the *real* Honourable Rag. The imposter's eyes had gone all strange.

I shook my head and slowly chose an outfit fit for the Lady's Day. I might be spending it traipsing around the hedgerows with my sisters collecting greenery before church this evening, but that didn't mean I couldn't respect the Lady all the day long.

I whispered a prayer of thanks for my safe delivery from the enchanted foods, and felt better for having done so.

Dark blue breeches, a silver waistcoat with blue embroidery— Master Boring's son had been partial to silver, which I also preferred to gold, which was convenient—my own shirt, linen worn soft, with an overshirt of fine grey wool, thin and warm. I put on my boots, which someone had polished for me since I'd last worn them, and carefully included my father's boot knife.

I tied my cravat in the full Waterfall and added a tie pin Mr. Buchance had given me two Winterturns before, silver with green beryls in the shape of a leaf. Then I took out the heavily embroidered blue wool coat that went with the breeches and headed out to see what was happening in my sitting room.

~

I was severely lacking in seats.

Mr. Dart sat in the chair he usually took; my father was in mine; and Ballory, Sela, and Lauren were all piled on the carpet, ignoring the chest I usually pressed into service as the third seat. I took it, and accepted the cup of coffee Mr. Dart handed me gratefully.

Sela was still trying to persuade Ballory to eat apples. Lauren was whispering to the kitten.

"Her name is Powderpuff," Lauren announced, showing the grey fluff to my father.

"So you've mentioned," he replied, his smile bright.

"Jemis named her."

"Did he indeed," Mr. Dart murmured. He was grinning rather viciously at me, I thought, and therefore deducted a point from the tally of our friendship.

"What's toward?" I asked. "Sela said it's the Lady's Day?"

My voice came out reasonably calm for all that I had to accept I had lost another stretch of time, again.

"You've been asleep for two days, yes," Mr. Dart confirmed. "Do you feel yourself?"

I considered, then nodded. "So far as I can tell."

Mr. Dart opened his mouth as if to speak further, then glanced at the two little girls and subsided.

My father followed his look, smiled, and said, "Ballory came in just after Perry knocked over the wine, and … Roald … took his leave."

I considered this as best I could. I didn't feel *alien* to myself, but I did feel somewhat discombobulated. Out of sorts. Odd.

Possibly hungover.

My father passed me a glass of water, which I drank gratefully.

"My brother's offered to host us for gathering greenery," Mr. Dart said. "I brought the carriage."

Dartington was really too far to walk with two children under seven, but the hedgerows and woodlots nearer town would be well scoured by mid-morning. I nodded agreeably, and sipped my coffee.

The Lady's Eve: shortest day of the year, when the Dark pressed close. We would start a dozen days of celebrations and church services tomorrow to do our part fighting back against the forces of death and destruction.

Usually this was entirely metaphorical.

Usually.

~

My father offered me a short sword when we had all climbed out of the carriage. The girls ran ahead with Ballory and Mr. Dart, calling and laughing as they stumbled through ankle-deep snow towards the nearest copse.

We were at the edge of the pear orchards. On Twelfthnight we would wassail the trees, reassuring them of our care and attention for the coming year. That was a Dartington tradition I had always rather loved.

I frowned at the trees, the upright pears and the high bulk, still garbed in russet leaves, of the ancient oak at the centre of the orchard. Dartington folk called it the Lúsa Tree, a name that went far back before anyone's memory of the word's meaning. It was the recipient of the last offering from the wassail-bowl.

I did not want to go to Fillering Pool in the least.

I looked at the old, worn leather scabbard my father offered me, the weathered belt. The hilt was shiny and smooth with the grip of many hands, plain wire burnished to silver. The tip of the scabbard was reinforced with tarnished silver.

"It's early for a Winterturn gift," I murmured, taking hold of the hilt.

He let the sword come free of the scabbard with a soft hiss. The blade was excellent, and half-familiar; I thought it might be the sword I had chosen from stores the Hunter in Green's gang had provided us.

"Did you retrieve this from Myrta the Hand?" I asked, angling the blade so the dim light caught it. It was another grey day, not too cold; flakes of snow drifted down intermittently, and there was a bit of a gusty breeze that ruffled my coat against my legs.

"It was returned, yes," he allowed. "Jemis … I would feel better to know you were properly armed."

It was unusual to wear a sword in Ragnor barony, unless perhaps if one were travelling alone along the highway. Wearing one in Ragnor Bella itself was considered the mark of an outsider, and a nervy one at that.

My father surely knew that. He would have seen how few people wore swords.

The fairy fox, the imposter wearing the Honourable Rag's face, the shortest day of the year. I nodded sharply, then grinned at him. "I *am* starting a new fashion."

"So you are," he answered, and with a gesture I hardly knew how to accept he girded the belt around me. I slid the sword back into its scabbard with a satisfying slither and thunk. He watched, and nodded: no longer simply my father, but the officer who had trained many soldiers.

"I spent hours practicing at Morrowlea," I admitted. The new coat hid most of the scabbard, and the slit in its length permitted the cloth to fall naturally about the sword. It must have been the style—the practice—to wear a sword when it was designed.

"One needs to," he replied in a low voice, and we marched over to where Sela and Lauren and Ballory were all excitedly pointing out the best holly berries to Mr. Dart.

~

We spent several hours tromping around the heath at the edge of the pear orchards, gathering huge armfuls of holly and pine and long streamers of ivy. My father added a few branches of yew, and a dozen of rowan, though the few remaining berries were wizened.

"Rowan on the window, iron at the door," he said.

Sela grinned up at him from where she was holding his hand and swinging on it. "I know that one! 'Rowan on the window, iron at the door; silver on your hand, and salt on the floor.' For the keeping away of all uninvited guests."

I met Mr. Dart's eye. He shrugged, and told the girls to run to the edge of the orchard and see if they could find any mistletoe growing in the pear trees.

"We might have to go around to the apples," he murmured, even as Ballory snorted at a small pile of snow and then sneezed when she got it up her nose. We all smiled, and I dropped my hand to the hilt of the sword. I hoped it wasn't making me swagger.

"Jack mentioned the fox's warning," Mr. Dart said in a quiet voice as we followed along behind my sisters.

"Three warnings," I replied. "Beware the false lover. Beware the false hunter. Beware the false friend."

"And then who should enter the bookstore but the Honourable Rag, who—"

"It wasn't he."

Lauren and Sela were arguing over something in the tree three rows ahead of us. Ballory was pawing at the ground just past them. I glanced up as a crow cawed; three crows were flying in a staggered line across the grey sky, in the direction of the Woods Noirell.

There was a huge rookery down there, so I had seen when I ran at dusk. There was nothing *unusual* about crows flying away home.

Dusk would fall all too soon today. We should be sure to be safe and warm indoors with the lights on and the rowan and iron and salt and silver in their places.

"Those biscuits were screaming ..."

"I knew they were wrong," I replied, somewhat nettled. "He didn't answer my questions properly ... and he was *compelling* me to take them. I did my best to resist. I was so relieved when you came in."

"I thought he was caught in it as well," Mr. Dart replied apologetically as my father came back from where he'd been examining a holly-tree with many stems. "There was so much magic in the room, I couldn't make head or tails of any of it except that you definitely ought not to be eating that food."

"His eyes were very odd at the end. Like the pupils melted."

"How peculiar. I didn't see that. I came in, but Ballory was out in the square with Mrs. Etaris. I was still working out what could have happened when they came in, and the stove ... *shrieked*."

"The *stove* did?"

"Yes. Like a ... dying rabbit. I'm sure *he* heard it too, whatever he was. The imposter. He dropped the biscuit and grabbed at his ears and bolted out through the door. Mrs. Etaris tumbled down, your father caught her, and Ballory came running over to you."

"I don't remember Ballory being there," I said, frowning. "There was silver dust all over my hands ..."

"You were not altogether yourself."

I gave him a dour look. "No."

Ahead of us, Ballory pounced down on something, her stub of a tail waving madly. She behaved more like a puppy than a horse, I thought absently; though then again I had not spent much time around foals, so for all I knew this was their usual behaviour.

There was something about Ballory and the wood stove—

The unicorn dug her nose deep into the pile of snow she had created, then gave a theatrical sigh and rolled in it. The expression in her eye, when I caught it by chance, was as blandly challenging as it had been in that strange midnight dream or vision or visitation.

I told my father and Mr. Dart about it. My father said, "You had a vision of her scraping her horn along the front of the stove?"

It sounded even odder now than it had seemed at the time. "That's what I can recall."

"How odd," Mr. Dart said.

"The Gentry are moving," my father said, and sighed. "I suppose it's to be expected, what with everything."

Sela and Lauren called us over, even as Ballory snorted and came trotting over to us, all innocence and wide eyes turned to Mr. Dart.

"There's a bird in that tree," Sela said. "It has a bow on it."

CHAPTER NINE

Sure enough, perched next to a clump of mistletoe was a plump hen pheasant. The bow was perched jauntily on the side of her head.

"It looks like it's wearing a hat like yours!" Sela said excitedly. "Is it yours, Jemis?"

I stared at the bird. The bow was in blue-green and silver, echoing my new hat's new cockade rather too close for comfort.

"Not as far as I know," I said slowly.

"Perhaps it's a present for you," Sela suggested. "Is it tied to the branch?"

It did seem to be. We could hardly leave a bird tied to a branch. The Darts' gamekeeper did occasionally lime trees to catch birds, but it was out of harvest season even for the latest quinces on the far side of the orchard. The Squire did not like to trap birds too often. He and Sir Hamish would take their dogs and go hawking when they felt like catching a brace of grouse or pheasants for the pot.

I looked at Mr. Dart, who shrugged without comment, and my father, who said, "We wanted mistletoe, at any rate."

Another holy wood, I thought. But like most of the trees sacred to the Lady, not entirely unknown to the Gentry either.

My father pressed a small sharp stake into my hand. I glanced at it, recognizing the grey bark and pale splotches of lichen. He had sharpened the end of a side branch from the rowan tree.

"Just in case," he said, smiling crookedly. "Girls, come away from the tree so Jemis can climb it."

Sela complained, but it seemed habit rather than any real desire to come up the tree—both she and Lauren were clearly starting to get tired—for she let my father gather her and Lauren together in his hands. I rubbed my hands together, once more wishing for the gloves the haberdashers had not finished, and considered how best to climb up to the bird.

The orchard trees were old and full of crooked branches, but pears grow much more upright than apples, and even ones as well-pruned as these did not branch for a good ten feet above the ground.

"I'll give you a boost," my father said, letting Mr. Dart take charge of my sisters and coming forth instead. Mr. Dart was, in truth, the better tree-climber, but his stone arm precluded it. My father was able to cup his hands together so I could set foot in them, whereupon he tossed me quite an extraordinary ways into the tree.

The bird shuffled and made a clucking noise, but otherwise did not move as I settled myself on the branch below it.

I regarded it dubiously. That did not seem a normal reaction.

I'd thought it a female pheasant from ground level, but up here I could see it was an unfamiliar member of the same family. I'd have to look it up in *Birds of Northwest Oriole*. Assuming it did, in fact, come from Northwest Oriole.

It had a short, stout, bright pink-orange beak, dark eyestripes on a white mask, and really quite remarkably pink legs. The body was mostly a soft caramel-colour, with darker stripes over the wings that looked rather like the gills of a fish.

It was really too much to hope it was a *normal* bird.

"Well," I said to it, "I don't suppose *you* talk?"

The bird just stared at me with the sort of blank terror I was familiar with from the chickens of Morrowlea.

Right. I slid the rowan stick into my sleeve and withdrew the knife from my boot. Then I considered the branch.

The tree was pruned into a kind of open goblet shape. I was on the lowest of the main scaffolding, with the bird and the mistletoe both on the one above, about a foot up but a quarter of the way around the tree. There was no evidence of whitelime on the branches, but I could see a fine dark thread tangled around the feet of the bird.

Mistletoe first, I decided. I could toss that down, and avoid having to climb up any other trees this afternoon. It was a shadowless sort of day, but was definitely growing dimmer as the sun sank behind the Gorbelow Hills to the west.

I scuttled out along my branch, which dipped alarmingly under my weight but did not creak or otherwise seem inclined to breaking, and with three slashes managed to cut most of the cluster's stems. The Squire was hardly likely to want his orchard infested with the parasitical plant. I looked around, and immediately noticed that only the edge trees had the telltale green clumps in their canopies, and by no means all of them.

That was clearly deliberate. How intriguing.

My father let Sela and Lauren run forward to gather the mistletoe branches. I called down to them, "The bird seems to be tied to the branch."

"You'd better cut it free," Mr. Dart called back. Ballory sniffed at the mistletoe in Lauren's hands and nibbled delicately at one of the berries.

Mistletoe is terribly poisonous, I wanted to say to the unicorn, but then again … unicorns famously neutralized or healed poison. Unicorn water was one of the legendary panaceas.

I turned back to the bird, which shuffled its wings and clucked but otherwise kept quiet and stared at me solemnly.

"Hush now," I said softly, moving slowly and smoothly so I didn't startle it. "Let me cut you free."

I slid my hand under its plump round breast. The feathers were soft, downy, and nearly hot on my cold fingers. Its heart was beating quickly, but not in a way that seemed terrified. All in all, it was uncannily calm.

Mr. Dart had some ability to sense magic, I told myself. There was a unicorn, however young, down below. It was the Lady's Eve.

My knife would not cut the black threads binding the bird to the branch.

It was good steel, and I'd sharpened it only a few days before. It had cut the mistletoe well enough.

Did I have to cut this line with silver? With a sword forged from starlight? Need I fetch the Red Company in some grand quest merely to free this bird?

The stick in my wrist-sleeve pinched, and I held still for a moment.

Well ... who knew?

I squirmed around until I could put the boot knife back, and instead tugged the sharpened rowan branch out of my sleeve. The bird gurgled, or that was the best I could describe the sound.

The rowan wood cut through the line as if it were shadows, which indeed is what it looked like, flakes of darkness falling down and dissolving long before they hit the snow-covered ground. The bird chuckled and did not stir.

It let me pick it up and draw it close to my chest. The jaunty bow looked even more like my cockade at close quarters. I truly had no idea what to do with that.

I was ten feet up. Not too far to jump, not when I was landing on snow and firm grass. I glanced around at the feeling of droplets on my face: it had started to snow again, picturesque large flakes. Fortunately there was already snow on the ground, so this wouldn't make it slick and dangerously slippery.

"All clear?" I asked. Mr. Dart nodded and tucked Ballory close against his legs. My father did the same with my sisters. I smiled and held the rowan stick point-down so I wasn't likely to stab myself, gripped the bird a little more securely around its feet, and leaped.

~

The world froze around me.

I hovered in midair. The snowflakes held still, twinkling in a light that did not come from the hidden sun.

I could move my head, at least. See through the snow that there was another landscape overlaying the familiar heathlands and orchards of the Dartington lands. This one was wilder: instead of neat rows of well-pruned pear trees there was a woodland as tangled and ancient as the oaks of the Arguty Forest. These were beeches rather than oaks, their boles that oddly attractive smooth grey, wrinkled around the collars of branches and roots in the way that always made me think of skin.

The snow hung there, twinkling in bright sunlight.

Not our woods, not our sunlight.

Looking down I could not see my father or my sisters.

But there, straight ahead, just where I had seen the Lúsa Tree, was a singular young oak tree, russet leaves like banners.

A thousand years and more ago, give or take a decade, if that were the same tree.

From the left, the heath in my time, a thicket of holly at the edge of the beech wood in this vision, a full-grown unicorn paced into visibility.

It was huge: sixteen hands high, surely, muscular and with white feathers on its pasterns and fetlocks. Its eyes were dark, gleaming, intelligent, and its spiral horn a shining pale gold. Not a narwhal horn such as had been displayed at Mr. Dart's college in Stoneybridge when I visited him there.

The unicorn looked less like a horse than Ballory did as a foal. It didn't exactly look like a deer, either; more like a horse uplifted, trans-figured, shining with the light of the Lady's smile.

It paced forward to what I now saw was a figure sitting on the ground. A man, I guessed from the breadth of his shoulders; his face was hidden.

He was sitting hunched over his knees, turned away from me. A broken sword lay to one side; he was wearing rusty chainmail with a torn and dirty surcoat that might once have been white over it. His hair was a curly copper as bright as Jullanar Maebh's. I had never seen such a picture of utter dejection.

The unicorn came to stand beside the man, and slowly bent its head until the horn lay gently on his his shoulder.

After a long moment the man lifted high right hand to cup the unicorn's muzzle. He wore a silver ring with a green stone; it caught the light in a bright, singular flash.

~

I landed on the ground lightly, the bird quiescent in my hands. Sela clapped. I made her an extravagant bow even as my thoughts whirled.

There were many reasons why I might be having visions.

My mother's family had fairy blood (whatever exactly that meant), and she used to dream truly; I had experienced a few of those dreams myself.

This didn't seem quite the same, somehow. That was almost certainly a vision of Sir Peregrine and *his* unicorn.

Was it entirely out of my imagination? I would have thought this was oak country here, not beeches.

I would probably have *imagined* the Lúsa Tee as enormous in girth and height, forgetting that a thousand years ago it would hardly be so large as now; I should not, I thought, have imagined it with a slender bole, not even twenty feet tall.

"Did anything strange happen just now?" I asked with an attempt at casualness that fooled no one except Lauren, who was once more preoccupied with Powderpuff despite us having left the kitten in Mrs. Etaris's capable hands.

Sela said, "Is that the bird? It *is* wearing a bow. The ribbons are just like yours! It must be a present for you."

The bird was resting comfortably in my hands, very warm under its feathers. "Perhaps," I said weakly. Mr. Dart and my father both looked at the bird and then at me.

"There was a faint sparkle," my father offered.

"And a kind of … splash," Mr. Dart added. "Like … a cymbal crash."

I wondered just how Mr. Dart perceived magic. All the books said it was personal to each great mage.

"Sela," my father said, "could you run ahead with Lauren and see if Mr. Lennox is ready to head back to the Hall?"

Sela appeared inclined to argue, until Mr. Dart added, "I believe he might have a flask of hot chocolate to share."

"Smart man," my father murmured as the two girls happily abandoned the mistletoe and ran to where the carriage waited, the Darts' coachman bundled up in woollen blankets and a book in his hand.

I described the vision I'd had, faltering a little when it came to conveying the utter despondency I'd seen in the seated man, which contrasted so sharply with the brilliance and power of the unicorn.

"It wasn't ... innocent, exactly," I said, not knowing why I was saying it. I could feel the bird's heartbeat, a steady fast pittering, somehow reassuring. "But it was ... pure."

"An interesting distinction," my father said.

We looked as one down at Ballory, who looked back up, all innocence.

"We should get back to the Hall," Mr. Dart said at length. "My brother promised us crumpets."

The fact that I had died and come back to life and therefore might well always be slightly counter to the world in future was likely rather too obvious to mention.

CHAPTER TEN

W hat does one do with a small, plump bird, clearly of that class usually considered game and equally clearly far too calm to be anything but a pet?

I carried it back to the carriage, and when I sat down it nestled comfortably on my lap. More comfortably than I was sitting, to be honest, for I had forgotten the sword. It twisted against the belt, not quite uncomfortable enough to require getting up and adjusting it, but certainly the sort of thing to keep breaking my attention.

Lauren and Sela crowded next to me so they could pat the bird with cautious fingers. The bird accepted their touch with quite remarkable equanimity.

"We should call it Pitrie," Sela said.

"Why Pitrie?" I asked, when no one else said anything. Mr. Lennox clucked to the horse and the carriage started moving with a slow lurch. The crows were calling again; when I chanced a look out the window a good score of them were passing overhead to the south.

"It looks like a Pitrie," Sela said, cooing at the bird. It cooed back and then closed its eyes and fluffed up all its feathers over my hands.

I leaned back against the tufted carriage seat and closed my eyes.

~

We had crumpets and hot cocoa with the Darts. Sela and Lauren were both on their best behaviour, and were much taken with both Hope and Jullanar Maebh.

"And who are these?" the Squire asked when we were ushered into the warm morning room with its bright fire.

"I am Miss Sela Buchance, and this is Miss Lauren," Sela declared, with something approximating a curtsey to the Squire, who bowed formally and with great good humour in return.

"These are my sisters," I explained to Hope and Jullanar Maebh, who both appeared confused.

"I have the same mama as Jemis, but our papas are different," Sela explained. "That's why we have different last names."

Lauren was far less interested in people. She had caught sight of the tabby kitten, and immediately tugged her hand out of my slack grip so she could go over to it. She turned to the Squire, who was less immediately intimidating than the tall and lean Sir Hamish, and said, "What is this cat's name? Is he Powderpuff's brother?"

I wondered how she had decided that the grey kitten was a female and this one a male. As far as I knew, it was nearly impossible to tell with kittens; and I could not imagine Lauren had any of the technical knowledge necessary, being all of five.

Anyway, weren't tabbies always female?

"I don't think it has a name yet," the Squire replied. "Would you like to give it one?"

"Crumpet," Sela declared, focused on the tray one of the servants had just brought it.

"Crumpet is a silly name for a cat," Lauren replied primly.

"Mrs. Etaris's cat is named Gingersnap." Sela took the bird from my hand and went over to sit next to Lauren and the tabby kitten on the settee. "Here, meet Pitrie, Crumpet."

"His name isn't *Crumpet*."

"Do I even want to ask about the bird?" Sir Hamish asked with due trepidation.

My father laughed and accepted a crumpet and a cup of chocolate. "It is the curse of the Greenwings striking again, I fear. Poor Jemis!" He added, shaking his head. "Can there be not one week without something happening?"

"Some months it feels as if there can't be a *day*," Mr. Dart murmured. "How was your day, Miss Stornaway?"

Hope blushed. "I wrote a letter to Hal—his grace, that is."

"I must write him as well," I murmured, then smiled at Hope. "Not for the same reason, I trust."

She blushed even harder. Jullanar Maebh sniffed, though that might have been her cold. Then again, she had taken quite against me after the extraordinary series of adventures between collecting her at Tara and arriving at Dart Hall.

"Will you be attending the service tonight?" my father enquired generally.

The service on the Lady's Eve was not one of the high days observed in the more popular churches in the barony, but it had always been one of my favourite services as a boy. My mother had always taken me—and most often Mr. Dart as well—to the tiny chapel tucked into the edge of the Coombe. We had lit candles there to help the Lady guard the passages between life and death through the long night.

No one else had ever gone to that chapel, I had fancied. We had always spent the first hours of the evening cleaning it out, sweeping out what seemed to be a year's accumulated dust and dead leaves, laying a new fire, setting out new beeswax candles. It would always be the remnants of the same candles the next year.

My mother had had some interesting practices, now that I came to think of it.

The priest at the Big Church did not like such 'country practices', as he decried some of the ancient traditions we still held to it odd corners of our remote barony. The old priest at the Dartington church had understood better; he'd blessed the candles for my mother, and blessed her for remembering that doorway.

I wondered if anyone had gone to that chapel since my mother's death. I hadn't thought of it the first years after her death: Mr.

Buchance had been pious in a bluff, hearty kind of way, going to the Big Church and giving his tithe, but not otherwise given to the more private depths of religious emotion.

(And yet he had been there, in the Wood of Spiritual Refreshment, himself. There were many paths to the Lady. She had said, *None who desire my table will be lost in the end*. What could I do but hold faith to that promise?)

"Would you go to the old chapel with me?" I asked Mr. Dart just as he started to speak. "I beg your pardon. What were you going to say?"

He smiled wryly. "Something not entirely unrelated."

My father regarded us with narrowed eyes, but he didn't say anything as Lauren started to demonstrate the edge of fractiousness, and I made haste to bundle her and Sela back into their coats and gloves. The Squire called for the carriage, and Mr. Lennox greeted them as if he hadn't see them for days rather than hours.

"Would you like me to join you?" my father asked quietly as Mr. Dart spoke to his brother. We'd agreed he would return to town with me so that we could head out to the old chapel together.

"Should you like to?"

He made a short, uncomfortable motion. "It was something your mother used to do."

"She used to take us," I replied, nodding at Mr. Dart.

His eyes cleared. "I see." A moment, then: "I used to walk the bounds through the night, while she was in the chapel. It was ... seemly, she said."

"She knew better than I do," I murmured. "Given everything, it seems ... important."

"Indeed," my father replied quietly. "I'll meet you there. There are a few things I shall need to bring with me."

~

Mr. Lennox drove the horses smartly, and we arrived back in town just as dusk became night. We should already have been at the old chapel, if I remembered my mother's old practices correctly.

There were so many things she had done that I had forgotten. She was the Lady of the Woods in a way that I suspected my grandmother the Marchioness had never quite been. It was my grandfather who had been of the blood of the Woods: the Marchioness was an upstart according to the ways of the region.

I deposited Lauren and Sela (having left Pitrie the bird with the Darts, to Hope's amusement and Jullanar Maebh's apparent dismay) with Mrs. Buchance, who appeared relieved to see them safe and sound and yawning sleepily. We'd had a sort of picnic in the carriage, courtesy of Mr. Dart who had brought warm sausage rolls and sweet chamomile tea with him, and both had fallen asleep long before we'd reached Ragnor Bella proper.

Mr. Lennox was a Dartington man, and when we told him our purpose he said he'd wait to take us to the top of the path leading to the chapel. We repaired accordingly to my flat, where I gathered all the new candles I could find. I managed seven, which was better than none but not so good as nine would have been.

"Seven is enough," Mr. Dart said, his head tilted to one side, his eyes bright and thoughtful. "Have you any honey?"

I did, in the jade crock my mother had left to me. I hesitated, then brought the crock as well as the honey. On this night we might need all the weapons against the Dark Kings we could muster.

"Honey and light," Mr. Dart murmured. "Salt and silver?"

Silver I had in my tie-pin, and he himself in the form of a letter-opener and a fine chain on which he had a locket containing a minia-ture portrait of his mother. I also had a silver florin from our journey to Tara. As far as I recalled from what my stepfather had said, it was nearly pure silver: that was why it was still used across half the continent.

I had a box of new salt from Orio City as well, and I placed that in the bundle with the candles. A fire starter was next, the new Ghilousetten lucifers, which only needed a strike and a flash of sulphur to start a flame.

Bread for supper, a broom for the sweeping …

Mr. Dart said, "Fire, salt, honey, silver …"

"Holly and hawthorn are at the chapel," I continued. "Fresh water as well."

"And the night is drawing down. Shall we?"

~

The old chapel was not far from road leading down into the Coombe, and consequently not far from the Ellery Stone near the Lady's Pools. Mr. Lennox took us to the old lichen-encrusted stone posts marking the path down.

Mr. Lennox handed us a lantern and then drove off. After the creak and clatter of the carriage and horse had faded into the night, it was very quiet.

The snow had stopped, but the clouds were heavy above us. No star or moonlight made it through their cover, and though the snow was faintly glimmering, the shadows were deep and dark.

Mr. Dart swung the lantern around.

The shrubs were hanging over the path, lines of snow along the branches showing that they had remained undisturbed by anything so heavy as a squirrel or a bird. There were no tracks in the snow to suggest anyone had come before us, not even my father.

It looked, in fact, as if no one had come this way since my mother had last brought us, seven years ago.

"Well," said Mr. Dart.

I rather wished he'd brought Ballory, but after eating several crumpets dripping with butter, the unicorn had lain down in front of the fire and refused to move, the newly-named Crumpet the kitten curled between her forelegs.

The night felt very cold and dark with the memory of that behind us.

An owl hooted, and I jumped.

"Barn owl," Mr. Dart said. "Look."

He pointed at a ghostly shape gliding down the road towards us. A dark figure moved behind it, like the shadow of a man cast against the dark landscape.

I remembered the Grim Crossroads, and stepped back so I was shoulder-to-shoulder with Mr. Dart.

"Owls are sacred to the Lady," Mr. Dart said. His voice wasn't trembling, and I admired him immensely in that moment.

The owl floated, wings motionless, a white disc of a face against the darkness. The figure behind it moved quickly. Not unnaturally quickly, surely, I thought, trying to keep the hysteria from overwhelming me. I was holding the broom from my flat, and switched it to my left hand so I cut put my right hand on the hilt of the sword my father had given me.

The owl floated past us. Its facial disc was so bright in the light of Mr. Dart's lantern that I had to blink away afterimages after it had passed.

"It's your father," Mr. Dart said, his voice absent and his eyes on the owl.

I shook my head as the dark figure resolved itself into the still-unfamiliar silhouette of my father. He was wearing a heavy cloak, the hood up. The sweep of the wool seemed a shadow given form.

It was his voice when he spoke.

"Jemis. Perry."

"Major Jack," Mr. Dart said, his voice warm and sure.

—I did trust him.

"Owls are sacred to the Lady," Mr. Dart repeated, as if to reassure me; behind us, the owl hooted again, three long, low notes that did not echo but seemed nonetheless to linger in the silent, dark, still trees.

I shivered and lifted the broom to brush aside the branches covering the path. Mr. Dart lifted the lantern, and my father clasped me on the shoulder with what was becoming a familiar gesture.

◇

The path was longer than I remembered.

Perhaps it was just that it was extravagantly overgrown. We battled our way through long branches: holly and hawthorn and yew and long snaking brambles. I mourned my beautiful coat and the snags that were sure to have half-destroyed it.

I couldn't see anything but the many overlapping shadows cast by Mr. Dart's lantern. No moon, no stars, only the crunch of snow and dead leaves underfoot, the rustle and snap of the branches. Our breathing, noisy in the dark. The owl, hooting behind us.

After interminable length we came out into the small open space in front of the chapel.

It was even smaller than I remembered, in the uncertain light of the lantern hardly seeming more than a cow byre. There was a story it had once been some such building, a pig sty for a long-abandoned farm or the like. Sir Peregrine, so my mother's story told, had taken shelter here one wild winter's night. His first miracle had been the spring of clean water that had ever after filled the font of the church.

It had one window, a black hole in a dark wall. There was not much sign of the door.

"It's all grown over with ivy," Mr. Dart said, striding forward to kick at the wall. His booted sole clanked against the stone twice before a hollow *boom* proved the wooden door.

Something rustled and called in the trees around us before falling silent again.

I walked forward, drawn by the memory of my mother, the basket of candles and salt, honey and silver over one arm, the broom back in my right hand. I pushed at the ivy until I found the ancient iron handle, cold as death to the touch.

Cold as winter, I corrected myself. Death had not been cold; had been bright and brilliant and full of light.

(The death we feared was that blighted crossroads where the monsters came. But Mr. Dart fought those monsters, in his dreams and in mine and in the Lady's name.)

The door was stiff, but the latch released and I was able to kick it open.

A great wash of musty, dank air came billowing out at us. I sneezed once, twice, half a dozen times in succession, the old familiar thickness overtaking my throat and nose.

I sighed and shifted the broom so I could fetch out a handkerchief. By the time I had remedied myself both my father and Mr. Dart were collected and Mr. Dart had lifted the lantern to show the interior.

As far as I could tell, it was empty.

Mr. Dart and my father were both listening. I imitated their postures, but heard nothing beyond my heart in my own ears.

"Well," I said, and brushed through the ivy curtain to enter the chapel.

I stepped—

CHAPTER ELEVEN

—I nto a vision.

A man knelt before an animal trough.

The trough was stone; the whole building was stone. I looked around. It was a stone shed, perhaps three yards by four. A shaggy cow was kneeling in straw, chewing her cud and watching the man with animal incuriosity. Her hide was deep red with a white band across her middle, just the same pattern as I had seen on the Banded Dartingtons the Squire raised.

Light came through the square window, sunlight streaming in and setting all the dust motes to dancing. It caught the man's copper hair.

This was Sir Peregrine again, I realized.

Again I could not move. I was frozen in a moment, my right foot lifted and not yet landed on the ground. The dust was not dancing; it hung still in the air. The man did not move. He held there, reminding me of nothing so much as the petrified villagers of St-Noire before we'd undone their curse.

No. He wasn't frozen. He was breathing: I could see his shoulders moving almost infinitesimally.

There was no water in the trough. There was no spigot for water to enter, either. Presumably whoever had built the byre, or who stabled the cow there, brought in buckets of water.

Sir Peregrine's face was drawn, narrow with fatigue and hunger. He was not in the chainmail this time, nor the dirty white surcoat. He wore rough homespun, the kind of dullish grey-green you could easily achieve by vegetable dyes. His hands were rough and callused but not with holding weapons.

He was very young. His face was freckled, his nose sunburned. His hair was short but untidy, as if he'd hacked it off with a knife; the curls sprang out in all sorts of angles.

His cheeks were hollow, his eyes sunken. They were a pale grey-blue, like a stormy sky.

I glanced again at the cow, seeing this time that she was not only shaggy but also gaunt, her hide matted and dusty. Her muzzle was as drawn, her eyes as hollow, as the young man before the trough.

He coughed, his shoulders racked with it, a dry, heaving thing that brought moisture to his eyes. He swallowed once, twice, and rubbed one hand across his mouth, streaking dust across his lip.

Then he spread his hands over the trough, palms up.

"Please, Lady, if you are real," he said, "give us water."

And the water came.

～

—My foot landed.

I stumbled forward and caught myself on the edge of a wooden pew that had not been there in my vision.

Of course not, I thought, my heart hammering in my throat. Of course it wasn't. The pew belonged to the church, and the church belonged to long after Sir Peregrine had performed his first miracle here.

Mr. Dart lifted the lantern to look at my face, but he said nothing and instead set it on the old altar. "Will you bring out the candles?" he suggested.

My mother had always lit the candles first, so we could see what we were doing.

"We clean out the chapel in the night," she had told us, "to clean out the shadows and show the Dark we are not afraid of it."

I had sometimes been afraid of the dark, but had never wanted to say so. My father was a brave man—my father had won the Heart of Glory from the hand of the Emperor himself for his bravery—and as a boy I had always endeavoured to follow him.

As a young man, also, albeit with far more complicated emotions.

And now that I knew my father *was* the courageous man I had always thought him to be, unstained by treachery or cowardice—oh, now I wished indeed to emulate him.

(I was not certain I would have been able to beat the bounds of this particular parish, this particular night; not when the Ellery Stone was so close.)

I turned my head, regarding the dim interior.

Had we come to the old chapel after the Fall?

Yes. We had come those two winters after the Interim and before my mother's death. That first Winterturn Eve had been a terrible mess, everything shattered but for the stone altar and the stone trough. Everything including the altar and trough inches-deep in dust, as if it had been centuries since we had last come.

I set out the candles, lighting the first one and using it to drop a puddle of molten wax on the altar so the candle would stay upright. We each took two of the remaining six candles and lit them from the first before setting them in the shallow embrasures carved into the walls. The lantern Mr. Dart set in the glassless window.

Those embrasures had not been in my vision, but this was recognizably the same cow byre. The pattern of stones was the same; and that trough against the wall, which we'd ignored so many times, was the same I had just seen filled.

"Is there something the matter?" Mr. Dart asked.

I heard him but felt bound by some deeper calling to cross the tiny chapel to the trough. The story my mother had told said that the cold spring outside was the water Sir Peregrine had called into being, but that was not what I had seen.

The trough was dusty. It had a hole in one corner for drainage, with a plug made of fired clay, a ring baked into its top. There was still no pipe, and the old bucket was by the door.

I looked at Mr. Dart. The chapel was tiny: the altar at the front, where the cow had been lying, was a narrow stone slab on top of two blocky piers. The pew was hardly more than a wooden stool, backless and equally narrow. A second lay tumbled against the wall, where my father was just picking it up.

Mr. Dart looked at me. In the light of the candles his auburn hair was gleaming much more brightly than usual. His eyes were ... well, *usually* blue, so that didn't seem so odd.

"There was another flash, wasn't there?" he murmured.

I nodded shortly, and tore myself away from the trough to meet my father, who had crossed back to the middle of the chapel.

Oddly, or perhaps not, after that vision I no longer feared it wasn't truly him. He had thrown back the hood, and the flickering shadows were kind: looking up at him, for he was still and would always be taller than I, he was every inch the beloved father of my childhood.

"I'll walk the bounds of the old chapel parish," he said. "It takes two hours or so. I'll stop by each time I come around."

"Thank you," said Mr. Dart, since I could do nothing but feel awash in sentiment. My father clasped me on the shoulder before ducking through the ivy again.

"Well," Mr. Dart said, surveying the room. "Your mother always made us sweep it out first, didn't she? Do you remember the song she used to sing?"

It was the same song we'd sung spring-cleaning our little cottage, and indeed all through the Interim when everything was shifting around us. I nodded, but took several tries to clear my throat before I could summon forth the words.

～

We swept the floor, using the stiff birch besom Mr. Dart found in one corner to scour the caked dirt from the corners. We pulled down cobwebs and chased the shadows out of the place with my mother's song of the Lady of the Green and White.

Sing of the holly and the hawthorn
Sing of the water and the sun
Our Lady of the Summer in her kirtle of green
Our Lady of the Winter in her mantle of white
Sing of the turning of the year
Sing of the sweeping out of the shadows
Salt and silver, water and sun
Berry and leaf, hawthorn and holly

I was warm while we cleaned. We used one of my handkerchiefs to wipe the embrasures around our candles, the polished stone surface of the altar, the dusty wooden seats. There was not much else to the space. Just bare stone walls and the bare stone floor, and behind the altar, a mosaic showing the Lady with water pouring out of her hands.

Eventually we finished the cleaning. I took my salt and Mr. Dart's silver letter-knife and walked around the inner perimeter of the building, marking first a complete circuit with the knife on the floor and following it with a circle of salt. While I did that, Mr. Dart wiped out the shallow stone dish carved into the altar and went outside to collect a few sprigs of holly and hawthorn.

One holly branch with berries; another with only leaves, to represent the male and the female and this season of light overtaking the dark, green growth and fruit in the cheerless time of the year. One hawthorn branch, bare of leaves, wicked of thorn, flower-buds quiescent, to represent the sleeping summer yet to come, the youth and the age of the year, all that which was neither male nor female, neither alive nor dead.

We wove together the holly and the hawthorn as my mother had shown us, pricking our fingers and offering the small droplets of blood to the Lady. Eventually we were able to join the two ends of our garland together to make a wreath that encircled the altar dish.

"I'll get the water, shall I?" Mr. Dart said after we had admired our wreath sufficiently.

"You could fill the trough," I said without thinking.

Mr. Dart looked at the trough, and then at me. "Jemis, there's a sacred spring outside."

I hesitated, long enough that he sat down on one pew and stared expectantly at me.

"Sir Peregrine ... I had a vision of him I came through the doorway ... he held his hands over the trough and asked for water."

"The trough?"

"That trough." I nodded at the ancient stone sink.

Mr. Dart swung around to look at it. His hair fell over his face, covering his eyes. His beard was getting rather long for the Charese style. Perhaps he was planning on introducing a new fashion as well.

Along with a renewed fashion for magic, that was.

"If I called it, it would likely be magic, not miracle."

I had no answer to that; only questions.

Mr. Dart expelled his breath explosively, then got up and with two steps was suddenly before the trough. He did not hesitate before kneeling.

It was the same flagstone as Sir Peregrine had used.

Of course, there were only two in the right position; it was hardly odd Mr. Dart would choose the same position, given the size and orientation of the trough.

He bowed his head and lifted his own good hand, palm up. He murmured something, too soft for me to catch the words.

A moment that hung suspended in the air, the same way I had hung suspended in the air: the guttering candles held still; the steam from my breath held in static cloud.

And then, with a shimmering, silvery sound, beads dropping on a cymbal, raindrops falling on a tile roof, the water poured out of the air and filled the trough.

The air broke: the candles flared upright, casting bright golden spangles off the water and all around the tiny chapel; and the mosaic face of the Lady seemed to smile.

"It's magic," Mr. Dart said, staggering to his feet and then sitting down almost immediately again on his pew. He was panting slightly but his face was bright, his eyes luminous. "Magic."

I smiled at him. "Before the coming of the Empire, people thought magic was the gift of the gods. Good magic from the Lady, wicked magic from the Dark Kings."

He had no counter-argument to that, and instead used the wooden cup my mother had left in the chapel long ago to fill the altar dish.

After the water stopped moving in trough and altar it was very quiet.

~

It was cold in the chapel.

I sat on my wooden pew, my hands tucked into my sleeves to keep them warm. Our breath steamed in the air, puffing forth. Mr. Dart pulled out his pipe from his pocket and spent a meditative period preparing it for smoking. I breathed in the mingled scent of beeswax and good tobacco.

He blew smoke rings. They hovered in the corners of the chapel, the vaulted roof that was of some much later date. I regarded the mosaic patiently. I could not recall the Lady's face in any particular: merely her expression, the brilliance of her eyes and smile, the dark chestnut hair and the skin as pale as Mr. Dart's or mine.

This Lady had dark hair and tan skin, dark eyes and lips pink as carnations. She wore a crown of holly, bright berries in her hair, and wore a green gown with a great white mantle over it, thus indicating she was here in her aspect as Lady of Winter. The mosaic was very old. My mother had told us that it had been made long before the coming of the Empire.

The Empire had brought its wizards, who bound magic into their nets and chains of spells and enchantments. They had wrought amazing things. I was child enough of the Empire to know that; to believe that. They had linked worlds together in trade and travel. We had coffee and potatoes and tobacco and maize-corn from that trade.

We had had laws and river-trade and wars and universities long before the coming of the Empire.

Now …

I was regretting not putting on another layer of clothing, to be honest.

I turned to Mr. Dart, who was staring pensively at his stone hand. He caught my motion, and turned enquiringly.

I, of course, could not think of a single word to say.

He laughed. "Cat got your tongue, Mr. Greenwing?"

"Something like that," I acknowledged, shoving the pew towards the wall so I could lean my back against the stone. The candlelight cast warm shadows.

Mr. Dart didn't say anything, but he didn't turn away, either. He simply puffed gently on his pipe and sent the smoke rings to hover and slowly dissipate above us. There was a cold draught coming in the open window, but a slow and incremental one.

"Do you think I should be worried about these visions?" I asked finally.

He pushed his seat back in turn so his back was to the opposite wall. Our outstretched feet still touched because the space was so small, but it felt more intimate. Confessional, even.

"I think it would be stranger if there were nothing changed in you. You died last week, Jemis." He knocked the pipe on the wall beside him. "Stone cold dead."

I hugged myself, hands still buried in my coat sleeves. I was reassuringly solid to myself. "I'm not a ghost," I whispered.

"No, nor a lich or an undead vampire. You came back body and soul from the dead."

"That wasn't magic," I said.

"No."

We fell silent again. I could see the trough of water, reflecting golden light up and around the room; the candles wavered and flickered. It was getting colder, for all that it was probably not yet suppertime according to the clock.

"You have changed," Mr. Dart continued presently. "You smile more than you did. Talk less."

"Not difficult," I muttered, glancing down. "So much has happened in the last six months."

"Tell me about it," he said; when I looked up again, he had tilted his head back and was watching his smoke rings drift and disappear. "Tell me about the past six months."

"You were there for much of it."

A gust caught the candles and made me shiver with a deep chill.

Mr. Dart regarded me with an almost puzzled air. I suddenly realized he was not wearing gloves either, nor an overcoat or cape, and yet showed no such hint of the cold as I felt.

"Are you ... magicking yourself warm?" I asked.

"No ... or not a-purpose." His voice trailed off as he held out the pipe into the air. The smoke rose up in fantastic curlicues. He glanced at me. "I will try, if you'd like."

"Please."

His eyes seemed to catch the candlelight first, candlelight and then the warm brown shadows; and then the air blossomed with warmth, slow as a sunrise on a winter's day.

I took my hands out of my sleeves and sighed with gratitude as my muscles slowly stopped shivering and unlocked themselves.

"Now," Mr. Dart said, his eyes once more their familiar blue, cheerful and bright with pleasure in his own power and skill. "I too have my thoughts about what has been happening."

"You can go first," I offered.

He grinned, and I remembered that this was the man who had guarded my soul against the Dark Kings at the Grim Crossroads, and caved.

CHAPTER TWELVE

I spoke of the bitter end of the bright dream at Morrowlea, and the slow unravelling of my health over the ensuing months.

Not simply health of body, but health of soul, spirit, mind.

"And then my stepfather died, and I hadn't told anyone where I was, and when I came home everything seemed to have fallen apart entirely."

"The chaos out of which all new creation comes," Mr. Dart said thoughtfully. "That's what Domina Black used to say. Sometimes the old order must be entirely brought down for a new one to be built in its place."

I regarded the gold ring on my hand, the simple flower picked out in tiny red garnets, and waited.

"You are learning the patience of the dead," Mr. Dart said.

A chill went straight down and then up my spine, and I shuddered. That was not merely the voice of my friend.

He tapped his pipe against the edge of the pew, sending a puff of ashes to dance in the candlelight. When he went on, his voice was more recognizably his.

"I received my degree in the spring. Highest honours, the Saltwell

Prize in History, half a dozen offers of second degrees, three offers of teaching positions, four for research."

He puffed out a smoke ring, which slowly changed colour as I watched it, from the usual grey to a soft, limpid lavender.

"I wasn't—I wasn't *angry* to come home, to be Tor's steward, to learn how to manage the estate properly. I had always known that was what I would do. Tor and Hamish had no children, of course, and there I was, the age almost a son of his could have been. I grew up knowing the estate was entailed and would come to me, and I wanted—I *want*— it to thrive. It was the gift of our ancestors to us, and ours to pass on to the future. There have *always* been Darts here."

I nodded. The air was soft and warm. My muscles relaxed despite the discomfort of the narrow pew. Mr. Dart blew another smoke ring; this one shaded incrementally into a soft evening-sky blue.

"You wondered why I said, when we had to confront our deep secrets, that I was jealous of you."

I could not deny that. It had, in fact, been my first question on seeing him at the Grim Crossroads between life and death. I nodded, watching him. His face was serious but not anguished. Solemn.

"Your life is so *interesting*," he said.

I could not help myself, and laughed.

He joined in, and when we had subsided, his eyes were bright with a complicated mixture of mirth and anguish. "I grant it is not always to your taste, but you must understand how it looks from the outside? How exciting all your adventures are."

"You have started several of them."

"I wanted ..." He stopped, and examined his pipe minutely. His cheeks and the tips of his ears were both pink. "I love Tor and Hamish, but they can be rather ... stodgy."

Stodgy was not the adjective anyone would use to describe me or my father, it was true.

"I didn't want to be stodgy," he went on in a lower tone. "I could see it happening. How I would come home and be Tor's steward and ... eventually I would be the squire myself. Oh, I would start a mono- graph and work on it, and in ten or twenty years I should have written a splendid account of someone else's deeds and have a thriving estate and be as solid and respectable as my brother. Married, very like, and with children of my own, being brought up to follow along me in their turn."

That this was my own dream, or something very close to it, went unsaid.

I sat there, my back against the cold stone but feeling warm as if I sat in warm autumn sunlight. I laced my hands over my stomach and tried to keep my thoughts well focused on him. For his part he stared very intently at his pipe, which was resting across the wrist of his stone arm.

"Everyone said we didn't need magic any longer, and I ... I had always hidden that part of me. I had always *had* to hide that part of me, so I didn't understand—I never understood—why it hurt so much to ignore it. I never listened to what *they* said, Jemis, I pretended there was nothing there."

There were a hundred accounts of why that was probably the very worst thing a mage of any power could do. Magic was like water, all the stories said: it always came out, eventually.

"You always seemed as if you had superficial hurts and—" He glanced up at me, face even more flushed. "That was ill-expressed. I do not mean that you had no griefs, far from it. Yet I always thought ... it always seemed to me ... that at some deep level you were fundamentally *happy*. I always thought it was because of how much you loved your parents."

I thought of his parents, Petronelle and Master Ricard, who had loved him dearly for all they had both died before he was fifteen.

I remembered his mother's death, how she had waded into the river and drowned herself, driven mad by the unbound and broken magic of the Fall. The memory was distant, all the emotions leached. Her face in the Lady's country, eager to hear my news of her sons, was bright and clear in my mind.

He sat there for a while. The air was warm as that autumn day, that spring morning, just the faint trickle of cold air from the open window to remind us it was the very turn into winter.

"I think what it is," he said finally, "is that you've never been afraid of who you are."

～

My secret, on that faery islet by which we escaped the inescapable Orio prison, had been that I was afraid of who I was without the wireweed. That I was not, after all, bright and brilliant and all that went with those.

I had come second in our year in the Entrance Examinations. By Winterturn of that first year at Morrowlea I had already fallen to Lark's guiles, her drugs and her magic and her social graces, and all that came after seemed to belong to her.

I had always been afraid of who I was. That I would never be good enough to meet the memory of my father; that I would never be good enough for my stepfather; that I would never, in the end, be enough.

I sat there with that knowledge settling into me. It had always been a cold and heavy thing, coiling in my gut like shame.

Now it lay there like a stone in the mosaic of the Lady granting water to the thirsty Sir Peregrine and his thirstier cow, softly glinting in the warm candlelight.

How could I be afraid of who I was, after I had looked upon the face of the Lady? I had looked upon her, and known all the pusillanimity of my soul; and she had nevertheless, welcomed me to her table.

"I think," Mr. Dart said, "that your expression might be the most convincing theological argument I have ever encountered."

I looked up at him, bewildered.

"I heard what you said to your double, as you heard what I said," he said. "You *were* afraid, weren't you? Before."

I nodded.

"Jealous that I had Tor and Hamish. Tired of all the things that fall upon you. Wearied with having to take up arms to defend your father again and again. Bewildered by the magic falling upon you. Miserable that you had stood up for your principles, and lost, you thought, everything important to you. You thought I was going to drop you as a friend, because you had lost reputation, position, wealth, family."

I nodded again, speechless with his insight.

He shook his head. "You know why I was jealous? Because despite all that, *you* never lost your temper. You lost everything, and you took up employment in the store and you smiled at every crow who came to tear at you, and were polite to everyone who gave you the cut direct, and ... you never stopped fighting. You were tired, but every time someone slandered your father, you lifted your arms again to fight for him."

"I could hardly do anything else," I said, uncertain.

He chuckled wryly. "Oh, trust me, Jemis, there are plenty of people who would not have bothered."

I smiled crookedly. "For good or for ill, I am my father's son, Perry."

"Yes. I admire that."

I took a deep breath. For all that the Lady's benediction might be all I *needed* (at least according to the theologians insofar as I remembered them), to have a friend, a peer, a man whom I admired, tell me *that* ...

The thought came quickly that perhaps he needed to hear the reciprocal statement.

"I admire you greatly, you know," I said. I wished it were as easy to be frank and candid as it had been in the bright country, when Ariadne nev Lingarel and I could speak to each other across time and space and learn how our souls had touched the other's.

I cleared my throat and tried again. "I admire how cheerful you are, how easy in yourself. How great a friend, no matter my own troubles and megrims. How brilliant, and how humble. And how you are starting to come into your magic ... you were so magnificent in that dark dream, at the Grim Crossroads ..."

My turn to flush, no doubt pink to the tips of my own ears. My face and neck certainly were hot and tight.

Mr. Dart fussed over his pipe, his face even redder. I could take looking at him no longer and jumped up to take a drink from the trough.

It was the finest water I had ever drunk in my mortal flesh: pure as the water in the Wood of Spiritual Refreshment. If this was magic, it was magic come of the Lady.

I turned to look at the mosaic of the Lady behind the altar. The water poured from her hands, blue and white streams turning into flowers, daisies and forget-me-nots, starry chickweed and the little blue-eyed Veronica that Hal had described so lovingly. Simple flowers; nearly weeds.

"What are you looking at?" Mr. Dart asked.

"The flowers," I said, gesturing at the mosaic. "The miraculous water turning into common, simple, flowers ... ones we dismiss as weeds."

"The Lady scatters her gifts widely."

I could wish Father Rigby at the Big Church had ever spoken such a simple message. He seemed to prefer learned tomes, convoluted exegesis of the ancient fathers of the church.

My mother had always told me the miracle stories, the legends and the songs, the *folk beliefs and country practices* dismissed by Father Rigby.

I thought of the Lady, laughing so the trees blossomed in the forest this side of Paradise.

Sir Peregrine had knelt before a simple stone trough—the same trough here before me—and prayed for water to save his dying cow, and the water had come.

For all that I loved complicated textual exegesis, I could not but think salvation was far simpler than that. It did not turn on an interpretation, but on trust.

"What time do you think it is?" I asked in lieu of faltering attempts at theology. It was not as if I were a priest, nor so pious or learned as Marcan over in Lind. I had no vocation for the church.

Mr. Dart set his pipe in the crook of his sling and pulled out a fine silver pocket watch from his waistcoat. "A quarter to eight," he replied.

"Seems later."

We dined on bread and honey, as my mother had always served us when we came to the chapel with her. She had brought blankets and let us make a nest in the corner away from the door, snuggled between the altar and the trough. I remembered waking every once in a while, warm and sleepy, to see my mother limned in candlelight and singing softly.

We had just finished eating when there came a knock on the door.

"Your father?" Mr. Dart suggested.

"Can you tell magically?" I asked curiously.

He looked startled, then closed his eyes and seemed to commune inwardly. I backed away from him to stand near the door, the new sword comforting under my hand.

The air moved, bringing a scent of honey and some sort of spice … cloves and peppercorns, possibly. I sneezed quietly and Mr. Dart laughed and opened his eyes.

The someone outside knocked again.

"It's him," Mr. Dart said. "I am coming to know the … feel of people."

I nodded and opened the door just as my father had lifted his fist to knock a third time. He had pushed his hood back. The night was very black behind him, but his face and eyes seemed almost luminous.

Mr. Dart's magic touching him?

I smiled at the thought, purely delighted, and my father smiled back. "May I come across your line of salt and silver, and drink of sacred water?" he asked, his formal tone at odds with his joyful expression. "I have circled the bounds with my branches of holly and hawthorn, and hawthorn and holly would I lay upon the altar to my Lady of the Green and White."

I glanced at Mr Dart, who nodded.

"Be welcome within the sacred circle," I said, the words coming from some deep memory. "Bear your hawthorn and your holly across the silver and the salt. Wash your hands with the sacred water, and be cleansed before the Dark of the year."

My father bowed, and stepped across the thin sprinkle of salt that lay before the threshold.

"I am surprised," he said, "that you recall those old words, Jemis."

"I must have heard Mama say them."

"Yes."

He had brought in boughs of holly and hawthorn, and he laid them upon the altar, hawthorn to the left and holly to the right of our wreath. He knelt before the altar for several moments, praying silently. Mr. Dart and I retreated as far as we could to give him privacy; I shut the door again, noting that it was once again starting to snow. The ivy slithered down against the outside of the wood with a sound like a snake moving through dry leaves.

After he finished his prayers, my father went to the trough and cupped his hands in it to drink. Then he unclasped his great cloak and let it fall over his arm in a great puddle of black cloth. He sat down on one of the pews and regarded the two of us standing by the door.

"I have walked the bounds of the old parish," he said. "The woods are silent and dark, even at the Ellery Stone."

The Ellery Stone was where the cult to the Dark Kings had first sacrificed a cow. They had chased Mr. Dart and I through the woods until we reached the Lady's Pools. I let out a breath of relief to know they weren't yet recovered from the blow given on the Fallowday of the Autumn, when the Black Priest had been taken by the Magarran Strid in its flood.

"That's good," I said.

My father looked at me, and then at Mr. Dart, and then he said, with infinite gentleness, "The lanterns are being lit along the Gentry's Road."

I had no idea what that meant, but before I could ask Mr. Dart said flatly, "The Wild Hunt is riding tonight."

CHAPTER THIRTEEN

"I don't know this story," I said, looking from Mr. Dart to my father in puzzlement. "What are the lanterns? What is the Gentry's Road?"

"You know the Savage Crux," Mr. Dart said. "The Giants' Road crosses there with the Gentry's."

"I always thought the second road was called the Lady's Way. Sir Peregrine and his unicorn chased the Gentry back along it."

"They came first," my father said. He bundled the cloak around him. "Do you have any food left?"

"Yes, we have bread and honey," I replied, reaching into our sack of provisions and passing him a selection. My father said nothing about the warmth in the chapel, though he clearly felt it; I could see his muscles relaxing the longer he sat on my former pew.

"What are the lanterns?" I asked presently. I ran the barony, and had seen nothing I could call lanterns—even ones belonging to the Good Neighbours. Mind you, I didn't run the Lady's Way; no one could.

"They're a kind of growth, like mistletoe," Mr. Dart replied. "They emit foxfire."

"What are we to do?" I asked.

"Stay inside," my father replied. I looked at him. He smiled crookedly. "You're keeping vigil tonight. That's what it means. You hold the circle in here."

"While you're out there?"

"So long as you hold the circle in here, I will be safe out there. So long as I hold the circle out there, you will be safe in here."

I stared at him. He met my eyes, quietly confident and fearless.

No, not fearless. But with the absolute certainty that he could hold that line because we could hold the circle.

The Gentry's Lanterns were lit. The Wild Hunt would be riding tonight.

They had never ridden in my memory, but there were stories of them hunting lost or erring souls … or … I frowned. They rode pell-mell through half a dozen legends, raiding deep into the mortal lands, down the valley of the Rag from the passes in the Woods Noirell, but … why? What were they looking for?

Would tonight be as the solstice vigil had been through my childhood, even the years after the Fall, when we needed simply to keep awake the night through?

"We will hold the circle," Mr. Dart said, forthright and true and also not fearless.

He had known what the Gentry's lanterns were, and what they portended.

I nodded, trying to emulate them. "Yes. We will."

"Of course," my father said, and stood up. He flung his cloak around his shoulders, a shadow that caused the candles to flicker and flash, but once the heavy cloth swirled about his legs it was no longer black and shadowy but a deep, rich brown, warm wool clasped at his throat with a pin bearing the sigil of two feathers crossed. The feathers were enamelled in green, and caught the light in winking flashes.

"That's the Greenwing sigil," I said. I knew it; my mother had made sure I knew it, for all my uncle had refused to let us have anything that bore it.

My father's hand lifted to the cloak-pin. "Your mother gave me this, one Winterturn night long ago." He smiled and as he passed us by clasped first Mr. Dart and then me on the shoulder, his hands warm and comforting. Proud even. "I will see you just before midnight. That is when the trials begin."

∾

We sat in pensive silence for a period. It was very quiet: the candles burned straight up, their scent pure and comforting. I tried to be patient.

Patient as the dead, Mr. Dart had said of me earlier. It was a strange thought.

The idea that I had died was both incontrovertible and inconceivable. I turned it in my mind, but it made no more sense than it had before. On the one hand, there was nothing but chance in that *I* had been able to return when no one else did without devastatingly wicked magic.

On the other hand, everything about my life and Mr. Dart's had been leading to that moment when he defended my mortal remains in his dream of the Grim Crossroads, and my soul had been permitted to cross back over.

That was indisputably a miracle.

I looked often at the trough, and thought of my two visions of Sir Peregrine, trying to balance them out. The old and the young man, the splendid unicorn and the dying cow.

∾

The candles should not have been able to burn the night through without burning out.

There was nothing special about them, save that I had made the probably foolish decision, given the state of my finances at the time, to purchase beeswax rather than tallow. My mother had kept bees; we had always had wax tapers, not tallow.

At Morrowlea I had been assigned to candle-making after burning through scores of them. I had enjoyed the process, which reminded me always of my mother, dipping the wicks into the molten wax, watching the tapers slowly take shape.

Golden is the wax and golden is the light, my mother had sung, teaching me how to keep my candles straight and even. *Golden is my heart in my true love's sight.*

She had had so many songs about bees.

I imagined it was Mr. Dart's magic keeping the candles burning without consuming. That, or another miracle.

I pondered the question. If he did not intend the magic, was it truly magic? Or was it the goddess working through him? Was there a difference?

In History of Magic, if I recalled correctly—it seemed so very long ago that I had taken the class, the first of my classes at Morrowlea—we had spent only a few lectures on pre-Astandalan magic. It was irrelevant, the lecturer had said, even to us who lived after the Fall of that great empire. Whatever native magic there had been was long since forgotten and dissipated.

The Dark Kings had not been forgotten nor dissipated, despite seven centuries of Astandalan rule and countless centuries before that of work by the church of the Lady of the Green and White. They offered power without price; or a price paid by others.

In the end, every story said, the cost was paid by the one who sought to cheat that fundamental law. If you would be powerful beyond the lot of mortals, you must trade something worthy of that gift. For the Dark Kings, it was said to be first the blood of others and finally the magician's own soul.

Astandalan wizards had held otherwise. They said magic was a natural force, no different than a gift for music or carpentry. Magic followed rules, principles, laws. Say these words, make these gestures, use these objects, perform this ritual, and the result would follow.

That had been the way of things through the centuries of Astandalan power. After the Fall that magic had no longer worked. Say those words, make those gestures, use those objects, perform that ritual, and ... everything went wrong.

Wild magic was different. Wild magic was the gift of genius, as far from ordinary talents as the storm was from the bellows.

The Lady worked through our lives, the priests said. Magic, true magic, was her gift.

Mr. Dart was already paying certain prices for that gift. He would never be the same; never be able to return to who he had been, back when he had not listened to the voices of the inanimate, back before he had called water into the trough, back before he had called me back to life.

"What do you think they want?"

The interruption to my thoughts was sudden, and I looked up, dazed and surprised to hear Mr. Dart's voice.

"What do who want?"

He made a gesture with his pipe overhead and outside. "Them. The Gentry."

"You didn't use to believe in them," I replied, gathering my thoughts together.

Mr. Dart gave me a sardonic sort of smile. "That was before all … this … started happening."

I straightened on my uncomfortable pew and regarded him more intently. "Let us be systematic about it. What would you class as part of 'this'? When do you think it started?"

"We had the cult, that first weekend you came home. That mermaid."

I had forgotten all about poor Miss Shipston. I hoped the Lady—the Lady of Alinor, in this case—had been able to help her. Perhaps I could ask Violet for news.

"And was that the first odd thing this summer? Did anything happen before I came back?"

I could see his immediate response was negative, but even as he started to shake his head and utter 'No' he caught himself. I nodded encouragingly, and could not but be glad that there was finally something that was not dependent on me.

"My ducks," he said slowly.

"You brought a new breed from Chare, you said. The brown ones."

"Buff," he corrected. "I had one particular duck that was a good mother. She had a notch in her beak so I could tell which one she was. She raised a hatch in the spring and I was taking note of the ducklings when one day she disappeared."

From what I remembered of the animal husbandry portions of my

Morrowlea education, this was an unfortunate but common element to raising poultry. People were not the only ones who found a plump hen or duck of great gustatory interest.

"Then she came back," he went on, "and she had a gold ring around one leg—which I had certainly not put on her—and ..." He paused for a moment. "And her eggs after that were gold."

I stared at him. "I beg your pardon?"

He shifted uncomfortably. "That duck's eggs. They were gold."

"Literal, solid, actual gold?" He nodded. I laughed incredulously. "What are you doing with them?"

"Nothing! What am I supposed to do with solid gold duck's eggs? They're clearly magical. And—" He stopped abruptly.

I waited, then offered a delicate, "And?"

His ears were pink again. "And they told me to keep them for later. They said I would need them in the future."

I considered this. "Do things ever ... lie to you?"

He looked startled. "I don't think they can. They don't ... it's not *words*. It's as if ... I look at something and it's blue, or red, or whatever, and equally obviously I know whatever it is they're saying. I looked at the first egg and I could see it was gold—it's so heavy—and I heard, clear as anything, *Keep me hidden*."

"So you did." I sat back against the wall. "Thank you for telling me."

He smiled reluctantly. "I think we're past those sorts of secrets, aren't we? You keep giving me the good news from the Other Side."

I didn't know quite what to say to that, so I simply nodded and returned to the main point. "Was that the only thing?—Not to say it's not quite astonishing, all by itself."

"There's also the two-tailed fox that's been running around. I've seen them from time to time since the spring."

I was momentarily confused. "The two-tailed vixen, I've seen her. Have you seen a dog fox as well?"

Mr. Dart sighed. "I don't think that fox is male or female the way we think of it. They're ... themself."

"Have you spoken to her—them?"

He was silent for a long time. I let him sit there, smoking his pipe and looking at the mosaic Lady. His face was even pinker, though I couldn't imagine why.

"They have another form," he muttered finally. "A more ... human one. They wear it sometimes on new-moon nights, and we've gone ... picking mushrooms together."

"You use that euphemism for far too many things," I said, hoping to clarify, though his incarnadine face suggested that in this case it was not poaching, seeking out illegal cults, or buying illegal whiskey that was intended.

"They told me that they're the child of a king on the other side of the Woods," he went on, his voice raspy. "They've told me all sorts of stories ... promised all sorts of wonders. I ... Jemis, I was trying so hard to fit myself into the mould I ... it was exciting."

"I am not going to judge you for an ill-advised choice of para-mour," I said. I remembered nearly his first question, that strange luncheon my first day of work. He'd asked me if I'd met anyone at Morrowlea; and told me that all the women he found interesting in Chare were running for parliament or disliked that his brother had a male lover. Or were his tutor.

I took a breath. Well, we could work this out. Clearly he was finally ready to talk about it. "Why is the fox—do they have a name?"

"They've never given me one. It's ... That's a deep magic, a great gift, for one of *them*."

"The fox, then. Is—are they courting you? Why would they be giving *me* warnings?"

Mr. Dart looked at me, then down again. "They can only have a human form in the night," he said. "Fox always by day." He put more tobacco into the bowl of his pipe. "I only ever met them in the night. This summer ... I couldn't sleep. I would do all the work I had to in the day, trying not to ... to ... *resent* it." He glanced at me. "I love Tor. I love Dart Hall. I wasn't going to break the entail."

"No."

"But you understand, don't you? How you have a dream that doesn't—that *can't*—be?"

I chuckled wryly. "I do."

121

He sat back, his good hand clenching. "I do apologize. That was unnecessary."

I waved off his apologies. Once—three months ago, perhaps—I would have been bruised by that thought, but I could not, considering it, now find it anything but amusing. My dreams were breaking up and reforming like storm clouds.

"I always told myself I wanted to be a Scholar. Be a professor at one of the great universities. Research, teach, write monographs." He shifted on his seat, his face suddenly intent, catching me with bright eyes. Magic in his eyes, I reckoned, remembering Domina Aurelia at Tara. Hers had caught gold when her magic stirred; Mr. Dart's were green and brown and blue.

"But that's not true, is it," he said. "I didn't want to be a Scholar. I wanted my magic."

Magic he had never told anyone he possessed. Magic he had been told to hide, to suppress, to stuff so deep down all the nets of Astandalan wizardry couldn't catch it.

"I didn't name it that. I thought of it as ... my art. I could see what it meant for Hamish to paint, and I wanted that. I was hungry for that. I couldn't find it—I don't have any of those skills. So I thought it was scholarship. History. And then this summer ... I was more and more restless. You weren't here, and Roald was irritating beyond measure. I learned from Tor and the factor and I took to walking nights. Not deep into the forest, but back of Dartington and upriver to the Coombe. Sometimes I would walk all the way up to the refuge at the crossroads up there, where the Coombe road meets the roads to Lind and Chare, and one new-moon night I met a person there."

"The fox."

He nodded. "Not that I knew that at the time. I could see they had come from ... somewhere else. And I was so hungry for some*thing* else that when they smiled at me, with these sharp, sharp teeth, and looked at me with their bright, bright eyes ... my magic woke."

He breathed hard, looking at me. "I didn't know that was what it was, not then. Jemis, you have to believe me."

I was surprised at his intensity. "I do. Why wouldn't I?"

He was startled into laughing. "Why wouldn't you? You can accept that I met a fairy at the mountain crossroads and went along with them despite being able to see how entirely dangerous they were."

I simply looked at him. "I fell in love with Lark with one look. For all that it turned out to be drugs and magic, that still was what I *felt.*"

"What a pair we are," he muttered. He tapped his pipe. The ashes fluttered around. The draught coming in the unglazed window was more obvious now, and colder. Little pellets of snow whirled in and disappeared into droplets of moisture. A kind of whine seemed to be rising in the trees. The wind picking up.

Or so I hoped. What a night for this conversation. The longest night of the year, when the Gentry's Lanterns were lit.

Mr. Dart packed more tobacco into his pipe, no haste or awkwardness in his motions as he braced his pipe against his stone wrist and opened the small tin with his other hand. I watched, mesmerized by his dexterity.

"I would meet them every new-moon night. They never said anything. I never said anything. We would ... visit with each other, high up on the mountain. The stars would stand around us as if they were watching. And then I would go back to my dull, respectable, ordinary life."

I regarded him. His colour remained high, but he was resolute: having decided to tell me this, he was doing so plainly.

"That continued all summer," he went on. "But the problem with *them* ..."

I thought of the stories my mother used to tell me about the Good Neighbours. The Gentry. Those from the other side of the Woods.

Oh, they can be beautiful, she had said. *Perilously so. You can drown in their beauty. No one who tastes fairy food can ever quite leave it behind.*

Food, when it came to the Gentry, probably covered a wide range of appetites.

"You understand about the wireweed."

He glanced up at me, with a too-familiar shame in his eyes, and nodded once, sharply.

"What happened? Why did it stop?"

The wind gusted, and something on the roof seemed to clatter. We both looked up, as if we could see anything through the stone vaulting.

"There are oak trees above the chapel," Mr. Dart said. "They might still have acorns."

"Indeed."

The candles were still burning sweetly, as tall as if they were new-lit. Magic and miracle seemed to swirl in the tiny room even as the wind subsided again.

"I met the fox on the new-moon of May. June, July, August, September, and in October I had a stone arm." He touched the petrified limb with his good hand. "They do not like imperfection, that folk."

His voice was calm, but the hurt was real.

I bit my tongue on all my reassurances and protestations. He had received that stone arm by saving me from a fascination cast by the priest of the Dark Kings. He had never complained about it to me, not once, in the months since.

"They would not come, though I waited the night through. And the next night the duck that laid the golden eggs was dead. Fox-tracks all around, but none of the other birds touched. The gift withdrawn, I realized."

"Did you ..." I didn't know what to say. His tone was odd. He might miss the fairy as I had missed the wireweed, with an ache and a hunger both desolate and shameful. I had *craved* the fulfilment of that hole the drug had left in me. I did not want to; but I did.

"No," he said, answering what question I did not know. His voice was soft but strong; his eyes were blue and white as the water turning into flowers in the mosaic. "I wanted my magic. Not theirs. Mine. *Mine.*"

And on that pronouncement the Wild Hunt came.

CHAPTER FOURTEEN

They crashed down upon the chapel like the Turning of the Waters in the Magarran Strid.

The noise was so loud both of us started to our feet.

I drew my sword, my father's sword, in a hiss and a silver shriek.

The lantern in the window opening tipped over and crashed on the stone floor. The oil spilled, burned, and went out.

A black wind gusted around, three times around the room, whipping our hair and clothes wildly.

The candles flared to the tops of the niches.

I stood there, facing the window; Mr. Dart, facing the door, closed his eyes.

This was not acorns. Not rain or hail either, surely. The sturdy stone building was shuddering, the roof overhead scratching and skittering like branches wind-whipped into frenzy, savage thumps and booms and wild, high, inhuman cries.

Mr. Dart was silent, his eyes closed and his good hand clenched into a fist.

The wind howled into the room, stirring my coat and tossing Mr. Dart's hair into chaotic disorder. I breathed it in—I could hardly avoid doing so—and sneezed.

Not a polite singular sneeze. No, this was the sort of debilitating, eye-watering, throat-clenching sneeze that had racked me all this past year. My body reacting to the wireweed burning my magic out of me.

My magic was now all burnt out of me, extinct as the lantern broken on the floor. I had offered it to the guardian of the passage, that dark nowhere bridging the faery islet and the hunting lodge of the King of Lind, and that offering had been true and permanent.

My body did not seem to care. I kept sneezing, barely able to get enough air to fill my lungs in between each stentorian sneeze. My eyes were swimming with silver sparkles and my ribs ached.

I staggered away from the open window. Mr. Dart was by the door; I could still see him, a bleary smudge of plum-purple against the golden flames of the candles. I cupped both hands around my face, trying to catch my breath, trying not to stumble outside of our circle. Silver and salt, holly and hawthorn—

The water in the trough.

I flung myself down on the flagstone where Sir Peregrine had knelt, where Mr. Dart had knelt, and asked not for water but for surcease.

Protect us, O Lady, I prayed. *Keep us safe this night through, from the hobgoblins and horrors of the night.*

It was a children's prayer, one my mother had taught me to pray as a boy. I had probably not said it since she died. Had I taught it to my sisters? They had other prayers, other lullabies, from the second Mrs. Buchance, who came from Ragnor Bella and did not know the legends and lore of the Woods.

Protect us from the hobgoblins and horrors of the night

I thrust my hand into the water—banged my other hand on the stone trough, stubbing my fingers with a brutal shock that nearly made it through the sneezes—but I was shaking so hard with the uncountable sneezes I could not cup my hands to contain the water in them.

Protect us, O Lady, I prayed, and dunked my head under the water Mr. Dart had called into being.

The sneezes stopped; all the noises stopped. My ears were stopped with water, sacred or profane as it might be.

Sacred, I thought, at its cold clarity.

Mr. Dart might have called it by his magic, but that was a gift from the Lady even so.

I could not sneeze underwater. But I could not breathe underwater either, and at length I had to lift my head, all my hair and nose dripping, and breathe the magic-heavy air once more.

One inhale, two; my breath hitched, but the sneezes did not recur.

I gasped properly, a fish in the air, a man out of water, and scrubbed my face with one of my handkerchiefs. Where was my hat, Mrs. Ayden's bonnie George's hat? I looked around for it aimlessly, my pulse shuddering and juddering in my throat.

Mr. Dart stood stone-still by the door. I rubbed at my chest even as I tried to make sense of the room. Seven candles burning with unnaturally high flames. The trough, brim-full of water despite my dunking my head into it. Water splashing on the floor ... and were those bits of green?—Shreds of leaf from making the holly wreath, I thought blankly.

Holly and hawthorn, salt and silver ...

Someone knocked on the door.

"Don't open it," Mr. Dart said. He opened his eyes, and they were the flat grey of the stone. "That is not your father."

It sounded like his voice, when someone outside called, "Jemis, Jemis, open the door."

"They know my name," I whispered hoarsely.

Mr. Dart smiled in a way that did not seem like his at all. He laid his good hand flat on the door, palm to the wood. I was sure the wood rippled, golden-green lines radiating out.

"Everyone knows your name. You stand in the world like a boulder thrown into a stream."

His voice was distant, too. Cool and abstract, as if he were reading off some academic list. It was not a voice I could question, though I wanted to.

I supposed it was because I had died and returned to life that made me stand in the world *like a boulder thrown into a stream*.

I did not feel like a boulder thrown out of its place, tumbling and tumbled by the water. I had felt Ragnor Bella to be *home*, no matter how hard it was to find my place there. It was still *my* place I was seeking.

The door boomed under some other hammering hand. The tiny chapel shook with the force of the blows. So had the drums beat when the Black Priest sought to raise the Dark Kings along the Magarran.

I had been the prepared sacrifice, unwilling and bound, forced, nearly broken: such was the difference between the power of the Dark Kings and that of the Lady. One sacrificed the unwilling, the other oneself.

What had the Astandalan wizards sacrificed?

"All that lay outside the Empire," Mr. Dart said.

I must have spoken aloud. "How so?" I asked.

"They bound more and more in their workings, edge to centre," he said, still in that eerie, distant, calm voice. "Outside the bounds the shadows were darker, the stars brighter."

So had my father said, once or twice. *The stars are brighter outside the Empire, but at what cost?*

"What do the Gentry want with us?" I whispered. Their voices cried and cackled and shrieked in unearthly tones dissonant with the wind.

"Banshee," Mr. Dart said even as a cry seemed to stab through the air and pierce me straight through the heart.

I staggered again, this time landing against the altar. The stone shivered but did not move under my weight.

"Do not cross the circle," Mr. Dart said.

My hand was on my breast, above my heart. My pulse was hammering wildly, and my blood felt as cold as the water in the stone trough.

I braced myself on the altar and forced myself to turn a head that seemed rusted in place to look at him. His eyes were not grey now, but white, white as snow, as ice, as light glinting off water. He had turned from the door, and stood with his back to it.

The ancient wood gleamed with verdant fire.

Dust shook down from the rafters as the knocking came again.

The third time of asking, I thought, in some deep, silent pool of astonishment. I was braced against the stone altar, my hair and face damp from the fresh water.

Salt and silver, hawthorn and holly.

What was the next line of that song?

Golden is the honey, and golden the light

Golden is my heart in my true love's sight

"Do not answer the door," Mr. Dart said. He stepped forward until he stood in the very centre of the chapel. The circle I had drawn with silver and salt was starting to smoke and sputter, white and silver as the froth of sparks Mr. Dart had thrust into the fireplace over in Lind when his heart had called magic into visibility.

My head swam. My throat was dry. I felt as if I had forgotten how to swallow. Silver had been the starry biscuits the imposter had tried to importune me to take. Silver had been the stars on the paper with which Mrs. Ayden the milliner had enveloped her bonny George's hat. Silver was the knife, and silver was the steel sword fallen on the floor.

The sword had fallen with its tip outside the salten circle. The sparks sputtered and rose, but the circle was not quite complete, not with the grains scattered by the sword.

"The circle," I said.

"I am holding it," Mr. Dart replied.

His voice was steady, and his eyes now were blue, his own bright blue, the colour of the forget-me-nots and blue-eyed Veronica in the mosaic.

"The sword—"

"Leave it."

The silver sparks sputtered and rose. Mr. Dart lifted his good hand, very slowly and as if against a great weight.

I dared not move. I stood there against the stone altar, the edge digging into the small of my back, my eyes on Mr. Dart as he did something I did not, could not comprehend. There was magic in the chapel, crowding the tiny space. It grew heavier and heavier, the weight of it like smoke in the air.

It tasted of snow and wintersweet, that fragile kind of scent from those few plants that flowered in winter.

Something scraped against the window.

I turned my head without volition, merely pure instinct.

"Don't move," Mr. Dart said, his voice no longer calm but grim, and yet as steady and as sure as he'd been in the Grim Crossroads.

I had been able to help him fight then. He had given me a weapon, and we had stood back-to-back and kept the monsters at bay.

The Wild Hunt howled outside the chapel and I could do nothing, nothing at all.

Some great eye was looking in the window.

I swallowed. *Do not answer the door. Do not leave the circle. Do not move.*

It was as large as a dragon's eye, and as intelligent, for all it seemed multifaceted as an insect's. My throat felt like shards of glass as I forced myself to swallow and not to move. It watched me. There were a hundred candle flames reflected in the facets of its eyes, and two smears of purple and blue for Mr. Dart and me.

My father was out there in the darkness, pacing the ancient borders of the parish. My muscles trembled; and then, with that plunge of relief, I was in the realm of mortal danger.

The heaviness in the room was no longer impediment but circumstance; even a tool. My eyes swept the space without haste or fear. There was the sword; there was the water; there were the seven candles; there was the one dark lantern.

Three motions and I could scoop up the sword and plunge it into the creature's eye before anyone else could move.

I pushed myself against the altar.

This was not my fight.

It was, oh, it was—all there was in me cried out for me to act, to move, to be what I could be in these moments between assessment and act.

I trembled, as if the wireweed was gone and I shook for its leaving.

But oh, Lady, Lady, this was all me. This was who I was.

The great and terrible eye was on me. It blinked once, a stone-grey lid sweeping down like a landslide, outlining the window with unholy light: and then it was the Honourable Rag perched there, every line of the body true to life but everything about the posture … wrong.

No human perched like that, crouched in a window embrasure

nowhere near large enough for a tall man. Either the window had stretched or he had shrunk. My mind was skittering, confused by perspective, by the strange lights of the flaring candles and the foxfire.

The imposter said, in that accent that was no part of the Honourable Rag's voice, "So, little wren, you are well protected this night through. Run well the year ahead of you, when we merry men go a-hunting."

His hair was glowing green, his eyes black but lit with the candle flames. I stared at him, aware of my fallen sword with every fibre of my being. One quick motion and I could grasp it—

The imposter laughed, and the great eye blinked again, stone scraping down the night air, and the figure was gone.

Mr. Dart was solid and steady in the centre of the chapel, his back to me, his hand lifting.

The circle spat silver fire and a sudden line of green and purple flared up along it and it stabilized, arc to arc under each of the seven candles.

I wavered. The sword was shining silver and gold. Gobbets of dark ichor were falling from the eye and dropping onto the stone ledge of the window opening. I could hear nothing: the wind and the banshee wail and the clattering of acorns and branches and hooves and hands were all one, all the rushing of my blood in my ears and the heavy warm weight of Mr. Dart's magic rising up, and—

I pushed myself back onto the altar, and stabbed my hand on the point of a holly-leaf.

The bright spear of pain lanced through my mind.

I gasped and fell as if my tendons had all been cut, but before my knees landed on the stone floor I—

— was somewhere else.

～

No.

Still the same place, the stone cow byre. The trough was there, as indeed it still was, but neither the cow nor the straw were in evidence. Instead there was a rough wooden table, and a three-legged stool. The table was in the middle of the space, where Mr. Dart stood now.

Sir Peregrine sat on the stool, one elbow on the table. He was on the other side of the table, and I could see his face clearly.

This was the older Sir Peregrine. His copper-red hair was still curly; it was longer, almost as long as Jullanar Maebh wore hers. There was white at his temples and threading through the curls, and his beard was a pure red roan. He had wrinkles around his eyes.

He was wearing the white surcoat over the chainmail. It was a bright white cloth, unmarked with any device. He didn't wear a helm of any fashion; instead he wore a circlet of oak leaves.

In his hand he held not a sword but a severed unicorn horn.

I gasped on seeing the horn. Its stump was still bloody; it had not been shed naturally, nor cut cleanly, but gouged out. My gorge rose at the thought, the idea that anyone could even *think* of doing something so obscene.

Sir Peregrine looked up and stared straight at me.

His eyes opened wide, and the unicorn horn rolled from his unresponsive hands. Blood spattered over the white cloth, but though he caught the horn before it could fall he seemed otherwise to ignore it.

"You," he said. His voice sounded as if it were echoing, the timbre normal but the sounds themselves doubled, trebled, echoing back over themselves as if a palimpsest of sound lay between his speech and my ears.

He was not speaking Shaian. He spoke the language my ancestors had known, whose name I could not remember.

I could not think of anything to say. I stared at him, at the horn, at the oak leaves in his hair and the blood on his garments.

"I have seen you before," he said. "The Lady sent you—why?"

I could think of nothing to do besides pray silently to the Lady for some direction. Nothing came: but Sir Peregrine regarded me with his tired, pleading eyes.

"Her champion called me back from the dead to fight the Dark Kings," I said finally, an answer that made no sense. But what else could I say?

However strange and useless a statement that was, the effect on Sir

Peregrine was extraordinary. He closed his eyes, but not in grief; in—dared I say it?—in *wonder*. In *relief*.

"There are others who fight," he said, without looking at me. "Others who stand against them, in the Lady's name."

It was not a question, but I answered it nonetheless. "Yes."

"I will not fail you," he said solemnly, looking now at me with eyes that seemed so ancient. Ancient, and fey. Holy.

"I have been fighting a long time and I thought there was no one left to stand with me."

I thought of Ariadne nev Lingarel, the ancient poet who had waited for me because *my* reading of her poem had brought *her* grace.

"We stand with you," I said, as solemn a promise as I had ever made my Mr. Dart.

"Take this," he said, holding out the horn. "It was meant as an insult but it is a holy gift."

I found I could move my hands, but I could not take that horn from him. I held my hands out, palms outfacing. The whorled ivory point touched my skin with a sensation like a burning coal.

"I cannot take that," I said. "I have nothing to give in return."

Sir Peregrine smiled: just the way the Squire did, the way Jullanar Maebh did, the way Master Ricard did. "You gave me hope. It is a banner I will fly until my death."

"Your name will not perish. Your line will not perish. Your fight is in not in vain."

He took a deep, shuddering breath, and his smile grew lighter, brighter. "Hope, and a promise—what faith you give me!"

Sir Peregrine harried the Wild Hunt from hill and dale, the Dark Kings and their fell shadows, the monsters that come from the night and those that slink in the corners of the day.

"You do not hunt a unicorn," he said. "You cannot; they are, or are not, by the Lady's grace."

"Peregrine and Ballory will ride again," I said, not sure if I meant this man before me or the one who stood where my own mortal body was still falling.

But I had seen the great unicorn come pacing out of the woods to bow his shining horn onto the shoulder of this man, older than he was now and bent in grief and woe.

"And where shall I find my beloved companion?" Sir Peregrine said, gesturing with the bloody horn in his hand. The point etched a rune in fire on my palm.

"North in Dartington," I said, my voice certain. I had seen it so, under the pear tree at the edge of the orchard. "Near the young oak, the Lúsa tree."

It would not be called the Lúsa tree *yet*—

"Hope, and faith, and a gift of grace," said Sir Peregrine, and pushed the horn against my hand until my fingers closed reflexively around it.

—and my knees hit the stone floor.

CHAPTER FIFTEEN

T he eye was gone, and the window was light.

Mr. Dart sat on one pew, and my father on the other, both of them watching me.

I was on my knees before the altar, my head bowed, my hands clasped before me in the deepest attitude of prayer.

I blinked. How did I know where they were? I could not see more than indeterminate shapes in the corners of my eyes. Yet I was absolutely certain it was Mr. Dart on the right and my father on the left. That they were watching me, with consideration and with care.

My left hand was throbbing.

I moved slowly, subsiding onto my heels. My left hand bore a red spiral as if I'd been branded; or marked with a unicorn horn.

There was no unicorn horn on the altar or the stone flags before it. There was, instead, a sword.

It was the sort of plain, sturdy weapon intended for hard use. The style was unfamiliar, though I had seen similar weapons in the small part of the University of Morrowlea's armoury devoted to historic weapons. Pre-Astandalan, at any rate.

(I knew it matched the one I had seen Sir Peregrine holding. I knew it matched his chainmail and surcoat, the period and the purpose and the look in his eyes. The thought was too raw to examine in more detail, yet.)

I rubbed my hands together and twisted to look at first my father and then Mr. Dart. My father said, "Do you need a hand?"

I considered the feel of my body, and nodded. He stood and came over without further comment, placing a strong hand under my elbow, on my shoulder, and heaved me upright. I staggered and caught myself with his support, and without apparently thinking further he wrapped his arms around me.

I reciprocated. My father was not so large a man as my stepfather had been (whom I had embraced in the Beyond, and never in this life), but he was bigger than me, taller and wider even without the flesh that seven years on the galleys had stolen from him.

"Jemis," he said, his voice muffled by my hair.

"Papa," I replied. My voice was rough, and I coughed, bringing my hand up to cover my mouth. My shoulders and ribs ached.

I coughed and coughed, bringing up some phlegm that stuck in my throat. Mr. Dart passed me a handkerchief—not one of my own, this was a finer cambric than any of mine—and I hacked it out. It was a disturbing black.

"Well," I said, folding the cloth over the mess. "Well."

"Here," my father said, passing me the wooden cup. The water was cold and sweet, tasting as fresh as it had earlier. The night before.

I hoped it was the night before. "It is Winterturn Day, is it not?"

"Yes." My father sighed and guided me gently to sit on the pew. I complied. I wasn't sure my knees would keep me upright for much longer. I felt incredibly shaky. The cup was a welcome weight to anchor my hands. A splash of water seemed to soothe the burn.

"What happened?" I asked presently, after several small sips of water.

Mr. Dart snorted. "We had thought to ask you that."

"I had another vision of Sir Peregrine. This time he saw me." I turned my left hand up, unfolding my fingers so they could see the mark. "He asked me why the Lady had sent me ... I said we stood against the Dark Kings. He handed me the unicorn horn. I suppose it turned into the sword."

We all looked at the sword. Mr. Dart went very tense, and then said, "The Ánhorn. It was lost; Sir Peregrine's final battle was with a lance and a borrowed sword. It's a famous story."

We had all heard the priests expound on it: the virtues of making do, of accepting assistance, of being not too proud or too attached to any one thing.

"He gave it to you," Mr. Dart said. "Across time and space."

I shook my head. "Not space. He was here. The altar wasn't, it was just a table."

My father regarded me with a strange smile. "The details are critical, of course."

"What happened on your side?" I asked, not sure how to respond to that. Of course the details were critical ... When were they ever not? I cleared my throat. "After the Wild Hunt came by. They knocked three times three on the door, and ... there was some sort of *eye* looking in ... but you did something with the circle, Perry."

"I held the circle on the inside, ensuring *you* did not leave it, as you seemed desperately inclined to. I know you didn't mean to eat any of those enchanted biscuits, but you did get crumbs on your lips and I think that made you more susceptible."

I rubbed my right thumb over the new scar. The burning sensation was diminishing now; it didn't hurt when I touched it. I smiled wryly at my friend. "I think this year's events have made it clear I don't need the Gentry's food to be susceptible to them."

My father cleared his throat. "Your mother said you took after that side of the family. I thought it was superstition, when you were a baby. She insisted we do all the old protections around your crib ... red thread and blue beads, silver and salt, hawthorn and holly, and rowan and iron over every door and window. Oak for the cradle, of course. She was entirely certain they would want you."

"But why?" I asked, bewildered.

"Olive said you were born under a contrary star."

Mr. Dart laughed. "I knew your propensity to calamity could not be entirely laid at the feet of chance."

I turned to him. "We've been friends since infancy. *You've* been hiding a propensity for wild magic all this time."

"It's nothing, really," Mr. Dart said, with a quick glance at my father, who's brow was furrowed as he listened.

"Did you not say you would declare yourself a great mage?"

"Jemis!"

I lifted my hands at his vehemence. "I think we can trust my father, don't you?"

Mr. Dart flushed, and he bowed in his seat to my father. "I mean you no insult, Major—"

"I think you can certainly call me Jack, Perry. Uncle Jack, if you must."

Like my stepsisters, I thought with satisfaction, and took another sip. The water truly was delicious. Refreshing. Satisfying.

"I haven't spoken to my brother and Hamish about it yet."

I blinked at him. "Did you not have to explain Ballory? I thought you would have discussed it after we left to go to town."

"We had other things to discuss," he said, glancing at my father, who nodded solemnly.

I felt I was missing something very important. "May I ask …"

They both stared at me incredulously. Mr. Dart said, "Jemis, you died and came back to life with messages from the Other Side. Even a unicorn is not quite so astonishing as that."

"But you were the one who called me back."

That, to me, was far the more important element. The Lady had been very clear it was no virtue of mine that I could return. It was the circumstances of my death, that I had been fashioned into a sacrifice for the Dark Kings and then sacrificed myself for precisely the opposite reason, combined with the incredible, incontestable fact that Mr. Dart was her Champion. *He* had kept he way open: he had been the vessel of the miracle. I was merely the object of it.

Object? Subject? Both, perhaps.

"At any rate, no, I have not discussed my magic with them."

I thought of his revelations of the night before. The duck that laid golden eggs; the fairy fox who had a human form each new-moon night; the magic slowly gathering force in his mind, under his skin, at his fingertips.

"What, then?" I asked, more subdued. "Last night."

"The Hunt was calling your name," Mr. Dart said, with another glance at my father. My father was leaning against the wall of the chapel, between two candles. They were blown out now, though their lengths were undiminished from the tapers we had brought.

"I heard them also," he said. His eyes were dark and sad. "I heard the banshee call for you."

I lifted my hand to my heart, where that cry had pierced it so sharply. "I heard it," I said.

"Fortunately you have already died," Mr. Dart said with renewed cheerfulness.

My father barked out a laugh at that. "That is one way of looking at it. I walked the parish boundaries, as I did for Olive every year I was home for the longest night. There have been storms and uncanny shadows before, but never a night where the Gentry ... came."

All those years my mother had placed Mr. Dart and me within her circle of salt and silver. She had had the gift of Sight, or so I had learned. Had she seen his power? Power was attractive ...

"Why me?" I asked again. "Why are they coming for me, and not Perry?"

"Your magic called a dragon out of the Woods."

"And yours called a unicorn." I looked at the wooden cup, the little scalloped scoops where the maker had gouged out the inner hollow. The last bit of water in the bottom settled into it like a hundred-petalled flower. "I have no magic now, and it was never so great as yours, anyhow."

My father stroked his chin pensively. "How do you know that?"

"Magistra Aurelia of the Faculty of Magic at Tara told me. She's a great mage ..."

Mr. Dart sighed. "I'll write to her."

"Thank you." I smiled at him. He knew the stories at least as well as I did. Surely he knew what he was risking by continuing untrained? There would be more than magic foxes after him as his power burgeoned.

My father said, "I do not have your sight, Jemis, nor your power, Perry. I saw dark shadows—wings and claws, horned riders, skeletal horses, dogs with flaming eyes. All shadows, formed out of wind and thunder.

They came thundering down the wind along the old road, following their lanterns. It crosses the centre of the parish … when they entered the circle of the boundaries they made for the chapel and circled it."

"Did they not continue along the road?" I asked. Where *did* the other end of that road go? The Giants' Road led from the Gap across the Gorbelow Hills to the standing stone in the Farry March. The Lady's Way, the Gentry's Road, led from the Woods Noirell to—where?

"Why would they?" Mr. Dart asked. "Everything they might want was here."

~

They had held their circles from midnight until dawn.

I had fallen to my knees, Mr. Dart said, as midnight rang out across the barony, parish to parish ringing the bells to call the Lady's attention down and scare off the Dark Kings and other forces of the night.

Only the old chapel, oldest of all in the barony—one of the oldest in the duchy, perhaps the kingdom—had no bell.

Instead it had Mr. Dart standing in the centre, and my father walking the perimeter, and me wavering, tempted, only prevented from lifting that sword and breaking the circles by Mr. Dart's voice and the vision of the ancient Sir Peregrine.

"And now it's Winterturn morning," I murmured. "We're missing all the services."

My father made an inelegant noise. "Are you proposing going to one of them? It snowed a foot before dawn."

"Good luck," I murmured, thinking again of the freakish snow storm centred on Master Boring's house on the other side of the mountains, where Ballory waited in a small box in the heart of a maze of uncountable things. "Good fortune, rather."

"Indeed. Are you feeling up to walking back to town?"

I finished the water and nodded. "I could do with eating something, I expect."

"There's a bit of bread and honey left," Mr. Dart observed. "We managed to save you some after we broke our fast."

"Thank you."

They were strange vigils that Mr. Dart had held over me, these past few weeks. One in the dark silence of death; another when I knelt transfixed in prayer. "Thank you," I said again, hoping he understood my meaning. "Thank you."

"Don't mention it," my father said, with a crooked smile.

~

It was one of those splendid mornings, where the snow has hidden all imperfections and the sun is shining bright as anything. My hat had fallen under the altar but had escaped any further indignities. I retrieved it and brushed off the dust, straightening the ribbons of the cockade so they returned to their jaunty angle.

My father shook his head as I examined the hat. "That is *astoundingly* out of date."

"It was a very kind gift from Mrs. Ayden," I replied, setting it on the altar so I could brush my fingers through my hair and re-plait it. My queue had been badly treated by the gusting wind and magic of the night.

"It doesn't go in the slightest with your coat," Mr. Dart said.

I smiled at him. "It does now. Come now, Mr. Dart, who are we to follow the fashions of Orio City?"

"Ragnor Bella being such a centre of fashion."

I tied my queue with the bit of black ribbon and set my hat on my head. My father's sword went in its sheath at my waist, but the Ánhorn I would have to hold as a naked blade, or else wrap it in the cloth we'd used to cover the bread.

"Cover it, I'd suggest," my father said when I hesitated before picking it up. "No sense asking for trouble."

"It'll come find us anyway," Mr. Dart murmured. "Along with those seeking fashion advice, apparently."

Ragnor Bella was the home of a new great mage, I thought, as I set the wooden cup on the altar next to the branches of hawthorn and holly. My mother had told us to leave the water, and that she would return on New Year's Day to scry for the fortune of the coming year before cleaning out the altar basin and trough.

I supposed that task would fall to me as well this year. I shook the crumbs out of the bread-wrap and carefully spiralled it around the blade and hilt of the Ánhorn. It felt good in my hand. My fingers ached to try the sword in practice.

I was the last one out of the chapel. The door was faintly warm under my hand as I closed it behind us. The ivy slithered down across my arm, no longer serpentine but healthy, hallowed by the prayers and green-and-gold magic Mr. Dart had wrought in the night.

Silver and salt, hawthorn and holly. Golden was the wax, and golden the light. Mr. Dart's eyes were blue in the sunlight; his auburn hair lit like stirring coals.

All the snow around the chapel was even and smooth, but for one line of human footprints leading to the door—my father's track, I presumed—and a small wicker basket that contained two cooing birds.

CHAPTER SIXTEEN

The basket was tied with a ribbon purple as a spring crocus.

We stood a little apart in front of the chapel, looking at the basket. There were no tracks of any kind around it.

"That wasn't here when I came at dawn," my father said.

He could not have missed it, as it was placed directly between two of his own footsteps. He would have stumbled over it even if the night was still too dark to see it.

Mr. Dart had his head cocked to the side, and his face bore the inward-turning intensity I was beginning to realize was him turning to his magic. The air hummed like when we had woken the bees of the Woods Noirell. I was surprised that when I moved my hand experimentally, the swaddled sword tucked under my arm, there was no visible response.

The light was heavy as honey. "I think it's fine," Mr. Dart said, the surprise audible. "It's a gift."

"From a very secret admirer," I murmured, even as my father bent down to pick the basket up.

"Ring-necked doves," he murmured, peeking inside at the birds.

"How curious," Mr. Dart said, and without further ado began stomping up the path towards the road.

~

It was a beautiful morning the whole way along.

There had been enough traffic along the road that we could stamp the snow off our boots and walk at a good pace towards Ragnor Bella. We passed a few people: farmers and families, the former in their rough working clothes and the latter bundled up in their Winterturn best.

The solstice was the more important theologically, but everyone's favourite day was Twelfthnight, when gifts were given and the New Year was wassailed in. That was a feast day for family. It was a wonderfully warming sentiment to think that this year I would have my father to share the meal with.

We did not speak much on the walk. After a while Mr. Dart began to sing Winterturn carols, and my father and I joined in. Mr. Dart's voice was hardly anything to celebrate, but that was one of the splendid things about this particular holiday. No one minded if he could hardly carry a tune, not with a Winterturn carol.

At the Ragglebridge we met one of the constant fishermen—the only other Jemis of my acquaintance, in fact, though he went by Jem. He asked what was in my basket and got misty-eyed when I showed him the ring-necked doves.

"I used to keep doves, racing pigeons, all them fancy sorts," he declared, brushing one gnarled finger down the back of the male bird. "Good Lady, they're beautiful."

I said, "They may be a gift from the Good Neighbours, but if you would like them, I would gladly give them to you, freely and with joy."

"And so do I accept them," Jem replied, immediately setting down his pole and starting to pack away his fishing gear. "My good wife will be pleased. She loved the birds herself, you know. Had to eat them through the dark times ..." He shook his head sharply, then crinkled back up at me as he coiled his lines and set them in the wicker hamper beside his pole. "'Tis a good thing to start up again with the old good things, isn't it? And new ones too, o'course."

I thought of Mr. Dart's magic shifting, stretching, waiting to come back, and smiled at him. "Yes."

~

When we reached town we found everyone smiling and full of cheerful greetings. No one seemed to find it odd we three should be returning from the Coombe road rather than the one leading to the Big Church to the north of town. By the numbers the main service had already let out and people were returning to their homes for the large midday meal that was traditional.

I wondered what I had in my pantry, and what I could offer. I had asked the milkman for eggs, had I not? Eggs and butter, and I had acquired several great wheels of cheese in Orio City ... and I had all that tea ... and Mr. Inglesides's bakery would be open.

"Will you join me for luncheon?" I asked as we entered the square in front of the bookstore and my flat. "It will not be a great feast but I can offer you omelettes and tea."

"Riches untold," Mr. Dart murmured. "I shall contribute something delicious from the bakery."

"I'll help you excavate your table from your boxes," my father offered with a sly grin.

We had just finished eating when a flurry of knocks on the book-store door sent me hurrying downstairs to find that the new edition of the *New Salon* had arrived and needed to be unboxed.

Mr. Dart came down behind me, leaving my father to sit by my fire upstairs and take forty winks, for, so he said, he was not so young as we, and could feel the sleepless night. We were invited to Dart Hall for that evenings' meal, so I was told, and he wanted to be in good shape for the traditional parlour games that would follow.

I brought the box in, checked that Gingersnap had sufficient food and water, and cleared the ash out of the stove before lighting it. Mr. Dart petted the cat and watched me with idle enjoyment.

It had been three years since I had last participated in the Darts' annual tradition of parlour games, and I considered the prospect with cautious excitement. I used to be reasonably skilled at Charades ...

"Are you going to open the box?" Mr. Dart asked, settling back in the chair next to the stove. "I am consumed with curiosity to know what it says about Jack Lindsary's new play."

I gave him a speaking glance, but he merely grinned and continued to pet the cat. I finished laying the fire with exaggerated care. To tell the truth our breath was steaming in the air.

Or mine was. Mr. Dart appeared to be unconsciously warming himself and the air around him again. No wonder the cat had jumped onto his lap as soon as it was practicable.

The fire caught, and I set the box of lucifers aside to fetch the crate instead. I set it upon the counter and fetched out the boot knife my father had given me. It was proving most useful; I wondered how I had gotten by without a pocket knife in the past.

(Had I had a pocket knife at one point? Mr. Buchance had given me a pen … had he also given me a knife? What had happened to it …?)

I shook my head. There were strange holes in my memory from that last year at Morrowlea and afterwards, when I had come perishingly near to a wireweed overdose.

Of course I had then actually perished of one.

Whatever the *New Salon* contained it could hardly be so astonishing as that. They couldn't have caught wind of the miracle in Lind in time to bring it to press for this week.

I levered off the lid and lifted out the first bundle. I slit the twine holding it closed and unfolded the first copy with the pleasant sensation of opening a gift. The scent of ink and paper rose up, and I breathed deep of the familiar, satisfying aroma. Not quite as splendid as old books, but pleasing nonetheless.

Then I glanced down to see what the cover story was.

Stories, rather.

DOWAGER DUCHESS POISONED

ORIO CITY IN REVOLT AFTER JEMIS GREENWING FIRST PERSON TO ESCAPE INESCAPABLE PRISON

FURIOUS DUKE CANCELS BALL

"Oh, this *is* good," said Mr. Dart. All I could do was laugh.

~

I could wish I had managed to find the time—though when precisely I wasn't sure—to decipher the code being used to pass messages in the Etiquette Questions Answered column.

I could also wish I had managed to get the Honourable Rag, in his persona of the Hunter in Green, to tell me the code *his* people were using to pass messages by way of the crossword puzzle.

I could wish I hadn't spent half the night transfixed in prayer and was consequently more than half-awake.

"Shall I read the stories?" Mr. Dart asked, reaching out for a copy. Gingersnap made a mewling sound of disappointment, then padded up to curl in the corner of Mr. Dart's sling, his stone arm being supported by the arm of the chair at the moment. "If you don't think you can stand the embarrassment."

I was morbidly curious. The only good thing about this was that as Mrs. Etaris's bookstore was the dissemination point for the *New Salon* in Ragnor Bella, only the Squire was likely to have read it before us.

And the Baron, I supposed.

And possibly also the Woodhills.

And—

"I don't suppose we can burn all the copies?" Mr. Dart asked, as I gave him one copy and sat down in the other chair with one of my own.

"It's not as bad as that, surely?"

He shrugged and flipped the paper open. "Perhaps not by the standards of a Greenwing."

～

It was a holiday, and therefore the bookstore was theoretically closed.

The fact that the fire was lit and Mr. Dart and I were quite obviously present through the window meant that the importunate knocking started approximately three minutes after we sat down.

I had not even begun to read any of the articles, being struck upon the headlines. In smaller print after *FURIOUS DUKE CANCELS BALL* was the claim that this was not in response to his mother's poisoning—

already a matter of some concern—but because of his sister having been abducted.

"Goodness," said Mr. Dart, setting aside the paper so he could dig in his pocket for his pipe. "The writers have truly outdone themselves this edition."

"Splendid," I replied dryly, as the first knock made me look to the door.

Mrs. Buchance stood there, peering in through the somewhat wavy glass. She waved when I stood and came over to unlock it.

"Oh, Jemis, I am glad to see you," Mrs. Buchance said breathlessly. "Ah—Mr. Dart, of course, good to see you as well—oh! And Major Greenwing, likewise."

I had not heard my father come down the stairs, but he seemed to have been roused from his nap.

"Mrs. Buchance," he replied gravely. "Can we help you?"

"I was hoping Jemis might be willing—" She turned beseeching eyes upon me. "Jemis, I don't suppose you would be willing to let the Embroidery Circle meet here tonight? It won't be everyone—Mrs. Henny and Mrs. Pritchard and perhaps Mrs. Etaris if she can get away … She's agreed we could use the space but she said you would have to be consulted. Something about a kitten? And a unicorn?" She laughed self-consciously. "Lauren and Sela haven't stopped talking about unicorns since they went out collecting greenery with you. I don't know what stories you've been telling them, but they adore the idea."

"Of course, I'm sure Mr. Greenwing will be happy to host," Mr. Dart said quickly.

I glanced at Mr. Dart and my father. We were supposed to be going to the Darts for supper and parlour games. I'd been looking forward to it. "Mr. Dart …" I trailed off.

"Mrs. Henny was stolen by the Gentry as a young girl, was she not?" my father said thoughtfully.

Mrs. Buchance appeared entirely scandalized, even as I turned to stare at my father in blatant surprise.

"Oh, that's a nasty rumour," Mrs. Buchance said hastily. "No need to rake up old gossip, surely?"

"Surely not," I murmured, thinking of the new gossip spread all along the front page of this week's *New Salon*.

The gossip couldn't be *that* old, came the second thought, if Mrs. Buchance—who was only five or six years older than I—knew about it.

My curiosity stirred. It wasn't as if I hadn't plenty of things to ask of the Embroidery Circle. Not to mention I'd bought that yarn, and once reminded of the craft of knitting was eager to make something using it.

"Thank you," Mrs. Buchance said. "They'll be here around seven. The host usually provides cakes or something of the sort. Nothing elaborate." And with that she bustled out, drawing the folds of her expensive fur cloak around herself as she went out the door.

I went to lock it, but someone else immediately started hammering. I sighed and opened the door again, this time to a strange young man. "Yes?"

He was holding a snorting and blowing horse, the reins loose in his hand. "I'm looking for Jemis Greenwing," he said.

"I am he."

He surveyed me, a certain skepticism in his eyes. "Did you truly escape from the Orio City prison?"

The only problem with this question was that we stood in the doorway of the bookstore and there were more than a handful of people crossing the market square behind the horseman.

The special messenger, I realized, taking in his livery. He wore the crossed-quills insignia of the Rondelan Post embroidered on the breast of his close-cut coat. He could not have been far off my own age, but his face seemed incredibly fresh and innocent. Cynical in expression, but innocent in its frank disbelief.

"I did," I said, setting my shoulders back. I did not recognize any of the people drawing close to eavesdrop on our conversation, which merely meant that the gossip would spread very fast indeed.

"There's an account in this week's *New Salon*," Mr. Dart said from my elbow.

"I read it," the special messenger said. "They say half of Orio City is on fire."

"I didn't light it," I stated, hopefully without defensiveness. "It was terribly foggy when we were there."

The special messenger shifted position, his expression transmuting into the smug joy of knowing news no one else did. I wondered if he had chosen his job because he liked that, or if it was an unexpected pleasure of a constrained choice.

"The fog's lifted," he said. "Trade has come to a complete standstill because everyone can see that the Lady's ships guard the Isle—and the pirates guard the coast. Ever since the *Blood Angel* was taken this summer things have been unsettled, but now ..." He shook his head. "No one can believe you led an escape. The Indrilline shouldn't have let it be known she'd captured you and the Duke Imperial. *He's* not happy, no, not at all."

FURIOUS DUKE CANCELS BALL, I thought, wondering just what lay behind that headline.

"Do you have a letter for me?" I asked, not exactly loath to keep hearing his news but also hoping there might be something more substantial on offer.

"Oh, yes," he said, unembarrassed. He tugged his horse and felt in an official-looking leather saddlebag, blue-dyed leather stamped with the Post Office insignia, from which he withdrew two oilskin packets. "That'll be a silver bee."

I raised my eyebrows at him, but it was common enough practice for someone to pay half the postage and require the recipient to pay the remainder. This was not always a matter of miserliness; there were certainly cases in which the messenger had pocketed the money and spent it on a spree rather than his commission.

"Here," my father said, pressing a coin into my hand. I forbore comment, as I'd left my wallet upstairs in my flat, and exchanged the silver bee for the two packets. One was addressed in Hal's familiar informal hand; the other was far more formal and entirely unfamiliar.

"Mr. Greenwing," the messenger said, touching his hat. He gave me one more once-over. "Is that the new style in Orio City?"

I gave him what I hoped was a nonchalant look in return, and spoke in what was, in immediate retrospect, perhaps slightly too clear a voice. "Why should we follow them? They're not the capital any more."

The special messenger's eyes opened wide with shock before he straightened his face and mounted his horse.

"That'll be around half of Fiellan before morning, you know," Mr. Dart murmured.

I nodded around at the people in the square. "The *New Salon* will be available tomorrow morning," I told them, before retreating with my oilskin packets and both shutting and locking the door.

The first packet was indeed from Hal. I set it aside, hoping it would clarify the *New Salon*'s headlines, and opened the second with due curiosity.

It was from the Lady of Alinor.

CHAPTER SEVENTEEN

H al's letter was relatively straightforward. He informed me he had returned safely home, only to discover his mother abed with a dreadful cold ("By no means poison!" he had clarified; "that was an ill-timed figure of speech") and his sister in the very process of eloping with her mathematics tutor.

At this point in the letter he started to scrawl.

I conclude in great haste, as the New Salon *was delivered here this morning and will be proceeding apace to you in south Fiellan. I enclose a note —alas, unfinished—for my dear Hope—Jemis, do tell her I would elope with her if she but gave me the word. My sister eloped in the north, to the Saint of the Lonely Isle: is there a saint in the south who might bless our union?*

As you will see in the New Salon, *I have cancelled the Winterturn Ball. There is tremendous news come out of Orio City in the wake of our departure. The Rainbow Isle has been seen, the fog has lifted, and the pirate fleets have closed in. Our friend is being harried into a box canyon: take care, for the stag is most dangerous when he turns at bay.*

We shall strategize anon. Do let me know what you learn of the New Salon *once you have had a chance to consider it more thoroughly.*

. . .

That suggested—oh, yes, that he too wished to know the results of my decoding, once I had decoded the cipher, that was.

I set Hal's letter on the table and turned again to the strange missive from the Lady Magus of Alinor.

To the Viscount St-Noire of the Woods Noirell

My dear Lord St-Noire,

I had the great pleasure of meeting your father, the notable Major Jack Greenwing, this past summer, while he recovered from the injuries sustained in the taking of the Blood Eagle. That was a great blow against our enemies, and I hoped it betokened a better year than the last several. Major Greenwing spoke most eloquently and movingly of his hopes of returning home to his son, memory of whom had sustained him through the long and gruelling years enslaved on the ship.

I should have loved you merely in admiration of your father; what then shall I call this emotion? When I woke to hear such news!—A fishing boat beached under cover of darkness and fog, smuggling two so dear to my heart, so long lost … and yet now found.

What an astonishing young man you must be, not only to escape from the hitherto-inescapable prison of Orio City but in so doing to rescue my son and my daughter, both lost to me many years since. My daughter speaks often of you: your academic brilliance, your wit, your great and good heart, and above all your courage, in which you stand surely beside your father.

As a mother and as the Lady of Alinor I stand in your debt. There are no constraints on what you may ask in return. From what my daughter has said, you will not ask for anything unmeet.

—Jessamine en-Annoré, Lady of Alinor.

As a postscript: I understand you desire to court my daughter. You have my leave and my blessing; even unto half my kingdom, should I still have one when she agrees to your hand.

Well.

I looked around blindly. I had been leaning on the counter; my father was in one chair, Mr. Dart in the other, both of them reading the paper. The cat had moved to sprawl before the wood stove, staring at the flames in the steady, slightly uncanny way of cats.

Mr. Dart lowered the paper. "Well?" he asked, neutrally.

"Violet made it home safely," I said.

"Did she write and send it to you by way of special messenger? I am amazed your suit progresses so quickly apace."

"It is from her mother," I said, trying not to show my embarrassment too obviously. I turned to my father, who had lowered his own paper and was regarding me with interest. He seemed more amused than aggravated by whatever was written in the *New Salon*, which was a relief. "It is from Lady Jessamine. She remembers you well, Papa, from this summer."

"Ah."

Mr. Dart looked intently at me, and then crowed immoderately. "Has she given you her blessing to court her daughter, the devastating and dangerous Violet?"

I, I am sure, flushed scarlet head-to-toe. My father lifted his hand to cover his smile. "You are looking to court the Lady's daughter? Nay, do not mistake me—it is an excellent match."

I could hardly do any better, as he well knew.

"You will be glad to hear that the opening of Jack Lindsary's new play has been delayed due to the 'unrest and uncertainty' in Orio City. The governor-prince and his affianced bride are barricaded in the palace." Mr. Dart smirked at me. "What are the odds of yon Lark being able to recreate your analysis?"

"She never read my final paper," I said, never so happy for that fact as this moment.

"So Hal has cancelled the ball?"

I passed on his news, and moved around the bookstore aimlessly, straightening books where they were resting incorrectly on the shelves. Mrs. Etaris had begun the process of shelving the new purchases, but there were several stacks that were sorted and priced but not shelved. I picked up a handful and found places for them.

The Discretion of the King, by A Lady: not the salacious novel it sounded, but an account of espionage and covert war in the kingdom of Lorgraine, on the other side of Ghilousette.

Three Recipes and their Variations, by S. Duval: a comprehensive account of the typical dishes of Furnai on Voonra, which had numerologically significant numbers of ingredients and astrologically inclined stages of preparation.

I flipped it open. The first recipe I landed on was supposed to be started 'on the night of a quarter moon', and had three sets of ingredients, the first containing thirteen, the second twenty-three, and the third forty-three items. The first direction was 'Begin by consulting the Seventree. If a major card is drawn, proceed to step four. ...'

I set the book on the shelf for Cookery, next to *A Guide to Late Imperial Decadent Dinner Parties*, which no one had yet acquired, and picked up the next book in the pile.

A Primer of Saints of the Lady, by Abbot Bollé of Gourande. I glanced at Mr. Dart and my father, both still engrossed in the *New Salon*, and opened it.

The primer was intended for children, or so it seemed from the general tone. I leaned against the bookcase, breathing deeply the familiar, friendly scents of wood and paper, leather and ink. Mrs. Etaris's potpourri added a faint floral note as the air warmed from the wood stove.

A dozen saints's lives were recounted. I paged through them, looking at the woodcuts of various men and women. They were so varied, these holy people: Saint Fiella, who had been a shield maiden and a duchess and a saint. Sir Peregrine, looking very unlike the real man. Saint Corovel, who had launched herself off the edge of the continent in a coracle, and found the Wandering Isle, the Rainbow-Girt Isle, and thereupon founded a great college of healing.

The introduction gave a brief overview of the Church of the Lady of the Green and White. It was the main religion of Northwest Oriole, the Abbot stated, evolved out of earlier pagan fertility cults.

(What made those *pagan*, and this true? I had seen the Lady; but I had also brushed against the power of the Dark Kings, much as I did not like to admit it. Who was to say that the religions of East Oriole or the less central parts of Northwest Oriole were entirely untrue? Let alone the gods of all the rest of the Empire and outside its boundaries.

Were those Mountains *only* the Lady's? Surely other people had other routes there, to our true selves?)

The religion was fairly simple at its core. The Lady of the Green and White oversaw the turning of the year. Over the centuries her saints had revealed pieces of her nature, each of them sharing a fragmented glimpse of the whole and thus assisting in the development of a religion aimed at teaching people what it meant to be happy.

The book was for children, I reminded myself. Yet I could not help but think I liked this abbot's view of faith far better than the majority of what the priests had taught in church services.

What, then, the Abbot wrote, *is a saint?*

Good question, I thought.

A saint is a person who has some special connection to the Lady. They are what we call holy: they have seen or heard or somehow been touched by the Lady, and share that knowledge with others for their joy and happiness. They fight against the dark in all the ways that can be.

The Linder Church has a system for determining whether a person is truly a saint. There are two categories, though both are called 'saints' in the common parlance. Ordinary saints are those individuals who show the virtues of the Lady in this life, and are usually known by their place of residence or another circumstantial feature.

Like the Wild Saint of the Arguty Forest, I thought, or the Saint of the Lonely Isle mentioned by Hal. I couldn't think of many more. I seemed to remember hearing some rumours of a saint in Ragnor Parva, down in the Coombe, but nothing ever seemed to have come of it.

Mind you, until this past fortnight I would never have considered myself particularly interested in religion. I attended church, as anyone might, but I would hardly call myself *pious*. Not like Marcan, or even Hal.

Criteria for ordinary sainthood are as follows:

First: The saint has performed at least three minor miracles, which include such wonders as: the healing of wounds; communing with animals; receiving visions of the future; etc. Second: The saint demonstrates through their daily life an insight into the nature of the Lady and Her relationship with Her people. Third, the saint may have a talent for true wild magic, unbound by the laws of Astandalas, which is a gift of the Lady.

There is also a second category, what is called High Sainthood. These are the saints who stand forth in the world as ambassadors from the Lady: not simply as virtuous men and women, who by their own efforts and the Lady's grace have become windows onto the true possibilities of life, but as doorways for the Lady to work in the world.

High Saints dramatically change the world.

There are several criteria that are incontrovertible evidence of sainthood. A Great Miracle, such as the famous Gift of Water (see Sir Peregrine), the healing of mortal wounds (see St Diamas), the Raising of the Isles (see St Corovel), or a clear blow given to the Dark Kings (see St Raspara) are all grounds for immediate canonization. The sending of a Unicorn is likewise considered evidence of the Lady's favour and love for her chosen saint and champion.

"What are you smirking at?" Mr. Dart asked, justifiably concerned when I glanced at him and said smirk only expanded.

"According to the Abbot Bollé," I replied, "you are incontrovertibly a saint."

My father broke off a guffaw as Mr. Dart started to his feet, his face flushing. The pages of the *New Salon* fluttered down around him, draping the cat with a tent of closely-written paper.

"Jemis!" Mr. Dart cried.

I read out the criteria, then lowered the book so I could raise my eyebrows at him, "You have the gift of a Unicorn companion; you performed what is undoubtedly a Great Miracle; and I'm sure you have *true* wild magic."

"Let me see that," Mr. Dart said, beckoning for the book. I passed it to him with a grin, collecting the scattered pages of his paper as I went.

Someone knocked on the door, hard, and seeing the Honourable Rag I tensed but nevertheless went to answer it. With my father and Mr. Dart in the room with me I felt far less concerned than I might otherwise have been.

"Mr. Greenwing," the Honourable Rag said. He glanced past me to see who was in the room, and both his shoulders and his vacuous expression relaxed. I regarded him thoughtfully. His eyes looked as they ought—none of that odd glint or the even odder spreading pupils.

"Roald."

"Are we back to our given names?" he asked, his smile broadening into something close to genuine.

"What did I give you, when you rode with us on the way to Yrchester?" I asked.

"What did you give me?" He held still for a moment, and I wondered—oh yes, I did—whether—But then he smiled even more genuinely. "A fair thistledown of a kitten."

"Don't let Jemis's sisters hear you call it that," Mr. Dart observed, though he didn't leave his position next to the counter. He'd set the saints book on the counter, and his good hand was not far from the Ánhorn. The sword was still swaddled in bread-linens but the handle was clear enough he could have seized it without trouble.

"Thistledown is not entirely ill a name for a cat," the Honourable Rag observed. "May I enter? Peregrine, do you vouchsafe my identity?"

I glanced at Mr. Dart, who nodded firmly. He raised his eyebrows at me. "I told him of our impostor."

"Come in," I said, and stood back.

Roald took off his hat and examined its brim. "I should bemoan your hesitation, but for that I have heard what happened last night."

We all looked at each other. "Last night? You mean at the Old Chapel?" Had I told anyone else about that eye and the strange wrong-sized impostor—

Roald coughed. "You haven't heard the news about the Wild Saint?"

CHAPTER EIGHTEEN

While we had been guarding the Old Chapel, the Wild Saint had been at his crossroads in the Arguty Forest.

"I heard," the Honourable Rag said, with a glance at my father, who was sitting in my usual chair with an unreadable expression, "that the Hunter in Green was present also."

Mr. Dart said, "I don't think you need to be so coy. Jemis here meets the criteria to be a minor saint."

"I do not," I said, diverted from the question of whether my father knew about the situation yet.

"Communing with animals—the bees. Visions—"

"They've all been of the past, not the future," I objected, relaxing from my initial surge of denial. "Moreover, both are clearly related to my mother's gift of the Sight, and *that* pertains to the Gentry, not the Lady."

I considered what the Lady had said, and my mother. There had been *something* ... but it was not in my conscious mind in any certain way. Merely the hazy knowledge that there was nothing frightful about the gifts from my mother's fairy blood.

Or at least, nothing objectively frightful. The fact that at least some of the Gentry knew me by name was worrying, to say the least.

"If this is about your other life, Roald," my father said mildly, "please don't concern yourself about keeping it a secret from me."

The Honourable Rag spluttered. "How did you know?"

My father shrugged. "I trained as a scout, you know. To read shape and body language, not just face and voice. You do a superb job of disguising yourself, admittedly. Also," and here he grinned, "several members of your gang are former comrades of mine."

Roald considered that, then nodded reluctantly. "I understand. Their loyalty to you was never in doubt, not from the very beginning. Many joined with me only if I promised to assist Jemis in clearing your name."

"You must have started before this autumn," I said, pulling out the stepstool and then leaning on the counter again when the Honourable Rag promptly took it for his seat, leaving Mr. Dart to return to his chair.

"We all knew you were hardly going to leave your father's name and reputation in tatters, as soon as you were of age and earning your own way you would obviously be starting. I was happy enough for such a solid reason for those men to join my cause."

"Which is what, precisely?" I asked, when no one else did. Roald looked at me with an almost sardonic eye, and I grinned back, undaunted. "I haven't had the opportunity to decode all the cross-words yet."

"Nor the Etiquette column, I presume? You will tell me what you find there, won't you?"

"Most likely."

He accepted that, no doubt in the spirit with which it was meant— that if he told me a few of his secrets now, I would tell him some of mine in future.

Not that I was all that likely to keep truly important matters to myself. As he also well knew.

"I told Jemis how I nearly fell into very bad trouble at Tara. Drinking, gambling, all that sort of folly. He'd warned me before we went up to university that I faced danger on those fronts … a warning I took hard at the time, but which turned out well for me in the end."

I nodded gravely. My father had taught me, that glorious long summer when I was nine, the signs of a dangerous habit. I had seen them in Roald, and not in myself, though in the end my own addiction was much the worse.

"By Jemis's timely warning and the grace of the Lady, I did not fall so low as to be caught by the snares of the Indrillines. I was close enough, however, to know—why are you looking like that, Perry?"

Mr. Dart was smirking. "Keeping a tally, is all," he said mildly. "To be a saint one must demonstrate a consistently virtuous life that provides windows onto the Lady's grace and the joy offered us in following Her."

"I think you're stretching," I retorted, and turned meaningfully to the Honourable Rag. "Do please go on, Roald."

He considered Mr. Dart a moment longer before shifting position on the step-stool. He wore his scarlet breeches and close black coat, with a cravat much closer to my style than he'd sported a month ago. I wondered idly how long it would take before he commissioned a long coat in the Artorian style. Or a cocked hat.

"Once I was out of my deepest folly, I became increasingly concerned about the state of things in Orio City. The university safe and isolated behind its high walls and the ancient magical protections … the Lady's Isle invisible and apparently helpless … the city increasingly mired in crime. People were looking to the new governor, but I met him a time or two and I could tell he was weak-willed and vain. Ripe for the picking, if someone could get close to him."

Lark had been that someone: she had caught him as easily as she had ensnared me.

"I began very quietly sounding out like-minded folk, and found myself directed at length to meet with a certain man." He showed his golden ring, the match of my own. "At that time they had no name or sigil. Just a network of rumours and safeguards before anyone could come speak to the man at the centre."

"And who was that?"

"Eamon," my father said, just before Roald did.

"Lady Jessamine's spymaster," Roald continued. "He was working in secret and shadows to fight against the increasing dominance of the Indrillines and the Knockermen and the even more dangerous but yet more shadowy players who were at that time just beginning to become noticeable."

The various priests of the Dark Kings, and the Dark Kings themselves, conceivably. "Hmm," I said.

"Over the next two years, we developed what we came to call Crimson Lake. I named it," he said with a decided lack of modesty. "We needed something to unify us properly. Eamon agreed."

"And the business with the Hunter in Green disguise?"

"Hunter in *the* Green," the Honourable Rag corrected.

"I think we decided that we should distinguish the player from the played by use of the definite article."

He laughed. "Very well. On visits home combined with news Eamon and others were collecting from other sources, it became increasingly clear that Ragnor Bella was an emerging locus for the conflict."

"There are three sides to any war," my father said. "Yours, theirs, and history's. Some wars have more."

"This one has several layers at work, and that was before the Good Neighbours decided to get involved."

"The Indrillines," I said, counting them off. "The Knockermen."

"Two criminal gangs duking it out for economic and, more recently, political control of the continent," Mr. Dart said.

"The Lady Jessamine," my father put in. "Whose focus has necessarily been the magic, and who has been hobbled by her abducted son and heir."

Her missing daughter, who was no mage and could therefore not be the heir, was not of political relevance, I supposed, and felt a pang of anger on behalf of Violet.

"The various existing rulers of the nations of eastern Northwest Oriole," the Honourable Rag continued. "We can leave out those west of Harktree and south of Chare, as they are caught up in their own squabbles. The main players are the duchies of Rondé, Lind, Chare, Orio City and the Tarvenol, Ghilousette, and West Erlingale. The Lesser Arcady is almost entirely consumed by its own magical problems."

"The most important are Lind, Chare, and Ronderell. Fiellan is not in itself important,, except for what's going on here."

"In Ragnor Bella, most boring town in Northwest Oriole," I murmured, staring unseeing at the box of *New Salons*.

"And then on top of the political situation we have the magical and religious parties. The cult of the Dark Kings, the Church of Lind, and the Gentry." Roald looked intently at Mr. Dart. "And now you."

Mr. Dart refused to say anything. He had pulled out his pipe earlier, and now fussed with it though it remained unlit. I supposed he must appreciate having something to do with his hands. Hand, I reminded myself.

"Those are the players," I said. "Hal said that half the kingdoms of eastern Northwest Oriole had important members taken hostage at the Orio City court."

"There's also you, Jemis," Mr. Dart said. "You're the newly acknowledged Viscount St-Noire *and* a hero out of storytales—slaying a dragon publicly, of all things!—even without being a saint."

"You can stop teasing me about that," I replied, nettled. "You are the sort to be a named saint. I'd just be the ... the Saint of the Book-store, to counterbalance the Wild Saint of the Arguty Forest."

"Speaking of whom," my father interjected, "What is the news there?"

Roald sighed, his brief moment of levity extinguished. "He was attacked last night. By a shadow with claws. He's unharmed, but ... sounded warning."

We were silent. *That* was a monster out of childhood legends. And out of the Grim Crossroads where Mr. Dart had beaten them back from entering the mortal world.

"Last night," I said slowly, "I saw the imposter again."

Roald held himself very still. "I was at church for the sunset service, and then supper with my family. When I reached the Savage Crux it was to find the Wild Saint in the aftermath of the attack. I was with him till dawn this morning."

"I didn't think it was you at all this time," I reassured him. "No one human could have sat in the window like that ... it was all very odd. There was the great eye, and it blinked, and the imposter, and then the eye blinked again and whatever-he-is was gone."

My father hummed thoughtfully. "Did he do anything? Say anything?"

I frowned. The vision of Sir Peregrine was much more brilliant in my memory. "There was something about a wren ... Yes, that was it. 'You are well protected this night, little wren,' he said. 'But run well the year ahead, when we merry men a-hunting go.' Something like that."

They all regarded me dubiously. Mr. Dart said, "Are you certain he called you a *wren*?"

"Fairly certain, yes."

"They used to sacrifice wrens," the Honourable Rag said, "in the old days."

I regarded him dourly. "Who did?"

He shrugged, as if to say, *Who didn't?* But the answer was evidently those priests to the Dark Kings; the Lady's priests had never sacrificed anything other than the first fruits and flowers of the season. She did not require the spilling of blood, our Lady of the Green and White.

"They sacrificed them on the solstices," my father said, frowning over the thought. "I remember Olive talking about it ... they do something ... not similar, more the opposite ... in the Woods. You'll be safe today, Jemis, but if they're interested ..."

"They'll come again on the Summer Solstice," I finished.

Which was, of course, a day when the boundaries between the mortal worlds and the Kingdom Between Worlds was very thin and easily passed.

"I don't recall a summer service in the old chapel," Mr. Dart said, and looked expectantly at my father, who shook his head. "Well," Mr. Dart continued after a moment, with forced cheer, "that's a full six months away. Plenty of time to research what *they* might want and what we can do about it."

"First my sister, now me," Roald muttered. "Yet *we* don't have the magic or history your families do. We're respectable, I'll have you know."

"So are the Darts," Mr. Dart replied sharply.

Roald laughed. "Respected, my friend. Not respectable. There's a difference."

CHAPTER NINETEEN

After Mr. Dart and my father departed for Dart Hall, I got ready for the Embroidery Circle. I made Outer Reaches style short-bread, which a student in the year below mine had taught us to make in my second year, and a kind of lemon-honey cake my mother used to make with poppyseeds from our own garden.

In my confused state in Orio City—the whole visit there seemed deeply surreal, as if I were looking back on it through warped and wavy glass—I had managed to buy a large pot of poppyseeds. I think I'd imagined planting them in a garden next summer, if I had a garden.

What garden had I been thinking of? The one at the dower house on the Arguty estate, where I had grown up ... it shone still in my memory, golden as the wax, golden as the light.

A pot of poppyseeds was about a pot-less-a-teaspoon more seeds than I would need to have poppies in my gardens for all time forth, if a mistake made by one of the other student-gardeners and Hal's reproaches bore any truth. I didn't even know what colour these flowers were. I looked at the pot. At least the container was attractive: tin painted with a rainbow of stripes.

The poppyseed and honey loaf was easy enough. Lemons were an ingredient from Astandalan days, this part of the world, but there had been a basket available at vast expense in one of the markets, and I had bought the whole thing.

I had vague plans to give one or two or three to all the people who had been kind to me, in the difficult days of the early autumn. Most of them were friends of my mother's from the Embroidery Circle. I'd always found them more than a trifle intimidating but they were the ones who had found me work and respectability when I myself was certain the future held neither fortune nor promise.

After my baking was well underway I spent a full half hour looking for the knitting needles and yarn I'd acquired at Mrs. Ayden's. Somehow the efforts to put away the things bought in Orio City had pushed all yesterday's purchases under cushions and the like.

At half past six I descended to the bookstore and set up. I stirred up the wood stove, cleaned off the counter and laid it with a couple of my extra clean handkerchiefs, then arranged the cake and shortbread in as attractive a manner as I could. My mother had always made this seem effortless.

I did not possess nearly enough serving dishes if I were to have guests, I discovered. It was not the sort of thought I had ever had before. Prior to this spring I had assumed I would be a gentleman, and one did not need to *buy* new serving dishes, at least not until one took a bride, in which case she would likely be the one doing the buying. And this autumn I had not imagined I would ever be in the social position to host anyone but Mr. Dart.

By a quarter to seven the stove was burning brilliantly and the kettle was singing. I set it to stay warm, and cleaned out the large teapot Mrs. Etaris had said was for black tea.

How had she taken hers? With milk, I thought; and she'd offered sugar.

I ran back upstairs for the milk and the sugar and spoons. We had four cups in the bookstore, and I brought down the three I had so far found for my own cupboards. How kind Mrs. Buchance and the Embroidery Circle ladies had been, when I set up this flat! They had been the ones to know I would need the practical necessities, and supplied them without fuss or embarrassment.

That done, I sat down to survey the room. It was clean and tidy—

I'd gotten the rest of the books Mrs. Etaris had priced put away, so that was fine—tea. I needed the tea itself. I jumped up to go upstairs and was immediately interrupted by a firm knock on the door.

Which I hadn't unlocked. I fumbled with the latch and even dropped the key, but managed it in the end.

It was Mrs. Henny the Post and Mrs. Pritchard, whom I knew only by name. She was married to the ironmonger, and was friends as a consequence with Mrs. Kulfield, whose son Roddy was a blacksmith but had gone off to sea on Hal's plant-hunting expedition. Mrs. Pritchard's children were all at least ten years older than me and I knew only that they existed.

"Good evening," I said, bowing them in. "Please, come in. May I take your cloaks?"

They were both wearing the heavy wool capes that had become both necessary and fashionable after the Fall, when the materials for the complex coats of late Astandalan days had been in short supply. Most of those items—a specific type of thread and whalebone and a few other more abstruse magical items once as common as wool cloth —were now available, or all of them but the magical buttons and sigils that would protect against wear and tear and moths and weather—

"Thank you, Mr. Greenwing," Mrs. Pritchard said, handing me her cloak and then working her hairpin out of her hat. The hat was even more elaborate than the sort Mrs. Etaris often sported, and her hatpin was eight inches long to accommodate the silk flowers. And real holly, I discovered upon pricking my thumb, to celebrate the season.

"A joyous and blessed Winterturn-tide to you," I said on that thought.

"And to you, Mr. Greenwing."

Mrs. Pritchard gave me a brilliant smile. She was perhaps in her late fifties, iron-grey of hair, both tall and broad-shouldered. She had a strong face with a prominent nose and freckles over its bridge; a woman, as Mr. Dart had once described her, *of character*.

Mrs. Henny the Post was about ninety. She had curly white hair and twinkling blue eyes, and my father had told me she was the best player of Poacher he'd ever met.

And, apparently, she'd been stolen away by the fairies as a girl.

She handed me her old-fashioned straw bonnet, which I placed carefully next to Mrs. Pritchard's hat on the hooks beside the door. I hung her cloak on the coat-rack and watched as they carried their embroidered work-bags over to their seats, with detours to consider my baked goods.

Despite tasting them to be sure they had come out as intended, I could not but admit to myself I was deeply nervous for their judgment. I did not have Hal or a dragon to help distract the judges this time.

Before I could do anything but stand there, another knock came on the door. This time it was very quiet and seemed to come from very low down. I opened the door, half-expecting the fox or one of my sisters, and instead met the somehow unrepentant but yet sheepish eyes of Ballory the unicorn.

"Does Mr. Dart know you're here?" I asked her.

She ignored me and trotted between my legs. Both Mrs. Pritchard and Mrs. Henny exclaimed, with tones that indicated that Ballory was once more winning all of them over.

Mr. Dart was going to fret, given that he'd already expressed concern that Ballory might have taken a chill after yesterday's adventures in the pear orchard. How exactly a unicorn might catch a chill—or how he would know if so—was something of a mystery to me, but he only laughed kindly at some of my foibles and so I felt obliged to reciprocate.

I looked out the door into the market square. It was quiet and dim, snow falling down in quiet, lazy spirals. It wasn't yet sticking on the damp cobblestones, but it wouldn't be long before it did, I reckoned.

There was no one else in sight, so I shut the door and turned my attention inside. Ballory was nudging at Mrs. Henny's hands, which were in her lap.

I blinked at the unicorn. How much had she grown? She was larger than a cat now; about as large as a small dog. Leaning up against the seated woman's side, she could lay her head on Mrs. Henny's lap.

Mrs. Henny herself was weeping as she buried her hands in Ballory's mane and stroked the soft muzzle. "Oh, you beauty," she was whispering over and over again. "I have not seen you for so long."

Tea. We needed tea.

~

When I came back down with the box of tea, I realized I had neglected to bring in a sufficiency of chairs for more than three.

"Are we expecting anyone else?" I asked as I set the kettle back on the wood stove and added another couple of logs to fire. "I can bring down another chair from upstairs if we are."

"Oh, dear, aren't there more chairs in the back room?" Mrs. Pritchard asked.

I was surprised she called me *dear*, but perhaps she was one of those women who called everyone *dear*. "I'll go look, shall I?" I said when she regarded me expectantly, and was only mildly surprised to discover that there was both a chair and a stool in the back room. I'd sat on at least one of them, that time the Honourable Rag had burst in to find me engrossed in a three-volume novel.

The kettle was boiling when I returned. Mindful of Mrs. Etaris's instructions, I first warmed the teapot before bringing the water to the boil again as I dumped it outside. The snow was settling now, and it was even darker in the square.

People would have lit candles in the windows of their homes, but it was rarely done for businesses, and I didn't think anyone else actually *lived* on the market square. Mr. Inglesides let out the room above the bakery for one of his workers … yes, there was one candle glowing up there in the air.

I had not wanted to leave candles burning unattended upstairs, but I had set three in each of the bookstore's big bay windows. The cat was sitting on the shelf of one, watching Ballory with slitted eyes.

I made the tea: "One spoonful for each person, and one for the pot," Mrs. Etaris had told me, and I measured the precious leaves out, amazed at this wealth at my fingertips. It might have been Master Boring's conscience that had given them to me, but it was wealth none-theless. It made me inordinately pleased to be able to share it with the older women. They could not have had much tea since the Fall.

Mrs. Pritchard was watching me intently, her back very straight. She'd opened her bag and drawn out a ball of wool the colour of clouds, all soft greys and white, with which she was knitting something that looked like socks. I watched her hands move deftly. She was using four needles to knit in the round.

Violet had once tried to show me how to do it, but though she had known how to spin and weave since childhood, knitting apparently had been as new to her as to me, and her explanation hadn't taken.

Hope, on the other hand, had been making her own socks and scarves for years before she came to university, and had been patient in teaching Hal and I. Come to think of it, her extreme patience in instructing me might have been to permit her to spend more time with Hal, who had learned in short order but pretended he hadn't.

I let the tea steep and sat down in the third chair with my own basket of wool and needles.

"What are you planning to make, Mr. Greenwing?" Mrs. Pritchard asked conversationally. She sounded a trifle startled, but not so much that I felt obliged to comment on it.

I glanced at Ballory, whose eyes were closed but whose upper ear twitched when I looked at her. I held up my first lot of yarn, the hunter's green almost as rich in tone as the holly leaves on Mrs. Pritchard's hat. "I was thinking perhaps a jumper for Ballory," I said, inwardly cursing the fact that my voice had a doubtful waver to it.

"Have you knit a jumper before?" Mrs. Pritchard asked as I unreeled a suitable length of the yarn and cast on.

It had been six months since I last knit anything, but there had been a period—most of second year and half of third, in fact—where I had knit whenever I wasn't running or actively doing something else with my hands. The nervous, fidgety energy from what I now knew was wireweed addiction had needed *some* outlet, and while I was willing to run in deeply inclement weather, it was not always possible.

"I have, but only once," I admitted. That had been for Lark, who had laughed mightily at my efforts and refused to wear the garment because it wasn't sufficiently fancy for her tastes.

"Well, we're here to help you, dear," she said placidly. "You'd best pour the tea before it becomes bitter."

~

I had plotted out the basic dimensions of the cardigan and begun knitting when Mrs. Henny stirred.

Mrs. Pritchard and I both looked over. Unlike Mrs. Pritchard I had to stop knitting first, as I knew all too well I was likely to lose my place if I started looking in other directions. Mrs. Pritchard's hands continued to flash, the yarn woven between her fingers like shreds of sheep wool caught on gorse.

"Would you like some tea, Mrs. Henny?" I asked politely. I'd set the pot on the warming shelf above the stove, where the refilled kettle also sat.

"Thank you, lad," the postmistress said, rubbing her knobbly hands together. I wondered if they felt better for having been petting a unicorn. Their horns were supposed to be instruments of great healing, after all.

The spiral mark on my hand was warm and comforting. I rubbed my thumb over it discreetly. And what did *it* portend?

I passed Mrs. Henny her tea, replete with milk and honey, and the old woman sipped at it as the unicorn sighed and lay down on her side next to the stove. I took the opportunity to use a length of yarn to measure Ballory's width; she twitched and snuffled curiously at me as I drew the yarn from withers to the swirl of hair between her forelegs. On a horse that would be considered a mark of good luck, to have a pattern like an ear of wheat there.

That famous racehorse, Jemis Swiftfoot for whom I was named, had borne it.

I offered Mrs. Henny my cakes and shortbread. She clearly had a sweet tooth, and took the honey cakes. Mrs. Pritchard accepted the shortbread with a gesture suggestive of placing it to the side. Her needles never stopped moving, for all that her eyes were on us.

"I suppose you are curious why we wanted to meet with you tonight," Mrs. Henny said. Her voice was thin and tremulous with age, but her eyes were sharp as ever. The greatest Poacher player my father had ever met, I recalled.

"It is an unusual night for such a meeting, I expect," I replied.

"I'm all alone in the world now," Mrs. Henny said simply.

"My Rob was taking iron oddments around the barony today, and will be home late," Mrs. Pritchard said.

"It is about the Gentry, then," I said.

Mrs. Henny nodded. Ballory whuffled. Mrs. Pritchard knit. I glanced down at the yarn next to my chair and selected the purple for the next stripe.

"My father told me that you had experience with them, Mrs. Henny."

"Aye, he'd know. Lady Olive would have told him. She was a great help to me, was your lady mother. A wise woman, in the old way. It was a blow to lose her so young, but she was never going to thrive so far from the Woods. It weakened her."

I gripped my needles. "What do you mean?"

"Surely you can see that you are much stronger—much *heartier*—now that you're home? And have been acknowledged by the Woods? Aye, lad, we've heard about the bees. That's a powerful old magic, that is. Slay the dragon and win—well that's the question, isn't it?"

"Is it?" I asked, bewildered. The dragon had told me it had been called out of the *Wide Dreaming* by my magic, but I did not have that magic any longer.

"You know that your mother had … their blood, I take it."

"I have learned so."

"You take after her," Mrs. Pritchard put in unexpectedly when Mrs. Henny paused. I glanced over at her. "That blood runs strong in you. It doesn't in every generation, your mother used to say. Depended on the star under which you were born."

And I, born on the come-and-go 29th of February, had been born under a contrary star.

"My people are from the Woods," Mrs. Henny said, leaning back in her chair. I found the step-stool and brought it over so she could put her feet up, which she did with a grateful smile. "All the way back. Mrs. Pritchard's grandfather also," she added, nodding at the other woman. "Woodlanders, you might say."

I settled back into my chair, my mind racing. This was why these two women had come, then. They were Woodlanders. (That word set off faint, echoing chimes in my mind. My mother had used that word, surely … but when? Why?)

Was *I* then a Woodlander? Their expressions suggested it.

"These are secrets rarely told," Mrs. Henny said. "You will never thrive if you dwell far from the Woods, lad. You woke the bees in the autumn. You will do well to wake them again in the spring."

"As I can," I said.

Was that why the wireweed had taken me so? I was too far from the Woods, for too long? My mother had never gone far from Ragnor Bella, which was not far from the Woods; except that she had never gone back, so far as I knew, after my father's reported death.

"There will be those who stand between you and the queen."

There was something about Mrs. Henny's eyes and the tone of her voice that sent shivers up and down my spine. A certainty for something that should not, surely, be that concrete.

"Your mother wove all the protections about your cradle that she might," Mrs. Pritchard said quietly. "I remember her doing so."

"Aye," Mrs. Henny went on. "She invited all the … fair ones, let us say, to your naming-day."

I felt a shivering dread settle into my bones. This was an old, old story.

Mrs. Henny fixed me with her sharp blue eyes. I could not look away.

"All except one."

CHAPTER TWENTY

I only got about half a dozen rows into my cardigan for Ballory, as the ladies departed soon after.

"There is little that we know," Mrs. Pritchard said. "Our kin in the Woods have been caught in the curse, and they were sore devastated by the Fall of Astandalas before then. Few were so wise as your lady mother, and none who survived the Fall or the Interim."

"The shadows had tooth and claw in the Woods then," Mrs. Henny said darkly.

They did again.

"What can I do?" I asked.

"We never heard what curse was pronounced upon you," Mrs. Prichard said. "Unless it was the curse of living in interesting times."

"That's a Greenwing trait," Mrs. Henny retorted.

I thought of how the doings of the Greenwings was the fundamental and perennial source of gossip in Ragnor Bella, and could pronounce no disagreement.

"There is always a way of finding out the truth," Mrs. Henny said. "*Someone* knows more than they have been saying."

The members of the Wild Hunt, who knew my name. The fairy fox, who gave me warnings. The imposter pretending to be the Honourable

Rag, who ... tried to give me fairy food. Whatever or whoever it was who kept delivering me gift-wrapped birds.

I sighed. There was far too much going on.

~

The next morning there were three white hens next to the milk and eggs and butter and cream.

~

I woke early, and since I was out of coffee decided to make tea instead.

It had not taken me very long, I reflected, to prefer tea on half the occasions I had been accustomed to drinking coffee. Coffee was rich and bitter and aromatic and strengthening ... but sometimes I wanted the rather more gentle effects of tea.

I lit the fire down in the bookstore, as it would be open today, collected my deliveries, and stared at the hens for a good few minutes before bringing them indoors. The feathery snow had continued to fall through the night, and the alley was covered four inches deep. The tracks of the pony-cart and the milkman's boots were obvious, touching my threshold and the lawyer's down the way.

Either the milkman was in on it, which seemed unlikely, or it was the fairy fox again.

It could have been someone else, but I didn't want to unnecessarily proliferate—

Oh, it was hardly *me* who was making these things proliferate. At least I was coming to have some understanding of why I might be afflicted by everything always happening to me. Part of it was surely my longstanding friendship with Mr. Dart, whose magic would be seeking ways out into the world.

And part of it was apparently because I'd been cursed by a fairy whom my mother had for whatever reason not invited to my christening.

I stared at the young flames in my own stove as I waited for the kettle to heat. Ballory had kept me company for the night, seemingly uninterested in returning to Mr. Dart by whatever mysterious method she had left him. She was still in my bed, in fact, nestled into the blankets. Her hooves had been very cold when she'd had some sort of dream of running and started kicking me around midnight.

I couldn't make my mind settle. For once I did not feel physically fidgety; I felt no strong yearning to knit or even to run. Instead I found the sheaf of transcriptions I'd made of the last year's worth of Etiquette Questions Answered, a notebook, my second-best pen (I *still* hadn't gotten my good one back from the Honourable Rag; I kept forgetting to ask him for it), and settled down at my table to decipher the code being used.

~

I was on the third cup of tea when Ballory came out, staggering as if she were drunk. Just tired, I realized, as she leaned against me, her head on my lap and her tail twitching slightly, one hoof cocked up. She didn't seem to want anything else of me, so I stroked her neck and scratched at the base of her ears, which she seemed to like, and continued on with the encryptions.

It was a doubled code, I discovered. Part of it was based on Hurtleman's Syllabary, which attributed certain pairs of letters to symbols in the ideographs in Classical Shaian on a set substitution. Those ideographs were then—

Ah, I thought, remembering a period in which Violet and I had played around with all these ancient codes. There were two known methods of using Hurtleman's Syllabary as a code, and one of them required one to have a paired book.

This cipher was clearly meant to be disseminated. The code was in both the questions and the answers, so it was not simply a matter of whoever wrote the column being the code maker. They were disseminating information both ways, unless of course they made up the questions as well as the answers. That seemed likely to be found out, however.

The Honourable Rag had said his people used the crossword. That meant two parts of the *New Salon* were being used for coded messages.

Were other parts? Was the entire paper intended for revolutionary purposes?

I felt mildly irked at the thought. I liked the paper—and I wanted to be part of the revolution. I paused, and amended the thought. Part of *one* of the revolutions.

One element of the code was a simple set of correlation between specific phrases—so much had I determined on my first pass when I was transcribing. That combined with Hurtleman's ... but the question was how the *recipients* were supposed to know when to switch ...

That was what 'seating arrangements' questions meant, I realized after I got up to add another log to the fire. There was always one question that involved that topic, a fraught one in real life.

Ballory huffed when I moved away and went to nose at the crate containing the hens, who were happily eating some wheat berries I'd acquired for tomorrow's gift-offering to the dead.

The question involving seating arrangements meant the reader had to count back not the number given but one *less* than it, and start the Hurtleman's Syllabary progression that number of items in. The *answer* given used the same number but one *more*, so that in each question-and-answer two sets of overlapping but not identical ideographs were to be used.

I fetched out my copy of the Syllabary. It was the sort of book you could find quite easily in bookstores, as it was a key resource for anyone studying Classical Shaian. It would not be considered odd in the least for nearly anyone with the smatterings of an education to own it, and those who didn't have said education could claim it was a gift for someone who did.

All in all, it was a brilliant choice for encoding such information.

I turned to the beginning of my stack of pages, and a new page of my notebook, but before I could proceed any further there was a heavy thunder of knocks on the door of the bookstore below.

The hens started squawking and Ballory emitted a surprised whicker. I left them to it and went downstairs, where Mr. Dart was the one hammering at the door.

"Good morning," I said, letting him in. "Ballory's upstairs, if you were wondering."

"Yes, yes, she said she was coming," he replied distractedly. "Jemis, who did you tell about the Ánhorn?"

I stepped back so he could come into the store, which he did with a great gust of cold air fragrant with snow and woodsmoke. I sneezed once and shut the door. The square, so pristine in the snow last night, was crisscrossed with tracks and slush. It wasn't a market day—the traditional Winterturn market would be held the fourth day after the Solstice—but the storekeepers were starting to open up, and of course the bakery was doing a grand trade.

"Er, no one," I said, pulling my thoughts back from Mr. Inglesides' baked goods.

"What have you been doing?" he demanded, pushing back the rich green cloak he wore over his usual grey-and-plum coat and waistcoat.

I felt as one does when missing a step on a stair. "I beg your pardon? This morning, do you mean?"

He gave me a look that said, *when else?*

"I was working on deciphering the code used in the *New Salon*. Why?"

"The air was ... reverberating," he said, which made very little sense to me. "If you didn't say anything, then it must be the sword itself." He nodded sharply, as if that solved the problem, and visibly relaxed.

I took his cloak. He said, voice much lighter, "Did you find out anything interesting?"

"I've figured out the cipher. I was just about to start working out the messages when you knocked."

"Hmm." He glanced around uncertainly, but seemed to find nothing amiss. "May I stay here a bit? The Dartington pageant is practicing," he added by way of explanation.

When he and I were boys we had participated gleefully. Everyone did—any child under the age of twelve or so was automatically included, and those a little older but not yet able to be considered *adults* (at least, by any save themselves; I was sure Mr. Dart and I had both considered ourselves very grown up at sixteen) were usually persuaded by dramatic inclination or familial blackmail into playing a role.

The Dartington pageant, like their Harvest Fair, was a relic of an earlier age still strongly alive and well in their village. The Winterturn Pageant—matched by the Spring Festival around Beltane—consisted of a series of vignettes from local history and the Lady's Church tales performed at certain locations around the parish.

In times past I had played one of the Fair Host belabouring Sir Peregrine, and Sir Peregrine's loyal squire, and the mysterious Lord of Shadows.

I gestured uncertainly for Mr. Dart to come in and take his seat by the fire as those memories resurfaced. Had they been signs, or omens, or simple coincidence?

I moved a stack of books I'd acquired in Orio City, and discovered one was a dictionary and grammar of Old Oriolan.

I nearly dropped the whole stock on that discovery.

I stood there, heart hammering, as I looked at the book. What coincidence or chance was *this*?

Mr. Dart added a log to the fire. Under his hand, the sigil Ballory had inscribed in my dream or waking vision glowed silver.

"A gift of good fellowship," he said, shutting the door. The sigil flashed and faded.

Coincidence, or wild magic, or the hand of the Lady, or all three, I decided, and opened the dictionary. It fell open to the section beginning with *n*.

Noirell was a very old word, cognate with *norë*, the Oriolan word for darkness and mystery.

The Woods Noirell: the shadowy woods, the dark woods, the place of mystery and magic.

Mr. Dart pulled out his pipe and was methodically preparing it for lighting. He always took his time over the act, clearly something he enjoyed.

I should run, I thought even more uncertainly. I had felt the desire to run since my death and resurrection, had I not?

—Yes. I had deeply desired to run that first morning after, when the frost limned every leaf and grass blade with silver-gilt fire in the dawning.

I left Mr. Dart to his pipe, closed the strange gift of the Oriolan grammar, and went up to bring my notes on the Etiquette Questions Answered down.

People came in seeking books on Ghilousetten cooking, the properties of trees, duelling traditions of the Tarvenol, and several dozen different novels in varying number of volumes.

I determined that the code in the Etiquette Questions Answered column dealt with the movements of men and goods.

People came in to gossip with Mr. Dart about the pageant and the rumours of the unicorn and this strange account I had died and come back to life. He fielded the questions cheerfully, never lying but also never stating outright anywhere near so boldly as I might have done for him.

I determined that the movements involved ships and small groups inland, scattered mostly amongst the Artificers—

Of course, I thought even as I counted out the change for the person who'd bought the Ghilousetten cookbook. Ghilousette was a country of artificers, of rabid hatred for magic and of deep-rooted witchcraft. They built automata out of cogs and metal and springs; artificial things.

People came in to buy the *New Salon* and tell me how pleased they were with my father's return to Ragnor Bella, and to ask leading questions for which I had no answer about his plans for the Arguty estate. Every time I thought of Arguty Hall I quailed, remembering the cold rejection of my uncle Sir Vorel.

No one was living in the old dower cottage that had been my childhood home. It had sat empty since my mother married Mr. Buchance and moved to town. I hadn't been inside it for years. It was probably half-decrepit by now.

In a quiet stretch between customers I re-shelved unsuitable books. Mr. Dart sat with the *New Salon* unfolded before him, his pipe smouldering in his mouth.

No one else came in, so I gathered together my notes. Reading over the snippets in order, one after the other, I began to see a pattern emerging.

"Anything of shattering import?" Mr. Dart asked lightly after I had stared at my notes for too long.

I glanced up at him. He had folded the paper and set it on the floor beside his chair, the better for Gingersnap to claim his lap. He was holding the pipe negligently in his hand, and smiling easily at me.

Not even a week ago he had called me back from the dead.

I shuddered to the soles of my feet. My resurrection might be uncanny to others, but from my perspective it was that he had held the gateway open that was by far the greater magic and higher spiritual calling.

"Mr. Greenwing?"

I started again, and shuffled my pages into a neat stack. "It's the code being used by the Knockermen to communicate and coordinate their movements."

"The Knockermen? The Indrillines' rivals?"

"Even so."

Mr. Dart tapped his pipe on the arm of the chair. "How intriguing."

Given that the Honourable Rag's group—Crimson Lake, fighting on behalf of the Lady of Alinor and more distantly the Lady of the Green and White—was reportedly using the crossword for their secret messages, that a second person was playing another spy network in the same publication was extraordinary.

Mind you, it wasn't as if there were any rivals to the *New Salon*. There were a few other publications with lesser circulation, mostly of academic or literary interest, but nothing with the mix of news, gossip, reportage, and diversions managed by the *New Salon*.

"You seem disappointed."

I smiled reluctantly. "I had hoped there might be another ally working in secret alongside us."

"If they are, they're not encoding their messages in the paper."

"Not in this column, at any rate." I considered my results. Who would want this? Hal. Hal's Uncle Ben, the General Sir Benneret Halioren and Lady Jessamine's advisor. Perhaps my father. The Lady Jessamine herself.

"Are you going to send it to your fair Violet as a courting-gift?" Mr. Dart asked.

I glanced at him even as the door opened to Mrs. Etaris.

"That's an excellent idea," I said. "Good morning, Mrs. Etaris."

"Mr. Greenwing, Mr. Dart." Mrs. Etaris swung off her cloak and handed it to me with a thankful smile before removing the eight-inch hatpin and hat from her piled-up mass of braided hair. "Dare I ask of your excellent idea?"

"Oh, I deciphered the Knockermen's secret code and past year's worth of communications, and Mr. Dart thought it might make a good courting gift."

"For the redoubtable Miss Redshank, indeed I expect it would." Mrs. Etaris smiled a little mistily, as mention of Violet often made her do, and moved past me to consider the boxes I had yet to open.

"Goodness me," she said mildly. "Is this the famously lost sword, Sir Peregrine's Ánhorn?"

CHAPTER TWENTY-ONE

I admit I stared in unflattering surprise.

Mrs. Etaris laughed lightly at my expression. "Oh," she said, even as she unfolded the cloth and gripped the sword in a decidedly competent hand. "I had a friend who was very keen on legendary swords."

She turned the Ánhorn in the light. I looked at her stance, judging it the way first my father and then Dominus Lukel at Morrowlea had taught me. Her weight was well balanced over her knees, which were slightly bent; her feet had assumed the separated perpendicular basic position of half a dozen schools of fencing; and she held the sword with a loose wrist and composed, not tight hands.

Someone, I knew immediately, had taught her very well.

"Several friends, to be honest," she murmured.

The light caught on the edge of the blade, splinters of gold and white spattering and spangling the room. From this angle Mr. Dart's blue eyes seemed to catch the light, as if stars had kindled in them.

He was staring at Mrs. Etaris and the Ánhorn. What was he seeing, I wondered. Or hearing? Did the sword speak to him, in whatever solid and irrefutable way inanimate things did for him?

What a strange thing, to walk through the world with the silent and unensouled crying forth.

Mrs. Etaris made a few slow motions, the sword sliding through the air to form positions I did not know—they were not any of the schools I had been taught—but which were clearly the poses of a set form. Like the Tarvenol style it seemed to start with a first position en garde, not the vertical or horizontal near the head of the Erlingalish or Charese forms I had learned at Morrowlea.

My father and the defence tutor at Morrowlea had taught me a dozen modes from across the Empire. Mrs. Etaris knew a thirteenth.

Suspicion began to unfurl in the back of my mind, but before it could do more than send a tendril of a thrilling sense of discovery—before I could learn what that discovery *was*—the door opened with a gust of wind and a customer came in. Mrs. Etaris stowed away the sword with impressive speed and discretion even as the customer glanced first at me. By the time he'd turned to Mrs. Etaris the Ánhorn was once more swaddled in the cloth.

"What is that?" he asked, politely curious.

"A Winterturn gift," Mrs. Etaris replied demurely, handing me the bundle. "How can I help you, Mr. Jenkins?"

∽

Mrs. Etaris informed me that she wished to tend the store that afternoon, so Mr. Dart and I retreated up to my flat with the Ánhorn, my notes on the *New Salon*, and this week's edition. And also the grammar of Old Oriolan, which I had paid Mrs. Etaris for; she had expressed mild amazement I had found such an apparently rare tome.

"Did the sword speak to you?" I asked him as I made another pot of tea.

Mr. Dart had opened the swaddling cloths and had the sword laid across his knees, the scarf falling on either side in green and gold folds. With his plum-and-grey clothes he looked like—

Well, like he belonged to the Lady in a minor key, ambiguous as so often in Northwest Oriole as to whether it was the Lady of Alinor as well as the Lady of the Green and White or only one or the other.

He stroked the central ridge of the blade. The hilt was made of well-worn leather, burnished splendid with the use of hands. The blade itself was plain and unadorned, straightforwardly what it was.

Except that it had been a unicorn horn gouged out from Sir Peregrine's companion when the ancient knight gave it to me.

"It is singing in a language I do not know," Mr. Dart said finally. "I think it is ... It does not seem unhappy to be here. It likes you."

"Surely it is for you?" I objected mildly as I brought over the tray—recent gift from Mrs. Buchance—with the tea things. I still had some shortbread and added a plate of that to the mix. It all felt both most domestic and luxurious.

"I think it is yours at the moment," Mr. Dart said, his head tilted as he looked at the blade. His hand had stilled, palm across the flat of the blade. The blade looked as if it needed to be sharpened.

"Yes. Perhaps it will come to me in future, but for now it is clearly for you."

I sat down in my chair. The powderpuff kitten—very well, Powderpuff the Kitten—scampered out of my bedroom, where it had undoubtedly been doing something I would regret discovering shortly, and skidded to a halt at my feet before mewing beseechingly. I scooped it up and set it on my lap. Even with all the fur it wasn't much bigger than my palm. It still managed to have an audible purr.

Mrs. Etaris had recognized the Ánhorn immediately. How?

I too had been interested—what was her phrase? 'Very keen', that was it—I too had been *very keen* on legendary swords since childhood. I had sought out stories and accounts of the famous blades of history and story. The starlight swords that Masseo Umrit had made for the Red Company in *Kissing the Moon*. Hoarblade, the white-jewelled sword of the Frost King in the story of Zolihar and the Seven Crows. Adony, the sword of the Lord of Ysthar.

I had *heard* of the Ánhorn, but I had never found any *description* of it. And I had looked: Sir Peregrine was *ours*, our saint and hero and legendary champion. Taddeo Toynbee did not mention him in his *Guide to Fiellan*, but that did not mean stories of the Darts' ancestor did not echo across our landscape.

What had Mrs. Etaris seen in the sword? The leather hilt was of an old-fashioned style but it was not striking, I didn't think. The blade itself was deeply ordinary.

Context would hardly help: even if she had been thinking of Sir Peregrine because of Ballory and Mr. Dart, no one had ever heard of the Ánhorn since his days. He had had it, and then it had disappeared.

Because he had passed it to me in a vision across time.

"May I see the sword?" I asked.

Mr. Dart passed it to me hilt-first and then settled back with a piece of shortbread. Powderpuff decided the biscuit was more interesting than the sword, and made a flying leap from my lap to his. I watched to make sure the kitten had landed safely, snickered quietly as Mr. Dart set down his biscuit so he could detach the kitten's claws from his leg as it tried to clamber up, and examined the sword.

There. In the pommel there was a button made of ivory and verdigrised bronze. It formed a spiral, the ivory prominent, the bronze a thin spiralling line. It was a clear identifying feature, if any song or story had ever described the sword accurately.

Where had Mrs. Etaris learned that lore?

Mr. Dart was stroking the kitten, his eyes far away. I set the sword on the floor beside my chair, safely out of the way. It did need to be sharpened but my whetstone was across the room with the sword my father had given me, and I reckoned that could be done this evening.

On immediate retrospect, I got up and fetched the stone. My father had too many stories of the difference timely preparation made.

I had always found sharpening a soothing, satisfying activity. No doubt the sound—so familiar from my father's visits home—made me think of being safe and surrounded by love. My mother would knit or embroider in her chair, my father would sharpen his weapons or mend the leather harness, and I would read or play with toy soldiers or the little wooden dog that was my favourite childhood toy.

Dogs made me think of our local witch.

"Do you know what's happened with Magistra Bellamy?" I asked.

Mr. Dart had tipped his head back and his eyes were closed. He did not move as he responded. "I believe she's back in her cottage. There was smoke rising when I passed it this morning, and the dog barked."

I nodded. The whetstone shirred across the sword, long even strokes as my father had taught me.

"It is the rhythm you can hear in Fitzroy Angursell's *Song of the Sword-Bridge*," he had told me.

That was one of the songs that was not banned: it was an account of how the Red Company had dared the castle of a giant to rescue someone caught inside. They had had to cross the moat on a bridge made out of swords.

Shirr, shirr, shirr went my stone; the rhythm and almost the rhyme of the song.

"He knew swords and the sharpening of swords," my father had continued. "You can tell in his songs. They sound light and humorous but there is much reality in there. He knew the sweat in your grip and the singing wave of battle madness and the smell of a battlefield. A great poet."

I had a friend who was prone to that kind of battle madness, Mrs. Etaris had said to me after the incident with Magistra Bellamy's dog and the arrow someone had shot at me. *He would start singing and you would know things were about to get ... interesting.*

I had doubted then that it was anyone at Madame Clancette's Finishing School for Girls, and I doubted now, despite Hal's assurances, that it was at Galderon either.

Galderon might have a library full of books on legendary weapons, but I very much doubted they would include the folk-blades of South Fiellan. And I should have found a reference to such a work, if there were one in their collection. I had *looked*.

Hal seemed to think that being caught at Galderon through that university's rebellion and successful attempt to secede from the province of East Oriole was sufficient explanation for Mrs. Etaris's more peculiarly clandestine skills.

When we—really Hal—had cleaned out the upstairs flat, we had found a set of adventuring items. A battered leather bag, which Mrs. Etaris's friend had left in her care many years ago. A tattered cloak; a set of lock picks; items I later learned were used to climb walls.

She had asked me to keep that bag. Where had I put it? Whose bag *was* it?

The answer slid into mind, intuition rather than any conscious logic: Fitzroy Angursell.

I examined the thought, which sat solidly in my mind, *true*. If she had *that* bag, why then—

"Do you reckon Mrs. Etaris is really Jullanar of the Sea?" I asked.

Mr. Dart stared at me. "I beg your pardon?"

I stopped whetting the Ánhorn, whose edge was now keen. "Mrs. Etaris. Jullanar of the Sea. It would explain everything."

He snowed, smoke puffing from his nostrils like dragon fire. "Except what she's doing running a bookstore in Ragnor Bella."

I didn't see this as any sort of a problem. "She's retired, undoubtedly. From the adventuring life."

That first afternoon in her bookstore, she had given me an odd smile and waved her hands in a gesture I took to mean all the books surrounding her, and said, "If there is anything I know, it is how to have an adventure."

Mr. Dart said slowly, "What prompted this?"

I explained my chain of reasoning, which evidently seemed somewhat precarious to him.

"I don't want to say you must be wrong ..."

"But you do think so."

He patted the kitten thoughtfully. Its purr somehow increased in volume. "I do think you might perhaps need some evidence before you accuse someone of being one of the most wanted criminals in the former Empire of Astandalas."

I regarded him. "I needn't *tell* her."

He regarded me, eyebrows raised. "Do you really think you would be able to keep the questions unspoken? To Mrs. Etaris, who reminds you of your mother?"

I could hardly deny that, though I had not phrased it so even in the privacy of my own mind. I set the whetstone and sword down on the floor beside me and took up my tea cup instead. "She's an estimable woman."

Mr. Dart muttered something about the firebrands of Morrowlea and my own criminal tendencies, which I pretended not to be able to hear.

I sipped my tea and ate several pieces of shortbread—it was quite good, I was pleased to determine—and waited.

Eventually he said, "There is that bag."

~

It was in the bottom of the wardrobe in which we had originally found it. I brought it back out to the sitting room and set in on the table. The kitten had jumped off Mr. Dart's lap to follow me into the room, no doubt concerned I would disturb the nest it had made in my pillows, and so he was free to join me at the table.

We considered the bag speculatively; even a touch reverently.

It was a brown leather item, deeply ordinary. The leather was supple, but also cracked and mended and burnished with use. The straps holding it closed were buckled with brass. I worked at the straps with fingers that were nearly trembling.

The Ánhorn was so legendary it belonged to the world of the visions and the talking fox and the Wild Hunt in the night, all of which seemed almost dreamlike in the cozy embrace of a winter afternoon by the fire. But Fitzroy Angursell's Bag of Unusual Capacity!

"It's supposed to hold *everything*, in the songs," I said.

He had written at least three *solely* about his bag. It was mentioned in numerous others.

Mr. Dart appeared doubtful. "This one doesn't seem particularly magical."

In the songs Fitzroy Angursell was forever bringing out amusing items that he was later able to triumphantly use for whatever problem the Red Company was facing.

One buckle, two. I worked the straps out, stiff as they were with such long disuse. How many years had it been since the Red Company went adventuring? They had disappeared the same year the Emperor Artorin Damara came to the throne, in an expanding bubble of rumour and story.

"Are you going to open it, then?" Mr. Dart asked after a period.

I took a breath. "We probably shouldn't ... it doesn't belong to us ..."

"You think it's Fitzroy Angursell's famous bag, being held by Mrs. Etaris because she's really Jullanar of the Sea."

"All the more reason—"

"It's a potential criminal accessory."

"I'm fairly certain that doesn't mean *we* should look at it. We should be calling the constable in, if we were going to take it *that* way."

Mr. Dart snorted, no doubt at the same thought I'd just had, that the chief constable of Ragnor Bella was Mrs. Etaris's husband.

"Look," he said, "if you're right it's the proof we need to be sure. If you're wrong then we will put it back. At any rate she hasn't looked at it for years, as she'd forgotten it was here."

"That logic doesn't follow," I objected. "It may be positive proof but it cannot prove the negative. It may not be Fitzroy Angursell's bag but that doesn't necessarily mean she is not Jullanar of the Sea."

"Oh, go and open it," Mr. Dart retorted.

I dithered no longer and grinned at him in conspiratorial delight as we opened the bag.

I don't know what I was expecting—light to stream out? Magic to fill the room? Music to sound forth in ethereal choruses?

A scent of flowers rose up; it made me sneeze.

Mr. Dart leaned back, his eyes starred and spangled as they had been down in the bookstore. He said to me, "That's it."

"Fitzroy Angursell's bag."

He nodded. I peered in, but the interior was dim and cluttered. There seemed to be the corner of a dusty book, and something like a wallet or a purse, and a fold of cloth … "How do you think it works?"

"Reach in and see what you pull out," he said.

"Go ahead," I said, hesitating.

Mr. Dart's voice was distant, his eyes on something I could not see. "It says … the bag says … that what it holds is not for us, but we may look. It has … gifts."

That was a kind of benediction, and to be honest no matter how bizarre it was to have it, I did feel better about reaching into the bag afterwards.

Mr. Dart pulled out a book. I reached in and pulled out the tangle of cloth wrapped loosely around something that crackled. I undid the cloth carefully. Something heavy thunked onto the table as the folds released it.

The cloth was a beguiling colour, silvery-green as moonlight on fish scales. It felt like the imagination of water in my hands, cool and smooth. Not silk, but some relative. I ran my palms and fingertips across the fabric. What an extraordinary material. I could barely see the individual threads in the weave. The iridescent sheen glimmered in the firelight.

It had been wrapped around a small draw-string pouch made of dusty brown velvet. That was the heavy item; when I weighed it in my palm it felt like a stone, heavy and round. The thing that had crackled was a furled sheaf of papers.

I unfolded them to find a song I knew only by title, as it was one of the pieces that had been forbidden on pain of death.

CHAPTER TWENTY-TWO

I glanced up at Mr. Dart, who was already deeply engrossed in the book.

I could not help it, and read the song.

Fitzroy Angursell—I presumed it was his own writing—had a strong hand, with a tendency to a rightward slant and extravagant ascenders and descenders. His letters were even and legible despite the occasional wild curlicue.

Someone had gone through with a different pen and edited it.

I had read a few autograph manuscripts of famous poems. Seen ones where the author had gone through and edited their work, or had other editors correct it for them. Seen the evidence of thought and reflection, of changed purpose or clearer insight.

I had not, for all that—not even for all of my efforts translating the Gainsgooding Conspirators' poetry—read a poem so utterly and shamelessly *treasonous*.

Let alone one that had been corrected to be *more so*.

I had seen Mrs. Etaris's hand enough to recognize the way she did her ascenders and descenders, with little spiralling finials.

It was not a long song, all told. Seven verses, each of eight lines. An elegant rhyme scheme, a twist on the ballad form: *abCDabba*, the strong rhymes in the third and fourth lines picking up middle words of the first two, and the next verse continuing on *cdEFcddc*.

I unfolded some of the metrical anomalies. How *brilliant* Fitzroy Angursell was as a poet. That seeming mistake, when his spondee broke into a dactyl, added a subtle emphasis on the key word of what was truly an excoriating satire.

Mr. Dart, it occurred to me, was suspiciously silent.

I tore my attention away from Mrs. Etaris's—from *Jullanar of the Sea's*—comments and directed it to him. "What have you found?"

He was slow to put the book down. His eyes were bright, not with magic but with wonder and a staggering relief. "It's a book by a great mage by the name of Harbut Zalarin, who was the father of Yr the Conqueror, on wild magic. With annotations by Fitzroy Angursell."

If the poem in my hands was a firebrand undoubtedly capable of igniting the smouldering tensions of Northwest Oriole even now, a whole reign and the Fall of Astandalas from the time when the specific law it decried had been passed, the book in Mr. Dart's hands was as unbelievably precious as an historical artifact.

Mr. Dart went on in a very low voice, "It's ... it tells me *how to do it*, Jemis. How to be a wild mage without destroying everything."

There was story after story in the Astandalan legendarium about the danger and disaster wild mages brought with them. It was a catastrophic and forbidden gift, it was said. No one dared mention wild magic, or not anything more powerful than the sort of small cantrips and minor blessings of a hedgewizard or country witch.

On the side of great wild mages who were renowned for their creativity and their splendid magic?

Fitzroy Angursell was the only name I knew. There were some stories about the present Lord of Ysthar, but hardly more than that he existed, was a wild mage, and was a great recluse. The only tale I'd ever heard with any certainty was that he had turned someone into a standing stone, and that according to Magistra Aurelia of Tara he wrote articles for their journal on the philosophy of magic.

"Look," Mr. Dart said, showing me a page.

I glanced down but was lost within three sentences. It appeared to be about the binding and unbinding of clouds. Or possibly curses.

Understand the nature of the one who cursed, or the one who was cursed. Then something about the *esharivalen* of the seven winds, whatever that meant. The most comprehensible sentence was a scrawl in peacock-blue ink saying, *Or the nature of knots.*

I passed the book back to him and gestured at the paper in my hand. "I found the text of 'The Law of Apposite Injustice'."

There were *dozens* of accounts of the censoring of that song. *Aurora* had been banned; *Kissing the Moon* had been banned; half a dozen other songs had been banned. People were fined or imprisoned for possessing them.

People had been *executed* for this song.

Reading it over again I could entirely see why. Seven verses was all it took to take down the legitimacy of the Astandalan government of Northwest Oriole.

The thought came that I could probably spend the rest of my life studying this one poem.

"What's in the pouch?" Mr. Dart asked, after he had given that statement a due moment of silence.

I set down the poem and turned to the velvet pouch. The drawstring was pulled tight and knotted, but the knot succumbed to my fingers eventually. I tugged it open and tipped the stone out onto my hand.

A diamond the size of my fist glittered there.

We stared at the stone. Another object beyond priceless, beyond famous.

"The Diamond of Gaesion," Mr. Dart said. "The Star of the North."

'That Party' was one of the banned-but-not-quite-censored songs. It skewered the entire imperial family and most of the court, and so was not *acceptable*, but it was also very funny and otherwise not particularly satirical.

Except insofar as the whole episode had been a grave scandal and caused the Red Company to go gallivanting off into the Kingdom between Worlds and—so said Fitzroy Angursell—off to court the Moon.

"Violet doesn't like that song," I said, setting the diamond on the velvet bag.

"Oh no? Not a fan of stealing six bottles of fairy wine, the Diamond of Gaesion, and a lady's maidenhead'?"

I grinned at him. "She says that 'maidenhead' is a terrible word, incorrect anatomically and relict of an outmoded and oppressive system."

Mr. Dart stared at me. "You talked with *Violet* about ..." He blushed and made a vague gesture.

(This from the man who'd barely blushed telling me about his affair with a fairy fox?)

"We were perhaps a little tipsy. We'd tried making beer, and were testing the batch."

He laughed. "Morrowlea was so much more liberal than Stoney-bridge. We drank in the pubs, but the men's colleges didn't mix with the women's outside of classes and clubs."

"What a pity."

"Indeed."

He smoothed out the velvet around the stone. "What an extraordinary diamond this is. I can see why Fitzroy Angursell might have wanted it."

The stone was truly the size of my fist, when I set it beside my hand. It was cut into facets, each of them catching the thin daylight streaming in my window. The diamond seemed to gather the light into a warm golden glow in its centre.

The Star of the North. The Diamond of Gaesion, though I didn't think I'd ever heard who or what or where Gaesion was. One of the largest diamonds of the first water ever found.

"This is Fitzroy Angursell's bag," I said, the realization coming into sudden sharp focus.

"I will concede to your argument that Mrs. Etaris is actually Jullanar of the Sea." Mr. Dart laughed. "And yes, that stone does belong to Fitzroy Angursell himself. It's humming his name."

"What a thought!"

We admired the diamond a little longer, but neither of us were avaricious in that way. I could see why someone might be inclined to take it, if they were lovers of beauty; though from what I knew of 'That

Party' from the song, Fitzroy Angursell's motives had not been simple greed, if greed at all.

I set the stone back inside its brown velvet bag and pulled the drawstring close before knotting it again. Then we looked at the long shining scarf, the manuscript of the poem, and the book. "We should go talk to Mrs. Etaris," I said. "Ask permission to borrow that book."

He nodded and turned immediately back to it. I rolled up the incendiary poem and folded the fabric. The scarf formed an incredibly small bundle; although unfolded it was wide enough to drape over one's shoulders as a near-shawl, folded it fit neatly into my waistcoat pocket with the furled scroll.

Mrs. Etaris was just finishing up with a customer as I entered from the back room. I nodded at her and busied myself with the small useful tasks an assistant clerk might do: mending the fire, returning a few loose books to their places, checking the back room for any stragglers.

I refilled the kettle and set it on the stove. Mrs. Etaris glanced at me, and smiled back in some surprise when I could not help myself and beamed at her.

"Whatever has you so cheerful, Mr. Greenwing?" she asked.

I had not thought through how to broach my discovery. Well—in that far country on the other side of the Grim Crossroads I had begun to learn to speak clearly and candidly.

"Mrs. Etaris," I said therefore, "I have recently come to the realization that you are Jullanar of the Sea."

She stared at me, then glanced once, quickly and incriminatingly, at the back room.

"No one's there," I assured her, but she had already regained her composure.

"That is quite the statement," she said, leaning back against the counter. Her lips were quirking up at one side in an expression I had found rather daunting when I first started working for her. "I assume you have something resembling proof?"

"Mr. Dart did say I should have some first," I agreed, but before I could explain any of it she started to laugh.

"Oh, Mr. Greenwing—my dear Jemis—" She cupped my face in her hands and kissed me on the forehead. "Your mother would be so very proud of you."

I was *slightly* disappointed. "You don't want the evidence?"

"Is it anything someone who does not have an uncanny facility for disentangling puzzle poetry would put together?"

I considered that. "Probably not," I conceded. "And no one else but for Hal even knows about Fitzroy Angursell's bag up in my wardrobe."

She tilted her head. "Did you open it?"

I hesitated. "Had you?"

She shook her head, her expression sad. "At first I didn't dare, and later it was easier not to. Not to mention that bag was always a bit ... temperamental."

"Mr. Dart said it told him it didn't mind."

I wondered then whether that particular skill of Mr. Dart's had been something we'd told her yet. I thought so, but it was hard to keep all those strands of confidences and discoveries clear. She asked no questions, regardless.

I reached into my pocket and pulled out the scarf and the poem. "We found a book on wild magic, this scarf, the Star of the North, and ... this poem."

Mrs. Etaris stroked the shining silver cloth. "Oh, I remember this," she murmured even as she unfolded the poem. Her eyes widened as she read it. "*Well* now."

"That's rather what I thought," I replied.

CHAPTER TWENTY-THREE

"You have no other questions?" Mrs. Etaris asked me, after I had given her due space to read the old forbidden poem. I did this by means of straightening various books and wondering if I had somehow managed to acquire a copy of *The Knight and the Unicorn* or *The Lady and the Dark* in amongst the rest of the books from Orio City.

If they were there, I did not find them that afternoon.

I glanced up at Mrs. Etaris from where I was reorganizing a set of shelves of histories to incorporate the new books. She was sitting next to the fire, her cat on her lap, the poem folded and set on top of the three green volumes of Durgand's *Valiance and Shock*.

There were so many questions I had dreamed of asking the Red Company that none came to mind.

I slid *A History of the Port of Inveragory* next to *Proceedings of the Society for the Preservation of Middle Fiellanese Historical Granges*, and considered.

All those stories. Those rumours, those songs, those scandalized reports. Cartoons and ballads in the broad-sheets. Excerpts of poems passed around like contraband. Gossip over their doings as if they were locals—as if they were *Greenwings*—or vehement arguments about the truth of the matter, as if it were a matter of purely academic interest.

"Did you really go to the Moon's Country?" I asked finally, remembering that line from *Kissing the Moon*, about Jullanar of the Sea dipping her hand into the River of Stars.

That Jullanar was this Jullanar, my own Mrs. Etaris.

Mrs. Etaris smiled at me, slowly, as radiantly as any of those in the Lady's Wood. "We did."

"With swords of starlight and cloaks of day?"

She laughed, as if that were a joke; but then she said, "We wanted cloaks of shadows, but Fitzroy never was very good at being discreet."

Her voice was so ... fond ... I could barely imagine the depth of friendship that lay there. Then I recalled that she had not heard from him for decades, that she had held onto his bag because she had *promised,* though she had long since thought he must have passed beyond the mortal coil.

"I didn't have a message from him, from any of them," I said.

Mrs. Etaris hesitated a moment. "I should think I was the only one to follow the Lady's Way."

I thought of those Mountains, of Ariadne nev Lingarel who had been so poor a governor of Northwest Oriole, and so great a poet. Whose efforts to understand her own prison had led her to grace.

"Those Mountains were not only for the Lady's folk," I said, the certainty in my bones, solid as my feet upon the ground. "That Wood was our way thither, but not the only way."

Mrs. Etaris's eyes were damp. She raised her hand to her mouth, biting down on her knuckles for a moment. I did not impose on her memories, but returned my attention to the books.

The History of Chimney Sweeps in Kingsford. The Seven Kings of Arcadia. The Development of Charcuterie in Chare.

I wasn't familiar with the term, so opened the last book. *Charcuterie* turned out to be dried and preserved meats, primarily sausages and terrines. I pondered whether it should therefore belong in Cookery, but there didn't appear to be anything in the way of recipes.

"It always seems as if one day one of them will simply ... walk in the door," Mrs. Etaris murmured, just loud enough for me to hear. I listened, but continued to shelve the books, moving them as quietly and unobtrusively as I could. She laughed in her throat, soft and a little sadly. "Fitzroy. I always expect *Fitzroy* to waltz through the door, looking just the same as he ever did, with that bright, conspiratorial grin and that glint of mischief in his eyes, and ..."

"Would you go?" I asked, after the silence had dragged on for a considerable time.

She wiped her eyes with her handkerchief. "Would you take care of my store if I did, Mr. Greenwing?"

"I would," I promised her.

"There would be no notice," she warned me. "There never was."

I turned to look at her. "Mrs. Etaris," I said plainly, "surely you have realized by now that nothing in my life happens with any notice."

"You were born under a contrary star," she said, nodding.

That was the third time someone had said that to me this week. I stood up, brushing the dust off my hands with one of my own handkerchiefs. "What do you know of that, Mrs. Etaris?"

She startled out of her teariness, her face turning intent, curious, delighted. "What do you mean?"

I told her what my father had said, and then, more awkwardly, what Mrs. Henny and Mrs. Pritchard had told me.

"It's a pity Fitzroy *hasn't* waltzed in with some mad story and an adventure to hand," she said. "He'd like you. And of course, he *is* a great mage." She snickered suddenly. "More or less."

That seemed to be a joke that had an antecedent decades in the making, so I let it go and instead described the book Mr. Dart had pulled out of the bag. Mrs. Etaris frowned at the story—"You found the Star of the North and *that* book? How curious!"

"Mr. Dart was hoping he might borrow the book."

"Of *course*. Though I should say ... please tell him to use his own judgment. You must recall that Fitzroy had something of an irrepressible sense of humour. We used to joke that he was secretly a trickster god come to be a gadfly to the world."

I felt as if I could probably spend a *great* deal of time unpacking that sentence.

The scarf had slithered to the floor. I picked it up and handed it to her. "Did this come from the ... Customs House?"

She turned the superlative cloth over in her hands. "No ... If I recall it was a gift from some lover or other of Fitzroy's after a night." She snorted and muttered something that was surely *not*, "Not that he was *that* good."

I tried not to flush, and was glad she was still playing with the cloth, and resolutely did not enquire of myself why Mrs. Etaris—why Jullanar of the Sea, even—might know the skills Fitzroy Angursell displayed in bed.

I cleared my throat. "Did—did you ever hear my mother tell of which of the Good Neighbours she might not have invited to my christening? And why?"

The question was out of a fairy tale; but then so too was my life. When it wasn't being a High Gothic melodrama from the pen of Jack Lindsary.

I really could not regret him having to delay the first performance of his new play because Lark was preoccupied with my having escaped Orio prison.

Mrs. Etaris scrunched the cloth up, her nose wrinkling as she thought over the question. "I don't know ... Your mother knew many people from ... *many* walks of life."

I glanced at her as she smoothed out the scarf again. The wrinkles fell out of the fabric as if it hadn't been mauled at all. "Did you know that my mother saw you once, as you rode to Astandalas? She was always so proud of being mentioned in one of Fitzroy Angursell's songs."

Mrs. Etaris laughed. "Oh, *White Stone and Ivy*? One of my favourites."

"And yet it had hardly anything scandalous about it at all."

She looked at the incendiary poem in its demurely folded innocence. "Well, Mr. Greenwing, it must be said that I am a woman of various inclinations, and only *some* of the time are they to burn everything down in frustration."

"I sympathize," I replied.

"I thought you might," she returned, and giggled. "Oh, my dear

Jemis. Let me think about your mother and your christening and the folk who might know, if the Woodlanders don't."

"Thank you." I meant for more than just that promise: for the work she had given me and the welcome made to me, for the gifts of the flat and her biscuits and her knowledge; and for being not only the splendid, wonderful, welcoming Mrs. Etaris of Ragnor Bella, but also the magnificent, the resplendent, the infamous criminal and folk hero, Jullanar of the Sea.

She grinned at me, eyes crinkling. "Don't mention it."

～

The next few days passed quietly. I worked in the bookstore, worked on the cardigan for Ballory, continued to decode the messages in the *Etiquette Questions Answered* columns, and began a study of Old Oriolan.

The grammar was frustratingly unfamiliar. The vocabulary was largely alien, but for outcroppings of sense in the form of familiar rootwords. There were moments I exclaimed, so *that* was why that surname or that place had the form it had … and why that children's counting song used *ân tvân teverâ*, for those were the ancient words for *one, two, three* … but in general Shaian had overwritten Oriolan to such an extent the few loanwords from the Alinorel language were invisible.

The Lúsa Tree was so called, it seemed, because *lúsan* was an old word for 'lord'. The lord of the manor, I presumed: that oak had been the centre of the Dart's lands since time immemorial.

(Or was it because I had told Sir Peregrine that was its name? The circularity confounded me.)

I could see kinship between Old Oriolan and some of the words and names from the Outer Reaches. I didn't see Jullanar Maebh during this period, and wasn't sure I wanted to interrupt this new beginning she was exploring with the Squire and Sir Hamish for such nebulous questions as on the history of languages. Mr. Dart came into town several times and reported that she was taking to the squirearchy like a duck to water.

"A curious choice of phrase," I replied, that particular morning.

"I've been following along behind them as a dutiful brother as they visit all the tenants," he said, flinging himself down into his chair by the bookstore stove. "Smiling as Tor explains about his daughter, and pretending I don't know why everyone suddenly frowns and then look pityingly at me."

"Are they sad you're not going to be the Squire after him?" I asked, trying to keep my tone neutral. Mr. Dart did not *want* to be Squire, but that didn't mean he wanted to be ousted, either.

He smiled wryly at me. "It seems it was more obvious than I had thought that my heart wasn't in the job."

I sighed. "I've not been to the Woods enough."

"Have you been to Arguty?"

I hitched my shoulders back. "My father has." That came out sharp and defensive, and at Mr. Dart's calm, questioning glance I looked down. "No. I should."

"You should," he agreed, and changed the subject to what I had learned so far of Old Oriolan.

~

The sixth day of Winterturn I ran to Dart Hall early and greeted the household before they had even finished breakfasting. The weather was fine in the early morning before dawn: the stars brilliant overhead, the snow glittering in the fields, a hoarfrost riming every leaf and branch. Still, crisp air, the sky inky blue with green rising in the east.

"What brings you here so early, Jemis?" the Squire asked politely when the butler showed me in, beckoning the maid to bring me coffee. The meal seemed to be kippers, but Jullanar Maebh was eating porridge and I was glad to request a bowl of that for myself as well. She looked mildly approving until I put sugar and cream on it.

"Salt is the better option," she informed me.

I glanced at her plain porridge and then at mine, which was frankly swimming in cream, and smiled at her, still exalted from the run through the bright, crystalline pre-dawn. "I shall be sure to try that next time, Miss Dart. Is that the Outer Reaches custom?"

She appeared surprised at my tone, and somewhat mollified. "Yes," she allowed, with a small, reluctant smile. "Many southerners find it too plain for their tastes."

"Mine can be somewhat recondite," I admitted.

"No textual criticism before noon," Mr. Dart said sternly as he came into the room. "Please."

"Must we make a similar rule for historical analysis?" the Squire asked mildly from behind his copy of the *New Salon*.

"No books at the table," Sir Hamish said. "That goes for you as well, Tor."

The Squire harrumphed, but he folded up the paper and was smiling as he did so. Jullanar Maebh was smiling; it made her seem much more the vivacious queen in her royal-blue robes than I had seen on the journey from Orio City.

I turned with a glad heart to my father. "I was wondering," I said, "whether we might go around Arguty together today, if you had nothing else planned."

He regarded me soberly, and nodded. "I'd be pleased to do so."

And so we did.

~

One of my uncle Vorel's more egregious sins, if not any legal crime, was that he had expelled the majority of the Arguty estate's tenants for the twin purposes of enclosing fields for sheep and producing a more pleasing view from the manor. He'd had some of the old cottages razed down, and grubbed out half the ancient hedgerows I remembered from early childhood.

The estate was much smaller than the Darts'. All but the core of the entailed property had been sold to cover debts from my gambling-mad grandfather and Vorel's ruinously expensive fish ponds. Almost all the rest had been turned into pastures for the sheep, but there was still something of a home farm.

We visited the farmers, dour taciturn men who greeted my father with cordial skepticism and regarded me with unveiled suspicion. I didn't know all the reasons behind the suspicion, as I trailed along behind my father, but I listened carefully and tried to commit their names and concerns to memory.

The cluster of houses around the home farm was nearly all that was left, but for two direly poor buildings on the far side of the estate, near the dower cottage, that I thought were derelict stables. They turned out to be inhabited by a cluster of vagrant men who had once been soldiers under my father's command.

"Your lady wife offered us the place, if we could maintain it," one of the men said, gesturing at the stable. I peered at him, but couldn't recognize him with any certainty. "We didn't at first, went off to try our fortune with the Lady's navy."

"Can't abide the sea," another said, coughing hard. "Give me dry land any day. So we came back."

"Aye," the third said. "We heard from old Harry Buck that your promise was being kept."

"We did our best," the first said.

I looked at them, and around the stable. There was old straw in the corners, made into what looked almost like nests. Old boots and raggedy garments hung on ropes strung over the fire, which was in a rough circle of stones in the middle of the floor, underneath a hole in the roof. It was cold despite the fire, and there was not much in the way of food.

"Yes, you always did," my father said.

He was easy with these men, his shoulders relaxed, his face friendly and confident, his words coming in a softened accent I didn't know. This was Mad Jack Greenwing, I suspected, beloved of his men. It was a camaraderie I did not know; that I had longed for as a boy.

My father spoke to them for a few minutes. I drifted around the stables, not too close to their private things but looking to see what the building needed to be habitable through the winter. It was freezing now. What would it be like in the truly cold weather of the New Year?

My father joined me when I circled to the door, his face serious but not unhappy. As we moved out of earshot, he sighed. "There is so much work left by your uncle, Jemis."

It was the closest he had come to asking for assistance. I ducked my chin into the collar of my coat, knowing I had wilfully ignored the Arguty estate because of the grief my uncle and aunt had given me.

That was a burden on my soul I should work to relieve before I returned to that Wood, I realized.

"There's the money from my stepfather," I said.

"To redeem my name? Yes," my father said pensively. "Yes, this would be a good use for that. Rebuilding Arguty."

I had meant the money Mr. Buchance had left me, the remnants of his vast fortune after his other bequests were filled, but perhaps they would not be necessary.

I glanced across the fields to the grey bulk of the manor, cold and silent against the snow, the leafless trees. The formal gardens showed none of their undoubted dishevelment from this distance: from here I could only see the lines of hedges and stone walls and the balustrades on the terrace. This side was open to the view across the fields, unlike some of the other approaches which were close-set with trees and shrubberies.

The Lady knew how much needed to be done. My father's older brother had worked hard to rebuild the heart of the estate, but Vorel had nearly gutted it again.

We continued on, past the cold cottage where Hagwood had lived until the autumn. Crows sat in the trees around it, cawing loudly at each other. I watched them, but they seemed engrossed in their own, inhuman affairs.

The cottage itself seemed dark and sad, longing for people to return. I gestured at it. "Is there any reason those men couldn't take over that cottage? No matter how Hagwood left it, it would be a sight better than those stables."

My father looked at the cottage, then at me, then cursed with his easy fluency. "As a Winterturn present? You're too clever by half, Jemis," he said, and accordingly we turned and retraced our steps.

Back to the derelict stables and the men who did their best with the hands they were given, to hand them another card from the deck of Happenstance and Chance to make of what they might.

CHAPTER TWENTY-FOUR

The middle few days of Winterturn were marked by the giving of many small gifts to acquaintances and casual friends. I spent most of one day making a bee sting cake for Mrs. Ayden, who teared up when I delivered it; though that might equally have been the cocked hat I was wearing with as much jaunty assurance as I possessed.

I presented oranges and lemons and similar small treasures from Orio City to the ladies of the Embroidery Circle, and sent baskets of food to the people of the Arguty estate and the villagers of St-Noire. These were mostly practical foodstuffs, flour and salt and sugar and lard and the like, but I made certain to also include some small luxuries, for I well remembered how it had been, that first time Mr. Buchance had come by after the Fall, when he gave root ginger as one of his courting-gifts to my mother.

I received gifts as well: biscuits and preserves, a few loaves of bread, ribbons for a new cockade, a bottle of good ink. My mother's voice in my mind made me write down the givers in a book so I could write thank-you notes in the new year. There were so many more gifts than I could possibly have anticipated when I returned to Ragnor Bella in September.

The eighth day of Winterturn was another snowy day, not as cold but pleasing to be out-and-about in. I woke early and made cardamon-flavoured cakes for my stepfather, and the candied lemon peel my mother had loved, and went out while it was still quite early to the graveyard at the Big Church to make my seasonal offerings to them.

It was a strange thing, this matter of praying to the dead.

The priests said that we prayed *for* them, and I well remembered those birds in the Grim Crossroads. The white birds of Marcan's piety; the green and crimson and violet ones of my friends' love and grief: all of them had helped with that matter of my return back through the blighted lands around the Grim Crossroads.

I loped down the road to the White Cross, where I made a brief prayer to assuage any spirits who might rest there, most particularly that unknown assemblage of bones intended to feign an ill enchantment. For years I had prayed for all the unquiet and criminal dead who were bound beneath the crossroads, not knowing if any of them were as wrongly accused as my father had been.

I prayed for them with a scattering of wheat grains and holly berries, and then continued across the river and up the hill to the graveyard.

There were a few people around, and evidence that others had already visited their beloved dead. I knew Mrs. Buchance had been by with my sisters the day my father and I had visited the Arguty lands. Sure enough, there were offerings at the shallow stone dishes before their headstones. Most of the seeds and berries had been eaten by the local birds and small animals, but my sisters had made wreaths of holly and felt flowers to lay on their graves, and I smiled seeing them.

I went to my stepfather's grave first. The headstone was as solid and permanent as he had seemed, as he had been. A large man, large in his business vision and in his voice and bodily frame.

I stood before the grave, not quite articulating any thoughts for a moment. Listening to the wind, to the quiet murmurs of other voices in more distant parts of the graveyard, the sound of birds above us. A robin was singing, sitting on the branch of a shrub planted next to my mother's stone.

She had loved robins; all the little songbirds.

I stood there, hat in hand, letting the burbling song fill my ears, my mind, even in some distant, odd way my soul. It had overtones of Paradise, this songbird in a graveyard during the Winterturn holidays, with the thin sun streaming through a high white overcast.

Eventually I knelt in the snow and laid the cardamom biscuits, Mr. Buchance's favourite 'cardy cakes', on the offering-stone, nestled like golden eggs amongst the bright felt flowers and sharp green leaves of the holly wreath.

And then I prayed. Not for his safety along the way to the Lady's Country, for he was assured of his place at her table; he had already passed through those dark countries and the dangers thereof.

(I did not remember passing through them on my way *to* the Wood of Spiritual Refreshment. I had tumbled out of my mortal frame and into that spiritual body without knowing it was happening until it was done. Were all deaths so unexpected, so ... easy?)

I prayed for his joy, and the grace of his soul, and that he would know those whose lives he had touched, who had touched his. And I told him of his daughters and his widow, and what I was planning on doing with the inheritance he had left me, as if we sat across from one another at the public house just outside the bounds of Morrowlea, when he had asked me for things I had not known I was already giving him.

I do wonder sometimes about praying. *I* felt better having done so, which seems somewhat backward, but then again, is it not better that good things are themselves enjoyable?

I enjoy the good gifts of the Lady of Winter: the cold crisp air, the bright sun, the cozy evenings, the candles in the winter, the fires in the hearth. The crows black against the blue sky, and the robin singing his winter songs, red breast bright against white snow.

After I stood up I patted the stone. "Enjoy the cardy cakes, sir," I said, and heard the echo of his laughter and his gently teasing comment, *Always so formal, Jemis?* from the other side of life.

I was smiling as I turned to my mother's grave. It seemed wrong that she was not buried in the Woods Noirell with her kin, but my grandmother had been caught in some curse or madness, and had refused to acknowledge my letter to her until I had broken the curse on the bees.

My mother had not requested me to see her bones moved. Mr. Buchance had ordered a knee-high flat stone to lie along the length of the grave, with a simple, elegant spire of stone at the head. It was an old, old style in south Fiellan, nothing like his own Charese-style square headstone, and I wondered if my mother had asked him for that design, or if he had come up with it himself. I had only been fifteen when she died, and not aware of such distinctions.

I brushed snow off the top of the stone and sat down on the flat stone, as if it were a seat at her bedside, and—well, this was not so much a prayer as a chat.

I told her about all the things I had done since returning to mortal life: about the unicorn and the visions of Sir Peregrine, the gift of the Ánhorn across time. The warnings of the fox and the gifts from the unknown admirer.

I told her too, ruefully, how I wished I'd asked her more about the Woodlander traditions, and how I wasn't sure what it meant for Mrs. Henny and Mrs. Pritchard to come speak to me with news from the Woods. There was something there, I was sure, more significant than just the comment itself. It felt as if I had passed some unknown test, and was being granted new privileges accordingly.

"I should have brought you tea, mama," I concluded, setting the candied lemon on the offering-stone, "but I haven't a good way of carrying it. I shall ask Mr. Inglesides if he has any ideas before the Fallowday of the Spring."

I felt a stir of wind in my hair, as if fingers were carding through it, and turned my face to the sun, squinting against its brightness. Not that Paradise had been in any way *up there*, but that was the closest analogy I could find.

One could reach it by one unexpected tumble, but to open one's heart to the Lady's grace in *this* life ... oh, I knew it only through the gifts of friendship and poetry, and the singing certainty of a sword in my hand and mortal danger surrounding me.

When I stood up from the grave I found that there were a few good citizens of Ragnor Bella attending to their own dead with all the solemn and serious expressions usually considered appropriate for the occasion. Some of them were looking sidelong at me, their faces shifting with suspicion and a strange, fearful awe.

My heart was too full of mirth and joy to be sober, though it was a solemn joy, like the sun shining through clouds in great beams and rays.

I put my hat back on so I could take it off when I bowed to Mrs. Etaris's sister Mrs. Landry, who looked as if she did not know at all what to make of me, but curtsied in automatic response when I bade her a joyous Winterturn.

~

The next morning, the ninth day of Winterturn, I helped Mrs. Etaris in the store in the morning. She closed up at noon, as the next day was a market-day. That afternoon I went for a run.

Mr. Dart was still avoiding being press-ganged into participating in the Dartington pageant by means of hiding out in my flat, so I left him and Ballory tending the fire and the kitten and reading about wild magic and set off into the crisp, clear air. The morning's snowfall was gone from the roads, which were soft underfoot but not unpleasant for all that.

I barely thought for the first few miles. I set off on the wide three-hour route: up the main road to the highway, along that to the Green Dragon. I swung around behind the tavern and onto the Greenway.

Past the Dragon Stone and its reflecting pool. A crow was sitting on the upright. It cawed loudly as I approached, its calls following me as I ran on.

By the time the sound faded—it was one of those still, crystalline days where sounds hung in the air, echoes caught in frost crystals, my breath steaming and falling away in clouds around me, my footsteps crunching on the ice rimming puddles—I had reached the other end of the Greenway and was turning left, away from the farmyard there and up to the bridge across the Dartwater. Past the Old Arrow; the water running dark and clear below me, beside me as I crossed the bridge and turned along the footpath that led along the river.

The riverside meadows were flooded, so I cut east to the higher ground where the Squire's herds grazed in the winter. The belted cattle, their fur as shaggy but their frames far healthier than Sir Peregrine's emaciated cow, raised their heads curiously as I passed. Another crow was flying overhead and paced me for a good mile, its caws falling into the air around me.

At the edge of the Arguty Forest I came across one of the old sunken roads and turned to follow it south. The flying crow veered off to the north; it was swallowed in a flock of jackdaws rising up in a sudden cloud out of the forest.

I followed the edge of the trees on a narrow path, more of a game-trail than a human road.

A fox-trail, perhaps: halfway to the Coombe I met the two-tailed fox.

They were sitting on a large flat stone to the side of the trail, tails tucked neatly around their feet. Black feet; white-tipped tails; a smart, pointed face with black ears and bright black eyes. They watched me arrive and slow to a stop a polite distance away.

"Good afternoon, Sayu Fox," I said.

The fox twitched first one ear and then the second. "Good day to you," they replied.

I waited, wondering why the fox was there; what they wanted with me; whether they had loved and abandoned Mr. Dart because of the stone arm.

"You have questions in your eyes," they said.

The words came from somewhere deep in the back of my mind. "Three warnings," I said, "and three gifts. Are three answers to come?"

"Ask wisely," the fox responded. "I am to be gone at sunset tonight."

I glanced to the west, where the sun was already touching the top of the Gorbelow Hills. I had not realized how close to sunset it was, but the shadows would find me soon enough, and I must turn my steps back to town.

Three warnings: *beware the false friend; beware the false lover; beware the false hunter.*

Three gifts: one bird, two, three.

Three answers, for three questions.

I could wish for Mr. Dart to be there, with his quick mind and cautious tongue. I could not think of any better questions than the ones that had come to mind on first seeing the fox. Would they know which fairy had cursed me, or what the curse was?

They might know how I might find out. But was that worth the loss of a question?

In Poacher, as my father had taught it to me, there was one card in the Happenstance Deck that was called the Oracle. The one who played it required the other to ask the question.

"What do I need to know?" I asked the fox.

It tilted its head. "What do you already know?"

Was sunset the moment the sun disappeared from view behind land, or behind the abstract line of the horizon? The sun was ruddy now, the light on the snow almost a lurid pink. The fox's fur glowed.

"What do I need to do?"

The fox tilted its head the other way. Both of its ears were pricked forward intently. "What are you already doing?"

I swallowed, and tried to rally my courage. I did not know why this was the third question to come to mind, but it was, and it obliterated all other consideration or concern. For some reason I *needed* to know.

"What is your true name?"

The fox laughed, high and nearly human. "Are you clever enough to follow my trail?"

High above us two crows called back and forth as they winged south towards the Woods Noirell.

CHAPTER TWENTY-FIVE

I ran home swiftly as the shadows leapt from the Gorbelow Hills and the stars started to come out above me. The sun sank and drew its red robes down behind it, the rich colour fading from the sky as it turned first pink and then pale lavender and then a deep, intense blue.

The fox had answered question with question, as was the wont of the Good Neighbours. I knew that from the stories.

Three warnings.

Three gifts.

Three questions.

Smoke rose in cheerful columns, straight up from chimneys of farm cottages. Most habitations were on the other side of the river, in the wide triangle between the Dartwater and the River Rag. This side of the river was always more debatable land.

There was Arguty Hall across the water, the windows dark and the chimneys cold. I was glad when it disappeared behind its oaks. The dower cottage by the river was also dark and overgrown; I was surprised by the stab of grief I felt on seeing it so cheerless.

It was good to see lights in Hagwood's old cottage, and smoke rising from its chimney. I had sent a large basket of food to my father's old men: coffee and sugar, flour and lard, butter, bacon, and eggs; cabbages, potatoes, parsnips; carrots and milk and apples, salt and a handful of spices, and my last lemon, plus one of the precious tins of tea. It was not enough for a winter, but enough, I hoped, for a good Winterturn.

There was an old stone bridge over the Dartwater about half a mile along from Arguty Hall. It was mossy and missing a few stones, but the river was shallow and noisy. Mr. Dart and I had often played in the shallows and shadows between its pilings, catching fish and building little weirs and telling stories.

There was snow on the bridge, clear of tracks in both directions; and a man standing there.

The night was drawing in, the shadows more blue than grey. In the glimmering twilight his green garments seemed to flutter like leaves.

He stood there, as tall as the Honourable Rag and as broad of shoulder and waist. His boots were brown leather, his hosen green wool, his tunic and his cloak both green as well. He had a wide brown belt with an ivory horn scabbarded there.

This was not the Honourable Rag pretending to be the Hunter in Green.

He had shadowy antlers rising up out of his curly brown hair. His eyes were blue as Mr. Dart's, bright and keen as the stars in the sky above.

He wore a beard like Mr. Dart's as well, close-trimmed around his jaw. He bore no sword, but had a staff in his hands, as stout and strong as the Wild Saint's, and a bow and quiver over his shoulder.

He watched me slow from my steady lope until I stopped at the foot of the arched bridge, at which point I bowed.

The air rose around me, lifting snow up in shining arabesques that were scented with the flowers that had bloomed when the Lady smiled in the Woods on the other side of life.

This was the Hunter in the Green.

"Bright the night, young one," he said.

His voice was deep and velvety. The stars above seemed to tangle in his antlers, as if he were draped with fireflies, dazzled with the coming winter. The Hunter in the Green, who harrowed the dark and blasted lands around the Grim Crossroads; who never lost his quarry, whether to hunt or to rescue; who had been caught up by the Lady as the winter constellation who pointed the way to the North Star.

"Good evening to you, my lord," I replied, as courteously as I could.

"Come up to me."

There was no compulsion to that quiet order, but I felt as compelled as if he had been my father uttering it. I climbed up the arc of the bridge, which seemed far higher and longer than I'd ever remembered it being. I was panting by the time I made it to the crest, my ribs aching with a stitch. I pressed my hand to my side, embarrassed.

The Hunter in the Green watched me until I drew abreast of him, and then he turned, gesturing to me to stand at his side. He smelled pleasantly musky, redolent of the woods and green growing things and the cold fresh air threaded through with homely woodsmoke and the thin, fragile scent of witch hazel.

The view from the bridge was not the one it usually was.

We stood high above the earth. I looked down but my feet were still on stone, steady and secure. I settled into my position and refused to be alarmed.

The Hunter in the Green said nothing, merely smiled and looked out over the world laid out below us like a patchwork quilt.

We stood with the Crosslains at our back. I twisted around to look at them, and there they stood, their peaks shaped out of starlit snow and dim grey shadows. Their forested laps spilled down behind us to the edge of the fields and copses, hills and rivers and dales and glens of the barony.

There to the south, my left, were the high peaks in the strange land between Fiellan and West Erlingale, which were tangled with magic and had never been well inhabited or explored. The road to Astandalas had passed through them. Faced with the mystery and magic of a passage between worlds to the golden and glittering city of the emperors, capital of a vast and glorious empire, no one I knew of had chosen to leave the road, go around the circular gate, and see what else might lie in those mountains..

Directly below us the land slanted down to the Dartwater and up again, higher in the south where the hills between the Coombe and the valley of the Rag proper rose up in their wooded capes. From here I could see the winking eyes of the Lady's Pools, and a glimmering silver shape. The Ellery Stone. The Woods Noirell were a hint of shadow and a few lights like earthbound stars, or jewels caught in a net of dark hair, mostly hidden from view by the folds of the land.

On the other side of the Hildon Wood along the Greenway was the larger fold of the valley of the Rag, mist rising from black water into the still air. Ragnor Bella was a cluster of lights and mist, like some dream of a fairy city, all the mundanity of human life hidden by the half-lights of twilight and distance.

Beyond the town, the fields and then the forests leading up to the Gorbelow Hills. The Leap was visible, a crack between two halves of a great mountain, the sky still red behind it, below the horizon of my position. From this vantage point the Giants' Road was clearly drawn, from the Leap back across the width of the valley to disappear in the dark and gloomy bulk of the Arguty Forest.

I completed the circle by looking up at the tall Hunter. The stars in his antlers were no less bright than the gleam in his eyes, nor any more distant.

It was a small compass, perhaps, this home of mine. I knew those roads; I had run them over the past months, re-learning the places I had known as a boy and learning new paths I had never before trod. I knew far more people by name and by sight now than I ever had, people who came into the bookstore or those who greeted me as I passed, knowing me for the scandal and gossip of my name, and sometimes for myself.

In the forests and woods were those who had served with my father, who had helped and hindered me. There were those who sought to bring the Dark Kings into the world, seeking the easy way to power and might; and those who fought the hard, grinding, endless fight against them.

In the town and the villages and the scattered houses of the barony were those who loved the Lady and those who bowed to the Dark Kings and those who followed neither, but were good or bad or indifferent regardless. In this small compass of the world had a dragon come to challenge me and a fox to warn me and the Gentry to steal me.

And the Lady and her servants to guide me.

I turned to the Hunter, who watched me steadily.

"What do I need to know?" I asked him. "What do I need to do?"

He smiled, with the whole of his being but for his eyes and his mouth. I remembered the glory of the Lady's smile, the reflected beauty of the smiles in the faces of those who sat at her table, and knew that his now would be too strong, too much for my mortal eyes.

Even on such a night as this, standing on an impossible bridge high in the air, with the Hunter at my side.

"What did the fox say?"

I was due for all my questions to be answered with more questions, it appeared. My tutor did much the same at Morrowlea. Something to do with being led to think for oneself.

I smiled at the Hunter. He was solemn and the air was full of portent but I could not but be mirthful, this season of the Lady of Winter.

My mother and stepfather were not *there*, in their graves of stone and earth; but they were there, listening, when I prayed. The very mystery of it was a gift.

"'What have you already learned? Where are you already going?'"

"And for your third question?"

I would never ask the Hunter for his true name. I was astonished at my own audacity for asking the fox.

"'Are you clever enough to follow that trail?'"

He nodded. For a moment I was sure the stars moved with the antlers, but they were back in their places when I glanced up.

"You looked first to see where you stood," he observed, "and then at the land from which you came and which holds your heart. Now look to the heavens."

I glanced at him—had I not looked at *him* first?—and then obeyed. As I tilted my head back an atavistic dread of falling seeped into me. I had not noticed the staggering drop two steps behind my feet when I looked *out*, but *up*?

He set his hand on my back, steadying me. "Do not fear falling."

I had been taught to give thanks to the Lady and her servants with every prayer I had ever learned to utter. The words came easily, if awkwardly, to my lips. "Thank you," I said.

"Look," he said softly.

I obeyed.

There was the winter sky in all its brilliance. The moon was a thin crescent to the west, hanging like a silver sickle in the lower sky. As a boy I had always wondered what the Lady harvested with that shining tool.

"Flowers of poetry for her garden," the Hunter said.

The sky behind the moon was still green with sunset. It transformed imperceptibly into a luminous blue, deeper and richer than any painted image, any earthly colour. The stars were scattered across it in their familiar constellations, though up here, away from the smokes and fumes of the lower earth, I could see far more stars than ever before.

I had not seen a night on the other side of life. What a splendour that sight must be, those stars in their fullness!

I picked out the constellations my father had taught me, the stories my mother had told me. The Hare and the Dog; the Stag and the Ship; the three Eagles; the great Unicorn; the Hunter himself. There was the Crown of the Winter, and the North Star.

And there, scattered across the sky, brighter and more beautiful than I'd ever seen them before, the four planets.

Except that this time there were five.

There was silver Kivroth, the Star of Even and Morn, always close attendant to the moon. A little higher lay blue Tazra, the Herald of Peace. Higher yet and still far to the east were the twin planets of red Dwile, the Harbinger of War, and green Heorl, the Bearer of Felicity. I had been born under the conjunction of Dwile and Heorl, my mother had told me once. A soldier's son through and through.

But to the south there shone a great golden planet I was sure I had never seen before.

"What is that?" I asked the Hunter. "It's not a comet, surely."

I had heard of comets but never seen one outside of a diagram in a book of astronomical marvels. They were called bearded stars for their long trailing hair.

This was not a bearded star. It was a shining beacon in the south, over the mountains, like the familiar four planets but larger, brighter, impossible.

The Hunter gave me a sad, grave look. "So long has it been since that planet last cast his light over the world, his name even has been forgotten and lies mouldering with the dreams of days long past."

I stared at the planet. A fifth planet. I did not have even a distant echo of something I had once read to chime in my mind. No story from my mother, no tale from my father, no poem of the classical poets.

"Long ago," the Hunter said, "our Lady walked the earth, which grew green under her feet. The sky her raiment, the winds her attendants, all good and growing things about her. She was the goddess of the morning and the evening, of the day and the night. When the seasons turned she was the Lady of the Winter as well as of the Summer."

I nodded. So said all my mother's stories.

"Her care and her charge was this hemisphere of the world," he went on, making a wide gesture from the west to the east, his hand arcing over the north. His horns caught the pole star and seemed to tug it out of its place. Shooting stars followed his hand, blazing down into the dim blanket of snow covering Middle Fiellan on the other side of the Arguty Forest. My breath caught at how *right* it was that the stars should follow his hand.

"To the South she had her partner and her friend in the Lord of the Purple and Gold; the Lord of Spring and Autumn; the Lord of Mountain and Sea."

I stared up at the Hunter. His eyes were as deep and fathomless as the sky above us, as brilliant with the stars. My throat was dry and my skin prickling with goosebumps.

"Two halves of the world, two hemispheres. They joined in the dance of the seasons, at solstice and equinox meeting and parting and meeting again. The world, blessed in their joy, peopled by their love. Magic in their meeting and in their parting. Lady of Green and White, Lord of Purple and Gold."

We turned to look at the great planet riding high above the south, with Dwile and Heorl and Kivroth and Tazra and the crescent moon his attendants, the southern constellations clustering around him.

The Hunter said, "There were those who lived in the Bright Countries, whose nearest edges you have glimpsed, who grew jealous that the Lady and the Lord would let the mortals whom they loved into Paradise. They strove against our Lord and Lady, and were cast out of the Bright Countries into the shadows between worlds."

"The Dark Kings," I whispered.

"And their servants."

I swallowed. "What then?"

"They waged war."

It was a simple statement. The source of evil, so said the Lady's priests in their sermons. I wasn't sure about that—surely there were those born to, raised in, those traditions who were not *evil*?—but it was true that the power of the priests of the Dark Kings as I had experienced it was unholy, broken, diseased.

"The Lord and our Lady fought, but by their very nature they brought the divine realms close. They held open the gates of Paradise with every step, every smile, every touch of their hands upon the world. Our Lady chose to withdraw so that those who had once joined her dance in the Bright Countries could no longer find their way thither. In her withdrawal she left behind what gifts she could, each to come in its own times and needs."

The Hunter himself. The unicorns. Magic. Sir Peregrine. Any of the saints, major and minor. Mr. Dart.

"And then you," the Hunter in the Green said. "Of this world, but yet not fully; kin by your mother's line to those who live in the places between worlds, neither of the Bright Countries or the mortal realms nor the Abyssal deeps. Friends with a champion, promising in his own right. There have been many such, over the years. Some of their names you know. Others were lost in the battle."

"I was lost in the battle," I said, and then the whole world seemed to lurch under my foot. The Hunter's hand was warm and strong on my shoulder. "Like my father."

"Another who knows the fight. And like him, you were not entirely lost."

"I came back so the gate would not open for the Dark Kings. Mr. Dart was the one who held the passage open."

The Hunter pointed to the glowing planet to the south, the Lord whose name no one now knew. "The Lady returned to the meads of Paradise, where she gathers those who seek her. I am her reeve and her hunter, keeping guard and keeping watch along the borderlands."

He was giving me metaphors and analogies I might understand, I knew that, grateful for the consideration. What was really happening … oh, it was an allegory for which we had no other words; the veil thrown over the invisible statue, giving us a glimpse of its shape and form.

"Just so," he said. There were clouds at the edge of the horizon now, black against the stars and royal sky. The shadows rising. And yet the bright planet, the Lord, in his place.

"You saw Sir Peregrine, and accepted his gift."

I swallowed again. This was what Mr. Dart had meant: that the sword, the Ánhorn, had come to me, and not to him. I clenched my left hand, the one marked by the spiral horn, the spiral scar. It was warm in my mind. "I did."

"You have found secrets."

Many; most recently that banned and lost poem of Fitzroy Angursell's, which had the key to unravelling half the magic of Alinor.

"It is only half," the Hunter said softly. "The invaders from other mortal worlds came. Our Lady was not unwelcoming, and the wizards of the iron roads did not like the Dark Kings either. But they bound both the green magic and the black, both the white magic and the red. What they brought into their sway was kept from the Dark Kings, but they did not bring *all*."

Half the world had never been conquered. South of Loe was an unknown continent. East of the Mountains of Desire on Eastern Oriole were countries whose universities had belonged to the Charter of Schools but which were merely names in the lists now. Westward over the ocean was the land—island? archipelago? continent?—which Hal had sent an expedition to find.

"And the Lord?" I asked, looking out at the fifth planet. "Did he too retreat to the Bright Countries?"

"He fought, and fell," the Hunter said. "Was caught and taken captive. Until he is freed, the world will never be more than half of what it might be."

I stared at the sky, the snow-capped mountains, the shadows and the starlight. The mysteries in those folds of land, the spine of the continent that wove from the Farry March in convoluted ranks into the southern mystery; the uninhabited, unexplored, unknown regions between Fiellan and West Erlingale, Ghilousette and Thourin south of Erlingale, and the countries beyond Loe.

What could catch and bind a god?

My father had fought his way through those shadows, those mountains, those darker nights and brighter days. He had not yet spoken of what he had seen and done on his way home.

"What do I need to know?" I breathed, the third time of asking. "What do I need to do?"

CHAPTER TWENTY-SIX

The Hunter's hand was warm, even hot on my back. The air was crisp on my skin, catching in my lungs as I breathed in the piercing clarity.

There might be shadows at the edges of the horizon, but nothing obscured the last light of the sun, the five planets set like jewels in golden rings, the crescent moon like the arc of the Hunter's bow.

"What do you already know? What do you already do?" the Hunter asked.

I should try answering questions with more questions, I thought, not crossly. It was hard to feel cross with my feet planted on the span of a bridge high above the world and intensely a part of it.

What did I already know? What did I already do?

What did I do *well*?

"Running," I answered. "Fighting." I paused, but then Ariadne came to mind, her poem that had so shaped my life. *Crescent and recrescent shadows,* just the shape of the sickle moon when the sun had been shadowed by an eclipse. Solving puzzles. But that was not the right phrase, was it? There were that handful of stories from before the coming of the Empire … "Answering riddles."

"Then answer me this," the Hunter said, bending his head to look me in the eye. I looked back, unafraid of the stars or the shadows there. The Lady would not forget me, should I fail in the tasks before me and be lost in the dark and blasted landscape around the Grim Crossroads. She had promised me her Hunter would harry out all those who longed for her table.

"Such faith," the Hunter murmured. "Let it burn brightly, son of twilight."

The twilit countries were those of the Good Neighbours, where neither Sun nor Moon shone, it was said.

"What riddle do you pose me?" I asked, though his whole presence was a riddle and a puzzle I should likely never fully be able to answer.

"We are always here, we who serve our Lady and those who oppose her," he said quietly in answer to my thought. "It takes a rare gift of sight for one to see us who has not been touched as you have been."

I nodded in understanding. I had looked upon the Lady: the memory, bright if blurry, lifted my heart every time my mind landed upon it. I held that in the treasure-chamber of my memory, that gift of grace and miracle.

What a gift of grace and miracle Mr. Dart was, to call me back across the chasm between death and life.

The Hunter turned me, his hand a gentle pressure on my shoulder, and guided me to the very edge of the bridge. I stood there, calm under his touch, knowing I would not fall.

"Would you jump if I asked?" he asked.

I had jumped the Leap for my father when he asked.

I pretended to consider it seriously, but the words came truthfully from my mouth. "Probably."

He laughed outright, and it seemed as if the stars could not help it, and laughed with him. I was sure the great golden planet, the fifth star, sign of the Lord we had lost, twinkled most brightly and brilliantly of all.

"Running, and fighting, and riddling you will have," the Hunter declared. "A desperate race to run, a good fight to undertake, and riddles piled upon riddles to unravel."

"My life is my Lady's," I replied, stepping away from his hand so I could turn and present him with one of my elaborate be-curlicued bows.

"Many are called, and few make it to the end," he murmured, "but each relays the torch a step further, though it be only a step. Do you understand?"

I remembered the drums beating in the gorge of the Magarran Strid as the waters turned. I remembered the high ululating wail that had changed the cultists from foolish to terrible. I remembered the taste of wireweed in my mouth, dissolving my inhibitions and burning my inner magic into firework-brilliance.

"I do."

"It is a simple riddle."

"Those can be the hardest ones."

It was easier to see that there was a mystery in a long and complicated poem ... harder in a short and tightly constructed stanza. But yet the Gainsgooding Conspirators had managed to plan the assassination of an Emperor through their poems, and it was only the fact that I had successfully escaped the Orio City prison that would convince anyone of the truth of my analysis of *On Being Incarcerated*.

"When is a trail not to be tracked?"

I looked up at the Hunter. That was apposite but hardly a very good riddle. Though, then again—

The first answer, *when it is a false trail*, was not necessarily *right*. One might need to follow the false trail to find out it was not the true one.

I looked out at the patterns of field and copse, hedgerow and road, river and human habitation. I could name half the fields I could see: there was the Ten-Acre Field which the baron spent far too long each year ploughing; there was the field in which the races were run at the Dartington Harvest Fair; there were the water meadows of the lower Raggle where Mr. Dart was worried the wireweed had washed down from the Talgarths' illicit operation.

When it leads into danger was another answer that, while true, was unhelpful. One did not always *know* that a trail did; and sometimes it was the only way, and one might have to hazard the danger to win the prize.

My father had gone into danger any number of times in order to follow his duty or save his life or those of his comrades and commanders. No, sometimes one needed to follow a trail no matter where it led.

I looked at the dark mass of the Arguty Forest. From up here I could see a lighter grey splotch I thought might be the hill on which stood that one singular tree, the Hanging Tree on which I had thought my father had been hanged to his death. The burial mound of the Bloody Queen. The location of Myrta the Hand's camp.

When is a trail not to be tracked?

When it was false; when it led into danger; when ...?

I looked down to the south, at the edge of the Coombe and the hills where the Lady's Pools and the Ellery Stone lay. There was a faint pale glimmer, some body of water catching the starlight. The spring behind the old chapel.

That night, solstice night, I had been required to stay in the circle while Mr. Dart and my father held the line. I was the weak point; I could neither run, nor fight, nor even answer riddles. I could only hold myself inside the circle and have visions.

I looked up at the Hunter. "When one is not the hunter."

He smiled without moving his face again. "It is a hard lesson for some."

To accept help. To await rescue. To allow another to fight on one's behalf. None of those were things I was good at.

"Why are so many things happening?" I asked, gazing out at this small diamond of land. Such a tiny portion of the world and yet stage enough for a lifetime of adventure. Surely it was impossible that it had been only four months since I came home.

A lifetime, indeed. Mine had ended and then ... begun again.

"Things happen at all times, in season and out of it," he replied evenly. "Many do not notice."

"I am noticing," I muttered. There was the Talgarth's house, in all its Late Bastard Decadent glory. There was the Little Church where Violet and I had tumbled in a fight. There was Ragnor Bella. There was Magistra Bellamy's cottage, with the smoke rising up in a steady spiral. There was Dart Hall, with all its windows lit. There was the Big Church and the White Cross and the Arguty Forest—

There was almost all the compass of my life.

I looked back at the golden planet. It gleamed, majestic and gorgeous, like the sunlight catching in Ballory's eye. It hung above the mountains behind the Woods Noirell, beyond the gate that once led to Astandalas.

"Where does the Gate of Morning lead?" the Hunter asked, his voice soft and full of portent. "Who holds the shield of the lost Lord? What banner shall be unfurled over the Lady's Champion?"

I stood a few steps away from him now, just over the crest of the invisible bridge. Far below us was Dartwater; far above us was the constellation of the Archer, with its stars caught in the Hunter's horns.

Answer questions with questions. I lifted my head. The air was moving about us, cold winds scented still with those flowers from the meads of Paradise. There I could desire nothing wrong, choose no ill path. That was not a grace given to us here in our mortal life, bounded and binding as it was; but yet—

"Who led my father home?" I asked in reply. "Why was the Ánhorn given to me? What am I to tell those who wait for me?"

The Hunter lifted his head and laughed, and the heavens shook and thundered with his laughter. The shadows curling about the horizon flinched and trembled. I could hear a joyous barking and baying coming from the heavenly hounds leaping through the sky, the stars in their eyes.

"You must choose your allies," the Hunter said. "The enemies test the guards at the gates. This is the year's midnight and its birthing-time alike, this passage from light to dark to light again. Not all trails are true. Some are false, laid to deceive; others are laid to test and teach."

"And some are red herring pies," I muttered.

The Hunter was not rumoured to be omniscient, and certainly did not seem to know what to make of my comment. After a brief flicker of hesitation he ignored it and went on.

"It is the time of riddles," he announced. "When the unicorn bloodies her horn will be time enough to fight."

"And to run?" I asked quietly.

He gave me a soft, steady glance. "You know well enough that there are many ways and times for that."

I met his glance. The wind was moving faster around us now. It reminded me of Mr. Dart's magic, powerful and uncertain, tentative but yet with such a steadily unfurling core of joy. The stars were bright above us, in the horns of the Hunter's crown, in his dark eyes, in his beard. I had imagined such stars when my father whispered of what the night sky looked like on the other side of the Border, outside of Astandalas.

"There is beauty there," he said very softly.

And knowledge and wisdom to be learned. Plants to be found, even.

"Am I ... to find it?"

"You might seek *him*," the Hunter said even more quietly, as if there were ears that might hear, high up on his magical bridge.

I looked at the golden planet, the unknown Lord, the lost partner of the Lady. "Where?"

It was not a real question, because if the Hunter had known surely he would already have gone searching. He did not answer, but merely looked at the fifth planet and then back to me. His curly hair was moving in the wind, and his antlers caught the stars in streamers and banners. I blinked, dizzy with the sense of otherness, of dislocation, of divinity.

"You must return," the Hunter said. "The world is calling you home."

He stepped forward and placed his hand on my shoulder again. It anchored me against the dizziness. It was also far warmer than before, hot as a brand. I braced myself against it, this touch of the divine against me.

"Go," the Hunter said. "It is time to run. The time to riddle and the time to fight come also."

I nodded. "Thank you."

An awkward human courtesy, nothing like the lauds and paeans I should have been pouring forth. But that was my way, was it not? To treat all equally, as souls before the Lady.

The Hunter was … his own being. Not the Lord whom he spoke of so fondly and so sadly, but the Lady's Hunter and helpmeet.

"When you run," whispered the Hunter. "Know I run beside you."

I looked one last time into his eyes, into the hair and horns and face that was dissolving into the wind, into the green and shadowed wind blowing out of the Lady's countries. He smiled at me, that brightening of the starry eyes, and he bent his great head and kissed me on the brow.

"When you fight," he said, taking my hand and pressing something into my grip. My fingers closed around the object, something hard and cool, strangely ceramic. "Know I fight beside you."

He stepped back, hand falling from my shoulder, from my own hand.

My head and hand were blazing, as if fires had been lit there, stars to beacon an army home.

"And when you riddle," he said, his eyes very keen, sharp as the winter wind that was rising around us. His dogs bayed joyously as they ran around the horizon chasing the clouds out of the sky. "Know that I guard the sacred circle around you."

He was not the patron of riddles and mysteries. That was not one of the noted gifts from the Lady: was it instead a field for the unknown god, the Lord of the fifth planet?

The wind rose, and the baying hounds. I gripped whatever it was he had given me and smiled at the Hunter in the Green. He stepped back, his garments fluttering and dissolving into a wind that was a nighttime wind, a winter wind, full of snow and sharp-tipped holly and running deer.

"Run," said the Hunter, in a voice at once commanding and delighted. "Run home, Jemis Greenwing of the Shadowy Woods. Run, and fight, and riddle your way home."

Somehow I knew which way to go. I bowed once more to the Hunter in the Green, deep and low and respectful, and then I turned and ran down the sky.

CHAPTER TWENTY-SEVEN

The stone bridge unspooled under my feet, arcing down like a moonlit rainbow, all grey and silver in the night.

I ran with the wind running beside me, my feet light on the stones of the air, thunder echoing in distant avalanches. The stars above me blurred and swept away with the wind-raised tears in my eyes. I squinted my eyes shut and opened them again to see that Ragnor Bella was rising up before me, mist and friendly candle-light and the scent of woodsmoke in the air.

I ran down, the mist around my feet. The stones were mist, firm underfoot and hazy to the glance, clouds springier than a fine greensward. Snow was rising, scattering under my steps, puffing upwards and whirling away into the night.

I ran down the wind, down the rainbow, down the arc of the evening, until my feet were running on the mortal cobbles of the road that was the spine of Ragnor Bella, and I was at my own front door.

The bookstore's door, rather. Close enough.

I slowed easily as I neared it. The candles were lit in the windows downstairs, upstairs in my flat. The fire was burning: smoke rose overhead, friendly as Mr. Dart's pipe tobacco as I descended once more into the world of mortal care.

The golden planet was hidden behind the southern mountains.

Of course, I thought, looking up. Only Kivroth was visible now, close behind the sickle moon, just visible over the roofs of the town. The rest were hidden: war and peace, felicity and that great mystery.

I knocked the snow and star-stuff off my shoes with the bootscraper and opened the door.

Mrs. Etaris was leaning on the counter, reading. She seemed to have been pricing new books, by the opened crates at her feet and the stacks beside her, the pencil behind her ear, but she had been caught by whatever work it was. I glanced at it as I shut the door behind me. Green cover; and there were two other volumes next to her.

Durgand's *Valiance and Shock*, on the deeds of the infamous Red Company.

Her smile was reminiscent, happy rather than melancholy. It was a treat to see it; and what an amazing thing to think that her reminiscences were of such deeds and crimes as those!

"Good evening, Mr. Greenwing," she said without looking up. "Your father is upstairs."

"Thank you," I replied, my joy audible even in my own ears. She glanced up, and caught her breath.

"Something has happened, then?"

I thought of what the Hunter had said. "Something is *always* happening, I am informed, though we may not always notice."

She paused. She was the one who had told me we never found out all the story. Then she smiled, a secret, delighted thing. Looking at her in that moment, I could see exactly how she was Jullanar of the Sea of all the stories.

"Anything in particular you'd like to share?"

"I met the Hunter in the Green," I told her, grinning in reciprocal delight. "Oh, and the fox."

"Mustn't forget the fox," Mrs. Etaris replied solemnly, and turned back to the book of her youthful exploits. From my quick glance she seemed to be reading about Fitzroy Angursell seducing the Moon. (Surely *that* wasn't true?) "Let me know if you need my assistance for anything."

~

My father was upstairs, dozing by the fire. He'd acquired a blanket from somewhere—Mrs. Etaris, possibly—and had his hands full of the grey kitten, which was once again purring loudly.

I mended the fire, filled the kettle of water, and surveyed my small store of foodstuffs. In the box on the windowsill was the jug of milk and the remaining butter along with the opened cheese.

I only had a few eggs left. There was plenty of honey, but not much flour. I had spices in extravagant array, but no meat. Dried beans, but nothing fresh. Half a loaf of braided fruit bread from the bakery.

For want of any better idea, I sliced the braided loaf and put it on a plate.

The kettle started to whistle and I returned to the sitting room to find my father rousing. I decided it was still a good time for tea and made another pot. My father watched me with bleary but amused eyes.

"Harry sent food over," he said, nodding at a covered basket on the table. "I wasn't sure when you would be back."

"I met the Hunter along the way," I answered, opening the basket to discover a cloth-covered dish of baked beans and pork, along with another pot of some sort of steamed pudding in a ceramic pot.

That reminded me of the Hunter's gift, which I had tucked into my pocket. I pulled it out and set it on the table: it was a miniature pudding basin in a fine glazed ware.

The pudding had a pleated cloth top tied into a sturdy knot.

I stared at it. That was not the sort of thing I really associated with the divinity of the woods and the wild.

"From your expression, I suppose it was not your friend Roald."

I shook my head silently, not able to state that Roald and I were not yet really *friends*, and then got up to set the pudding on the mantle. *Gather your allies*, the Hunter had said. That meant Mr. Dart and Mrs. Etaris and my father at the very least, and probably also Roald and Hal and Violet and Hal's Uncle Ben and—

I stopped, thinking of that list in satisfaction. What an array of allies I was gathering. Lady Jessamine had offered me an unspecified favour.

My father had links to various highwaymen, and then there were the folk of the Woods—the Woodlanders, Mrs. Pritchard had called them —called *us*—

And there was the Embroidery Circle and the Chancellor of Morrowlea, and perhaps Magistra Aurelia of Tara, and Mr. Dart's tutor too. Hope, the Ironwood Heiress. Master Boring, if his conscience remained susceptible to mild blackmail.

Mrs. Etaris probably knew whereof she spoke when she warned me off getting a taste for it. Perhaps not Master Boring, then.

I turned to my father, who had risen and was setting out plates and cutlery from my cupboard. It pleased me inordinately that he knew where to find them, that we could sit together and share this meal in my own flat.

"I passed the Dower Cottage and Arguty House on my run," I said. "They were both dark. Hagwood's old cottage was lit."

My father passed me the salt and a little pot of mustard, and we both sat down. "You don't like the Manor, do you?"

I grimaced apologetically. "I don't have many good memories of it."

His face was sad, but also understanding. "You'd be happy with the Dower Cottage, wouldn't you?"

"That was always *home*."

One of the things I had found hard to forgive my stepfather for had been moving us to town. It had been *hard* in the cottage, through the Interim and afterwards, but that had always been my family home. Moving to town had been the final rupture with my father.

Or so it had seemed. Seven years later and here he was, alive and well and sitting opposite me in my little flat above the bookstore.

"Tell me about the Hunter?" he asked softly.

I smiled, and poured the tea, and as we ate together, did so.

❧

After supper we retired to the comfortable chairs by the fire. I fed the kitten and ran downstairs to put a note out for Mr. Sifton the milkman for more eggs and butter and cream in the morning. There were no foxes, fairy or otherwise, in the alley. The sky was still clear, the stars bright overhead, but a fine crystalline precipitation was sifting down.

I went back upstairs and took out the knitting needles and wool. My father laughed soundlessly and then asked if he might borrow my whetstone, if we were going to be so very domestic.

Once we had settled into our places he said, "I have never heard of the Lord, either."

I was disappointed, but not surprised. "I will have to write to people. Scholars, librarians, any authors of books that seem useful."

"And are still alive."

"That too." I smiled at him. "I doubt answers to those questions are the sorts of visions I will have."

"It seems unlikely," he agreed lightly. "Far too useful."

The stone made a shirring rasp on his sword. The air was full of the scent of our supper and the faint metallic tang of the steel, the lanolin of the wool in my hands, the beeswax from the brace of candles on the side table.

"The Lord of the Purple and Gold," he said thoughtfully after a long, companionable silence. "The Lord of the Mountains and the Sea."

"That was all the Hunter would, or could, tell me. That, and that he is Lord of Autumn and Spring, as our Lady is Lady of Summer and Winter."

"Green and white, purple and gold." His hands stilled, stone and sword. "The Loëssie had a phrase they used. A password, and a ... proverb. It never made sense to me, but they said it as if it were the truth of all things. *Stone speaks to stone, and water to water.*"

The words fell into the room with a kind of portentousness. I shivered, feeling them land hard, like the strike of steel upon steel, sparking ... something.

I repeated the words quietly "Stone speaks to stone, and water to water."

"They could speak to stone, stone and ice. Their artistry was astonishing. They built palaces and fortresses out of the living mountains, out of the glaciers and the stone. Water and stone, ice and caverns. They did not do well with living things. We made overshoes of reeds to hide from their sight, their magic."

He shivered and fell silent, hands gripping the stone, the hilt of the sword, anchoring himself.

"Where does the Gate of Morning lead?" I asked, the riddle posed me by the Hunter.

"Bloodwater," my father replied. "On one side, at any rate, the side with the Border with Astandalas. Our side."

"And on the other?"

He let his hands relax. Stone fell to his lap; sword rested on his knees.

"On the other," he said, with a great sigh. "I cannot tell you, Jemis."

I stared at him. For all the conversations we had had, all the questions posed him, he had never yet answered what exactly had happened to him between being left to hold the Gate of the Morning against an army and returning home three years later after the Fall of Astandalas.

"Why not?"

He leaned back against his chair, closing his eyes in what almost seemed a prayer.

"I have never heard of the lost Lord," he said, "but I think I did see where he was bound."

CHAPTER TWENTY-EIGHT

I put another log on the fire. It flared up in golden sparks, warm against the winter night pressing close outside. I loved this kind of cozy evening, with a hot drink to hand and someone I loved close by.

My father watched me settle back down with the incipient cardigan. "Who are you knitting that for?" he asked. "One of your sisters?"

"No, I bought things in Orio City for them. It's for Ballory."

"You're knitting a sweater for a unicorn?"

"If she doesn't outgrow it before I'm even finished."

He laughed, rich and robust. "Oh Jemis! How glad I am I have this opportunity to know you."

It was one of the great, unfathomable gifts. I flushed, looking down at the thick green wool, soft and warm twisted around my fingers, in the small patch of cloth forming on my lap. "I am glad to know you," I replied, after clearing my throat.

He sat back with his coffee and the last piece of shortbread. "My tongue is bound," he said, an explanation that was not one. "I cannot tell you, tell anyone, unless they should ask precisely the right question."

"The Hunter did tell me it was the time for riddling." I worked the needles for a few stitches, thinking. Knitting was not quite as good as running for helping me settle my thoughts, but it was a good indoors option. As the loops formed, twisted, were caught on one needle and slid over to the other, I let my thoughts follow them.

All my questions had been answered with questions. Perhaps I should throw them back into the world and see what others replied.

"When is a trail not to be tracked?" I asked my father.

He sipped his coffee. Where did the beans come from now? Was there still *some* trade between worlds? Or did it come by way of merchants trading outside the bounds of the former empire, to the mysterious countries under those brighter days and darker nights?

Where did coffee even come from?

"When is a trail not to be tracked?" my father murmured out loud, turning the words in his mouth as I had in my mind. "When it is not your business, I suppose. What did you say?"

"Much the same. When you are not the hunter."

He grunted. I knitted. The fire crackled. He picked up his whetstone and turned his attention to his daggers, and started singing some of the old Winterturn carols.

I came to the end of the first ball of yarn and hesitated there, the end held pinched in my fingers. I had several balls remaining. They were smaller than the ones I had been taught on and I hadn't been sure of quantities.

"I think," my father said meditatively, "that I should like to see what the cards do in your hands now. Shall we play a game of Poacher?"

~

Halfway through the game my father hesitated and said, "Jemis."

I had to concentrate, for he was a far better player than I, and my experiences in the Bright Country seemed to have changed my response to the cards, or perhaps their responsiveness to me. From the Happenstance deck I picked up Crows and Crowns and Silver Swords and all sorts of other strange and wonderful things that rarely came more than once or twice a hand.

Magic and myth were in my hands tonight: a Golden Hind, with the crescent moon above her. Six Geese with their eggs below them, one of them as golden as the one Mr. Dart had said his duck had laid …

"Jemis," my father said again, and I looked up at him to see his eyes fixed intently on me.

He had laid down the Salmon of Wisdom.

We had spoken of this. My mind jumped back to his comments about *why*—but then it was my turn. I considered my hand. Considered the cards so far played.

My father set down the Seven Swans.

Seven Swans: there was an old fairy tale about them. The seven brothers turned into birds, and their sister who had to endure a year of silence and weave them all shirts of nettles to rescue them, and she had almost, almost succeeded when the magic caught up with her, and so her youngest and closest brother had forever after a swan's wing in place of his right arm, for she had not quite finished his shirt.

Salmon of Wisdom. Seven Swans. And third … third he laid down the Net.

Now the Net was a strange card to draw and a stranger one to lay down. Rounds of the game were often called Nets, but the version of Poacher my father had taught me held that the Fish were only the smallest part of the hand.

Salmon of Wisdom. ("When do you discard it, Jemis?")

Seven Swans. (Disguised brothers. A slightly-botched rescue. A brother with only one good arm.)

The Net … which catches, binds, holds together.

I met his glance then returned hastily to my cards. This was the time of riddles, the Hunter in the Green had told me. And the riddle that had landed directly in front of me was why my father *could not* tell me what had happened after Loe.

I considered my cards. If this were my father's code … if this were a curse … speaking aloud would likely trigger it. Therefore, cards only. In my hand I held the Crown and the Crow and the Golden Hind, the Six Geese; the Eel broken out of an eel-trap, the School of Minnows; and the Two Carp.

I set down the Golden Hind. *Is it to do with the Good Neighbours?*

239

We each drew our cards. Mine was the Fish Eagle, with lightning in its talons.

My father laid down the Flood.

Stone speaks to Stone, and Water to Water, he had said. Not the Gentry, then. The Loëssie.

My turn to lay down three cards.

Two Carp. The Eel. And for the third … I met his eyes and laid down the Six Geese.

The Two Carp, for my uncle Vorel again, whose wife had been conspiring with the priests of the Dark Kings. *Confirmation.* The Eel, escaping from its trap: *How?*

And the Geese, setting on eggs as they were … What were the fruits of this escape?

My father smiled slightly and laid down Friend with Boat.

Hal's Uncle Ben, my father's old commanding officer and great friend. The one whose rescue had stranded my father on the other side of the Border and the wrong side of the Fall of Astandalas.

Except … it was Friend with *Boat.*

We had to use the cards we drew; that was the joy and the trouble of the game. I studied the cards in their spreads on the table, and then we both drew.

Two from the deck of Fish, one from Happenstance for me.

I nearly dropped my cards as I glanced down at them. My father had laid down the Salmon of Wisdom, and here came the Grail, the cup which the Lady had blessed. A Great Storm followed; and the third card was Leviathan.

One of my earliest classes at Morrowlea had been the history of magical divination. Haruspexy had never worked for me, though I hadn't been entirely unsuccessful at dowsing. I should have been using cards.

I glanced at my father, and he looked down at his cards with nearly as troubled and triumphant an expression as I myself felt on my face.

"Show our hands, then?" I asked lightly, as for any game coming to its end.

He nodded and we laid our spreads down on the table, one card at a time. One always began with a Fish card.

He set down The Crab-Pot.

Captivity, or perhaps *Grasping Avarice*. Captivity seemed more likely.

I responded with the School of Minnows. *Confusion, Misdirection*; more literally, I was at school, at university. What was *he* learning?

A Happenstance card was next. His was A Special Messenger.

Assistance or *News*? Something surprising, something unexpected, at any rate. I thought back to the special messenger that had brought that unexpected letter from Mrs. Dart and set off our journey to Orio City. Or that other special messenger who had brought me letters from Hal and Lady Jessamine, promises of aid and alliance and also great upheaval in the wider world.

I set down the Crow. The calling birds following me as I ran across the Dartington lands towards the bridge where I had met the Hunter in the Green; the great rookery at the edge of the Woods Noirell; the crows that were supposed to be sacred, yet we had never heard to whom.

Were they sacred to that Lord who had been lost? Birds of the spring and the autumn, pecking corn and insects, gathering in great numbers. Birds of mischief, uncannily intelligent; never to be hunted, according to the ancient country practices.

My father laid down Sunset.

Sunset: when the fish rise; when the dew falls; when Astandalas, whose sign and symbol was the Sun-in-Glory, had fallen.

I was captive, but with surprising result, or *in surprising company*, the cards told me; *and then Astandalas Fell*.

And then, indeed.

I considered my remaining cards. The Crown, the Fish Eagle, the Grail; Leviathan; and A Great Storm.

I placed A Great Storm down, trembling with superstitious awe. The cards were not supposed to do this, for all that my father had always told me you could see the truth of a soul in the course of a game.

The truth of a soul, quite possibly: the truth of a past?

He set down The Wild Wood.

I closed my eyes, thinking hard. In the Interim, the great storm after the Fall, my father had been … lost, perhaps, in the forest. What forest? There were so many overtones to *the wild wood* in literature.

He had taught me ideographs with his book of haikus.

(He had kept that book of haikus through all the trials and tribulations, through the captivity and the sunset and the storm and the forest.)

The Wild Wood: the wood of confusion, of the body, of mortal confusion, of shadows, of sin. The wood of matter, of creation, of abundance; of fruitfulness and joy and earthly pleasure.

The wood of the Gentry, perilous and fair alike.

The Wood of Spiritual Refreshment, at the near edge of Paradise.

After the Storm, the Wild Wood.

To the Wild Wood … I hesitated, then set down the Fish Eagle with lightning in its claws. *How did you escape?*

He was ready with his next card. A Pearl Oyster.

He had far too many cards of the sea for my taste. Or—*no*.

I looked again at the sequence. The Crab-Pot: Captivity. A Special Messenger: Someone helped him escape or gave him what news he needed to do so. Sunset: the Fall. The Wild Wood: ambiguous. The Pearl Oyster: Treasure from the Sea.

He had come home to find his reputation in tatters and his wife married to another man, and been lost—we had thought at first by suicide, and then, much later, by murder—in the Arguty Forest. He had been sold to the pirate fleet and spent nearly a full seven years as a pirate slave on the *Blood Eagle*.

We had jumped ahead in his life, over the mystery.

An effective and insidious curse, I supposed. We would have to continue on and hope some unregarded comment would prove the necessary key, the metrical or poetical anomaly that showed the depths of meaning lying below the surface.

Against the Pearl Oyster I placed Leviathan.

They had not known what they had, those pirates; and the events that followed his time on the sea were ever more and more proving themselves not the fish we had expected to catch, but the great monster and wonder of the deeps rising in its own time, for its own purpose.

He set down his final card: The Wishing Fish, with a golden ring in its mouth.

I could not stop myself from smiling. So yes: the golden rings of Crimson Lake. And also the golden planet? Was this my father's circuitous answer? He had thrown away the Salmon of Wisdom to tell me what game we were playing, and presented me with the answer that one could never throw it away truly, for the ring would always return, one way or another.

He had come back from the reputed dead twice.

My last card was the Grail. I set it down with shaking hands.

I had come back from the literal, true, stone cold dead.

We paused there, looking at the spreads. In a proper game I had probably won.

"Good show, Jemis," my father said, something rueful in his eyes.

"Thank you, Papa," I replied, going to gather the cards together. He assisted me, but one card left in the decks caught on the edge of his sleeve and went flying into the air.

It landed face-down at my feet. I bent down to pick it up, knowing with a sudden, incontrovertible certainty that that had been no accident, no work of chance: it was the work of either the gods or my father's own indomitable will.

I scooped the card up and flipped it casually in my hand as I returned it to the deck.

The Dragon.

CHAPTER TWENTY-NINE

The Dragon.

Metaphorically—well, we returned to that question of the Crab-Pot. Avarice, gold-lust, blood-lust. Riddles and treasure hoards. Mortal peril. Magic. *Pre-Astandalan* magic.

What did I know of dragons?

Enough of their anatomy to kill one with a cake knife.

I shuffled the cards together, Fish with Fish and Happenstance with Happenstance. The Dragon was a Happenstance card. In the picture it sat on its gold, fire in its eyes and smoke rising from its nostrils. The mountain reached above it, sharp peaks and sharper shadows.

A dragon: wisdom, and the dangers of seeking too much knowledge.

What did I *know* of dragons, really?

"Thank you for the game," I said politely, handing my father back the cards. Message received, I hoped my expression said. I wasn't good enough with either the counting or the shuffling to be able to force a single card for him in response.

Prestidigitation was a skill in which I was lacking, really.

"Thank you," my father replied, and yawned. He covered his

mouth with a disappointed air. "I'm sorry. I think I must head back to Dartington."

It was six miles in the dark, and the night was cold. My father was hardly *old*, but then again—"You could stay here," I suggested.

"You've only the one bed," he pointed out.

I shrugged. I did not feel in the least sleepy. And besides, there were extra blankets. "I'll be fine," I assured him. "I'm not tired."

"Have you slept since you … died?" he asked after a moment. "Not just the swoon you were in after that strange episode with the biscuits."

For a moment I didn't understand what he could possibly mean, then hastened to reassure him. "Yes, I have slept. Eaten, too, and … the other bodily functions. Needed to shave, and, and so on."

He relaxed and chuckled wryly. "I apologize."

I thought of the cold sludgy doubts that had coiled through my own gut when he had first returned. Partly the curse, and partly … not. Thought of my own doubts, reassured in my turn by Mr. Dart. I stepped forward and embraced him. "I am corporeal, blood and bone and breath," I said into his chest. He smelled of iron and smoke and the outdoors. "Returned by the gift and grace of the Lady. No sorcerer raised me, no sunlight burns me, no silver scars."

"The banshee called for you but did not take you," he murmured back, his breath on the crown of my head. "I thought my heart would stop when I heard it crying, and its call was not for me."

Involuntarily I lifted one hand to rub my breast, where that cold cry had stabbed. "I felt it," I replied, even as his hands slipped to hold onto my shoulders as I lifted my head to look at his face. "Mr. Dart would not let me break the circle."

His hands clenched tight. "I am grateful to him."

"As am I."

He exhaled hard, and we stood there for a moment longer, his hands no longer clutching but resting strong and secure on my shoulders. I thought of the touch of the Hunter in the Green, supporting me and reassuring me as I turned to look at the sky above, the land around. I had trusted the Hunter because I had had this: I had my father to stand beside and behind me, to go before me, to be my model and my teacher and my guide.

And yet—my father had a riddle to give me, that *I* could unravel it for *him*. I was no longer a child, and even if I had not yet come officially into adulthood, yet I was coming into my own. I could stand beside and behind him, go before him even in those areas I had studied and he had not.

"I'll sleep here tonight, thank you," he said finally, and let me go.

∾

I sat before the fire, the knitting in my hands and my thoughts full of many questions.

There were the ciphers in the *New Salon*, which I was well on my way to decoding. I needed another few hours with Hurtleman's Syllabary to finish off the transcriptions, but I had enough to be sure of what they contained. Movements of ships and men, goods and information, all on behalf of the Knockermen.

I tugged the ball of yarn away from the kitten, who had sleepily begun to play with it. Powderpuff meeped quietly and then curled up in the small basket I had found to hold my work. Well, I didn't suppose Ballory would mind much if there were a few stray cat hairs on her cardigan.

I shook out the cloth and decided it was just about long enough for the purpose. Two more rows and then the sleeves. I was doing *them* in the easiest fashion, further rectangles which I would then sew together into tubes. Watching Mrs. Pritchard knitting in the round the other night had made it very clear I was nowhere near ready for that level of craft. The stripes had been daring enough.

The fairy fox was a mystery. If we—Mr. Dart and I, that was—were clever enough we could find their name.

I thought about the fox. The two-tailed fox ... who had been the one to talk about seeing the Twa-Tailed Vixen earlier? Was it Hagwood the Arguty factor, who had been swept away by the Magarran Flood in the wake of throwing his lot in with the priests of the Dark Kings? Or was it one of the Dartington folk?

If it was one of the Dartington folk, they might well know more stories. The Gentry were somewhat local: those whose realms bordered ours were known in our histories and legends. There would be stories *somewhere* of the two-tailed fox and what they portended.

I finished the main body of the cardigan and tied off my yarn. There was more to learn about the Hunter in the Green ... the obvious place to start there was with the Honourable Rag, who had chosen him as his alias for a reason. Presumably.

I cast on the yarn for the first of the sleeves. Legs? I tilted my head. This was a cardigan in effect, so sleeves. I could wish I had thought to measure Ballory's legs while she was here last, but, well ... if I made them sufficient for my forearm that would surely work.

The needles clicked soothingly. I was getting better at looking up while knitting, and stared at the flames in the wood stove. Counting the stitches was a calming as counting the feet of a metre, my steps as I ran a measured length. Down the arc of the rainbow, the stone bridge over the Dartwater, the Hunter's Road.

The Wild Hunt had come on the longest night, the Lady's Eve. They had come howling down the wings of the storm, down the path marked by their lanterns, from the passages in the Woods Noirell along the Lady's Way, the Gentry's Road, until they hit the circle of safety walked by my father, held by Mr. Dart.

There they had stopped and circled, testing the protections woven around me.

The fire crackled and a spray of sparks flurried up. I jerked and lost a stitch, had to stop and count it over again.

I had been born under a *contrary star*, my father had said. Under the conjunction of Dwile and Heor, my mother had told me as a child. My mother had bound protections around my cradle, fearing *they* would come to steal me away.

Mrs. Henny and Mrs. Pritchard had told me that my mother had invited 'all the fairies save one' to my christening.

I would have been christened in the Woods. It was *necessary* that such ceremonies were done in the Woods. That was why I was my mother's legitimate heir and Sela was not. Not so much because of the second marriage, bigamous according to Fiellanese law, but because the marriage to Mr. Buchance had not occurred within the Woods, at the hidden chapel only certain people had ever found.

I had been taken there that once, when I was nine. It was a natural cave turned into a church, the living stone walls damp with condensation, strange fungi and plants growing at the edge of the light. It had been beautiful, perilous, of the Lady but not only.

Of the Lady but not only … and the lost Lord was Lord of the Mountains and the Sea.

I turned the wool in my hands. The kitten was purring. The night outside was quiet. My father snorted and rolled over and then began to snore.

I smiled. My father had a mystery tangled around him, a curse and a question. Or a gift? He might be bound with the Lady's grace as I was; might have seen *too much* for mortal eyes. He had not known of the Lord, but he thought he might have seen where the god was bound.

What *could* bind a god, beyond their own will?

Were the Dark Kings gods? Theologically that was a bit suspect, I was sure. I started another row of the sleeve, the short lengths coming quickly, my wooden needles flashing gold in the firelight. Green and purple were the yarn, rich in the gloaming.

Our Lady of the Green and White. Our Lord of the Purple and Gold.

Purple and gold. The saffron crocuses came to mind, lavender petals and fire-orange stamens, scattered along the verges of a road, a place where Hal had never expected to see them.

Vernal crocuses were a rich royal purple and a flaming egg-yolk yellow, blazing heraldic colours across the greensward of the spring landscape. Yellow laburnum, golden chain trees, blooming next to certain wells; purple windflowers, purple bluebells in every half-shaded dell, yellow primroses at their feet. Purple heather on the mountains; yellow gorse, autumn bracken blazing gold.

Purple seaweed on the beaches of northern Fiellan, of Ghilousette. Yellow amber washed up from who-knew-where. Hal had shown me an ancient heirloom in his treasury, amber and amethyst in a crown older than his family's records

The lost Lord was everywhere, now that I knew to look. If I followed the colours, the heraldry of universities and ancient families, would I find out the footsteps of the god on the land before he was lost?

Gather your allies.

I did not have to go to each of those libraries, each of those universities, each of those stately houses myself. The Darts were an ancient family—Mr. Dart's predilection for wearing purple came inching to mind, even if I did not know what to do with *that*—

He was the Lady's Champion. Chosen, and choosing, to be that.

Chosen for *what*?

The bindings of Astandalas had broken in the Fall. They had bound worlds together; they had bound the Dark Kings.

They had not, if I had understood the Hunter correctly, bound the Lord. That did not mean that the loosened bindings and changed magic had not affected whatever kept him captive.

Mr. Dart. Mr. *Peregrine* Dart. With his unicorn, Ballory, sent as the Lady's Champion, sent to fight against the dark, sent to guard the way, protect those who needed it.

And me?

Sent back from the Bright Countries with messages from those gone ahead of us. Sent back to close the gate opened by my death, by my chosen sacrifice and that unchosen one the dark priests had intended.

Sent to stand beside the Champion; sent to riddle, and to fight, and to run.

Riddles first.

The fire sputtered again, and I looked down to see the sleeve a good six inches longer than was likely necessary. Well … perhaps not, if Ballory kept growing. I cast off anyway, added few more logs to the fire, and started in on the second sleeve.

Lark and the Indrillines, the Knockermen and the wireweed, the Lady and the Rainbow-Girt Isle, now emerging from its fogs and mists. Hal the Imperial Duke and I, new Viscount St-Noire, allies in politics and also in magic.

I smiled as my eyes fell on the hat Mrs. Ayden had given me. Allies also in fashion, and changing that fashion. Magic was out of fashion, but that did not need to be permanent.

Allies I had, and continued to gain. I would not spurn those who had no apparent political might to wield. This fight was not only in the back rooms of Swordage's club for gentlemen, not only in the Parliament of Chare and the court of Kingsbury, not only in the hostages held in Orio City and the prisoners who had escaped thence.

The Embroidery Circle held wisdom and cunning. Mrs. Etaris held not only the wealth of her bookstore and all the knowledge and wisdom contained therein, but also all the skills and courage and memories of being Jullanar of the Sea, one of the greatest heroes of Astandalas. Of Alinor.

Jullanar of the Sea, who had *dipped her hand into the River of Stars*. Jullanar of the Sea, who had been courted by a fairy king. Jullanar of the Sea, who edited Fitzroy Angursell's poetry to be *more* revolutionary. Jullanar of the Sea, who had *started* the rebellion in Galderon.

Jullanar of the Sea, who had reached out her hand kindly to help me up when I was slipping.

My mother, and all the folk of the Woods. Mr. White, the innkeeper from another world, holding a faint faith that his family had not all perished in the Fall, that he might yet be able to receive word or send it. The Bee at the Border was the heart of the village of St-Noire. There would be much to learn there, if I could.

The wool moved under my hands, the tension more even than it had been. The green thread forming green sleeves, green for the Lady, for the Hunter, for the holly in winter and the hawthorn in summer. Green for the unicorn come as herald and agent of change. Purple for violets, for Mr. Dart's favourite colour, for the spring and the autumn of the year.

We had until the unicorn bloodied her horn, the Hunter had said. The Ánhorn, that bloodied horn, lay on the mantle next to the plum pudding given me by the Hunter. The time to fight would come.

The scar on my hand tingled. That had a purpose and a meaning to it, too, that I would need to uncover.

Are you patient enough to await the truth? the Wild Saint had asked me.

Three warnings had the fox given me, and three gifts, and three questions in answer to three questions of mine. Nine was a magical number ... but somehow it did not seem quite *right*.

The Lady and the Lord. Winter and Summer, Spring and Autumn. Four seasons; twelve months of the year—

Twelve days of Winterturn.

Three days for the fairy fox. Three days for the Hunter. Three days for mortal festivities—

And then three days for the *servant of the unknown*.

CHAPTER THIRTY

I fell asleep in the chair and woke with a crick in my neck and a thrill of excitement, the tenth day of Winterturn.

At some level below my conscious mind I had solved a puzzle.

I knew from past experience that I would need to be patient —*patient as the grave*—in order for the answer to surface. Or perhaps it was that I already knew the answer, had always known the answer, but had not known the question.

All those questions I had been asked this week. All those questions I myself had asked in turn. One of them was the key to *something*.

The dragon on its hoard; the binding on my father's tongue; the fairy fox's name. Where to start looking for the lost Lord of Spring and Autumn.

Something.

~

My father was already up and had managed to relight the fire, boil a kettle of water, make coffee, and was in the process of frying bacon, all without waking me despite my close proximity to the stove.

"That smells divine," I said without thinking, surprising him into laughter. I pushed the chair back from the wood stove and stretched, yawning as I watched him stir the pan.

"Was there bacon and coffee in the Lady's Country?"

"There was *some* sort of food," I replied. "I don't remember that part very clearly. What time is it?"

"Time for you to be up," Mr. Dart said from the doorway. A clatter of hooves indicated Ballory had accompanied him. I glanced down hurriedly, but my father had bundled away the cardigan and wool so it was out of sight. I cast him a grateful smile; he winked conspiratorially.

"You are in an excellent mood this fine morning," Mr. Dart observed, sitting down at the table and looking hopefully at the bacon. "Is there enough to share? I've been up since long before dawn. It's market day, you know. Your Mrs. Etaris is looking somewhat frazzled."

"I *am*," I said, with rather too much emphasis. They looked at me. "I have realized something," I said, but it was too tentative and too glorious to share without a smidgen more proof. I was as certain of my intuition as I had been for Ariadne's poem, for Mrs. Etaris's true identity, but I knew well enough from those two announcements that no one would believe me without having all the facts well arrayed.

But that Hunter! He was just as clever as in all the stories.

~

I went downstairs and took over running the bookstore for the market, leaving my father and Mr. Dart (and Ballory) to go out and report back on the various minor excitements and disasters of the day. I was too busy to think much: customers came in looking for last-minute presents for their friends and families.

They gossiped about the unicorn foal clattering along behind Mr. Dart as he examined the stalls on offer. They talked about my hat, and my long coat, and reminisced about the days when the great lords and ladies of Alinor had passed along the old Imperial Highway on their way to Astandalas the Golden.

Seven different people told me that Father Rigby didn't know what to make of the account of Mr. Dart's miracle, and four more asked, in all earnestness, if that 'lady friend who dressed as a man' was the one who'd rescued me from prison.

I sold books of poetry, of fiction, of scholarship and humour, on the history of gate hinges and the many kinds of efts.

Jullanar Maebh and Hope came in around midday, just at the tail end of a great rush. I smiled at them as they entered and continued helping Mrs. Kulfield gather up the change she had dropped.

"You haven't heard anything of the expedition, have you?" she asked.

"Hal hasn't said," I replied. "I don't think he's expecting word until the spring at the earliest. The last point of contact was the Fury Islands, I think."

West of the Fury Islands was the great ocean. There were rumours of a continent on its far side—the great sailors of the Outer Reaches had gone so far in their old stories, seeking fish and fur—but no one had anything more substantive than stories of green hills and schools of fish so thick the boats stood still in the water.

She smiled sadly, but also proudly. "He was so excited, my Roddy."

"I'm sure he's a great asset to the ship. I'll let you know if Hal tells me anything, Mrs. Kulfield."

She patted me on my hand and took her change and little parcel of books. She'd been a good friend to my mother, and a good neighbour to me in that tempestuous period after my mother's death and before I went to Morrowlea, when I feared I was of no pleasant company to anyone.

I'd given her lemons and a small book on the *Legends of the Far West* I'd found in Orio City. She now set a small tin on the counter. "Biscuits," she said, smiling at me. "Keep well, Mr. Greenwing."

She went out, and Jullanar Maebh and Hope drifted over. Both had found a book, and Jullanar Maebh's expression was less pinched than it had been the last time we'd spoken. She also looked considerably less peaky. "You're looking well, Miss Dart," I said, smiling at her. "Miss Stornaway."

"Mr. Greenwing," Hope replied, her eyes glinting with amusement as she curtsied. "I'm surprised to see you … work here?"

"Mrs. Etaris very kindly gave me a job in the autumn, before I learned of my inheritance," I replied. "I enjoy it. My stepfather was a merchant, you know."

Jullanar Maebh looked as if she suspected me of mocking her, though I could not think why, and set her chosen book on the counter with a firm slap. It was *A History of Southern Fiellan*. I picked it up, unfamiliar with the author's name.

There was a map of the three baronies in the frontispiece. I looked at the familiar roads and rivers. It had been done before the Fall, and the tiny hamlets that had once been scattered along the land between Ragnor Bella and the Woods Noirell were still shown.

There was the Coombe, and Ragnor Parva. I traced my finger down the line of the river that ran out of the Coombe to join the Rag near Dartington. There was the bridge where I had met the Hunter.

There was the Old Chapel, which was marked; the Ellery Stone and the Lady's Pools were not, no doubt of little interest to the Astandalan historian who had written the book.

But there was the dotted line of the Gentry's Road, the Lady's Way. It was labelled *Sir Peregrine's Ride*.

It drew a line from the *other side* of the Woods Noirell straight through the Old Chapel to the Savage Crux—there was the cross-line of the Giants' Road—and north to end—

There. The Fourfold Stone, where Lind and the Farry March and Fiellan and Ronderell all met.

"Did you find something interesting, Jemis?" Hope asked. Her tone was much the same as it had always been at Morrowlea when I got going on some splendid discovery in a poem and she and Hal would listen politely before decamping to talk about natural philosophy.

I grinned at her. "I did. I had wondered where this track ended up."

Another answer to the Hunter's question: One might not be *able* to follow a certain trail.

Right now I could not follow the Lady's Way, Sir Peregrine's Ride, the Gentry's Road. Not *yet*. Not yet. When Ballory was grown perhaps Mr. Dart might be able to ride her, if she grew to such a stature as the grand unicorn stallion in my visions, but that would not be the way I ran.

I thought of the air under my feet, the arc of the sky holding me up, as I ran down the Hunter's path. There might be some gift—

"You're looking rather fey again," Hope whispered softly as I moved to wrap up her book, a perishingly dull account of the stratigraphic profile of the Crosslains I had bought in Orio City. I glanced at her; she gave me a small, bright, dimpled smile. "Just so you know."

~

The Honourable Rag blew in that afternoon, after my father had come in with cheese rolls courtesy of Mr. Inglesides the baker. He had brought mulled wine as well, from the vendor who always set up for the Winterturn market under the statue of the Emperor Artorin, and I was feeling warm and cozy when Roald arrived. He was dressed in his scarlet breeches but he had a new coat, still black but in the early Artorian style; it was embroidered in gold.

I grinned at him. "That was quick."

"It's m'grandfather's," he admitted, running a hand down the embroidered wool.

"It fits well."

He accepted the compliment with a wry smile, which shifted immediately to vacuity as several matrons came into the store, chattering like crows. "Can't let you run too far ahead of the rest of us," he said, with a wink as he collected a copy of the *New Salon* and threw a Taran florin down on the table in excessive payment.

I flicked his change to him, a copper bee spinning through the air to be snatched easily in one large hand. He paused, a hand at the door. "Aye?"

"Come back when you've read that," I said, nodding at the paper. "I have some gossip for you."

He laughed in his penetrating fashion and whirled out. I could only assume he'd taken my meaning, and turned to the good matrons, who'd heard the word 'gossip' and were all ears.

"You're in the headline," one gasped, unfolding the paper to see *JEMIS GREENWING ESCAPES INESCAPABLE PRISON.*

Oh, Lark, I thought, nearly fondly, and leaned forward to tell them all about it.

~

We sold out the entire run of *New Salons* over the course of market day, which was entirely unsurprising. That evening I joined Mrs. Buchance and my sisters for a meal. My father was back at Dart Hall, but Mr. Inglesides and his wife and their children were there, along with a man a few years older than I whom Mr. Inglesides introduced as 'Johan Klyme, my good friend from when I studied pastry-making in Cullorth.'

I had not known Mr. Inglesides had studied pastry-making in Cullorth, and finding out the details of that was an acceptable and quite interesting topic of conversation, especially when I eventually clued into the fact that Mr. Inglesides had invited his friend to meet his widowed sister.

Six months of full mourning had passed, and Mrs. Buchance was now in the same position Mr. Buchance had been with my mother's death: alone with several small children, a strange if not estranged older stepson, and a goodly fortune.

With that in mind I turned the conversation more to Mr. Klyme. I trusted Mr. Inglesides with his sister's heart and fortune, but these were *my* sisters.

Mr. Klyme was obviously a bit taken aback by my sudden interest in his family back in Cullorth, his training as a affineur—someone who aged cheeses, it turned out—and his present occupation as an importer and exporter of fine cheeses.

"And you," he said finally, as we moved on from the main course of roast chicken to a selection of cheeses he had brought as a hosting gift. I was pleased to determine they were all excellent. "You're a … bookseller, I understand?"

I had begun the conversation that evening with a humorous account of a few incidents from the store that appealed to Sela's somewhat bloodthirsty sense of humour (Lauren was only interested in news of Ballory, Powderpuff, and Crumpet), so I supposed that was a reasonable question.

I did glance at Mrs. Buchance, who blushed, and Mr. Inglesides, who only grinned. My presence at the table had been explained by my relation to Mrs. Buchance as her late husband's first wife's son by her first marriage, and Jemis was not, as my mother had assured me, an unusual name in Mr. Klyme's part of the world.

Mr. Klyme was looking somewhat confused and a little unhappy about our reaction. If he'd been merely a visitor I should likely have left it at that, but seeing as Mrs. Buchance did not seem averse to his potential courtship, I gave him an empathetic smile.

"I do apologize, Mr. Klyme," I replied cheerfully. "I am so used to my doings being known I forget that not everyone is conversant with our village gossip. My surname is Greenwing, and I am the Viscount St-Noire. I do, however, presently work in the bookstore."

Mr. Klyme stared at me, his jaw loose. He was a tall, rangy sort of man, good looking in a dour way, with dark hair and a strong jaw. He was good with the girls, and even Sela seemed to like him. Mrs. Buchance could certainly do worse; and Ragnor Bella really *could* do with a cheese shop.

The children had been sent up to play after greeting us earlier, but now came thundering down in an exuberant chaotic mess.

They stumbled to a ragged halt in the doorway, my sisters and their cousins, all making cows eyes after Lauren ascertained that I had not somehow produced either Ballory or the kittens since she had been gone.

Sela was, as always, the boldest. She made a curtsey, almost a proper one, and then giggled and rushed up to tug at my sleeve.

"Are you done, Jemis? Will you come play Milkmaids? Jemis, if you play with us we'll have enough for a full game. Jemis, we haven't seen you in *ages*."

I looked down at her with amused skepticism. Sela twisted the end of her braid and grinned up at me. Her fine, fair hair was coming out of the plaits, but her expression was so much like my mother's in the Lady's Country I could not resist for long.

Well—I *was* the youngest of the adults, by all of five years from Mrs. Buchance. I grinned at the table, begged excuse of my absence, and let Sela lead me upstairs to play a noisy and complicated game of tag.

～

It snowed the next day. Mrs. Etaris had decreed it a proper holiday, for a reason I wasn't entirely sure of—the eleventh day of Winterturn was not one of the high days—but which I did not contest. I slept in and then went for a long run along the snowy roads of the barony.

Down to the Woods Noirell first, where I checked to ensure all the ordered supplies had arrived as planned. Only one cartload was yet to arrive, Mr. White the innkeeper told me, and that was the second load of hams.

"All the staples have arrived," he assured me over a glass of his mead. It was a fierce drink, spiced with nutmeg and something fiery, and he served it in tiny crystal glasses. The inn had been a rich place once, famous in song and story. It was all closed up now, but the taproom was clean and merry, the three fireplaces roaring and a goodly number of villagers gathered there.

There was always firewood, at least. I well remembered my mother telling me that the villagers had *rights*.

The more I learned of my mother, the less surprising it was that I had come to be such an ardent revolutionary in temperament. Even my father, for all he had fought for the Empire's banner, was no stranger to thoughtful political criticism either. He had nothing to say against the Emperor Artorin, whose wars he had fought; but he did not shy from speaking against the last governors of Northwest Oriole.

I thought of Fitzroy Angursell's poem, still folded in the pocket of my coat. What an inflammatory piece that would be, if I found the right moment and the right means to publish it.

"I couldn't find word of any letters sent astray," I told the innkeeper, who did not seem surprised by this news. "I did find that there are many ways to mis-say *St-Noire*, however, so I have a few places to write for to try."

"Don't take too much trouble over it," Mr. White said. "There's probably nothing, after so long."

At least he would see his family on the other side, I hoped, whatever his faith and theirs.

"I'll write, at any rate," I said, "in case anything new comes. There hasn't been any post since you awoke, has there?"

He shook his head. "Only the wagons you sent." He frowned down at his mead, then forced a bright smile. "For which we are all grateful."

This was the season of family and coming together in thanksgiving against the dark. I was sorry not to have better news for him. Another set of letters to add to those I would need to start writing soon.

"Where are you from?" I asked hesitantly. "If you'd like to tell me, that is."

He glanced around at the cozy, snug room, the snow falling in large flakes outside the diamond-paned windows, the fires roaring in the hearth. The scent of venison roasting on the fire, and the honeyed mead in our glasses.

"An island very far away," he said, his eyes crinkling with a secret mirth. "I'd never seen snow before I came here. My cousin wrote about seeing the first snowfall in Astandalas, how at first he thought someone had ripped open a bag of feathers in the floor above above him and was shaking them down. I didn't believe him when he said people wore *gloves*. The thought was inconceivable."

Gloves *inconceivable*? I stared at him, but he didn't seem to be joking.

"It's a warm country, then?"

"Aye. Islands in a sea the colour of your coat. The most beautiful place in all the Nine Worlds ..." He cast a look towards one of the back rooms of the inn, and his face shifted from wistfulness to a gentle, sorrowful smile. "Except for where my wife is. And my brother died before the Fall and then ... my cousin ..." He sighed. "He was in Astandalas when it Fell. I have more family at home but ... it wouldn't be the same without him. I'm not sure I could find my way back to living there if he wasn't there with me."

Mr. Dart was my bear-baiter, Hal had said: the one who led where I followed. Mr. White had followed his cousin to Alinor and stayed where his heart had found its home, but without his cousin to call him home?

I would not have come back from *my* heart's home if Mr. Dart had not called me.

The subterranean realizations were stirring, nearly come to my waking mind. I had to let them come in their own time. Soon. Soon.

"I'll write again," I said, wondering if Hal was right and the Zuni ambassador to Nên Corovel could be of assistance. "What is the name of your ... island?"

Something sharp flashed in his eyes at the question. "Loaloa," he said quietly, with an astounding certainty. He smiled slowly. "Loaloa in the Vangavaye-ve."

CHAPTER THIRTY-ONE

I had a dream that night, Twelfthday eve.

It began in the Dower Cottage; which was, and was not, the one of my childhood. There were herbs hanging to dry and preserves lined up in neat rows on the shelves of the pantry, but the dishes were not those my mother had chosen, and the jars were those designed by my stepfather.

In my dream I was washing dishes when someone knocked on the door.

I set the goblet in my hands on the drying board, noting with an absent-minded air that it was the Grail from my father's deck of Poacher, and wiped my hands on the shining silver-green scarf I had found in Fitzroy Angursell's bag.

At the door was the Hunter, and on his arm a woman dressed all in violet except for her veil, which was gold. She was barefoot, with rings on her toes and golden bells jingling on her ankles.

I bowed to them, my cocked hat falling into my hand as I gestured them to come in.

"Be welcome across my threshold," I said, the words my mother had used with all those importunate men, my father's old soldiers, when they had come hat in hand to beg her assistance. "Come in peace and felicity and be welcome."

In the sky outside the door I could see the five planets shining: Kivroth and Heorl, Dwile and Tazra, and the fifth golden planet, the jovial sign of the lost Lord.

The Hunter's horns reached the ceiling, bearing streamers of stars and mist with them, and he wore garlands of ivy and hawthorn blossoms, their scent heavy as summer.

The veiled woman had primroses and violets springing up around her feet, cowslips and crocuses. She stood before the Heart of Glory on the wall, her face hidden.

I wore the Ánhorn at my belt, not the sword but the bloody unicorn horn.

The Hunter said, "What have you already learned? Where are you already going?"

And the veiled woman, in a voice that was in my mind alone: "Are you daring enough to hear the truth?"

〜

My tutor at Morrowlea had taught me to start with the obvious, just in case.

When I woke the next morning the first thing I did was to check the Ánhorn, and the second to do my dishes. The sword was a sword; and none of my cups had turned into the Holy Grail.

I had finished the cardigan for Ballory and had enough yarn and time left over to make a matching scarf for Mr. Dart. I wrapped them and the other presents for my various friends and family in brown paper and used the ribbons I had bought off Mrs. Ayden to close the parcels.

That done, I went downstairs and looked in a map of the barony I had found the day before.

There was the River Raggle coming out of the Coombe. And there was the smaller stream Mr. Dart and I had always called the Dartwater, which was not the same water at all.

I traced its course. Downriver into the East Rag, of course; it joined the larger river opposite Dart Hall.

Upriver it meandered through the Darts' water-meadows to the upper pastures and the edge of the woods cloaking the lower foothills of the Crosslains. And there was the bridge where I had met the Hunter.

That portion of the track I had been running, which I had run so many times before, was part of the Lady's Way. The Gentry's Road. Sir Peregrine's Ride.

I traced the path marked on the map. Northwards it ran to the thousand-year oak at the upper corner of the Darts' land. That was where I had joined it, coming up the lane from the Hartlebees' farm to the old sunken road that disappeared in the woods as they imperceptibly became the Arguty Forest.

South to the bridge, and if one continued on the path, the road took one straight across the fields to a dry oxbow bend and a second thousand-year oak that stood sentinel at the southern edge of the Squire's land.

Beyond that was a jumble of rocks that might once have been a building, or perhaps a bridge, and on the other side of that the path was marked *impassible*.

I returned to the Dartwater. It ran very nearly down the middle of the space between the two great oaks.

And eastward?

Eastward the stream's course was marked as far as the ring of nine standing stones known as the False Witnesses. You went there, Dartington people said, when there was no other recourse.

The modern Shaian *False* sounded rather like *Falaist*, the Old Oriolan word for *Star* according to my new grammar.

The map did not mark any of the standing stones, but I plotted them out using coins from my pocket.

The Ellery Stone. The Dragon Stone. The False Witnesses. The Fourfold Stone.

I considered the pattern starting to take form, and used smaller coins to mark the market cross in Ragnor Bella, the pile of the Giants' Castle at the bight of the river, the White Cross.

The Lady's Cross, the stone at the mouth of Ragnor Parva in the Coombe.

I was missing some, that was clear. But what was also clear was that the standing stones marked two arcs whose centre was somewhere on the Darts' land.

I reckoned, estimating directions and distances, that it would fall somewhere about the middle of the pear orchard. The Lúsa Tree. The Lord's Oak.

Are you brave enough to seek that answer? the Wild Saint had asked me.

Are you clever enough to follow that trail? the fox had asked in their turn.

Do you dare to hear that truth? had been the question of the veiled woman in my dream.

My hand was tingling. Before I could begin to answer the questions in my own mind there came a knock on the door, and Mr. Dart entered. It was Winterturn morning, and I was surprised to see him so far from Dartington.

"I'm collecting you for lunch, you ingrate," he said at my inquisitive look.

I laughed, as he wasn't able to keep a straight face for even that statement. "Ah yes, nothing to do with avoiding the pageant."

"Tor's showing Jullanar Maebh off to everyone," he muttered. "I've been supportive and shown myself pleased to see her and have her here, but people have started to realize she's Tor's heir, and ... I don't know how you do it, Jemis, I really don't."

I remembered his confessional in the dark of the solstice night. I smiled crookedly at him. "At least you already know you have something more exciting ahead of you."

He slumped against the counter, playing with the coin I'd used to mark the False Witnesses. "Do I?"

His hand brushing against the map had jolted the coins out of their places. They had bounced—was it his wild magic working on them?—to form a loose circle centred not on the orchard but on Dart Hall itself. He glanced down, following my gaze.

"Have I thrown it all out of alignment? My apologies."

"Not at all," I replied, scooping up the coins and replacing them in my pocket. "I'd already seen what I needed to. Shall we?"

"You are looking disgustingly pleased with yourself," Mr. Dart murmured.

I collected my basket of gifts, tucked the Hunter's plum pudding in the top, and refused to answer.

"Come now," Mr. Dart said, giving up on extracting a response. "Let us be off, unless you have more to do today?"

"Merely to lock the door," I replied, and accordingly fetched my hat and my long teal coat. "I noticed that the Honourable Roald Ragnor is sporting a more complex cravat these days. And his grandfather's coat."

Mr. Dart settled his sling on his shoulder as he held the door for me. "One must be to the point," he replied in a fair imitation of the Honourable Rag's most irritating tone. "It would not do for the baron's son to fail to follow the lead set by those in the foremost rank."

I rolled my eyes and greeted several passersby whom I recognized from the bookstore. The square was busy with people setting up bunting and greenery for the festivities that night. Ragnor Bella mostly celebrated the newer parts of the holiday, the ones that coincided with the Astandalan holiday of Silverheart. That was a holiday for family, for feasting and singing and a bonfire in the market square.

The bonfire was older than Astandalas, I guessed. Dartington would have kept theirs burning every night since Solstice Eve until New Year's Day tomorrow.

We would be feasting the new year in and exchanging our gifts at Dart Hall tonight.

But first—

First the feast at Dart Hall, and then the Wassail to rouse the orchard and reclaim the night for the New Year to come and the Lady's work through the coming winter. My hand tingled with some strange anticipation.

～

Mr. Dart had brought his riding horse and a spare mount for me.

It had been months since I last rode, and it was a pleasant surprise to get to do so today. I mounted the chestnut, who was in a frisky mood but not entirely unresponsive for all that. Mr. Dart's own fine blood bay was in excellent form, obviously eager for another six-mile run. I empathized. Still, I had a sack full of presents and was glad enough not to be carrying them myself.

I let Mr. Dart lead the way, through town and up onto the road leading uphill from the humpback bridge to the highway. He took it at an easy canter despite the slope. My horse followed without strain or apparent effort, and I was reminded of how much I had loved riding when I was younger.

"Will you be buying yourself a horse?" Mr. Dart asked as we slowed to a walk at the top of the hill. I urged my horse abreast of his, and considered this. "You can afford one now."

Since I had inherited the half of Mr. Buchance's fortune, indeed. "I hadn't thought," I replied truthfully. "My father might like one."

He had been a cavalry officer, once upon a time, though it must have been many years since he had last ridden himself. I did not think he had done so since arriving back in Ragnor Bella, and it seemed unlikely he had on his way there.

Mr. Dart rode easily, balancing the weight of his stone arm without difficulty. It had been nearly four months since he received it, in that strange mist the Grey Priest had used to try to capture me.

No word of complaint, though no magic user or physician had yet to even begin to heal it. Perhaps he needed a miracle; or perhaps he needed Ballory to grow older, so that her horn could cause the stone to dissolve once more into flesh and blood and bone.

At the White Cross we came across one of the many portions of the Dartington Winterturn pageant, this one a large group of drummers and pipers playing in loud cacophony to scare off the haunts.

Which no longer included my father, or at least not in spiritual form, as he was standing amongst the crowd of observers.

I dismounted and walked my horse behind the crowd to join him. He was a little by himself, not quite part of the throng but not separate from it either. I could see that there were those keeping a wary eye on him.

"I think they're concerned I might take a scare from the pipers," he murmured by way of a greeting, then yawning. "It's too early for this. I must be getting old."

I grinned at him. "Would you like to ride the rest of the way?"

"So you can run?" He considered the horse, and then Mr. Dart, and then shrugged. "Very well. Are you on your way to Dart Hall?"

"Yes," I said, happily.

"You know something," my father said without heat.

"I've realized something," I corrected him.

He paused in the act of letting the horse sniff his hand. The horse, intrigued, lipped at his fingers. I patted it on its velvet muzzle and wondered once more if Ballory would grow so tall as this, or if she would stay the size of a small dog.

"Realized what?" he asked suspiciously.

But I could only pass him the reins and smile, and look at the basket of gifts in my hand.

CHAPTER THIRTY-TWO

F or Winterturn lunch there was Master Dart, Sir Hamish, Mr. Dart, Jullanar Maebh, Hope, my father, myself, and Mr. Dart's Aunt Millicent, who had always disapproved of me.

She still did, it was evident, but my title had mollified her to my presence.

"I had thought," she said when I greeted her in the parlour before we sat down to dine, "that you had decided no longer to follow our old country customs."

I had spent Winterturn at Morrowlea all three years of my degree, partially due to my own alienation from my awkward family situation and partially due to the exhortations of Lark.

"Winterturn at Morrowlea was magical," Hope put in, smiling winningly at Aunt Millicent. The old woman softened and actually asked Hope for more details.

"She's entirely won over Aunt Millicent," Mr. Dart murmured in my ear. "I'm inclined to add it to the tally of your minor miracles."

"If it were one of mine," I said, "she'd like me better."

"You don't know Aunt Millicent," he replied, shaking his head. "She doesn't believe in extravagant displays of piety. Thinks they're vulgar."

~

We ate a fine roast goose and all the trimmings: braised red cabbage and apples, bread sauce, onion stuffing, gravy, carrots, parsnips. Afterwards we had a great flaming pudding.

It was literally on fire, burning with alcoholic blue flames. We all regarded the arrival of the dish with some amazement.

"It's an Outer Reaches custom Jullanar Maebh has shared with us," the Squire said, with a fond smile at his daughter. She smiled back at him, and I was glad that Mr. Dart's discussion with her about her traditions had borne such fruit as this.

"We light the Winterturn pudding on fire," Jullanar Maebh said, "to remind us of the light in the dark that the Lady brings, and that we share."

"I believe the pudding is the one you brought, Jemis, and thank you," the Squire added, turning an almost equally fond smile on me. "It is a great gift and appropriate to the season to share our traditions and our foods along with our company and our gifts."

"Hear, hear," Sir Hamish replied, raising his glass of wine in a toast.

I regarded the pudding. It was at least four times the size of the one the Hunter in the Green had given me, but then again—what did I know of a divine gift? All I knew was what I had myself experienced and what I had learned from Abbot Bollé's book about saints, which claimed that every instance of a miracle was the expanding-forth of what the Lady always wrought.

She was the Lady of the Summer and the Winter, of bounty and of hunger, of the quickening sun and the darkest shadows.

The pudding sat in its puddle of brandy, the blue fire dancing across the glistening dark surface. The scent of brandy was thick in the air: brandy, and fruit, and sugar, and warm spices. All the good things of this time of the year.

The butler set the pudding before the Squire before returning with a jug of thick cream and another of fresh custard. Plum pudding and yellow custard, I thought, smiling at the image. White cream and green holly in the sprig placed on the top of the pudding, in a wreath around the plate.

The Squire used a silver spoon to serve the pudding; it was traditionally served at table. In an ordinary pudding there would be a small silver or pewter ornament mixed into the batter, which was considered good fortune for the coming year to whoever received it.

I looked down at my portion when the bowl was passed to me. The blue fire was fading and going out as the bowls passed hand to hand, the brandy burning off. The candlelight seemed very yellow in comparison.

I poured a measure of cream and another of custard, rejected the hard sauce, and with some nervous anticipation watched as everyone took a polite mouthful, even Hope whose custom this was not at all.

For a moment there was no sound and no response. I took a bite myself, wondering what I would say when someone inevitably asked me if I had made this myself; for it tasted of that far country.

Mr. Dart raised his eyebrow at me as he took a second or third bite and then had to spit out a small object back into his spoon, where it landed with a silver chime. As if that had been a signal, Aunt Millicent declared it a 'fine pudding, indeed', and the Squire cautiously took up the threads of the conversation.

I closed my eyes and focused on enjoying the dish to the fulness of my ability.

∾

I was indeed asked if I had made the dish, by Hope who had spent time in the kitchens of Morrowlea with me. Mr. Dart's Aunt Millicent had been mellowed by the brandy and the brandy-infused pudding, and merely gave me a jaded eye at this further evidence of my odd ways. Jullanar Maebh visibly braced herself for the truth of the answer.

"I was given it by the Hunter in the Green," I said. My father and Mr. Dart both considered their empty bowls with due wonder, but Aunt Millicent took the opportunity to declare how ridiculous it was for people to dress up and pretend to be folk heroes.

"He's a lesser divinity," I said mildly.

"That is *one* view," she allowed, if doubtingly.

"He serves the Lady," I stated, which was a theologically neutral statement that came out as ringingly as if I'd thrown down a gauntlet.

"Very true, and let us toast him for his generosity," the Squire said hastily, with a sharp glance at Sir Hamish, who duly lifted his glass and made a short and witty speech in honour of the Hunter in the Green. At the end the Squire nodded more happily. "Excellent, excellent. Thank you Jemis, for the pudding. Now—"

"Presents!" Mr. Dart said, with brandy-lubricated enthusiasm.

～

We adjourned to the library, which was well festooned with the greenery we had acquired on the Lady's Day, and brilliantly lit with candles. Our various gifts had been piled on the large table that usually stood against the wall, now pulled into the centre of the room before the fire. Ballory, who had stuffed herself on the roast apples and plum pudding everyone had been pretending not to give her under the table, was snoring softly beneath it.

I had never spent this particular part of Winterturn with the Darts, and wasn't sure of their tradition. I sat on a sofa next to my father, with Hope on a chair to my right. The Darts were distributed in their usual chairs, their Aunt Millicent ensconced in a great chair of state next to the fire.

The Squire smiled at his daughter, who sat next to him and was regarding the pile of gifts with mild astonishment. "We're a large party tonight," he said genially, "with much to celebrate for the year that has passed, and the year that is to come. Traditionally we give things intended to help with the year ahead."

"Or simply to delight the heart," Mr. Dart put in.

"Or that," the Squire said, reaching out and patting his brother's shoulder with more expressiveness than he usually showed. He harrumphed a moment later and said, "We have one solemn round, and begin with the one who came farthest. Now, we had some discussion as to who that might be," and he glared lightly at Mr. Dart and Sir Hamish, "with each of us arguing for someone else. In the end we decided that it was Jack."

He reached forward and picked up a box wrapped in brown paper. "This is from Hamish and I, Jack."

My father accepted the box thus passed to him, and we all watched as he opened the lid to find a set of what seemed to be ledger books.

"Thank you," he said. "I'm sure these will be very useful in the coming year."

"Look under the ledgers," Sir Hamish said, his voice dry.

There were several bottles of very good wine, and we all laughed.

Next was Jullanar Maebh, who was presented with a set of keys to the hall and all its outbuildings, and who accepted them as the gift of home they were obviously intended to be.

Hope was given a handsome leather-bound notebook, which she accepted with apparent astonishment that she'd been included.

I was next. The Squire nodded at Sir Hamish, who gave me a a small flat object of familiar dimensions. I unwrapped the paper covering to discover it was one of Sir Hamish's miniatures, this one of my stepfather just as I remembered him.

The Squire next fixed Mr. Dart with a stern eye. "Perry," he said solemnly, "Hamish and I decided we wished to give you the dining table."

Mr. Dart stared at his brother. "That was built *in* the dining room, Tor. I don't think it could be moved. Even if I had anywhere to move it to."

"Just so," the Squire said, and we all pretended not to look as Mr. Dart went first red and then white, much as Jullanar Maebh had done shortly before. Something solid, immovable, built in the house and for the house ... my heart swelled with pride in the Squire for having thought to ensure Mr. Dart would never feel outcast in his own home.

"We also have this for you," Sir Hamish said, passing him a box. Mr. Dart opened it and took out a set of what looked like well-loved hand-made notebooks. "They were Mother's notes on magic," the Squire rumbled. "We thought you might ... appreciate them."

"Thank you," Mr. Dart said quietly, as his Aunt Millicent woke up from her doze, snorted magnificently, and informed him she had decided to make him her chief beneficiary now that he wasn't getting the estate. Mr. Dart thanked her handsomely and she nodded sharply, told Jullanar Maebh that *she* was getting all her art collection, and after a dismissive glance at the rest of us, who evidently did not warrant gifts, took a great gulp of brandy and went back to sleep.

~

I had never spent an entire evening opening gifts before, one at a time, as if each was to be cherished, witnessed, some sacred ceremony.

It was rather lovely. After the first, formal round, we went round the room. Jullanar Maebh and Hope barely knew us, of course, and their gifts had been largely acquired in Ragnor Bella itself.

Hope gave me a set of lovely pottery mugs; Jullanar Maebh, a red-and-purple cockade for my new hat. I gave Hope *A Practical Guide to Creating a Plant Nursery*, which made her smile at me even before she found the note inside informing her I'd do my best to assist with an elopement, if she and Hal decided on it. Jullanar Maebh had been more difficult, but the bookstore had come through with a beautiful illustrated edition of *The Rivers of the Empire*, which Mrs. Etaris had assured me was mostly accurate.

Other gifts had been sent from town, though by whom I wasn't entirely certain: from the villagers of St-Noire I received a bottle of Mr. White's mead and a crock of that autumn's honey; from Mrs. Etaris the first volume of *Valiance and Shock*, which I closed very hastily upon discovering she'd already begun annotating it; from the Honourable Rag, my good fountain pen which he'd stolen months ago.

My father gave me a deck of Poacher of my own. "You never buy a deck," he said, shuffling it in one arc from hand to hand. "The cards come to you when it's time. This one came to me along my journey, the second of my decks. I held onto it, knowing it was meant for someone else … hoping it was for you."

I accepted the deck with tears springing in my eyes, and could hardly bear to give him the box I'd prepared for him. "Look at it later, please," I told him. "It's … letters I wrote you, when you were … gone."

He went pale, and for a moment we were silent, and it was everyone's turn to pretend to ignore us while we recovered our composure.

I felt a little embarrassed to give Mr. Dart the slim volume on wild magic that had all I'd been able to find on the subject, but he accepted it gratefully. What could I give to one I had sworn fealty to?

When he gave me in turn a little pewter amulet in the shape of a unicorn, the sort of thing a pilgrim might acquire to show they'd been to visit a saint or a shrine, I could only laugh. "Is this to commemorate your first great miracle?"

"No, to stop me from having to do it again!" he retorted.

"It's perfect," I said, though in truth it was a marvellously ugly thing. Nowhere near as graceful as the real unicorn slumbering under the table. On which thought I took up my second gift, the cardigan and scarf, and passed it to him.

"I don't think this will fit me," he said, laughing as he held up the cardigan.

"It's for Ballory," I replied, tucking the amulet in my pocket. I would have to find a chain to affix it to. "The scarf's for you."

Mr. Dart gave me a strange look, but Ballory had apparently heard her name, and came clattering out to nose at the cardigan with much interest. After Mr. Dart had managed to wrestle her front legs into the sleeves—which needed to be rolled up a time or two but were of adequate width, I was pleased to see—I nodded in satisfaction to see that she looked quite natty in the purple and green stripes.

No matter that everyone else was trying not to laugh at the sight.

Ballory liked the cardigan, and the rest of them could go hang.

"Here's my real gift," Mr. Dart said, wrapping the scarf about his neck in a gesture of solidarity and then passing me what was obviously a book. I raised my eyebrows at him, for surely he knew that I would never be able to reciprocate the gift he had given me—not though I had a hundred visions and insights—and opened the book to find it was a brand-new book with the distinctive sewn binding of academic works published by Stoneybridge.

"Look inside," Mr. Dart instructed, with barely suppressed eagerness.

The title page read:

A New Translation and Analysis of the Gainsgooding Conspiracy Poems by Peregrine Dart of Stoneybridge and Jemis Greenwing of Morrowlea.

"Congratulations on your first publication, Jemis," Mr. Dart said. "It'll serve you very well when you publish your account of *On Being Incarcerated in Orio Prison*."

CHAPTER THIRTY-THREE

After the rest of the gifts were exchanged, we went a-wassailing. The Squire's custom was for his household to go out at dusk to the bonfire that had been burning at the edge of the orchard all week. There the villagers had set up a great wooden chair and a huge cauldron full of wassail, which here was the Dartington perry, spiced and spiked with pearjack against the cold.

Persiflage, the drink was called at the Green Dragon. A cupful was usually more than enough to set everyone to merriment.

The Squire sat in the chair and accepted the wishes of the season from his tenants, who came and in their turn received a cup of wassail for themselves and another to give to their lands or houses. When everyone had drunk, anyone staying at the Squire's household dipped our cups and went out into the orchard near Dart Hall to sing to the trees.

"What is the purpose of this?" Hope whispered to me as we stumbled after the men holding lanterns ahead of us. I was feeling warm and replete after the wassail cup, my thoughts sitting easily in my mind. I could feel a soft call, like Mr. Dart's voice in that other country but somehow just the opposite without being at all the opposite moral valence.

The Lady's calling in this world, perhaps. The air was full of the scent of Paradise.

"We are protecting the orchards against the hobgoblins of the night," I told Hope, "and encouraging the trees to be bountiful next year."

"We don't do this in my part of Chare," she murmured, taking my arm as I led her to a tree no one else had yet greeted.

"Some places do it for the apples only, but it's always been pears here," I replied, bowing to the tree.

I flicked a few drops of persiflage onto the ground before the tree and sang the verse of the song.

Pear tree, pear tree, we all come to wassail thee
Bear this year and next year to bloom and to blow
Hat fulls, cap fulls, three cornered sack fulls
Hip, hip, hip, hurrah
Holler bys, holler hurrah

By the third tree Hope was tipsy enough to sing with me, even though she did occasionally mutter that Hal was not nearly so sentimental about his plants, an opinion I rather doubted. The gardens at Morrowlea had not been *his* gardens, after all.

We made our way through the orchard until we came across everyone gathered about the ancient oak that stood at the centre of the orchard.

The oak, not the pear trees, was the oldest tree on the estate, if estate was quite the right word for something as old and venerable as the Darts' relationship to their land. Like the Lúsa Oak, they had been here since long before the coming of the Empire.

We formed a loose circle around the oak. It was old enough that Darts past had set up struts and braces to support the branches, which bent and curved and recurved again. Old enough that generations of Darts had played in its hollow trunk, or sheltered there from invading armies, or spoken secrets to their friends.

Hope squeezed my hand and went to stand beside Jullanar Maebh, who was close to her father. In the lantern-light Jullanar Maebh's unbound hair streamed like fire, a blazon and a beacon in the dark. She stood straight and tall next to the Squire, her face strong and pale in the night.

"She is much better at this than I ever was," Mr. Dart murmured in my ear. "All the tenants love her already."

His voice was relieved rather than chagrinned, which I expected but was still glad for.

"And she?" I asked quietly. "Is she settling in?"

"I think she misses the sea," he replied, "and her mother and friends, but I can see … the land acknowledges her, and she feels that. Knows it. She told me she can be happy here."

What an extraordinary gift his magic was.

"What did you find in the pudding?" I asked him curiously.

He glanced at me, then offered me the small silver token, dropping it into my upturned palm. It was a silver arrow.

"Apposite," I said, handing it back to him.

"Very," he replied, extremely dryly.

The Squire made a toast to the oak tree, his voice loud and sure, the ancient nonsense words falling in my ears in a cadence that was surely not nonsensical at all, but rather words passed down over the generations long after Shaian was the tongue spoken in the land, words older than empires and even, perhaps, older than this tree. The Lúsa Oak. The Lord's tree. I had called it that to Sir Peregrine, when it was a young tree, as yet unnamed and insignificant.

I tilted my head back. The stars were tangled in the oak's branches as they had been in the Hunter's horns.

We drank down the last drops of our cups, all but the Squire, who wet his lips and then poured the rest into the hollow between the exposed roots of the oak, where gifts had always been laid.

The cups were wooden, as wooden as the Grail in my dream, in my father's deck of cards. One of the Squire's tenants made them each year, out of a fallen or cut pear tree from the orchard. We would place them on the bonfire before returning to Dart Hall for the late-night supper and gift-giving.

Before we did that, however, we joined hands around the oak and sang the wassailing song in one last variation. I glanced around and like the others set my cup into my pocket; but unlike the others I took

Mr. Dart's as well, and moved around so I stood on his right side, my left hand taking his stone right.

The stone hand was cold in mine.

It was made of marble, Hope had said. The spiral scar on my palm burned against it. My father was on my right, come out of the darkness to stand beside me, his hand warm and strong in mine.

Oak tree, Oak Tree, we all come to wassail thee
 Remember us, O Oak Tree, in the spring and the autumn
 The winter and the summer
 All the turning of the year

Oak Tree, Oak Tree, we all come to wassail thee
 Bear this year and next year, to bloom and to blow
 Acorns full of gold and green
 Hat fulls, cap fulls, three cornered sack fulls
 All the land around thee
 Ours and thine remembered be

Oak Tree, Oak Tree, we all come to wassail thee

It didn't make all that much sense, I thought. My thoughts were on Mr. Dart's stone hand and the feel of my father's living flesh on my other side, and the oak tree and the crown of holly and hawthorn the Squire was wearing, which I had not noticed before.

The oak was a Dartington tree: their coat of arms was an oak with an arrow in its branches and a river at its feet.

A silver arrow for Mr. Dart, from the Hunter in the Green, whose bow was an arc of stars across half the sky.

An oak for Sir Peregrine and his lost unicorn friend, whose bloody horn had scarred my hand and granted me some gift I did not yet know.

But I did know. The world was shifting under my feet, but Mr. Dart's cold hand was steady in mine, stone like the bridge underfoot when I had tipped back my head to regard the glory of the heavens.

And a river ... we had not yet plumbed that mystery. *Stone speaks to stone, and water to water,* my father had said, a riddle he had never quite unravelled. A curse or a wonder that bound his tongue still. Stone speaks to stone, and water to water.

Golden is the wax, went my mother's song. *Golden is the light. Golden is my heart in my true love's sight.*

We finished the wassailing song and my father squeezed my hand once before letting go. He turned to walk with Sir Hamish, who was not far from us. The circle of men and women broke up into smaller groupings, friends and neighbours chatting merrily, the perry and pearjack loosening tongues and warming hearts. The air was cold and crisp, but when we turned the bonfire was bright and not too far distant. We could see people gathered around it, dark shapes against the flames.

Mr. Dart held still, not moving. He was looking at the tree.

I looked down at his stone arm, the pale marble striking in the dimness. The lantern-bearers had gone now, but as my eyes adjusted the night did not seem dark. There were stars tossing in the branches of the oak, and stars glimmering on the snow.

The intuitive certainty with which I had woken so many days ago was nearly clear in my mind, some underwater or subterranean creature coming to the surface. Strands of thoughts and insights came to my mind: what it meant to be a saint, and what the great mages in Mr. Dart's book had said about undoing curses, untying knots. What it meant to be a friend, and what the Hunter and the fox had said and not said.

Purple emperors were the butterflies of an oak wood in the springtime, and golden were the acorns in the wassailing song.

There would be another tree for the lost Lord, as the Lady had both hawthorn and holly. There would be other clues to find, by research and by riddling, until it was the time to run, the time to fight.

My hand was burning.

Mr. Dart said, "The oak tree says you know what to do."

Did I?

What do you already know? What do you already do?

I thought of all the stories of the Wild Saint, that he received what he was given and gave it away again. Was that not the fundamental way of the Lady of the Summer and the Winter? She guarded the turning of the year, the hunger in the winter giving way to the fruits of the summer; the abundance of the summer providing all those good things through the leanness of the winter.

A unicorn horn was an instrument of healing. What had Sir Peregrine said? That the bloody horn was meant as an insult, but it was truly a holy gift?

Are you clever enough to follow my trail?

I turned my hands upright. The spiral scar on my palm was throbbing, not painfully but with … readiness.

"The Ánhorn did that, did it not?" Mr. Dart said.

"Yes. Before it turned into the sword."

There were shouts and laughter, more carols being sung, over at the bonfire. The oak tree above us creaked, the dry leaves rustling, almost on the edge of words even for me. Mr. Dart cocked his head. "The tree remembers you," he said.

Sir Peregrine of my vision was not *my* Mr. Dart. That great unicorn I had seen beneath this very tree in its youth had been a stallion.

And yet Sir Peregrine had passed me the Ánhorn across time.

"I think," Mr. Dart said slowly, "that you might *actually* be a saint, Jemis."

It was cozy, despite the dark and the cold, under the Lúsa tree. The Lady's smiling eyes were in my mind, her laughter shaking the world into blossom. Snow started to fall around us, intricate crystals, each one a natural wonder, ephemeral as any moment.

It was not *I*, I thought, who was the saint.

"In that case," I asked, "what do *you* want me to do?"

He looked down at his hands. He wasn't wearing a glove on his good hand; the stone arm was supported in its sling.

"You could try my arm," he said thoughtfully.

"Does it bother you?"

He gave me a flat, sardonic look, and I realized just how much he had bitten back.

"You're allowed to complain," I said, placing my hands underneath the sling, lifting the weight of the stone arm. It *was* heavy, surely nearly a—heh, a stone.

"I don't mind the loss of dexterity so much," he murmured as I placed my hands around the cold, unresponsive marble. "I've gotten used to that. It's the … weight of it." He twisted his neck, gesturing at the knot that held the sling in place.

"I've never done this before," I said, though the burning in my hand seemed to know what I should do. I shifted that hand to his elbow, just where the stone became once more flesh. Mr. Dart hissed and said, "Your hand is cold."

"So is yours," I retorted, and he laughed.

Above us the wind rustled in the oak leaves, and the snow drifted inexorably down.

The first gift of the fox had been bound by a ribbon of shadows a rowan branch could cut. I had given the bird to the Squire.

The second, the two doves, I had given to that other Jemis at another bridge over another river, waking some distant memory of joys known before the Fall, that could be known once again.

The third, the three hens, I had given to Mrs. Etaris, for she kept chickens and could make good use of them. No golden eggs from those hens, but riches nonetheless in the giving and the taking.

Mrs. Etaris, who was really Jullanar of the Sea, whose life was far richer than anyone could rightfully have expected.

To unbind a curse, that book had said, the only sentence clear to me amidst the mass of abstruse magical theory, *one must know the truth of the one cursed or the one who cursed*.

Or, Fitzroy Angursell had scrawled beside the paragraph in peacock-blue ink, *understand the nature of the knot*.

This curse was not of magic, or not of human magic. The one who cursed was the Grey Priest, who served the Dark Kings, and his power came from them, from those who had fallen and twisted the glory of the Bright Countries.

And Mr. Dart, the one cursed, was mage and Champion.

As for the knot … *I* did not need to understand it. I merely needed to let the one who *did* work through me, through the door we had already made, the gifts already given, the path already laid.

The certainty thrilled through me. It was Winterturn, the Twelfthday, the last night of the year. Once upon a time wrens had been sacrificed to bring back the light.

The wheel of the year was turning. This was a moment of balance, of revelation: of transformation, of change. The death of the old, as the fires burned down the old year and called for the new.

I closed my eyes and bowed my head, and as I had seen Sir Peregrine do in that vision of the cow byre, that miracle of water, I prayed to the Lady that she could work through my hands.

The oak tree rustled in a wind that blew from Paradise, and I heard the Hunter's hounds baying distantly in the night.

I held Mr. Dart's stone hand, not striving, not doing, simply holding myself open, patient, waiting.

What do you already know? What do you already do?

I knew the grace of the Lady. I followed Mr. Dart where he led. I had no magic; I had sacrificed it; but I did not need magic for this.

Are you patient enough to await what comes?

Are you clever enough to follow that trail?

Do you dare to hear that truth?

I waited, remembering the wind blowing in the living woods on the other side of death.

Almost, almost, I seemed to hear, *this is almost the task for you.*

Almost, and not quite, but a token—an earnest of things to come—would be given: not for me but for the one whose faith was stronger than mine and who had, crucially, *asked.*

Under my hands the cold stone warmed; and a heavy strain seemed to go out of his shoulders, no longer braced against a counterbalancing weight.

Mr. Dart took several deep breaths. We looked down: the arm was still petrified, but now only the *appearance* of marble, not its weight and chill. Even under my hands I could feel how much lighter it was.

The snow around us was sparkling silver, and even the oak tree was quiet, listening, attentive. I gave silent, heartfelt thanks to the Lady, and a tentative offer of thanks to that lost Lord I did not know. If it was not my gift to heal, then I could only be grateful to have achieved anything at all.

"What did you realize?" he asked me.

Somehow we were still in that moment between miracle and mundanity.

I turned, turning him, and there, between the branches of the oak, shone the five planets in their staggered line. The great mystery was framed by dark rustling leaves. It looked about the same size as the Star of the North, but rich gold like candlelight.

Golden is the wax, golden is the light. Golden is my heart in my true love's sight.

"What do you already know?" I asked Mr. Dart. "What do you already do? Are you clever enough to follow that trail?"

"The fox's questions to you—"

I shook my head. The wind caught the branches, all last year's leathery leaves, shouting so loudly even I could almost understand them.

"Three warnings. Three gifts. Three questions. Three *riddles*."

"And their answers?" he asked. His eyes were shining in the starlight.

Understand the nature of the knot.

I did not need to understand magic. I understood riddles.

"Three warnings: Beware the false hunter. Beware the false lover. Beware the false friend.

"Three gifts: One bird bound by shadows. Two birds caged in a basket. Three birds sitting calmly."

Mr. Dart looked up at the five planets in the shimmering arc of the southern half of the sky, the white-peaked mountains stark in their magnificence. Behind us the bonfire snapped and people were singing the wassailing songs. The oak was quiet now, as if the venerable tree were listening.

"Three questions," he murmured.

"The same questions," I said, "the Lady's Hunter asked me."

"The Gentry do not belong to her," he objected.

I smiled at him. I did not know the fox's true name. I did not know their purpose in loving and then leaving Mr. Dart. I did not know why they could come into human form only on new-moon nights. But I had been granted the promise of riddles.

"They do not," I agreed, and nodded at the fifth planet. "The fox belongs to our lost Lord."

"And those were clues by which we might be able to seek—to find —to *rescue*—him?"

The world held its breath for a moment, and then there was a distant tolling—the churches ringing in the new year—and with a great thunderclap the oak let loose all its acorns. They clattered down around us like hail, frost-shining nuts catching the golden light of the bonfire as they bounced against the orchard's close-cropped grass.

Some bounced off my hat, but Mrs. Ayden's masterpiece kept my head safe. Mr. Dart's magic shimmered protectively around him, like the mist at the edge of a waterfall.

I could swear the oak was laughing at us.

"Mr. Greenwing," Mr. Dart said, sighing.

"Mr. Dart," I replied, grinning, and we returned to the circle of light cast by the bonfire and the songs being sung to welcome in the new year.

ABOUT THE AUTHOR

Victoria Goddard is a fantasy novelist, gardener, and occasional academic. She has a PhD in Medieval Studies from the University of Toronto, has walked down the length of England (and across that of Spain), and is currently a writer, cheesemonger, and gardener in the Canadian Maritimes. Along with cheese, books, and flowers she also loves dogs, tea, and languages.

Read more at Victoria Goddard's site, www.victoriagoddard.ca.

CPSIA information can be obtained
at www.ICGtesting.com
Printed in the USA
LVHW100424210323
742114LV00005BA/27

9 781988 908465